"With breathtaking lyricisr   en
in flux brilliantly. This profound book complicates the impose   al-
ism and throbs with life. *Inside the Mirror* is an extraordinary novel."

—JENNIFER MARITZA MCCAULEY, author of *When Trying to Return Home*

"*Inside the Mirror* is an extraordinary and moving story about twin sisters
Jaya and Kamlesh as they struggle to pursue their passion and independence as women artists from a conservative society. Crafted with elegance
and precision, and heartrending in its exploration of family drama, this
novel is a beautiful and ambitious work of fiction."

—BRANDON HOBSON, National Book Award finalist and author of *The Removed*

"A sparkling jewel of a novel, *Inside the Mirror* follows twins Jaya and
Kamlesh as they pursue artistic ambitions. Battling their own fears, the
young women wrestle with the familial and cultural expectations holding
them back. Even as relationships splinter and trust is broken, Jaya and
Kamlesh bravely seek lives without limits, lives in which they attain the
grace they have long deserved."

—HEATHER BELL ADAMS, author of *Maranatha Road* and *The Good Luck Stone*

"Parul Kapur's compelling debut novel, *Inside the Mirror*, explores the
tension between family bonds and the pursuit of artistic passion. Set
against the backdrop of post-Partition Bombay, this meticulously researched
story follows twins Jaya and Kamlesh as they grapple with the quest for
self-expression within a tightly knit community that has predetermined
their life paths. Kapur expertly recreates the social complexities of 1950s
Bombay, illustrating the profound impact each twin has on their family
and community as they pursue their chosen vocations—painting for Jaya
and dance for Kamlesh. Every decision they make comes with a sense of
guilt and shame. In eloquent prose Kapur explores themes of women's
roles, the power of art, familial obligations, and the sacrifices entailed in
seeking self-determination."

—GEETA KOTHARI, author of *I Brake for Moose and Other Stories*

INSIDE THE MIRROR

INSIDE

THE

A Novel

MIRROR

Parul Kapur

University of Nebraska Press
LINCOLN

This book is the winner of the 2022 AWP Prize for the
Novel, part of the AWP Award Series. The Association of
Writers & Writing Programs is a nonprofit organization
dedicated to amplifying the voices of writers and the
academic programs and organizations that serve them.
Please visit www.awpwriter.org for more information.

The University of Nebraska Press is part of a land-
grant institution with campuses and programs on the
past, present, and future homelands of the Pawnee,
Ponca, Otoe-Missouria, Omaha, Dakota, Lakota, Kaw,
Cheyenne, and Arapaho Peoples, as well as those of the
relocated Ho-Chunk, Sac and Fox, and Iowa Peoples.

Library of Congress Cataloging-in-Publication Data
Names: Kapur, Parul, 1961– author.
Title: Inside the mirror: a novel / Parul Kapur.
Description: Lincoln: University of Nebraska
Press, 2024. | Series: AWP prize for the novel
Identifiers: LCCN 2023028611
ISBN 9781496236784 (paperback)
ISBN 9781496239297 (epub)
ISBN 9781496239303 (pdf)
Subjects: BISAC: FICTION / Literary | LCGFT: Novels.
Classification: LCC PS3611.A6946 I57 2024 |
DDC 813/.6—dc23/eng/20230621
LC record available at https://lccn.loc.gov/2023028611

Set and designed in Sabon Next by N. Putens.

For Krishan
beloved son

Nothing is far away,

Everything is near;

The universe

And the painting on the wall.

—CHANDIDAS

PART 1

The Witnesses and Their Dreams

I

INSIDE THE GUNNYSACKS were the makings of a man. There were two bags, roughly dividing the bones for the upper and lower halves of the body, and Jaya had not wanted them inside the bedroom. But her father said they should not be stored on the balcony during the monsoons, where she'd kept them last month, because they might start to smell in a heavy rain. The servant boy had climbed a stool and placed the sacks on top of the wardrobe at her father's instruction, her mother grimacing as the thin boy raised the bundles overhead. Jaya had been told to ask the servant to retrieve the sacks for her whenever she was ready to work in the afternoons. Instead, she had moved the rootless bones once again. She'd removed a pile of household wreckage from the corner between the wardrobe and the wall—a broken towel rack, loose shelves, boxes of childhood belongings—and pushed the bone-sacks into the space, where she could easily reach them.

Today she had pulled out both bags, not only the one containing the bones of the upper body, which she had to mark up. She hesitated before removing the rib cage and placing it on an old sheet spread over the dhurrie on the floor. She glanced behind her—the door was shut. No one liked to see her laying the bones on the bedroom floor and taking her red chalk to draw a line where a muscle originated, and marking in blue chalk where the muscle inserted. Now she took out the brownish basin of the pelvis, searched for the long shaft of the thigh, and found a fully formed foot, all the knotty bones threaded together. These were new bones to her; she had not dared to assemble them like this before.

The first couple of times she'd set out to do her assignment, she had asked Kamlesh to stay in the room on the pretext of holding open *Gray's Anatomy* for her. Searching inside the sacks was frightening, all sorts of forms coming into her hands, rough protrusions and smooth cavities. She'd have to pull out a number of bones until she found the ones for the arm that they were dissecting in college. Her twin had frowned and asked to leave, looking so distraught that Jaya realized she would have to do her work in privacy. If their grandmother happened to be in her alcove at the back of the bedroom, which the three of them shared, Jaya would ask her to shift to another room and Bebeji would rise from her bed, taking with her the many newspapers she read religiously. Bebeji found it indecent for a person to handle human remains.

From her writing table, Jaya fetched her pen and ink bottle and tore a sheet from a tablet of drawing paper. She tacked it to a small plank she used as an easel. She sat on the floor, leaned against Kamlesh's curio cabinet, and considered the skull with its clenched set of teeth and hollow eyes, the winged whole of the rib cage, the rod of a femur, and beneath a gap of white sheet the fanlike foot. The morgue prepared the bones from the bodies of the unclaimed dead found in the roads and railway stations; each first-year medical student was partnered with a fresh skeleton.

Here were the pieces of a man. Who had he been? Jaya drew the rib cage with a slower hand. The trunk of the sternum and looping branches of ribs needed close attention to be given form as a whole, with lines and shading. A splotch of ink spread on the half-made foot, the toes sharp as pincers. A thought came to her: *How do you become someone?* She wrote the words like a banner in a fluttering script and capped the pen, lifting the board from her lap.

For a moment she let herself drift, closing her eyes, as she tried to feel some connection to the man. Moving onto the bedsheet, she slipped a few feet away from the fragmented figure she had laid out. Aligning her body parallel to his, she lay down, wondering if she could assess the man's height, discern something about him.

The bell rang, the front door banged shut. Heerabai must have answered; Jaya could never hear the maidservant's barefoot movements in the flat. Clicking steps hurried down the passage. Their mother called out, "You've come, Kamlesh?" Jaya was pushing herself up when her sister opened the door and caught her sitting beside the partially assembled skeleton. Her twin made a face, clutching a parcel to her chest. "What are you doing? Making the whole thing up?"

"I wanted to try drawing it." Jaya stood up and arranged the pleats of her sari. Her nervous hand went to her hair, which was bound in a neat plait down her back.

"They want you to draw the full skeleton?"

"No. I wanted to see how the bones fit together."

"Just like that?" Kamlesh squinted at her.

"Yah—just like that," said Jaya, bending over to gather her art materials, then the bones.

IN THE DARKNESS of a hissing rain that night, she wondered if she should try sketching each bone as an exercise to become familiar with the anonymous man in the room, to gain some understanding of him. Listening to the downpour from her bed, she opened and closed her fist in front of her face, her fingers bursting open like petals, but nothing could be seen. She had vanished into the night, become formless, inert, existing only in her thoughts. It was difficult to talk about the things she saw in college, so it was an altogether lonelier time. She told no one in any detail about the cadavers in the dissection hall, not even her twin—who could speak of such things? Sometimes when she slept, the face of the man her group was assigned to dissect came to her unbidden—he would break into a dream, like someone she was running away from. At daybreak, she filled with dread, realizing she would be returning to him. Her father didn't ask about the dissection hall. It was something she was meant to bear alone.

When the exam results for Inter-science had been published in the paper a couple of months ago, they knew her marks, her first class first, had earned her a seat at Grant Medical College, which took only the top one hundred and twenty applicants. A renowned institution, it attracted premedical students not only from Bombay state but from other parts of India and even some African countries. Her father had never looked happier, medicine his choice of profession for Jaya. Just twenty-three girls had been admitted. He'd laughed in relief, having tutored her occasionally from his collection of books on the body and disease. Though he relied solely on natural remedies to treat his asthma and digestive ailments, he believed in the power of allopathic medicine. As a reward for her achievement, he had presented Jaya fifty-one rupees. She had felt a swell of pride, then, holding so much money in her hands.

She heard her name in the dark, her sister calling. Kamlesh must have heard her shifting around in bed. Rain pelted the coconut trees that fringed their building, fronds sputtering in the wind. The curtain flapped in the doorway. They'd left the balcony doors open for the breeze when they went to bed, before it started to rain. Now she could hear the waves thrashing the seawall, as if it were just inches away, a rhythmic pounding of water on stone. Some mornings they awoke to find Marine Drive flooded, cars gliding slowly through saltwater like boats.

"Jaya?"

She didn't reply. Kamlesh would want her to close the doors, although the wind whisking through the room was lovely. She was always asking Jaya to do things she could do herself, as if she were younger by years, not just twenty minutes. Jaya groaned in protest, hearing her name again. She knew she ought to get up, at least to bring in the painting she had left to dry on the balcony.

"Should I close the doors?" Kamlesh's clear words startled her. "I'm shivering. Just see." Her sister sounded wide awake, eager to talk. "Feel my legs—they're ice cold," she urged Jaya. "Come here. Where are you?"

Jaya got up, blundering in the darkness, clutching her pillow and sheet. It was hard to go on resisting her sister's voice. Clumsily she climbed in from the foot of Kamlesh's bed, because of the curio cabinet pushed along its side like a defensive wall, rising a foot above the mattress. Once it had been meant as a barrier against her, because she was considered "too strong," as their mother used to say. It was true she'd tried to dominate Kamlesh. And yet, no matter how much they'd fought as children, they had found comfort in sleeping with their beds joined together. Now, on the narrow mattress between the cabinet and the wall, they adjusted the sheet over their doubled bodies, Kamlesh scraping her chilled feet against Jaya's for warmth. Jaya pressed her hand over her sister's mouth, reminding her of their grandmother—"Bebeji!"—asleep in her alcove, a deep enclosed balcony, at the back of the room.

"No, don't," Kamlesh cried, catching Jaya's hand tightly in hers to keep from being silenced again. All Kamlesh's strength was physical, her hands iron-hard from the gestures of her dance, her spine straight as a plank of wood. For a full hour, she could be heard slapping the stone floor with her bare feet, practicing adavus in the bedroom. She would shape her hands into Krishna's flute at her lips, or set them quivering to mimic the movement of flowery arrows shot by the god of love, sometimes demonstrating mudras for Jaya to draw. Kamlesh began whispering about a friend from college who was teaching herself to drive her father's car on the sly, promising to take their group to Juhu Beach one of these days. The same Meher who danced every Thursday to Chic Chocolate blowing his horn at the Cricket Club. Did Jaya know what a "tag dance" was? Jaya laughed. How could she know? They didn't go to clubs like Meher. Parsi girls had all the freedoms. "It's when another boy is allowed to cut in on your partner," Kamlesh replied, delighted.

Closing her eyes, her hand grazing her sister's, Jaya imagined painting two curves of rounded female hips and thighs. The dancing figure burned in her head, a sudden lamp, then vanished. "You know what else she was saying?" Kamlesh lowered her voice. "She wants to have a love marriage. She wants to 'experience the rapture of falling in love'—that's what she called it. *Rapture*. Such rubbish she talks."

"A mad hatter," Jaya agreed. "Hema's just like that." Though, really, Hema wasn't. None of her classmates at medical college were anything like Kamlesh's friends at Sophia College or their old friends at St. Anne's—purely social girls, competitive about clothes and family standing. Medical college girls had not an ounce of glamour in them. Shy, bookish students from conservative families, they hesitated even to answer a professor's question. What made Hema different from them was her low, mannish voice and bravado. "I don't know how she does some of the things she does," Jaya confessed.

"What things?" Kamlesh asked.

"Some things," Jaya replied vaguely, hesitating to say any more. Silence had become her shelter, a comfortable place to conceal her thoughts. These days she floated in a state of mind that kept her at a distance from everyone, even her sister. The things she used to think awaited her at the threshold of adulthood had never appeared—her admission into medical college was nothing she had wanted for herself. Growing up, she'd dreamt of becoming a different person. In the library at her old school was a mural of Mother India in a pristine white sari, atop a pyramid of village emblems—a cart-wheel, a farmer in a turban, a scythe, a pulsing sun. The figure of the artist painting the portrait, his palette in hand, stood at the bottom of the mural. She had always pictured herself there, in his place.

Gingerly Kamlesh laid an arm over her, as if touch might enable her to speak, but Jaya remained quiet. Kamlesh had always studied among girls, even her college was a girls' college, and all her notions of romance came from the cinema hall. Still, it was to tell her twin about something unset-tling, Jaya realized, that she had come to her bed. "There's a Parsi fellow a few years senior to us, Mr. Wadia," she began. "Hema's gone out with him for tea a couple of times. Telling fibs at her hostel that her aunt or her cousin has come to town and taking permission to leave the campus."

"Does she want to marry him?"

Jaya didn't know. "Probably," she surmised. She knew of no other couples at college, and Hema didn't speak of what she hoped her clandestine meetings with Farrokh Wadia would bring. *We're just coming to know one another*, she would say. He was a soft, plump, deeply courteous boy with gold-rimmed spectacles. It was hard to imagine Hema, who was demand-ing and quick to speak her mind, married to him.

Jaya turned away, onto her side, pushing herself to say what she was burning to. "This Mr. Wadia has a friend, and his friend, if you please, has been asking about me. 'Who's that girl who's always with Hema?' 'The one who's always wearing yellow clothes?' Can you imagine some fellow taking notice of your clothes and such?"

"Who is he?"

"I've seen him in passing, I think. A Bengali chap. Some Mr. Dasgupta." She wouldn't give away everything about him, not the strikingly dark impression of his face, not his remarkable height. She didn't mention that she'd come to a fourth-year boy's attention only because Hema had goaded her and a few other girls in their batch to trespass inside the Boys Common

Room in the second week of college. Hema had charged in ahead of them like a campaigner for social justice, saying, "A 'common room' should be for all students—we girls also require a place to hang about in." Some of the boys looked amused, and others tried earnestly to correct them— "Gentlemen only." After that initial incursion, their group summoned the courage to stride into the dim Gothic hall a few more times on the pretext of playing table tennis despite the looks they got. How embarrassing to chase after errant balls in their saris. The other girls dropped away, one by one, even the adventurous Gujarati girl from Kenya, until it was only Jaya left following Hema into the hall, her feelings shifting between emboldened and mortified. Once she felt someone's eyes piercing her back and turned to catch the Bengali boy, standing among his friends, staring hard before he looked away. Aggressive eyes under thick black brows. A giant of a boy. Must be a six-footer.

"Do you want to meet him?" Kamlesh said.

Jaya laughed softly without answering. An image came to mind again: a painting of a long, dim room with a vaulted ceiling, in shades of gray and soft yellow, a cathedral window at one end. The window filtered a beam of light that lay over empty tables and chairs, that paled as it lengthened, ending at two figures, a man and a woman, speaking in an inner doorway. She lingered over it for a moment then turned to her twin, reaching into the blackness and smoothing Kamlesh's heavy tresses, which lay along her arm like strands of her own hair.

A watery ripple of light shifted over the bed from behind them. Their grandmother's torch dipped down to the top of the curio cabinet, grazing a trio of black porcelain cats linked by chains and Kamlesh's film magazines spread out in a fan.

"Did we wake you?" Kamlesh sat up, shielding her eyes from the beam with her hand. The torch darted up to her face, illuminated lush hair falling over the shoulder of her lime-green nightdress, her eyes glistening with a vitality Jaya hadn't imagined in the dark.

"First the rain woke me up. So much noise, as if the sky is falling down," Bebeji said in her rough voice. "Then I could make out your khuss-puss going on. What's so important that you have to talk in the middle of the night?" The beam jerked across the blue wall, and Bebeji grew visible in her white widow's garments, dragging her feet as if she found her body a burden. Her thinning gray hair was pulled away from her face in a plait, exposing heavy jowls and earlobes that drooped with stretched-out holes.

"You shouldn't walk alone—it's pitch dark," Jaya said.

"Go to sleep now. You'll be too tired for your classes tomorrow." Bebeji shifted away, saying she would shut the balcony doors, the rain was too loud.

Jaya stopped herself from objecting. The room belonged to the three of them—she couldn't demand they keep the curtains open to the breeze. Bebeji took a few steps and uttered a startled moan, reaching her hand back to the cabinet for support.

"What happened? Did you hurt yourself?" Jaya said.

"Some pain—here—in the inside of the knees." Bebeji bent over, pressing the spots on her legs. Her arthritis seemed to grow worse in the rainy season, the pain sharper. She winced as she raised her broad face, etched with a map of deep lines. Rolls of flesh hung over her petticoat, her nightshirt gathered around her cascading stomach. Sometimes she would pound her belly as if she wished to dissolve herself. Almost by habit, she slept poorly and little, getting up at five-thirty every day to sing her muffled hymns in the puja corner in her alcove. In the mornings, she sat in a whitewash of light, staring at the empty sea from the front balcony. "Everything lost," Jaya had heard her mutter to herself. The lively, willful, energetic person she'd known her grandmother to be as a child had vanished.

Bebeji moved toward the balcony doors, calling to them as if they were small girls. "Go to sleep."

Jaya got up and slipped the torch from Bebeji's hand, seating her at the foot of Kamlesh's bed despite her protests. Bebeji might not notice if the balcony floor was wet; she would struggle to reach the latch. Her composure was slipping with August looming close, the month of the death anniversaries: her husband's and her eldest son's.

The torch in Jaya's hand swung across the bulky wooden wardrobe, darted to her stale drawing on the wall of a footbridge in a snowy wood. The gold nucleus slid onto the dressing table's triple mirrors and, in the murky surface of the glass, she glimpsed volumes of hair, her flowered orange kameez, the imprint of Kamlesh's fine features. Though Kamlesh was the more beautiful one, her skin as bright as a child's, her face a fine oval, they had the same large, light brown eyes—like a doe's eyes, Bebeji said—thin noses that pleased Mummy, and abundant hair that fell below the waist. Strangers sometimes mixed them up, and in photographs the impression was of identical twins.

Their clothes were the easiest way to tell them apart. Kamlesh still dressed in a schoolgirl's skirts and blouses, or in loose salwar suits; Jaya wore a sari to college like a grown-up woman.

The torch beam skimmed a slippery patch of rain that had blown onto the balcony floor. Jaya leaned over the rail to view the burning eye of a gas lamp on Marine Drive, rain drawing silver streaks in its glow. The headlamps of cars swept around the bay, and a dull light burned in a window in the next building, but she could see nothing of her city beyond these faint illuminations. She untwisted the ropes, letting the heavy chiks down. Her painting of roses, beaded with water, stood timidly on top of a sideboard containing her paints. The cabinet, missing a leg, was raised on bricks. She traced the beam over blotchy stalks of painted pinkish-red roses against a clotted blue ground, the flowers crammed into a narrow vase with a glass frill around its neck. Handles curved along its sides like a pair of brittle arms. They were another dead thing in her life, these flowers stiff in their urn. Though a canvas could open out on many images, she had confined herself to painting still lifes, trapping herself in a garden of vases, just as she was encircled by the fourteen gates of the hospital every day, as she was closed inside the bedroom with her twin and her grandmother at the back. She hadn't signed her name to the picture after she finished it yesterday, only noted the year on the back of the board in black oil color: *1953*.

Stepping back inside the room, Jaya banged the doors shut and pulled the damp curtain over them. "Everything is soaking wet," she called to Bebeji and Kamlesh, her wounded tone implying some damage had been done. Without the wind blowing inside, the room was already tight, already close, but she said nothing as she ushered her grandmother to bed.

THE NEXT MORNING, she climbed the outer stairs of the anatomy building with a habitual apprehension and opened a door to the sweet, charred odor of the dissection hall. It struck her first as a cloying bakery aroma, something sugary and smoky, then strongly chemical. As she walked into the hall, the smell ripened in her nostrils to the pungent stench of rub-bish heaps fermenting in the heat. Two crows flew around in the arches of the ceiling, high over the rows of tables laid with bodies. The boys were shouting, one batting the air with a bamboo pole they kept to shoo birds back out of the open transom windows.

Jaya paused to watch for a moment before following a shallow gutter in the floor all the way through the hall to the lockers at the back, where she kept her apron. She buttoned her white smock over her sari, dismayed to see the front smeared with the fat and grime of previous dissections. When she returned to the hall, the uproar over the birds had subsided—one of the crows apparently had been expelled; the other nervously perched on a rafter, surveying the graveyard below. Making her way over to her group, she was relieved she could now walk almost casually among the dead. At the start of college last month, in June, the nude bodies lying flat on their backs on white marble tables had horrified her. A dozen dark, shriveled men, their skin glistening wet with formalin, their lips, teeth and eyes intact. Some had scalps shaved to stubble. Others retained bushy heads of hair. The cadavers dripped their fluids into a hole cut in the center of each table, the liquid draining onto the floor, then dribbling into the gutters crossing the room. Second-year students left bodies halved or in pieces on their tables. A torso propped face down on wooden blocks, shedding flakes of charred skin. An open abdomen packed with the pale tubing of intestines. A worker with a bucket scrubbed an empty, yellowing tabletop, nodding to her as she walked by. Jaya greeted the other girls warmly as she passed their groups.

Hema looked up from the book in her hands, smiling brusquely, thick black kajal making her eyes dramatic. Jaya stood next to her, clasping her arms behind her back. The only two girls in the group of six, always side by side. The ambitious boy, Mr. Nigrani, drew his blade obliquely across the cadaver's left forearm, making two transverse cuts like bangles at either end as Hema read sternly from *Cunningham's Manual of Practical Anatomy* to guide him. The other boys leaned in to watch Nigrani pull the tough mahogany skin back, cutting away the sticky fat and cellophane of fascia with vigorous flicks of his knife.

Jaya could look and not think the body human. Despite the reek of formalin mingled with flesh, the cadaver didn't seem as if he'd been a real person until she had to lay her bare hands on him. The boys had been quite chivalrous, offering her the easier dissection or allowing her to miss her turn, knowing it alarmed her to touch the corpse. On their first day in the hall, six weeks back, they had all gathered solemnly at the cadaver's feet with their heads bowed and scalpels in hand, like devotees before an idol. When the buxom lady demonstrator announced that they would begin their study of gross anatomy with the superior extremity, they had all moved guardedly up the table and Jaya had dared to look the dead man in the eye.

His eyeballs were a jaded yellow, his face compact, a sleek Marathi man with a mustache flaring under his nose. Soiled brown teeth protruding from a mouth left permanently open were his only flaw. Pushing her knife into his skin for the first time, she felt light-headed, her stomach convulsing so sharply she was afraid she might vomit.

"Chalo, why don't you take over, Miss Malhotra?" Mr. Nigrani half smiled and gestured to the cadaver, as if he were presenting her a valuable opportunity.

Jaya was startled by the invitation—was he challenging her? He was a cocksure type. None of the other boys offered to step in for her. Maybe they were fed up of protecting her from her work. Hema located the appropriate section in *Cunningham's* and began to read how Jaya should separate the muscle to reach the passage through which the median nerve was threaded. Jaya studied the man's taut, smoothly angled jawline. He wasn't old, probably no more than thirty-five. Medium height, slender of build. No blemishes on his body. What had happened to him? They said the mortuary was packed to the ceiling with unclaimed bodies. The corpses of poor men and women. Students occasionally fell ill with the diseases still alive inside some of the dead.

Jaya clutched the man's hard, knobby wrist with her free hand, trying not to think of what she touched, pressing her blade below the double head of the pronator teres into the swell of pinkish-brown muscle. She let herself imagine she was tracing the bowed edge of his arm, taking a charcoal stick with its twiggy protrusions around his knuckled fist and one pointing finger. In the end, a person was nothing more than flesh, gristle, and bone—pure matter. What he'd thought or felt or tried to be didn't seem important, only the body remained. She had to get used to touching him, to become comfortable handling him without dissolving in a panic. Her left hand slipped around to cradle his leathery fist, to accept the connection to him.

"Friend *banarahi hai?*" One of the boys laughed. *She's making a friend!* Mocking her as if she were trying to hold a boyfriend's hand. It wasn't Nigrani, but someone else. A few of them were smirking. Jaya dropped the rigid hand, too embarrassed to say anything.

At noon, when she and Hema left the Anatomy Hall, the gardener was burning a pile of leaves and rubbish in the yard, sending up a smoke so acrid they rushed across the grounds, past the Court of the Coroner of Bombay and the hulking stone castle of the Pathology School. Jaya pressed the edge of her sari against her nose as if she could block out the morose hospital campus around her by snuffing out its smell. Past the red dust yard of the eye hospital crowned by battlements and blinkered by massive date palms, they came to the grim centerpiece of Grant Medical College: the smutted black-stone facade of J. J. Hospital, which sprawled in the form of two crosses joined together. Each long wing was marked by a row of arched glass doors that offered glimpses of patients plodding around in their white gowns.

Jaya wouldn't feel relief until they reached the Lady Students Hostel, where Hema stayed and the girls' canteen was located. Only as they walked down a paved path overhung by the wide boughs of mango trees did she realize they were headed in the wrong direction. She had been following Hema without thinking, lost to that terrible moment she'd clutched the cadaver's hand—how strange and repulsive the hard, slick crust of his skin had felt against her palm. Ward boys pushed trolleys piled with boxes. The sick walked in front of them with a painful slowness. A stooped man dragged a wooden handcart behind him loaded with bundles of hospital laundry. "Why are we going this way?" She turned to Hema.

Hema suggested stopping in at the Boys Common Room for a few minutes. She thought Jaya wanted to look for him, claiming Jaya had turned in this direction. Jaya denied this—she hadn't been paying attention to where they were going. Some older boys passed them and Jaya shrank a little. The church-like building that housed the Boys Common

Room stood a short distance ahead, just beyond the tin-roofed cottage of the C.C., the canteen where the boys ate. They could hear radio music playing in the mess. Jaya hesitated. No one had taken them to task for it, but every time they entered the Boys Common Room, they were violating college rules. The Bengali boy, Kirti Dasgupta, was probably inside playing teen patti, gambling for his pocket money as the older boys did. She was tempted to stop in, but also reluctant. She didn't want to appear obvious about courting his attention. She could spoil her reputation. She had seen girls on campus turn right around and walk away when a boy tried to talk to them.

"They've all remarked that you don't say a word, Farrokh was saying. Not a peep out of you." Hema shut her fingers like a beak. Her gaze was blunt and probing. A Marathi girl from Poona, she didn't soften her tone or offer pleasantries like the girls Jaya had gone to school with. Many things set Jaya apart from Hema: her convent school education, her fluency in English and smattering of French, her cosmetics and flame-colored sandals. Hema copied her remorselessly, down to her coral lipstick and dark glasses, though she'd make the look louder and sloppier with her dark eyebrow pencil, her big earrings, and her hair pinned up in a large, showy bun, her springy curls poking out from the sides.

"Why should I speak to every Tom, Dick, and Harry who comes around?" Jaya affected a superior tone but her face warmed. Had the tall Bengali boy complained about her? Inside the hall, some third- and fourth-year boys had come around to ask her stupid questions like what was the time. Her own class boys kept a respectable distance from girls; they were always "Miss" and "Mister" to each other. No one was accustomed to studying with the opposite sex in school; but a number of colleges in Bombay, not only medical college, were co-educational. Her mother said that would be unthinkable in the North. No one would accept it. Girls only studied among girls. The last few times in the Boys Common Room, Hema had not hesitated to accept Farrokh Wadia's invitation to play table tennis, leaving Jaya bewildered and without a purpose. She'd found herself sitting alone at a table, her head bent over her *Atlas of Histology*, a paper laid inside on which she sketched the angles of boys' faces. *Where is he?* Until she spotted him, she remained in a restless state of waiting.

A network of paths took them around in a circle past the Anatomy Hall, and Jaya began to regret denying herself the chance to see Kirti Dasgupta. At the Lady Students Hostel she went up to Hema's tiny shared room. Hema complained about her roommate's dirty habits. Two bones had been left out on the writing table, the batons of the humerus and ulna laid in a straight line beside a half-drunk cup of tea. Jaya felt desperate to take a full bath before lunch, as she'd done once before in Hema's hostel.

Hema offered her a stiff towel and a chunk of used soap. Quickly Jaya removed her sari and laid it on Hema's bed, then hurried down the corridor with Hema's dressing gown belted over her blouse and petticoat. In the washroom she undressed and squatted on the floor in front of a brass bucket brimming with cold water, lathering her thighs, arms, and head. Traces of the sugary smoke aroma coating her neck and hair came off on her fingers. She could still smell the cadaver as she flung cups full of water at herself, trying to wash away the lingering sensation of mucking about in a dead man's flesh.

2

KAMLESH BOWED TO touch her teacher's feet before taking her position in the middle of the dance floor. Pulling her shoulders back, she stood as straight as she could hold herself in her knee-length sari, her hands tucked in at her waist and bare feet joined together. She waited as Masterji settled back on his cushion on the floor and readjusted his weight, seeking a level of concentration. Across the curve of his forehead he'd drawn powdery bars of ash taken from the incense he burned for his morning puja. An off-white lungi was wrapped neatly around his legs, and his sagging chest was bare, a white cloth draped over his shoulder for use as a hand towel. A few feet to his right, in a corner, Jaya sat on the floor, a drawing pad open in her lap, a pencil box at her side. She'd surprised Kamlesh by asking to come along for her Saturday lesson, but Masterji had readily accommodated her, changing the lesson time from ten in the morning to four in the afternoon so Jaya could still attend a half day of college.

"Not seen you in a long time. Good you've come," Masterji had greeted her warmly, and they'd agreed it must have been at least two years since she'd attended a lesson to make drawings of Kamlesh dancing. "Now she moves so fast, you won't be able to keep up." Jaya had smiled, accepting his teasing.

Kamlesh waited, breathing deeply. They heard feet running in the corridor, a shriek from Masterji's young grandson. Masterji smacked his stick on the rosewood plank at his feet, a noise like the crack of a whip. "*Indendu Vachitivira?*" he said, without looking up.

Her feet thumped the drumhead of the stone floor as Masterji's song pierced the air in a high, ringing female timbre. "*Indendu vachitivira? Alladamillu eneedhikaadhu popora?*" *Why did you come here? That girl's house is not in this street. Please go away!*

Holding her palm out like a mirror in which she admired herself, Kamlesh posed with her eyes half closed and her head thrown back, one hip turned away and the opposite knee thrust out. She stamped her foot, drew a tika on her forehead with her free hand, traced crescents of kohl under her eyes. She was Krishna's haughty younger wife, Satyabhama, adorning herself at her toilette. Her hands made the rolling motion of crushing sandalwood to a paste, then she dotted the salve on her wrists and neck. Earrings were hooked on, bangles slipped over both hands. Kamlesh mimed knotting her sari at her waist, pulling the loose end across her breasts. Hearing a knock at the door, she hurried to the window, parting imaginary curtains to see Krishna standing in the moonlight—God and husband, her unfaithful spouse. His hair was tousled and his clothing crushed. Her eyes narrowed in dismay. She made a gesture of pushing him away, stamping her foot down fiercely.

"*Majiga thoduna manascu chellaga jesi, gurchi kaugilinchina,*" Masterji sang plaintively. *Why don't you go away? I'm not the girl you just embraced.*

Rubbing her eyes, Kamlesh mockingly asked Krishna to remove the cinders from his own so he would recognize whose house he had come to. Jealousy and wounded pride mingled in her expression: love in its angry mood. She missed a step, bounding to the right rather than backward at a diagonal, setting off a series of missteps in a segment new to her, breaking the triangular pattern of the dance. Masterji motioned for her to stop. Jaya watched intently, looking dismayed at Kamlesh's mistake. She turned her drawing paper over. Though Kamlesh had been vaguely aware, as she danced, of her twin turning pages in her pad, it had not disturbed her. In her mind she was in a different place—a make-believe world of gods and goddesses, a river flowing behind her and mountains rising in the distance.

Masterji stood, smoothing the ripples in his soft muslin lungi, and stepped into Kamlesh's place on the floor as she sat down next to his cushion, perspiring, breathing hard, quivering with energy. Her teacher spun out the adavus lithely, one bare shoulder jutting up in a flirtatious pose as he coyly averted his gaze, then turned longingly to Krishna with eyes glowing like a woman's.

Lessons sometimes progressed in silence, she and Masterji communicating with gestures and glances, an extension of the mime language of dance. But Kamlesh was worried now, asking, "What about my eyes, Masterji?" A brilliant technique might thrill an audience, he'd told her, but nothing moved people like a dancer's expressions. The eyes conjured the mood of a dance, yet the look of love in padams, especially, emerged only with maturity, he'd said, and she feared her expressions were shallow or exaggerated or fraudulent, a college girl's imitations of true emotion. Sringara was the essence of dance. Erotic love. All emotions, from peace to envy, existed within this complex feeling only a married woman had knowledge of. Masterji alluded to it in front of her as "romance" or "the heart's desire."

"You're gaining finesse," he assured her, shaking his head from side to side. A musician and scholar, Masterji was versed in Sanskrit and Telugu, had written a book in Tamil commenting on the theory of drama and dance contained in the *Natya Shastra*, and was so highly skilled a violinist that esteemed musicians like Srinivasan Iyer chose him as an accompanist on stage. His name, Pillai, was a second name for the dance itself—his forefathers the famed choreographer brothers who had revived Bharata Natyam a century back, giving it its present forms. A friend in her former dance class in Colaba, who envied how quickly she picked up steps, had told her of this legendary Bharata Natyam teacher staying way out in Matunga. His ancestry had so fascinated Kamlesh she had pestered her mother to take her to meet him. It was the year after Partition, when her father bought his first car, an ancient Vauxhall in which he could drive her there in half an hour. Her mother was happy to listen to her excited retellings of Masterji's tales of the gods, since she was afraid in those days that her daughters' health was being compromised by the terrible stories they heard from their relations who'd fled Punjab and taken refuge with them. So afraid was her mother, Vidya, that she was willing to pay some extra rupees a month for Kamlesh to take solo dance lessons. Masterji didn't offer group classes, teaching in the old way, by which a dancer had the freedom to develop her own idiom through her imagination, he said, rather than being tempted to copy others.

Masterji glanced at Jaya, gesturing with his eyes and chin to indicate he wanted to see what she had drawn. Jaya turned her pad toward him. "Just some rough sketches," she said hesitantly. A cascade of markings fluttered across the page.

Kamlesh could not make sense of the picture, viewing it from the side. She stepped toward her sister. Each sheet Jaya held up showed her spilling in curves—not quite a figure, but the sweep of a body's shifting forms. "One has a sense of her movements, yes," Masterji said. "I told you her timing is too good now. You require a camera to capture her jumping hither and thither."

Jaya laughed, looking down, saying that was all right, she wanted to make her hand move faster too. Kamlesh knew that was the reason she'd come to watch the lesson—to free her hand, as if she were hoping for a jolt to pass through her in the practice room. At home, she sometimes sketched Kamlesh dancing, demanding she hold a pose for ten or fifteen minutes. If Kamlesh complained of an ache or broke the stance for a moment, Jaya would remind her that models in art school posed for five hours in one sitting as though she had drawn them herself. Hurriedly Jaya flipped through the last pages of her drawing pad, giving Kamlesh the impression she was watching herself dance, her body taking definition, the sketches making her palpable to herself. Masterji was amused and asked Jaya to move through the pictures like that again.

Kamlesh reclaimed her place in the center of the floor, repeating the sequence Masterji had demonstrated, the dance passing fluidly between them as she mirrored her teacher—her audience and master both. In the ash markings on his forehead, in his austere dress, in the wooden shrine in the corner that held his sacred nattuvangam, the finger cymbals he struck to conduct his students' debut recitals, and rows of deities she didn't recognize—one goddess holding an enormous brass spoon across her lap—in all these elements she found signs of a sublime world. Coming to Masterji's quiet, Tamil-speaking locality with its great temple in the market replicated a journey South for her three times a week, giving her entry into an older, more intricate Hindu religion than the one she knew at home.

At the next verse, Kamlesh jumped, praising Krishna's prowess in raising the great mountain Govardhana, his valor in slaying the snake Kaliya. Then she wondered, putting on a pained look, her eyebrows curling inward, how the Divine One could be as untrue as any mortal.

AFTER AN HOUR'S solitary dance practice at home the next day, Kamlesh sprawled across her bed in a blissful state of fatigue. One foot was propped against her curio cabinet, her head raised on a pillow set against the wall. At home, too, with the bedroom door shut, Bharata Natyam became an enchanted story world she inhabited, a mythological house of gods. By the time she finished, she was exhausted and disoriented, pulled out of her dream world into the flatness of life.

Today the empty feeling had subsided, her friends having come over for lunch and the three of them planning on a matinee. They faced the usual dilemma—*which picture?* And a new worry had arisen about Leela's marriage coming up, in November, to a boy she knew only by his photograph. Leela, a softly maternal girl, milk-skinned in a baggy salwar kameez, sat at the foot of Kamlesh's bed, paging through an issue of *Silver Screen*.

"What about *The Master of Ballantrae?* 'A dashing picturization of Robert Louis Stevenson's thrilling adventure story,'" Meher read from the cinema listing in the *Times*, which was spread open on the writing table. Neither Kamlesh nor Leela had any interest. Not *Viva Zapata!* either. Their taste in films ran to love stories starring Madhubala, whose beauty made them swoon, or any funny romance. Lately Kamlesh had become enchanted with Bina Rai, who played the dancing girl in *Anarkali*, this year's big hit. She'd seen it three times already, mainly for the last scene, which was the saddest, most horrifying scene she'd ever watched in a movie. Beautiful Anarkali stood in the open, singing her mournful farewell song, while the king's laborers built her tomb up around her block by block, until she fell silent, sealed inside, death her punishment for having fallen in love with the prince.

"He's a good dancer, his cousin was saying. He knows the waltz, the foxtrot, the rumba." Leela's mind was on her fiancé, and her gaze dropped to her lap.

Kamlesh tried to laugh, despite the catch in her throat. She felt the depth of her friend's qualms about the future—her marriage to a boy living two thousand miles away, in a quarry town in the jungles of Orissa. A blue-eyed boy, Leela's father called him. He worked for a British managing agency on the same level as a British manager, lived in a bungalow in the British section of town. Very few were given the privileges of Europeans. For such a boy Leela's father had pulled her out of college before they began their BA last month. So she had graduated with just a two-year faculty of arts degree, Kamlesh and Meher facing two more years of study. Following her BA, Kamlesh knew further studies lay ahead, her father keen for her to do a teacher's training course.

"They haven't said anything to you?" Leela asked, looking at Kamlesh softly.

"About what?" Kamlesh couldn't help grinning, embarrassed by the suggestion of marriage. One day, through no doing of her own, it would happen: the future. It would be arranged by her parents—she would receive a husband, a home. A destiny.

Leela brought up her fiancé's cousin again, the one who had visited him in Birmitrapur, accompanying him to an elite club across the river, where they had danced to a live band. Giggling, Leela suggested she could ask her mother to speak to Kamlesh's mother about his cousin. What a lovely couple they would make—two such good-looking people.

"Don't talk nonsense," Kamlesh said, frowning. It unnerved her to think of an actual boy to whom her marriage might be arranged. She wouldn't know how to be herself around a man. "It's too early as yet." She pretended to complain about the years of study her father had plotted for her and Jaya, deciding they should both be professionally qualified—a doctor and a teacher. People admired Harbans Malhotra as "farsighted" for insisting his daughters be able to provide for themselves if the need ever arose. No one mentioned that would be necessary only if their husbands suffered some misfortune. Nobody wanted to cast doubt upon their futures.

Meher proposed a Marlon Brando picture playing at Eros—she preferred English films. Just then, Jaya pushed the bedroom door open and walked in, an old smock buttoned over an old salwar kameez, the front blotched with dried paint. She'd pulled her hair back in the same thick plait Kamlesh did when she danced. Her face showed strain, each eye marked with a thin black rim of kajal, accentuating the dark circles beneath.

"We're going to a matinee—coming?" Kamlesh proposed, hoping to stop Jaya from spending time alone painting on the balcony and growing dejected over what she'd made.

Jaya didn't reply, letting Kamlesh's invitation drift by in small talk with Leela and Meher—it surprised Kamlesh how brusquely Jaya answered, "No, I don't know any older boys," when Leela mentioned the name of her fiancé's brother. He was at Grant Medical College, in the final year of his MBBS.

Jaya quickly stepped outside, shutting the double balcony doors behind her. After a moment, Meher said to Kamlesh, "We'll drag her along with us, don't worry." Looking smart in her navy pleated skirt and dotted pink blouse, Meher kept fluffing her hair self-consciously, having cut it without asking a single friend's approval. How they'd all scolded her for neglecting them. Only a Parsi girl would dare such a chic cut.

Meher tossed the paper on the bed, saying, "Here, you two decide. You don't seem to like anything I suggest." Kamlesh guiltily offered to see the Marlon Brando picture, but Meher shrugged and said a Hindi film was all right. Kamlesh opened the disheveled paper, her glance falling on a fashion illustration of a tall, busty lady perfectly draped in a lace-trimmed sari. She read, "A most stunning example would be black Chantilly lace crisscrossed on a lemon yellow satin. It would be enhanced by a matching taffeta choli trimmed with black lace panels."

She felt the lush satin slipping against her skin. *My goodness.* Meher tapped out a rhythm on the top of her curio cabinet. "So? Any ideas?" She complained, as usual, about the cabinet's odd placement against Kamlesh's bed. "Why do you box yourself in like this? I'd have bad dreams at night."

"I like having my things close by." Kamlesh gestured to her film magazines. She'd first asked to have the cabinet placed against her bed in their old Colaba flat, long after their mother had pulled their joined beds apart. She and Jaya had been fighting a lot in those tense days after Partition. That's when Kamlesh had accidentally cracked the glass on a beloved picture from childhood that still hung over her bed—a golden-haired English girl gazing sweetly at a kitten pawing a basket of wool.

Meher picked up one of her magazines as Leela asked if they wanted to see *Gardish*. "Cursed," Leela said she thought it meant. She spoke a purer

Hindi than Kamlesh, who often mashed up Hindi, Punjabi, and English together. "I see you've ticked off some very important names," Meher said, holding up an issue of *Starlight*. It was the back page, bearing a list of addresses of producers and directors. Adverts for small roles. Kamlesh's pencil marks dotted the page. Meher discovered a loose sheet of paper between the pages. "'My Dear Sir, It is with the utmost interest I am writing to you in regard to your advertisement for one girl in your film . . .' One girl? For which film? Why didn't you finish the letter?"

"What? Let me see," Kamlesh demanded. Meher surrendered the piece of paper and magazine. It was Kamlesh's handwriting—her letter. Once in a while she wrote to inquire about a role, tore up the letter before she could send it. Now she folded the thin writing paper into a small square, into nothing. "Must have been thoroughly bored one day."

Leela didn't say anything, to save her more embarrassment. She admired Nayantara's photo on the cover, her long black curls set off by a pale rosebud pinned at her ear. Leela asked if she'd spotted Nayantara again—Kamlesh had recognized her green Buick with white curtains sailing down Marine Drive. Nayantara lived just down the road. Meher said tartly, "You could pass for an actress, if you just dolled up a bit. Why don't you drop by her place? Let her show you how to put on some lipstick and rouge at least," which elicited a surprised laugh from Kamlesh.

On the balcony later, after Kamlesh had tucked the letter into her cabinet, she stood beside Meher, who announced to Jaya, "We're taking you with us. You can't say no."

Kamlesh waited for her sister's response, having put Meher up to it, thinking Jaya might yield to an outsider. A board on which Jaya had lavishly painted yellow and white roses in a copper jug, some petals scattered below on a table, was screwed into her easel, a wooden bar across the top. Other boards of various sizes were stacked against one end of the sideboard, scrap materials Jaya had asked their father to salvage from the factory to save on canvases. A tall table at Jaya's side held her palette, dented tubes of paint, and cloudy jars of solvents.

Jaya gave Kamlesh a sharp look when Kamlesh blurted, "I thought this was finished." A flare of her nostrils meant Kamlesh should not push her in front of others. There was a raw spot in the picture, a small brass figurine of a crawling baby Krishna beside the jug of roses that had been painted over too many times. Kamlesh slipped across the balcony and leaned over the parapet for a view of the sea between the buildings. The road below flared out in a crescent, containing the brisk flow of the salt water under a heavy monsoon sky. Despite the whistle of traffic on Marine Drive and the constant stares of a bored old man in the next building, Jaya had created a studio for herself out here. Their mother used every bedroom balcony for storage, since the flat lacked a proper storeroom, but Jaya had managed to clear half the space of the broken things Mummy clung to by piling them at the back—cracked wooden pelmets, shattered light fixtures, bottomless cane chairs, and bundles of curtains. At the top she'd heaped the boxes and other junk she'd carted out of the bedroom weeks back, her awful sacks of bones now kept in their place.

"Come with us. What will you do here all by yourself?" Kamlesh appealed to her twin in Punjabi, the family tongue.

"I must introduce you to Persis," said Meher, her tone tentative despite her words. The degree of Jaya's quiet intensity made people careful around her, as if they felt she was silently appraising them and they were coming off badly. But Jaya appeared very interested in Persis, who, Meher said, had studied at the J. J. School of Art and excelled at portraits. "She's done a painting of my father, standing at his table, holding his pipe," Meher reported. "It's absolutely lifelike."

Jaya grew enthusiastic, hearing that Persis, in her final year at J. J., had won a painting prize. "She must have done Western painting. Was it the five-year course? I want to try figure painting sometime—not just the head, but the whole figure. They have a class for casual students in the evenings. I don't know if Daddy would let me join."

Kamlesh smiled. Normally Jaya kept silent about the things she wanted. Jaya picked up a brush, mucky with blue paint, but walked away from the canvas rather than toward it. "My drawing master learned in that British style." Kamlesh gave her a puzzled look, wondering why she spoke of Mhatre Sahib as if he were still her teacher. He used to come to the flat to give Jaya weekly lessons, then suddenly quit, leaving her feeling utterly lost. Without a teacher, Jaya stood alone here on the weekends, sketching, painting, reworking a picture and growing angry with herself. Sometimes she produced something beautiful.

Jaya sketched people with a crayon or charcoal twig hidden in her hand when she thought they weren't looking, and the likenesses were startling. Kamlesh nearly blurted this out to her friends when they returned to the bedroom. "She's drawn my face," was all she revealed about her twin, however, thinking Jaya wouldn't want them to know about her furtive portraits.

Voices escalating in the passageway stilled Kamlesh's gaze on the dressing table mirror. Bebeji could be heard growling in Punjabi, "What have I said to you? Tell me."

Mummy's plaintive reply curled up like smoke—"Am I always the one at fault? Why?"—and her chappals came flap-flapping down the passageway. Often an argument erupted in the kitchen. But why now? Lunch was finished. Heerabai, the maidservant, cried out in Marathi, trying haplessly to mediate between them. No one in the family spoke the local language except Kamlesh, who'd easily picked it up as a child.

Manu, their younger brother, stepped into the corridor, asking what was going on. "Don't ask me," Mummy cried out. Kamlesh saw the streak of her mother's beige house sari, heard the slam of her parents' bedroom door. She stared into the mirror's central panel, stunned, aware her friends had heard every word. Even worse, Leela's parents were friendly with hers—part of the same Punjabi circle in Bombay.

Bebeji's withdrawn expression changed with a jerk of the head as she entered the bedroom; she'd clearly forgotten about the other two girls. Immediately she drew her sari over her head, as if to reassert her dignity, and nearly walked away after the hellos, but Kamlesh tried to engage her in conversation. A little chatter to dissolve the tension. Rocking her head from side to side, Bebeji pretended to make a joke of her disapproval— "Picture, picture always? Can't you girls these days find anything else to do?" Her Hindi came out contorted by Punjabi intonations. Kamlesh tried to smile. Bebeji said she was going to take rest and lumbered toward her alcove, the white khadi sari she'd worn as a freedom fighter now her widow's white dress.

In the drawing room, where Kamlesh took her friends to escape the hostility at the back of the flat, Jaya's oil paintings sent a pulse of life through the chalky blue room. In one picture, yellow dahlias were piled high beside a bowl of plump, gleaming blackish-red cherries. On the opposite wall, a composition of pink and gold mangoes in a basket, ripe and flat, was a rich splash of color against a hollow black space. Kamlesh went to turn on the radiogram on the corner table, only then seeing her father hunched forward on the blue sofa that had its back to the door. He looked up from his papers spread on the center table, his file unlaced. Several typewritten letters bore the same letterhead—a long surname "& Sons." Perhaps a supplier or customer for the glassworks. "Come, I'll drive you to the cinema," Daddy proposed, hearing they were going to see a film at Regal.

Her friends, embarrassed, asked him not to trouble himself. "Dipi said he'll take us, Daddy." Kamlesh explained the arrangement made with her cousin to drop them off after he returned home from a lunch out with friends. Still, she was touched by her father's offer. He gathered up his letters, methodically putting his papers in order into the file to leave the drawing room to them. He wore a long-sleeved shirt to cover his extraordinarily thin arms. There was a time when he would have pointed a finger and ordered Kamlesh out of the room, furious at being disturbed. His high, arched forehead and thin lips, his scholar's gaze, he'd inherited from his father—his temper, everyone said, he'd gotten from Bebeji.

When Kamlesh was young, she'd felt the sting of his slap at the least irritation, because he thought her stupid compared to Jaya. Then the pressure on him had eased after Independence. He no longer had to answer to British superiors in the government—"my masters," as he used to call the engineers who demanded Indians meet standards of industry and punctuality they themselves fell short of. A way to make themselves feared. Then three years back, a remarkable opportunity had presented itself. Mr. Khosla, a factory owner who was an acquaintance, had lured him away from the Central PWD with an offer to manage the glass factory he was putting up. This posh flat on Marine Drive, twice the size of their old place in Colaba, was provided by Indus Glassworks.

Standing on the front balcony with her friends, Kamlesh took in the greenish-gray expanse of the Arabian Sea, thick clouds hanging low over the water, the chop of American piano music playing on Radio Ceylon behind them. Which was Nayantara's building? Leela wanted to know. Babylon, lilac blue, stood a short distance down the esplanade—Kamlesh leaned over to point it out among the apartment houses curving around the bay. All the modern six-story buildings along Marine Drive had pastel facades and fantasy names. Akbar Khan, the director, stayed in Kohinoor, three buildings to the left. In the evenings, Kamlesh and Jaya strolled past the Hotel Oceana, where actors and actresses gathered at the famous kebab restaurant. It was the most glamorous thing in the world, living in a film city.

As they stepped back into the drawing room, anxious that Dipi hadn't yet returned home, Leela was struck afresh by the fear that she'd be gone forever in four months' time. In November her fiancé would come home on leave, and she would be married. "I'll never even have a chance to see you on the stage," she lamented to Kamlesh.

"I don't know when that will be," Kamlesh admitted. "Normally a girl studies Bharata Natyam for seven or eight years before her arangetram. I've only been learning properly, from Masterji, for five."

Leela brightened, remembering that every year she'd come back to Bombay on a month's leave with *him*. She never took her fiancé's name, abiding by custom. A husband had to be shown deference. Kamlesh had never heard her mother call her father by his name either. "You must have your debut during one of my holidays," Leela implored her. "I'll bring him with me."

Kamlesh smiled. It occurred to her that she ought to ask for more lessons, go to Masterji four or five times a week to make herself into a real dancer. "You're a natural dancer, it's a grace within you," Masterji had told her not long ago, and she clung to his words, without knowing what they might bring her. Sometimes she pictured herself on stage, dancing, acting, becoming a presence others looked to instead of being the one always looking to others, but she couldn't imagine the story of her future. The future had no story.

BECAUSE THE MORNING'S dance practice had left her fatigued, Kamlesh closed her eyes, listening to a flute echoing birds in a forest, a girl humming to herself.

Meher nudged her. "Hey, don't fall asleep before the picture's begun—"

The girl, hearing a noise, looks back to see if someone is following her. She sees no one and continues walking, pushing aside the thick branches closing in her path.

He watches her from behind a cluster of bamboo. She sways as she walks, her hips flaring out in a ghagra, her breasts caught in a tight choli. Her shapely arms curve up to support a clay water pot on her head. Now that a gap has grown between him and the girl, he stumbles onto the path behind her, dodging her backward glances by jumping behind trees, running to keep up with her.

Angry hoots from the men in the stalls as the screen bleached to white, revived, then faded. Crackling lines appeared across the girl's mouth before she disappeared again. Was she cursed? Or was he? Kamlesh wondered. Or would their love be cursed? Cheers and whistles blew from every direction as the picture returned in full contrast.

The girl backs away from him, her eyes filling with fear.

"Don't be afraid," he tells her, taking a step forward. "I don't mean any harm. For so long I've been admiring you. Every time I come back to the village, I look for you." Hailing from the city, the hero wears pleated trousers and a corduroy cap with a bill.

She has a round face, thick arched eyebrows, a small silver O dangling from her nose. "Stay back," she commands him, stepping back herself, her grip on the clay pot tightening as if it were a weapon.

He moves toward her, music sweeping into the stillness to lift him into his song. Her pot falls to the ground as she tries to run, spilling water over black earth.

Kamlesh tilted her head back in her chair, exposing herself to a breeze stirred by the oscillating fans mounted in the upper corners of the balcony. A wind was blowing through the film, too, shadows fluttering in its airy light and dark atmosphere. In a forest, a man would approach her from behind, his hands slipping down her shoulders to the swelling of her breasts, spreading softly around them. She gazed into the window of the film, in which the hero, holding one hand out after the fleeing girl, was still singing. If she approached him, he would pull away her sari slowly, unwinding satin between his fingers like a golden river.

3

EARLY ON THE day of her grandfather's fifth death anniversary, Jaya unraveled flowers from their newspaper wrapping and climbed a chair in the drawing room to hang the garland of bright marigolds around a portrait of Lalaji. The photograph, in a heavy wooden frame, tilted away from the wall, a small monument looming over the radiogram in the corner. She remembered the day Lalaji died, 11 August 1948, when Bebeji couldn't wake him from his sleep. He couldn't bear to mark his own son's first death anniversary the following week, Bebeji told them; he wanted never to see that day.

Behind her, Bebeji bent slowly to the floor, setting down a silver tray bearing a mound of samighiri, herbs as dark and soft as soil that they would later feed to the fire for their fragrance. White sheets had been laid over the carpet for guests to sit on during the havan, the furniture pushed away to the sides of the room. "Tell Manoj to open the windows," Bebeji said, meaning the servant boy should push open the transoms over the balcony doors. Once the fire was lit, they would need to let out the smoke.

Rain was coming down in torrents, and the sky was soot black with clouds, so they'd kept the windows latched and the lights blazing all morning. Running just a few yards from the car to the florist's stand, Jaya had gotten drenched. Her hair was still wet, but she hadn't wanted to leave the task to Heerabai or Manoj. It was important to her to pick up the garland they had ordered for Lalaji herself.

Bebeji settled herself on the floor to Jaya's surprise, bowing her head as if already in prayer, swabbing at the perspiration around her neck with the edge of her sari. "I'll get you a glass of water," Jaya offered, uncertain what to say to her grandmother on a day when the deaths in the family would be heavy on her mind—her husband's and her son's. Two other children had died long ago when she was a young woman.

Bebeji shook her head. "Nothing," she said. She wanted nothing.

Jaya lifted the solid and weighty dining chair she'd used and carried it back to the dining table. In the windowless room, Dipi sat alone, his back to her, his head dropped forward. Jaya paused, setting the chair down as lightly as she could. Was he crying? If ever he sat alone, it was in the drawing room with the radio on, the newspaper spread out on the center table. Since yesterday he'd been subdued. No ready laugh. Next week they would mark his father's death anniversary. His hand fell to his side—something caught between his fingers. Was he smoking? Surely he wouldn't dare to smoke inside. Once, she'd found him with a cigarette on the side balcony where she painted. He'd held his finger to his lips, begging for secrecy. Of course he didn't want her father to know of his vice.

A pencil. He had a pencil between his fingers. Writing something perhaps. He wouldn't be doing his personal accounts today. Dipi turned to her with a startled "Uh" and ran a hand through his curly hair. "Good," he said when she mentioned she'd placed a garland on Lalaji's picture. No brightness in his face today—how could there be? She was used to Dipi offering a cheerful word, a silly remark to make her laugh. He didn't like to dwell on things.

After Partition, he'd shuttled from college to college, Amritsar to Simla to Delhi, in the hopes of finishing his B. Com. in the least possible time, to cut down on his widowed mother's expenses. Daddy had brought him to Bombay to establish him in his career, introducing him through a friend to a chartered accountancy firm. Once he finished his articles, he would be made deputy to the chief accountant at the glassworks. Dipi had been amenable to that. Everything was agreeable to him.

They never spoke about his father's death. Girdhari Lal had "died in the Partition"—that's how it was always phrased, without elaboration. Daddy wouldn't speak of his brother's murder in any other way. How did Dipi feel, trying to find a second father in Daddy? Never had Jaya paused to fully contemplate his agony.

"Will you have some cold water?" she asked, going to the fridge in a corner of the room. She removed a frosty bottle. "Bebeji's feeling very hot with all the windows closed."

"I'm all right, Choti." Dipi lifted his head from the block of paper in front of him. One of the rhyming nicknames he'd given them, to tease them with when they were younger—Choti and Moti. Tiny and Fatty. Neither description fit, but sometimes out of habit—or affection—he remembered those old names.

Jaya took a glass from the crockery cabinet, poured water for Bebeji. She was pleased to see the servants had set stacks of plates and a clutter of spoons on the table. Bebeji had been stirring the kheer herself this morning, keen to provide a good meal to all the family members who would gather in Lalaji's memory. The servant boy had been told to collect poor children from the roads nearby and bring them to the gate, so they could also be fed. In the drawing room, Bebeji stood sighing by the cloth-bedecked table on which the radiogram was stationed, gazing at a small display of family photos in metal frames. She massaged one arthritic hand with the thumb of the other. She was sixty-seven, yet she seemed even older. After Partition she'd aged ten years, Jaya's mother said, but some sorrows were far older than that.

Bebeji accepted the glass, sipped thirstily. "What did you say to the people at these rallies?" Jaya asked after a moment, trying to divert her grandmother's attention. They had a single photo of Bebeji's time as a Congress leader in Lahore. In it, she stood on a dais, the stalwart Nihal Devi Malhotra speaking into a tall microphone, the other leaders seated behind her. All of them men except Bebeji's friend Satya, who had served with her on the executive of the Lahore Congress Committee. A crowd covered the open ground in front of Bebeji—a sea of dark heads in the pure white dress of freedom fighters. Thousands of people must have gathered.

"The people in the villages showed a lot of affection when we came to them," Bebeji replied after a pause. "They were not used to having any outsider support them. They were intimidated by the English, by any government officer, who normally came just to take their money. We told them they had a right to expect more from the government."

Bebeji had been jailed twice for her speeches. When Daddy worked in government, in the Central Public Works Department, he couldn't display this photograph because any jealous colleague who saw it might have reported to their British higher-ups that Harbans Malhotra's mother was leading anti-government protests in Punjab. In any case, the British uncovered the connection and stopped promoting him. He was brilliant, a gold medalist who had been top of his class, but they stalled him in a middling position. Ex. En.—executive engineer. His junior was appointed superintending engineer above him. Those were the Englishman's tactics.

"The government doesn't help you with agriculture, we would say," Bebeji went on. "They don't provide you canals, despite the heavy taxes they charge you. They don't offer you loans or fair prices for your grains and vegetables. At Shahdara we spoke to men from a number of villages about forming a farmers union and some were afraid the tehsildar would arrest them for organizing illegally—" She broke off with a vague gaze at Lalaji's portrait.

A white turban crowned Lalaji's head, tied into a stiff blossom of cloth at the side. In his portrait Jaya's grandfather, newly promoted to income tax inspector, sat squarely in an armchair in the brick courtyard of their Lahore house on a twisting lane in Gowalmandi. He looked younger than she'd ever seen him in life, free of his round wire spectacles, wearing a fresh white suit. Bebeji, who was well versed in the intricacies of caste, had once pointed out that Lalaji belonged to a higher subcaste than she did, Dhai Ghar Khatris—Malhotras from Chiniot. Many Hafizabad girls were married to Chinioti boys. Her father had never expected to marry her so well, but at sixteen she was thought a beauty. Lalaji taught her to read and write English, a language she didn't feel comfortable speaking.

Making a partial fist with her right hand, Bebeji opened and closed it as far as she could to improve flexibility, the crumpled tissue paper of her skin stretched shiny over a dark branch of veins.

"Is it paining you?" Jaya winced to see her grandmother's effort in trying to unfurl her hand, her fingers stiff with arthritis like her knees.

Slipping out of Punjabi, Bebeji murmured a Sanskrit phrase as if she were offering an answer—"*Na tweva jatu nasem, na tvam neme jhanadaipa.*" Jaya asked the meaning of the words. "'*Never was there a time when I was not, nor you, nor these kings of men ..*'" Bebeji's voice fell away for a moment. "Krishna says, 'The truly wise grieve neither for the living nor the dead.'" She shook her head, as if refusing a thought that came to mind. "He was only forty-eight years old. Out of four children, I have only one left."

Though the radio had warned that India would be partitioned at Independence, and rumors circulated that the western side of Punjab would fall to Pakistan, no one had known what the final boundary line would be. Bebeji's son Girdhari Lal, a solicitor with a thriving practice who had lived for years on Lalaji's ancestral property in Chiniot, had never considered leaving home. Like most people, he thought the division of Punjab would amount to nothing more than a change in administration. The British would break the province, giving half to India, half to create Pakistan. What difference would it make in ordinary people's lives? Even Bebeji had believed Hindus could continue living as easily in Pakistan as in India, having lived under Muslim rulers for centuries before the British took power. The Punjabis were one people, whether Hindu or Muslim.

Girdhari Lal never foresaw the violence. None of them did. He was a fair man, an optimist, and his wife, Lajwanti, still spoke admiringly of him. He'd advised their Hindu neighbors against locking the gates to their lane at night—as some families had proposed, frightened by the news of killings in the province—because it would hamper the access of the Muslim laborers who lived in shacks outside the perimeter wall and did odd jobs for them. They could be seen in the lane every day, some leading donkeys loaded with sacks of bricks and mortar.

On the night of August 19, a few days after Partition was announced, violence spreading like a fire from place to place, Girdhari Lal slept in a charpai in the courtyard, the house stifling in the heat. Lajwanti lay asleep in the cool hay room with their youngest daughter, Premi, the only child left at home—Dipi was a college student in Lahore then; his two elder sisters were married and living in other cities. In the middle of the night, the screams of their horses woke them. When Lajwanti opened the hay room door, she saw men pulling the animals away by ropes. Girdhari ran toward the sheds, shouting at the thieves. The same laborers who made small repairs around the property dragged him into the house—she recognized some of their voices. Her husband cried out the name of a man he favored.

Lajwanti shut the door, covered Premi with heaps of straw. Hearing Girdhari Lal's shrieks, she didn't know whether to run out to help him or stay to protect her daughter. Mother and daughter remained in hiding all night and all day. The next evening, Lajwanti crept into the house, hoping her husband might only be injured, but she found him on the floor. His throat had been cut—to Bebeji, she only said, "they killed him." The cupboard had been ransacked, all the jewelry taken. Lajwanti ran to her daughter, and they fled the house, the lane, the city, under cover of darkness, joining a group of Hindu families escaping Chiniot. That was the story Jaya remembered hearing through an open door when she was twelve. Lajwanti and Premi had come to stay with them in their Colaba flat soon after it happened, crying with relief to find Dipi already there, not knowing where the two older girls and their families were. Not knowing where they could make their home.

Bebeji's fingers went to the corners of her eyes, as if pressing away tears. Jaya laid a hand on the soft flesh of her grandmother's back. So much was gone. Bebeji was fifteen hundred miles from Punjab, far from her only brother and three elder sisters, far from her friend Satya, whom she called her younger sister. She was cut off forever from west Punjab, their homeland, feeling so out of place in Bombay she called herself a "refugee," even in her son's home, saying the English word crudely as if to spit upon herself—*Ref-oogee*.

A short while later, Jaya—along with Kamlesh, still damp from her bath—sought their mother's help in selecting appropriate saris for the havan. Vidya looked through their wardrobe. Bebeji came into the room with an air of purpose, looking more robust than earlier, carrying a plate of blanched almonds leftover from her kheer with some honey and fresh butter. She made a round with her plate, poking the almonds rolled in butter and honey into the twins' mouths, exhorting them to build up their stamina. "You both should have red, red cheeks glowing with health," she commanded.

"Do we look pale?" Seated at the dressing table, Kamlesh untangled webs of damp hair with her fingers, carefully pulling apart the knots.

Bebeji snatched up a comb. "I'll do it for you. Stand up."

The ancient dressing table with its deep drawers and stepped surfaces had been passed on to them by their mother when she had a new one built for herself. Its tall center mirror, flanked by two narrower panels, seemed to expand the dimensions of the room. Bebeji had objected to its presence, frowning if she caught either of them lingering in front of the triple mirrors. Their weakness was this vanity of looking at themselves, she scolded them, of showing themselves off—in drawings, in dance. If she found Kamlesh making the eye expressions of Bharata Natyam to herself in the glass, she admonished her with a sharp word.

"What does Gandhiji teach?" she demanded at unexpected moments, and then sternly provided the answer herself: "Once you become selfless, you become strong."

"Their health is all right," their mother said, as though defending herself against an accusation of failing her daughters. Her hair was pinned back neatly in a bun, her face made up with a dusting of powder, a tentative composure easily cracked by Bebeji's criticisms or habit of questioning her. Mummy took pleasure in the praise her friends offered up at her daughters' artistic talents—at Jaya's paintings hanging in the flat, and at Kamlesh's impromptu dance demonstrations, which she would put on at their mother's insistence for the ladies gathered in the drawing room for tea. Bebeji would chastise Mummy for coveting the admiration of her friends. They wouldn't admire her daughters' "artistic talents," she said, if they knew how art could unbalance a girl, leave her lost in her fantasies. Unlike Mummy, who'd grown up with great privilege until her father's death and been given piano and drawing lessons to cultivate her talents, Bebeji spoke of art as a dangerous thing, as if it might injure the twins. Jaya, too, sensed a danger in art, though it didn't deter her. A real artist, she thought, could belong to nothing else. But Mummy would say, "Don't be an extremist, Jaya," if she spent a few hours by herself drawing or painting. "A girl has to be good in many things. In studies, in her dress—later on in keeping a house, in cooking, in looking after a family." But an artist, Jaya thought, had to be an extremist.

"The girls in our family have to be careful about maintaining their strength," Bebeji now declared, coming over to feed Jaya more almonds.

Jaya accepted the honey-coated morsels, worrying her grandmother mistook her and Kamlesh in her mind for her daughter, Shivan Devi, who had died at the age of thirteen—a little older than they were when Bebeji and Lalaji came to live with them after Partition. Bebeji spoke of Shivan vanishing like a bird flying from its perch, when she contracted meningitis. The only thing that remained of Shivan was the picture Bebeji kept on her shelf in the alcove: three of her children posed in a photographer's studio—Shivan's hand resting on the shoulder of her little brother Harbans—sometime in 1917 or 1918.

From her cupboard, Kamlesh took out the ivory-yellow voile Mummy had suggested, seeking Bebeji's approval. Any light-colored sari would do for the ceremony, Bebeji agreed, only she was obliged to wear pure white. Returning to the cupboard, Kamlesh began hunting through the shelves for something else, pulling out shawls, stray chunnis, stacks of neatly pressed salwar kameez. Then she found it—a fringed scarlet muffler she draped over her hand. "Lalaji bought this for me in Lahore. It was so chilly one winter when we went to see you. We hardly had a sweater each, coming from Bombay." She remained standing by the cupboard, as if she didn't want to come too close to Bebeji with the memory.

"Lalaji was always buying us things in the bazaar, like those Bakelite dolls," Jaya added, pronouncing it "Bac-you-lite," as her grandfather had. With his long fingers he would dole out exact counts of pistachios and dates into their palms from the jute sacks he kept in a storeroom. He'd been forced to go into business, finding his way to the wholesale trade in dry fruits. Bebeji's leadership role in the Lahore Congress Committee, the name "Nihal Devi Malhotra" in the papers, had cost him his job as income tax officer. Government service—assistance to the British rulers—had been the primary source of employment for educated Indians so Lalaji had considered no other option.

Stepping across to examine the scarf, touch the coarse wool, Jaya was pleased Kamlesh had thought of it, a reminder for Bebeji that they'd been tied to Lalaji's life in Lahore too.

The Khoslas were the first to arrive for the havan at eleven. Portly, garrulous Khosla Sahib, their father's business partner—the owner of the glassworks—offered a solemn greeting to Bebeji, his head bowed. Mrs. Khosla, always formal, turned to everyone with a prim "namaste." Khosla Sahib took Daddy aside a few minutes later, and Jaya heard him mention a discussion he'd had with so-and-so at a bank about extending their line of credit by a certain amount.

In the drawing room, where arriving guests were served refreshments, the pandit cracked mango wood into smaller pieces, building a pyramid of sticks in the iron brazier. Everyone had removed their shoes outside the door to keep the space for the ceremony pure. Jaya and Kamlesh posted themselves beside their grandmother, feeling protective of her, although almost all those invited were family members. It was a Sunday so the men were free to come. Some of these distant relations had stayed with them in their Colaba flat for a few weeks, some for a few months, about fifteen people in all finding refuge with them during Partition. Jaya wondered if Kamlesh felt an instinct to guard herself, too, from the memory of that time when what they heard in any room they entered were tearful stories, urgent whisperings, or open sobbing. Men had argued over how to find accommodation and jobs or consoled each other. Everywhere in their old flat had risen the cries of family people whose very lives had been torn from them.

Now no one said anything remarkable—"How are you?" "Children all right?" "Yes, yes." Some fondly remembered Lalaji: "He was a gem of a person." "How good he was to us, after all he'd been through." The wrenching stories Jaya remembered about people couldn't be guessed at by their ordinary appearances, their small talk. The ladies gently smiling, the men restrained.

Rarely did the family gather in such a large group. Jaya could recall meeting everyone like this only a couple of times, for the marriage of someone's son or daughter. Modest functions on the outskirts of town. The girl she knew best, Sarojini, a mother of two now, asked quietly about her new college—did she find medicine a tough subject? Another five years of study? Jaya wanted to know how the babies were.

A plain girl with her sari draped over her head, Sarojini didn't smile. She had a flat, neutral gaze; it was hard to know what she felt underneath. When she'd stayed with them, as part of her husband's extended family, she'd worn an expression of pure devastation. Pathans armed with swords had stormed the family's apartment in Karachi some weeks before Partition, and her father-in-law, a relative of Lalaji, had cried out for her to fetch the locker key, shouting its location in a drawer in his room. The family, clutching all the brothers' children, ran down the stairs and past a neighbor lying in blood in a common washing area, his head nearly severed. On their way to catch a boat across the sea to Bombay, they rushed to the bank to retrieve all their gold jewelry, silver, and cash, to start a new life in India. But they couldn't open the locker. Sarojini had brought the wrong key. She lay in Jaya's old bedroom one afternoon, whispering that she could understand why the whole family hated her.

Everyone's grief Jaya remembered—even those family people who hadn't sheltered with them but with other close relations in Bombay. The retired civil surgeon from Dera Ghazi Khan, who was taking a glass of water from Manoj's tray, had climbed on top of the boundary wall of his haveli along with his neighbors, throwing pots of boiling oil on the mob below trying to break down their doors. A doctor and his stocky gray-haired wife burning people with oil. The mob had run. A military transport truck arrived the next day to rescue Hindus, and it dropped them in a field near a remote railway station. They waited for three days in torrential rain for a train to arrive. The doctor's right eye constantly flickered in spasms, a nervous affliction he'd never had before Partition, according to Bebeji, who was his first cousin.

Sarvi Singh, son of Bebeji's dearest friend, Satya, a slim man with hair flecked bright silver, spoke earnestly to Manu. Sarvi was a subeditor at the *National Standard*, and Manu wanted to write for a newspaper when he grew up. Sarvi used to repeat the story of his escape from Pakistan like a fable whose ending he couldn't quite believe. The train for Hindu refugees he, his wife, and three children had managed to push into in Multan had braked to a sudden halt in the countryside. A horde wielding swords and axes jumped on board, slaughtering passengers—he could hear wailing and ferocious screaming in his bogey. Nearby, a man threw open the door to his private compartment, ushering in as many people as could fit. Sarvi's family jammed inside with about forty others before the door was bolted. Six Baluchi soldiers bearing rifles stood guard outside. The occupants' safe passage to India had been ensured by his best friend, a Muslim police official who could no longer guarantee his safety in their home city. When the train reached Amritsar, Sarvi and his family had to walk through a red river running in the corridor, the blood of fellow passengers whose bodies they had to shut their eyes to as they made their way out to the platform.

Her father helped Bebeji sit on the white-sheeted floor, taking his place opposite her as her only surviving child. The two of them turned to the pandit, an elderly man with a shining head as hairless as a stone, the iron pot of fire between them. Jaya joined Kamlesh, Manu, and Dipi, making a row of grandchildren directly behind Bebeji. The four of them were absorbed into a larger circle formed by their mother and the other family members. Against the lash of rain, the pandit sang his hymns, his voice expanding on the final vowel of each Sanskrit verse like a bell reverberating in Jaya's ear, holding them in an ancient spell of sound: "*Om mitraya svaa-haaa.*" On the last swelling syllable, Jaya watched her father drizzle a spoon of ghee on the flaming sticks. A sizzle and flare, followed by wisps of smoke rising. Bebeji spooned up the samighiri in her right hand and dropped the mixture of crushed bark and leaves into the fire, which released its sweet, earthy aroma.

Jaya pressed herself against Kamlesh, hearing Bebeji's sighs, afraid the many deaths her grandmother had known were colliding in her mind. Not only Lalaji's passing, but her son Girdhari Lal's murder and her daughter Shivan Devi's death of typhoid fever. And before that, the loss of her first child, who died a few days after she gave birth to him. They had wrapped him in soft cloth and cast him in the Chenab River, Bebeji once whispered, in Chiniot.

Chiniot, Hafizabad, Jhelum, Oakara, Sargodha, Lahore—these were places in the Punjab, now lost to Pakistan, whose names circulated in the family talk. Jaya and Kamlesh had been born in Sargodha, a city famed for its luscious oranges, a place they had no memory of. They had lived in a couple of towns in east Punjab, too, before their father was transferred to Bombay when they were five. The house they knew best in Punjab, their grandparents' home in Lahore—where they spent their summer vacations—was a mud-brick building with a large courtyard, a few doors down from the Bharati School. Bebeji had found them playmates among the schoolgirls when they were young—the daughters of her friends and neighbors. Traipsing between the house and the school, waiting for their friends to be let out, they had a joyous feeling of belonging to their grandparents' lane, to the Gowalmandi neighborhood.

Three days before Partition, men came at night and set fire to the entire line of Hindu houses and the girls' school. Bebeji's front room burned first; she and Lalaji, assisted by Dipi, who lived with them while attending college, managed to climb up the back boundary wall to escape. The family next door perished inside their house. The Muslim fire-tenders had sprayed water away from the flames, people said, to let the fire spread. Jaya felt as if she herself had seen the black ruins smoldering the next day, when Lalaji and Bebeji went to retrieve their things, the houses disintegrated to mounds of ash. Her grandparents and Dipi arrived in Bombay, numb and silent. When Jaya heard that the fire had blazed across the whole lane, she'd wanted to burn down the houses of the men who'd burned Bebeji's house. She'd wanted those men to burn.

The pandit's verses swelled and surged, sank and surged again, his burnt sticks speckled with a crust of white ash. Bebeji bowed her head deeply, and Jaya saw her shut her eyes against the flames. *"Sarva shanti. Shantirev sa mam shanti redhi. Om shanti, shanti, shanti,"* the pandit sang the final blessing. At the invocation of peace, Bebeji broke into a spasm of coughing. A moment later, she rose clumsily, dabbing her eyes with the edge of her white sari. Her face was covered in a bright sheen of sweat. They moved to make way for her, saw her head drop, heard choked sobs. Her elderly cousin, the civil surgeon, flung an arm out, rushing forward, crying, "Catch her." Jaya lunged to grasp Bebeji, who stumbled, her legs giving out beneath her. Daddy ran across to keep her from falling backward, and Dipi assisted, kneeling down and bringing their sobbing grandmother to sit up against him. Stroking Bebeji's back, Jaya felt her shuddering helplessly. Kamlesh clasped her hands, asking, "Why are you so cold, Bebeji?"

"Bring water," their mother ordered Manu, but it was Sarojini who rushed out of the room to fetch it.

"Leave me, Vidya," Bebeji murmured to Mummy, who tried to dab the sweat from her forehead. Water ran from Bebeji's eyes and nose and mouth.

"You must take rest," Daddy told her. He and Dipi helped her to slowly stand and walked her down the passageway between them, Jaya and Kamlesh following a step behind. "The children will be coming," Bebeji remembered in a small voice. To calm her, Vidya said they would tell her when the children were at the gate.

Their father ushered his mother through the bedroom to her alcove. Sheets of rain struck the back wall of windows, slipping down in blurry waves. Manu drew the curtains that separated their grandmother's alcove from the main bedroom, and the small space grew hollow and dim, vibrating with rain. Mummy helped Bebeji lie down, positioning the pillow under her head.

"Rest. Sleep if you can," said their father.

Inside the alcove, Jaya and Kamlesh stood by the curtains, mutely wiping their eyes. Together they sat down at the edge of Bebeji's bed. Lifting a corner of her bedsheet, they began to press her dry, cracked feet. Bebeji peered at them as if they were very remote, the great distance of the past separating her from them like a wide body of water.

4

CLOUDS DESCENDED ON the open land behind the factory, trapping odors of dung and mud, and as they walked through the thick, humid air, Jaya and Kamlesh brushed against each other without noticing, their eyes cast down to the wet field that streaked their feet with ocher-red clay like henna.

"Jaya-Kamlesh! Come on, you girls!" Dipi shouted from a distance, waving them forward with a baton of rolled drawings in his hand. Jaya waved back, urging her sister to hurry. Bebeji was with him, a stout figure in pure white, a worker from the factory clinging to her side. He'd been pleading with her to bless his newborn son. His hut lay somewhere out here behind the factory, he said, not more than a twenty-minute walk. Manu ran in great circles around the group as if he were playing in a sporting match, all of them dwarfed by the fractured hills thrown up against the dingy sky.

The atmosphere at home had been tense since Lalaji's death anniversary a week back. Mummy had urged them to leave the flat and see the glass tanks in operation, which had so impressed her, and everyone had been eager for the outing. Only Bebeji had protested, saying an hour's drive to Thana was too long, but Jaya and Kamlesh said they wouldn't go without her. They had come in the scorching heat of afternoon, unfortunately, since Jaya had a half day of classes on Saturdays.

Figures materialized in the empty landscape—spectral men crossing through the tall grass, goats scattered around a stand of palm trees, a faraway herd of buffalo tended by a shirtless boy striking the ground with a tall stick. Jaya loved the great wilderness of Thana, thirty miles north of the city. Somewhere in the middle of this lush land tilting up to the monsoon-green hills lay the site of Indus Glassworks' proposed workers' housing colony. A pamphlet she'd seen promoting the new industrial belt illustrated a thriving manufacturing city of the future, sleek chimneys billowing smoke into the air. At present, perhaps a dozen factories had gone up. Table fans, ball bearings, kerosene stoves, tractor parts—Dipi could recite the products made by the units neighboring Indus Glassworks Pvt. Ltd., which occupied the largest industrial compound in Thana after the Kilachands' automobile plant. At each phase of its development, they were taken to visit the factory and offer their impressions. It was virtually a family business—all of them calling it "our factory"—though their father could afford to invest only a small amount, having been a government servant all his life.

Dipi called out again. Jaya turned impatiently to Kamlesh. "Look where they've reached. Let's hurry up." She hated being left behind, being the slow one. She bent down to roll up the stiff cuffs of her salwar, shaking off her slippers. Kamlesh stopped to do the same, letting out a whimper when her dainty clutch purse fell in the muck. Carrying her muddy chappals, Jaya sprinted across the pebble-strewn slush, spraying wet mud onto her kurta.

"Wait! Don't run off like that!" Kamlesh cried out.

Jaya paused, looking back, giving her sister a chance to catch up. The factory compound was not far behind them, closed off by a high boundary wall topped by jagged shards of glass. Above the serrated iron roof of the furnace shed, twin chimneys rose into the sky, one expelling a red flame and the other plumes of hot gases. A three-month trial phase of production was underway, an engineer brought over from America to train the workers. The whole enterprise filled them with pride—it would be the third largest glass factory in the country, eventually employing four hundred workers. Jaya could faintly hear some laborers' children screaming as they jumped off large pipes stacked beside the back gate. Kamlesh had stopped to talk to them earlier and asked where they lived. In those hills, the children said, pointing to the distance. Jaya and Kamlesh were puzzled—"Those hills? So far away?"

"Come on, let's run up," Jaya scolded her twin, gesturing ahead to the others. She began walking quickly, still agitated by the tension at home. For two days after the ceremony for Lalaji, Bebeji had refused to eat. Only in the last few days had she started taking a chapati with some dry vegetables. She kept saying she was born in Punjab and she wanted to die there, asking Daddy to buy her a train ticket to Ludhiana, where her brother Lekh Raj lived, the eldest of five. Finally, their father had ordered her to stop talking like that. Jaya had sat at her writing table, listening, the old dread coming back to her—that sense of being trapped in the despair of the people she was bound to. The same sensation that had shaken her after Partition, when the family people's stories caught like hooks under her skin, forgotten only during the hours she was at school. She had been eager to come here and walk in the open for distances that weren't possible in the city, to free her mind by wandering.

Lifting her gaze to the hills, Jaya realized what she had taken to be croppings of black rock amid the flourishing greenery were probably clusters of shanties, spreading like a wild rainy-season growth, their zigzagging lines tracing the ridge's ragged stone contours. "People are living up there, it looks like. Just as those children said," she remarked to Kamlesh.

"Where?"

"On that big, long hill—there are jhopadis up there." She gestured to the dark blots along the front ridge. Behind it the rocky peak of another, taller hill was sheared off at a steep angle. Within the folds of the ridge were what appeared to be black holes that might be openings in the stone. "I wonder if there are caves in those hills," she said to Kamlesh. "It would be interesting to go up and look."

Her old drawing master, Mhatre Sahib, had explored the hills outside Bombay, searching for caves decorated with rock sculptures and the frescoes of Buddhist monks. As an art student in the twenties, he had been taken to the Ajanta caves to create facsimiles of the ancient paintings by the light of flaming torches. For months, he and his class fellows had copied those sublime images of dancers and musicians and gods, an experience so vivid he dreamt about painting in that firelight for years afterward. Going into the caves, Mhatre Sahib said, he came to know himself as an image-maker. Hearing his story, Jaya wanted to submerge herself into drawing something as intensively as he had, to turn herself into an image-maker like him. She settled on flowers after viewing Mhatre Sahib's enchanting little book on flower paintings in history.

Everything she drew or painted, she did to please Mhatre Sahib. Everything he said, she took to heart. When Daddy enrolled her in Inter-science at sixteen, in the premedical section, Mhatre Sahib dismissed her. "Go, go into medicine—you've made your decision. Why do you need me?" He had chided her for betraying her talent, though he knew science wasn't her choice. At her last lesson he predicted she would never be an artist, and every day she fought his curse inside herself.

"Are you interested in going to look for paintings?" Kamlesh knew Mhatre Sahib had searched the hills in the area himself. "Forget all that. Don't think about him." They heard a shout. Dipi swept his arm across the air, beckoning them, and Jaya ran across the sucking mud like an animal taking flight.

On the way here, the main road past the grimy cotton mills of Parel had been blocked by a religious procession, people shaking tambourines, so Dipi had cut across to a smaller road. In the swollen traffic they came to a halt in front of a tenement with blue-painted galleries, where women lurked between lines of washing. On the opposite side of the road stood a Hanuman shrine. Jaya recognized the blue chawl opposite the Hanuman Mandir as Mhatre Sahib's building. Mummy had once taken her and Kamlesh to his home to view his work on his invitation. Mhatre Sahib had welcomed them grandly. His strangely shaped face, indented at the temples and bulging at the jowls like a pear, had glowed with pleasure. Every inch of his walls displayed pictures he'd made over the years, each done by a different hand, it seemed, in every style from the streaky seaside paintings you found in French art to tribal folk figures to copies of the Buddhist murals he'd made in the Ajanta caves. Each picture was lovely in its own right, but taken together they were a mirror image of a man who didn't know who he was. Jaya had protested fiercely when her mother suggested letting Mhatre Sahib go, distressed by the way he'd shouted at his wife and children for making a noise behind the curtained area where he'd hidden them. Even a disturbed guide was better than no guide at all.

Dipi waited for her to reach him. Her grandmother, Manu, and the electrician from the factory were about forty feet ahead. "Even Bebeji walks faster than you two," Dipi teased.

"Did you know there were huts up there?" Jaya pointed to the shanties along the ridge and he nodded. She breathed in her cousin's fresh cologne, matching her stride to his. In his cream trousers and white bush shirt, his hair lustrous with a sheen of Brylcreem, he looked ready for one of his restaurant outings with friends, although his clothes were old and he was wearing worn-out leather slippers. There was a gleam of wild enthusiasm in Dipi's eyes, a speed to him Jaya relished. He was the only one in the family who hadn't been pulled down by the quarreling at home, cracking his silly jokes, trotting out his old nicknames for them. Now he put a hand on his hip, observing Kamlesh's slow progress with a wry smile, and chided Jaya, "Why do you leave your sister behind like that?" They watched Kamlesh suddenly stop and reach down in one of her sinuous dance curves, a sculpted woman plucking a thorn from her foot, tossing it away.

"Bebeji, just wait," Dipi called ahead. He pointed out to Jaya the short stacks of bricks in the distance that Mr. Khosla had ordered be laid at regular intervals to mark the far boundary of the workers' housing scheme. Here, where they were standing, was the approximate center of the site. Her father had planned to come show them the new layout of the buildings, per the architect's revised plan, but Khosla Sahib had dropped by the office without warning. So it was left to Dipi to lead them here. Once he took his chartered accountancy exams, he would become part of management. He had already familiarized himself with factory operations, his nightly conversations with Harbans revolving around the glassworks.

When they'd all gathered around Bebeji, Dipi held open a crackling blueprint of the housing colony that would be set up as a small township, with a primary school, a dispensary, and a recreation ground in the center of four blocks of flats. He'd directed the electrician, Madan, to wait off to the side; the family had something to discuss among themselves. No need to reveal the details of the housing scheme to laborers now, he told them in Punjabi, and inadvertently encourage further demands. They glanced at Madan, a short, stunted man in his factory uniform—dark-blue half-pants and bush shirt—bristling with energy, pacing a short distance toward the hills and back, waiting to be summoned.

"The first housing block won't go up for another four years, at least," Dipi said authoritatively, "but I can guarantee no factory in Thana will offer anything like this. Ninety-five percent of their workers will go on living in jhopadis. More than half our labor force will be given one-room accommodation with a small kitchen—electric connection, running water. Those staying on that hill now will have pukka cement buildings to live in."

Bebeji asked to see all the drawings. Based on their architect's revised plans, they expected Bombay state to allot the factory ten acres for the housing scheme at nominal cost. Kamlesh helped Dipi unfurl another drawing. The front elevation of a block of flats was drawn in violet ink—a long cement carton three stories high, marked by rows of barred windows shielded by slab-cement overhangs. Tall, blossom-like coconut palms sketched in the background softened the impression of a barracks. "*Bauhat vadiya*," Bebeji said heartily. Her enthusiasm made them smile. *Wonderful*.

"If Bebeji has approved the scheme as good enough, Bombay government will also have to approve it," Dipi quipped.

"The workers' housing is not guaranteed." Bebeji shook her head doubtfully. "We don't know how Khosla will actually end up using the land." A familiar bitterness crept into her tone as she remembered Mr. Khosla's remark a short while ago, in the offices, that the Malhotra family wanted him to construct a "model factory" with every amenity for the worker—lifting the worker up on a throne! He'd pretended to joke, but they knew he was warning them to curb their demands. Perhaps he'd only sanctioned the workers' housing scheme to acquire a tract of government land virtually free of charge, Bebeji sometimes speculated, land that would be ambiguously earmarked "for the factory's future use" and might be appropriated for the expansion of his own facilities. Bebeji looked away from the plans, suspecting Khosla might only be using the architect's drawings to mislead the government about his intentions. "As if we're asking him to bring heaven to Earth for poor men. Don't the workers in such a big factory deserve to have a roof over their heads?"

Earlier, as they drove into the factory compound, newly planted Ashoka trees poking up along the boundary wall, the sight of the completed office building had astonished Bebeji—"My God, it's all finished." Jaya, too, was impressed that three years of construction had come to such a successful end. She hadn't been to Thana in months. The chalky smell of whitewash saturated the new offices; fans on long rods hung from the ceiling; modern furnishings decorated the reception area. Her father sat behind his massive desk, cardboard files arrayed in front of him. Mr. Khosla, occupying a visitor's chair, immediately stood up to pull a chair out for Bebeji. Jaya saw her grandmother's smile extinguish. Khosla Sahib normally sat at his office in town, her father in charge of the factory. The rest of them found seats, too, in the long row of chairs in front of Daddy's table.

Mr. Khosla brushed away the hair falling in his eyes like a disheveled boy and immediately announced his big news: a property developer putting up an eight-story building on Nepean Sea Road had just awarded him the contract for all the window glass. Naturally, they were all excited. "Eight stories, is it, Uncle?" Manu said. Jaya had heard her father speak about this particular project and imagined he was instrumental in securing the contract—all the big developers and engineering firms in Bombay were well known to him. For twenty years, he'd been a civil engineer with Buildings & Roads in the Central PWD, intimately knowledgeable about the boom in government construction projects after the British left. Everything from refugee housing to government offices was needed. When his friend Khosla mentioned his desire to invest in a new business, Harbans suggested manufacturing sheet glass. Only two suppliers existed in all of India, and since multistory buildings were going up everywhere, sheet glass would be in great demand. Jaya liked seeing her father in his new domain. He wore the relaxed expression of a man who had been away on a long holiday, an enormous burden set down behind him. His hairline was receding at the sides, but otherwise he looked almost youthful, his hair gleaming black. The pocket of his white linen shirt was appointed with two fountain pens, a sign of his fastidiousness.

"One has to earn a lot of money to build the model factory you idealistic Malhotras aspire to. Gandhiji's dreams don't come cheaply." Mr. Khosla laughed a dry laugh, sprawled in his armchair. He gestured to the full-length oil portrait of Mahatma Gandhi that hung on the bright blue wall behind Harbans's table. It was the most beautiful picture she'd ever painted, her father had told Jaya when she presented it to him for his new office. An image of Gandhiji walking bent-backed, supporting himself with a poor man's cane, a copy of a beloved picture that hung over her father's prayer nook at home. In front of them all, Bebeji praised Jaya for making such a fine reproduction—perhaps to avert her attention from Mr. Khosla. After a moment's courteous pause, Khosla Sahib continued his complaint, "Accommodation, primary school, medical care. Men will be queuing up for jobs at Indus Glassworks."

Bebeji bristled. Mahatma Gandhi called for building up India's villages, she corrected Khosla Sahib, he didn't see much value in industrialization. Didn't Mr. Khosla know it was Pandit Nehru who said 'We have to build up the country brick by brick'? That Nehru was the one who called hydroelectric plants and factories our new temples? Underlying Bebeji's bantering tone was an unmistakable edge of disdain.

Mr. Khosla sat up and pushed himself toward Bebeji, excitedly thrusting a finger out to make a point. "What I would like to know is, did any of you who were fighting for freedom imagine that one day something like this would be possible? An Indian factory employing the latest American technology? Manufacturing a product as good as what's made in the West?"

Bebeji's hands adjusted her sari palla over her head, a habit Jaya recognized as an effort to keep her composure. After a moment, she said, "How could we have predicted these things? Our struggle was to cut away the chains the British put us in. We thought of ownership in general terms— the ownership of the country changing back to our hands."

Supplying packing crates to the British during the war had made Khosla Sahib a rich man, Bebeji would say cuttingly at home, that's why you never heard him speak against them. She had spent three and a half years in jail after denouncing England for declaring India at war, coercing its participation in European battles without asking for its consent. Standing in front of Queen Victoria's statue in the center of Lahore, Bebeji had spoken out against the government of British India. "The English use our money and our men to fight their war! Let them rely on themselves," she had cried, attracting a crowd of passersby. "Our battle is with England: free us from bondage." Although the British had outlawed public protests during wartime, Congress had launched a campaign of individual rebellions. Protestors of conscience like Bebeji and Satya fully expected to be arrested. Bebeji later felt proud to tell her grandchildren her words had inspired the crowd to cry out vehemently: *"Inquilab! Zindabad!" Long Live the Revolution!*

She and Satya were imprisoned together in a filthy women's jail in a rural area, Bebeji losing her health until her bones showed through her skin, her life slipping out of her body, she said, in the absence of home. When the girls saw their grandmother after her release, she had already started to put on weight, Lalaji feeding her well to restore her vigor. She went on eating, she later said, because the extra weight made her feel solidly attached to the earth. What she feared most was the frailty she had experienced in jail that made her feel as if she almost didn't exist.

Mr. Khosla sent an office boy to summon the American engineer. Fifteen minutes later, Mr. Hunsinger, a long, loping man sent over by the American collaborators, his face bright red with the heat and eyebrows blanched gold-white, led them out for a tour of the factory. He was acquainted with them all, having come home for dinner a couple of times. "This is good curry," he would say enthusiastically, and Mummy would insist he have more. In the smoky darkness of the vast shed, Jaya couldn't hear his question to Bebeji over the growl of machinery, the hammering, clanging, and hissing noises resonating from the dim corners. Workers in half-pants, their faces glistening wet, yelled into the shadows occupied by the vague shapes of equipment. Bebeji stood absolutely still, listening to the noise as if it whispered a message to her. Jaya and Kamlesh flanked their grandmother, and Jaya leaned across to catch the engineer's joke. "Is it hot enough for you?"

"Yes, quite," Bebeji agreed in English, smiling. She couldn't be discouraged from climbing up a catwalk with them when they moved back into the depths of the shed. The engineer called the tank furnaces "the two volcanoes." This was the remarkable thing about their factory—the tank furnace technology from America. Other glass factories, not just the little cottage industries, but the large, organized works, still used pot furnaces. The soaring brick facades of twin thirty-ton tank furnaces, elevated on platforms and surrounded by a grid of catwalks, formed a second story within the building. Fired up to three thousand degrees Fahrenheit, Mr. Hunsinger cautioned, casting a warning glance at Bebeji. Nor could Dipi talk her out of climbing up, though they were already sweating profusely.

High above the shop floor on an elevated platform, they faced the massive wall of a tank furnace built of American refractory bricks. A worker used an iron rod to pry open a brick shutter outlined by the orange glow of fire. It was possible to look inside the tank for a moment. They each took a turn. Jaya stepped up, then sprang back a few feet as the heat hit her, holding up to the small window a paddle fitted with a pane of purple-blue glass to protect their eyes. A primal violet-blue sea of molten glass undulated inside the tank, thick bubbles slowly rising to the surface. Jets of white gas blew in from the corners like furious winds, and the tank walls shone like blue marble. Jaya was mesmerized and struggled to keep looking for as many seconds as she could, despite the infernal heat, until it felt like her body was wrapped in a shell of fire. She ran to the railing in a violent sweat. Bebeji was there, wiping rivulets of sweat from her face and neck with Dipi's handkerchief.

Returning to the production floor, they watched lengths of molten glass slide down the roller beds from the furnaces like sheets of fire. In the maintenance department, an area caged off by wire-mesh walls, they encountered the electrician. A small, bustling man, with a pockmarked face grained like rough stone, he switched on and off for their approval the focused beam of a lamp he had just repaired. Working overtime, he told Dipi. When he heard Bebeji was Malhotra Sahib's mother, he attached himself to her like a servant, offering to bring them cold drinks from the canteen. Later, as they wandered to the outbuildings in the compound behind the shed, Madan acted as Bebeji's interpreter with the workers who spoke only Marathi.

Men on their breaks squatted everywhere, smoking bidis, eating out of leaf wrappings, sleeping on piles of gunnysacks stuffed with soda ash and borax. A few perched atop tall mounds of white quartz sand. The ground glittered with crushed glass, and a luminous white crust of minerals spilled everywhere like salt. The grandchildren looked to each other, surprised to see Bebeji engage the laborers enthusiastically, asking what their job was, where did they come from. "What did you do before you came here?" she wanted to know. A young man offered to show her the batch house where he weighed raw materials, and she said, "Show me!" and went off with him for a few minutes. Kamlesh was as amazed as Jaya to watch Bebeji move from conversation to conversation, spontaneous exchanges that seemed to bring back the vigorous, spirited grandmother they had known in Lahore.

At the back gate, which framed a view of the hills, Madan implored Bebeji to give her blessings to his little boy. His only son. Born three weeks back. His hut lay in the same direction they were walking in, he said, gesturing toward the workers' housing site—just a little further away. Despite Dipi's protests, Bebeji agreed, and her grandchildren followed her.

A hot breeze ruffled the architectural drawings Dipi was winding into a tight tube. Kamlesh helped keep them in order. The wind swept the fronds of the palms off to the side like a woman's hair. Ahead, the clouds glowered over the hills. Straying a few paces from her family, toward the wild palms, Jaya wondered how this tilting landscape could be given form on canvas. How could a painter create its green sculptures, the hot mist hanging in the air? It was lush and beautiful—was that reason enough to paint it? Mhatre Sahib had said the pursuit of art was beauty. Modern artists didn't care about beauty only, she knew. Was fear something to paint? She wanted to find a new master and speak to him about it.

Dipi raised his voice harshly. She heard him shout, "No. Nothing doing. How can you ask such a thing?" He was rarely so angry. The electrician stood before him, folding his hands, bobbing his head. Jaya walked back, alarmed. Madan turned to say something to Bebeji, and she nodded. "That's too far for us," Dipi declared. In Punjabi he told Bebeji it was out of the question for her to climb up that stony hill. From here it looked green, but in the dry season you could see all the rock. And the ground was so mucky now, she might slip. He invoked his uncle Harbans—how furious he would be to know she'd taken such a risk.

No concession came from Bebeji. She seemed to weigh her options, looking ahead to the spur of isolated hills thrusting up from the ground like an illusion. Draped in bright shawls of monsoon greenery.

"It's hardly a fifteen-minute walk, Mataji, half a mile from here." Madan called Bebeji "Mataji"—Mother. A man from the North, like them. "A lot of people stay there; it's become like a village. Ganesh Murti Nagar, we call it. There's an old statue of Ganesha at the top. The shrine has fallen down, but the statue remains."

"How many people stay there? Why have you put up your jhuggies in such a difficult place?" Bebeji readjusted her coarse khadi sari, lifting the pleats as if she was ready to set off.

"What about your knees, Bebeji?" Jaya asked, because she ought to raise some objection. This wasn't a sensible thing to do, yet she thrilled to think Bebeji was on the verge of rejecting all their arguments. That she might again turn into the indomitable figure she once was.

No joint pain today, Bebeji reported. Despite Dipi's admonitions, echoed by Manu and half-heartedly backed up by Jaya and Kamlesh, Bebeji's determination to see the shanty colony hardened into a fierce emotion they could not deter.

Dipi was silent and angry on the walk. Jaya swung her slippers in her hands, asking about caves. Madan had seen no caves, he told her. There were three hills, one behind the other, he said; you could walk between two of them on which people had built their shanties. A dense girdle of trees enclosed the base of the long hill in the distance. From there a narrow tract ran across the wild grass, and a trickle of women and bashful children coming down from the hill passed them along this corridor. Dipi looked back to the distant acreage to be allotted for the workers' housing scheme, scolding Madan that the hills were more than half a mile away. Folding his hands, accepting his mistake, Madan sought forgiveness. "I only asked for the child's sake, Sahib."

"Let's carry on," Bebeji said.

They found little shade, walking under the palpitating light breaking through the cracks in the clouds. Crows screeched in the air, drawing Jaya's eye up as they darted furiously from the shelter of one lonesome tree to another. Leafy branches littered the ground in places, struck down by last night's rain. Crossing the sodden ground toward the hill, Jaya realized Kamlesh was so close beside her, they might have been holding hands.

The path winding uphill came as a relief, at first—broader than Jaya imagined, almost half the width of a lane. But sharp stones thrust up from its surface like blades. She and Kamlesh had to slip their chappals on, each gripping Bebeji by an arm. They climbed slowly, their feet slipping back in the red muck at times. Manu ran ahead in his sturdy shoes, stopping at intervals to look back at them. Dipi feebly insisted it wasn't too late to go back even now, shadowing Bebeji from behind as though he was ready to catch her if she fell. "Where's your hut?" he demanded of Madan. The electrician gestured vaguely ahead. "Just there—a little further."

Bebeji sighed, out of breath. People in the first line of shanties noticed them and came down, a crowd collecting in front of them, then people came up the graveled slope, appearing from nowhere, gathering behind them. The people and Bebeji exchanged questions and answers, Madan translating for both sides, though his Marathi was not much better than Kamlesh's. Kamlesh smiled, joining in the translating. The only one in the family who knew some basic Marathi.

"How long have you been living here?" Bebeji asked a group of women carrying earthen water pots on their heads. Three months, five months, a year, they heard. A woman carrying two spherical pots stacked like a tall clay crown lamented in Hindi, "More than a year, Ma, and for water I have to walk three-four miles to a well near some Agri people's huts. Sometimes, they won't let me take water, and I have to go further away to a pond near the Agra Road." Their sons were beaten if they were caught filling cans from outdoor taps in the factory compounds. Other women, holding their chunnis across their mouths, were reluctant to speak in front of Dipi, the young sahib from the factory brushing mud from his white trousers.

The crowd observed with great interest their ascent to a row of huts moored to a weedy green shelf of earth. Roofs of shaggy, dried palm fronds were littered with rotten baskets. A few insolent-looking boys in lungis joined the group of onlookers, and a couple of small girls strutted giddily in the commotion. One wore a glass bangle and no shirt, her coppery, dust-dry hair falling around her dirty face. Other children came traipsing down the slope to see what the noise was about. Madan called to a pretty, sharp-eyed girl in a torn skirt. She wound herself into her veil, a fraying wave of light-green fabric falling from her head to her ankles. "My daughter," Madan said, "a very capable girl." She fetched the firewood every day.

Kamlesh beckoned her, beckoned the other children. They regarded her in fascination. One girl wanted to touch the long necklace of red and silver beads she wore over her old shirt. Popping open her leather clutch, she offered two toffees, promising the disappointed faces she would bring enough for all of them next time.

"What is your name?" Jaya smiled at Madan's daughter, who replied in a small voice. "Lakshmi?" said Jaya. "That's a very pretty name."

The sisters took Bebeji by the elbow, one on each side, as Madan climbed further to a second congregation of shanties, the path a thread of red mud spattered with human excrement. "Horrible smell," remarked Kamlesh as they ascended steeply to a turn. A pale, hairless dog, his pink skin broken in patches seamed with blood, padded very slowly in the muck. Jaya pressed her hand against her mouth at the sorrowful sight. Suffering without dying, he appeared almost motionless yet continued to plod ahead.

"Take us back," Dipi shouted imperiously. The electrician had been charging ahead, leading the way, but now he took steps back toward them. "What do you think you're doing, making Mataji climb so far up? You have no sense?"

Jaya bent over to support her grandmother, who winced and grabbed her right knee. The reality of their situation struck her—Dipi was right. It was dangerous to have brought Bebeji up here. "How will we climb down with her?" she cried to Dipi. "It's too steep."

Again, Madan folded his hands. "Forgive me, Sahib, I didn't mean to make you suffer the hardships of a poor man. I just wanted Mataji to give her blessing to my boy. He's not been keeping well."

"It's not your fault," Bebeji said. "Come on, quickly take us to your house—let me see your child." It was like a village up here, she told Jaya and Kamlesh in surprise. No one was native to it, of course; it was an orphaned community, with this fellow Madan running around like the prince. To Jaya it seemed no village, but a collection of hovels taken out of a Bombay slum and scattered precariously across the stony shelves. A third line of shanties was cobbled together from timber scraps, rusted patches of tin, and tarpaulin, their roofs weighted down with crooked lines of stones and shards of clay pots. Bebeji paused, crying out again as she clutched her knee. She remained bent for a long moment. Then, straightening up, she seemed to want to forget the pain and asked the people whether there was a school available for the children. Did any of their children study?

"We're too far from Thana city, too far from any village school, we don't belong anywhere," said a woman clutching a wide-eyed little boy on her hip.

A stooped woman beside her, with a shriveled face like a spoiled plum, replied in trembling Marathi that the younger woman translated into

Hindi: "This is one place where we knew no one would throw us off the land, no one sees us here. No one will bother us . . ." Jaya leaned forward as the old woman angled her head up, gasping for air, showing them the blind whites of her eyes.

"Form a group. Go to the municipality and tell them to put up a school for your children," Bebeji said. "You pay the government their due, they must provide for you."

"Why don't you speak out for us, Mataji?" Madan demanded, a canvasser stirring the sentiments of the crowd. "Mataji is a freedom fighter from Punjab. She fought with Gandhiji and Pandit Nehru to throw the English Sahibs out of India," he proclaimed to the shanty dwellers, "so poor people like us wouldn't have to go on living like insects—"

"You know everything, do you? Don't talk too much," Bebeji admonished him, but Jaya could see her lips twitch with a buried excitement. Madan might have overheard them happily talking among themselves about how it seemed like the old Nihal Devi Malhotra, general secretary of the Lahore Congress, had returned, rallying people as she went around the factory compound, speaking to the workers on their breaks.

"Do something for us, Ma," the woman carrying the small boy cried out. "We're a thousand, two thousand people up here. We have nothing."

Others echoed her, closing around Bebeji.

"That is what the English left us with—nothing." Bebeji spoke animatedly. *Loot liya.* "They took all our wealth, took it all the way to England with them. Left our people starving."

"Bring us water, Ma," someone cried.

"Mataji is tired after all these years." Dipi said, as if in Bebeji's defense. "Show your strength by forming an association and go to the tehsildar with your demands—"

Jaya gave her cousin a sharp glance—why did he puncture Bebeji's spirits? She didn't seem tired here; she seemed herself.

Bebeji remained quiet, as though recognizing in Dipi's words that her time had passed.

"Where is your house?" Jaya inquired of Madan, to shift her grandmother's attention. Madan's daughter eyed her in puzzlement from beneath her soft green veil bitten with holes. *Are they coming to my house?*

The gashed bed of rock and dust on which Madan's jhopadi stood looked across the sweep of fields, toward the long shed and double chimney pipes of the glassworks. A small thatched roof was raised on bamboo poles to shelter a mud stove and a few cooking utensils. Madan planted his hands on his hips, shouting inside the hut for his wife. "Ram Shree! Bring the child. Sahib and Mataji have come!" His daughter turned her head expectantly from person to person, smiling, watching for some drama to unfold.

An infant was carried out. He squeezed his hands into tight fists, opened his mouth in a soundless shriek as he emerged into the light in the arms of a woman who reached no higher than Jaya's shoulder. Her sari was pulled low over her face like a veil, covering her eyes. When Bebeji tried to talk to her, she giggled, so Madan spoke for his wife. The child began to whimper, bundled in a dirty cloth, his eyes outlined in sooty smudges of kajal. His sister pulled on her mother's arms to hold him lower, and she stroked his face to calm him.

They had to have Bebeji inside their home. Bebeji pulled Kamlesh and Jaya along into the windowless black shanty, which smelled of soil and musty wheat. A corner devoted to the gods was on display, Madan lighting an oil lamp in front of a few blackened metal idols. The twins joined Bebeji in bowing their heads to the deities. All Jaya could make out in the prayer lamp's dim light was bedding open on the earthen floor and the globes of two water pots leaning against a wall. Madan pushed Lakshmi forward: "She attended school for a year." He found the wooden writing board she'd used behind some bundles. Its dried-mud surface had crumbled away.

"You learned handwriting?" Kamlesh leaned down to touch the board. The girl spoke up, a little more sure of herself, saying she had learned to write the alphabet in Hindi, but she'd forgotten it now. "That's all right. You can learn it again," Kamlesh murmured.

Outside there was a loud commotion as people laughed and called out, crowding around the narrow doorway, craning their necks to catch a glimpse of the "factory owners" inside one of their huts. Boys pushed down on each other's shoulders to jump up for a look.

"You must sit down," Ram Shree said to Bebeji in a soft voice, finding composure inside the shadowed room. "You've come so far by foot, you must be tired."

Get a stool, find a stool! They wouldn't allow Bebeji to sit on the bare earth floor. The English word "stool," uttered by Madan, darted through the crowd. Within minutes, a short, boxy stool appeared, lifted over the heads of the onlookers and passed inside to Madan. Ram Shree dusted the seat before spreading a cloth over it. Bebeji bent her knees slowly, clutching Kamlesh's hand as she sank to her low throne, her white sari flaring out on the dusty ground. Madan's family arranged themselves around Bebeji and her granddaughters, his wife asking Jaya to place the infant on Bebeji's lap. Holding him, Jaya felt a livid heat, and she touched his moist face, whispering to Bebeji that he was burning with fever. Bebeji frowned, pressing her hand to the boy's forehead, saying they would take him to a clinic in Thana.

They lifted their gazes, smiling, composing a portrait in the absence of a camera—the men, women, and children gathered outside pressed forward into the doorway to take a good look. Then their laughter diminished and everyone quieted to behold the moment: the occasion of the stool.

5

THE SIDE GARDEN, shadowy and deep, drew Jaya away from the wedding guests on the lawn into a patch of ebony trees. In the dark, the soft hiss of the sea hundreds of feet below the rocky slope called to her. For a girl to disappear alone into the darkness to behold the sea would seem strange to others, so she stopped herself from going farther. At the opposite end of the long garden was Leela's building, divided into four apartments, a handsome and solid mansion. Strands of blue lights were draped down the back facade—the same blue lights that glowed in the hedges and shrubbery, leaving only this small grove of trees unlit. The wedding tent, roaring with noise, stood some yards away. Jaya found it pleasant to stand between the voices and the silence, taking both in.

A mural of Mughal arches entwined with colorful flowering vines was printed on the shamiana's fabric wall. Jaya walked back up toward the crowd, pausing to look into the tent's wide opening. Chandeliers shed a gold light on bearers in fanned turbans carrying trays of food to the boy's people, who were eating their dinner at long, cloth-covered tables. Leela's family members milled around, attending to them. There was Kamlesh, to Jaya's surprise, among a group of girls escorting Leela in her heavy red bridal sari, shimmering with spirals of gold gota, to the groom's table. An older man beside the groom rose so Leela could be seated in his chair.

People turned to look at the unusual sight of the bride coming to her groom's side before the wedding ceremony. Leela's friends hovered off to the side of the couple, curiously studying the groom's face.

Jaya watched as Kamlesh, in her flickering sequined blue sari, leaned eagerly forward for a closer look. Earlier, the veil of flowers hanging from the groom's ceremonial turban had concealed him, but at the table the long strands of jasmine and marigold blossoms had been pushed away to his shoulders, exposing his face—narrow, with a thin mustache. Serious, intelligent, friendly. He regarded Leela with concern as she hung her head helplessly before a pedestaled bowl of fruit. Jaya considered joining Kamlesh and her college friends, who were trying to listen in on what the groom was saying to Leela, but she'd felt out of place in their clique earlier. They had all gathered around the bride in her flat, recalling the great fun they'd had together in their Inter-arts course—incidents which Jaya had to try to feign interest in.

Jaya walked away, threading between shifting clusters of people on the lawn. No circle of familiar faces she might join. Ten yards away, her father looked handsome in his Nehru jacket, his head thrown back in a hearty laugh. There was a new ease about him these last few years. The friends he stood among were government servants, as he had been—how astonished they had been when he traveled to America with Mr. Khosla to sign the partnership agreement with Eerie Glass. People were known to sail to England, but who had ever flown to America? So many stops he'd made on the way—Cairo, Bahrain, Rome, London. Her eyes lingering on her father, Jaya felt privileged and lucky at that moment as she swept across the lawn in her sand-colored silk.

"Jaya, come, come." Her mother had spotted her. Looking glamorous in sea-green silk and pearls, she was surrounded by a familiar group of Punjabi ladies. One smart lady Jaya didn't recognize spoke haughtily of her search for a cook: every candidate had been put through a "soup and soufflé test." A well-to-do businessman's wife most likely—no government servant's family Jaya knew of ate soufflés and soups. The woman's hair was cut and curled in waves, like a European. The traditional ladies in Mummy's crowd were large-hearted and "god-fearing," as Mummy called them. Jaya offered a smile to the wife of Bebeji's cousin, the retired civil surgeon, whom she had greeted earlier. Auntieji might have been a society lady from the glow on her face, past hardships momentarily forgotten, her squarish figure sheathed in a mauve and silver sari.

Immediately Jaya found herself being shown off by her mother. "Every evening she studies so late. I asked Malhotra Sahib, 'Why did you make her do the most difficult course?'"

Jaya merely smiled, telling the gathered ladies in their bright winter silks that she was adjusting to medical college. "It's fine, auntie," she kept saying to expressions of concern. "Not too difficult, no." She had her pride. One auntie asked if she knew the medical college boys who were here—Prakash's friends, the groom's brother and his crowd. Jaya professed not to have seen them. Coming downstairs from Leela's flat earlier, she'd nearly run into a group of college boys at the back veranda. Senior fellows. She'd seen a tall figure in profile behind them, who might have been the chap from the Boys Common Room, and walked swiftly past. After that she couldn't stop wondering if he was here. She had wandered through the crowd of a few hundred people, then walked in the direction of the sea, trying to gather her thoughts.

Big-hipped and busty, Shuli Auntie, radiating old-fashioned Punjabi warmth and care, inquired about Bebeji—why hadn't she come? Bebeji didn't keep late nights, her mother said; she liked to go to sleep by nine-thirty. Normally it worried Jaya when her grandmother avoided social functions and isolated herself at home, but Bebeji was in a different mood now, active and consumed with creating a scheme to improve conditions for the people on the hill. Jaya had sketched her grandmother writing in a cardboard-backed register that contained her evolving blueprint for the shanty colony and had produced several accurate likenesses. All motion in Bebeji's static poses was psychological—a vitality Jaya tried to capture with charcoal pencil by showing the forward tilt of her massive head and her puffy, bespectacled eyes, while the rest of her face fell away in shadow. "Bebeji's quite occupied with some work these days," she mentioned to Shuli Auntie. "She gets tired by the evening."

Leela's aunt inquired where Kamlesh was when she spotted a particular lady walking up the lawn with a group of young people. How nice it would be for Kamlesh to meet them, Shuli Auntie confided to Jaya and Vidya, waving exuberantly to the small group. That was Mrs. Bakshi with her daughters and her son, Vikram, the groom's cousin. Leela thought he would make an excellent match for Kamlesh, Shuli murmured. She waved to the group again and they approached. Jaya glanced at them, a nice-looking family—three adult sisters and the brother, a young executive in a suit. Kamlesh had complained that Leela kept going on about this boy to her, as if she fancied they could pair up as the brides of two cousins, living together in that remote quarry town in the jungle.

Shuli Auntie made the introductions to Mrs. Bakshi and her children. Jaya was described as Leela's good friend Kamlesh's sister. "Both look just the same," Shuli Auntie declared. "Identical twins." Jaya didn't contradict her. She averted her glance from the boy and smiled broadly at his sisters, feeling like she was standing in for her twin. Mrs. Bakshi smiled faintly, a subdued lady with low, hooded eyes that seemed to carry a burden. A moment later she murmured that she'd heard Kamlesh's name. Leela had been talking about all her college friends, Kamlesh especially, and how much she was going to miss them.

Vikram Bakshi had a well-shaped, broad Punjabi face, thick black hair, and wide shoulders. The same gentleness of manner Jaya had sensed in his cousin, the groom. "A very handsome boy" had been Leela's emphatic description of him to Kamlesh. That much was true, Jaya could attest to her twin. "You're working in Bombay?" Mummy asked Vikram. He offered a very long name in response—British India Steam Navigation something. Not a shippie, a sales manager.

Mrs. Bakshi grew more animated with Mummy, the two of them court-ing each other, it appeared, on behalf of their children. They discovered they'd both attended Kinnaird College in Lahore, Mrs. Bakshi passing out before Mummy in 1928. Memories of college fluttered between them like reminiscences of a vanished paradise. They'd both enjoyed acting in the historical dramas the college was famous for putting on. They grew girlish in manner, slipping back to the delights of their youth—this picnic, that jovial teacher, the endless rehearsals for their plays. The other women were silent; probably none of them had attended college.

Jaya almost blurted out that Kamlesh must have gotten her love of performing from Mummy, but she refrained. Some Punjabis shunned girls who danced, regarding any woman who performed in public as a sort of prostitute. Though the Bakshis seemed to be enlightened people, Jaya kept her silence, not wanting to spoil their good impression of her sister, who Mrs. Bakshi, being discreet, said she would like her daughters to meet.

Sometime later, after the Bakshis drifted away, Jaya left her mother and looked around for a group of young people to join. Not Dipi and his friends—older boys who looked too keenly at her when they dropped in at home. She kept wandering, coming upon Kamlesh and her college girls at last. They'd all fed Leela with their own hands, Meher reported excitedly; she'd been too nervous to eat on her own. The whole big group of friends stood near the building's back veranda, eight or nine girls, small blue lights glittering down the facade. Meher looked like a grown-up stranger in dangling earrings set with precious stones, a prominent brooch pinning her exquisitely embroidered jade sari to her shoulder. Then Shuli Auntie had burst into the room saying *he* was asking for her, Meher went on, filling Jaya in on the high drama she'd missed earlier in Leela's flat. No one could believe it! What a modern fellow, the groom! Wanting to eat his dinner with his bride!

Jaya smiled. She wished she could shift closer to her twin, to tell her about the steamship navigation boy. Leela was right—how handsome Vikram Bakshi was! She kept trying to catch Kamlesh's eye, but Kamlesh was caught in a silly conversation with a friend, constantly laughing. When she turned back to Meher, some medical college boys joined their group—white shirts, thin ties, dark trousers. The groom's brother's friends. One of the girls was apparently related to one of them. Good excuse for the rest of them to push their way into a girls' group.

A bearer in a white coat and fanned white turban came around with a tray of soft drinks. "Hey, what happened to you?" a boy called out to someone. After a moment, Jaya realized she was being spoken to. A boy with oiled hair and black-framed spectacles. She recognized him. "You don't play table tennis anymore?" He stood with his hands on his hips like an authority, announcing to the others with an air of amusement, "She and her friends used to barge into the Boys Common Room and brazenly take over the T.T. table from us."

Jaya looked away toward Kamlesh, too stunned to reply. Kamlesh gave her an encouraging half smile. She'd played table tennis only a few times, in any case, and a couple of months ago she had stopped going to the common room altogether to protect her reputation and save herself the embarrassment of the Bengali chap's silent gaze, which left her uncertain about what he wanted from her.

Wagging her finger at Jaya's accuser, Meher broke the strained silence. "Don't tell tales out of school!"

It helped Jaya find her voice. "We gave up such silly pranks," she muttered, trying to sound dismissive. The boy chuckled, looking a little chagrined over humiliating a first-year girl so easily. He turned his sights on someone he considered more of an equal. "So, tell us the film world gossip, Ashok. Which picture is your uncle making next? Who'll be his heroine?" He glanced around at the girls, pleased to offer a new entertainment. The other boy, Ashok, had been looking between Jaya and Kamlesh, trying to figure out their relationship. As their large group had broken in two, he'd maneuvered close to Kamlesh, and the bespectacled boy's question had caught him off guard.

Eyes blazing, Kamlesh asked, "Your uncle makes pictures? Which are his films? I might have seen some of them." Her interrogation of the boy amazed Jaya. Normally their presence intimidated her, leaving her too inhibited to speak.

Lush black locks grazed Ashok's brow. Jaya knew his face from college—he was part of Farrokh Wadia and Kirti Dasgupta's crowd—but she hadn't known of his illustrious connection to the director N. D. Narula. Ashok Narula beamed gently at Kamlesh—his uncle's latest picture was a Laila-Majnu story, a doomed romance. Smiling, considering the tragic possibilities with downcast eyes, Kamlesh said it sounded lovely.

Had he seen *Anarkali*, Kamlesh wondered—and when he said yes, she told him she'd seen it five times now! The last time, the men in the cinema hall had showered the screen with coins when Bina Rai danced for the prince in the hall of mirrors. Oh yes, Ashok said, what a scene that Sheesh Mahal scene was, their mutual reverie about Kamlesh's favorite movie interrupted by others joining their group.

The very handsome boy who worked for the steamship navigation company greeted Kamlesh with a cordial smile, like a gentleman, when Jaya made the introduction with proper formality: "Mr. Bakshi, please meet my sister Kamlesh. She's Leela's friend." Her twin acknowledged him with a shy whispered hello. Then Vikram Bakshi turned fully toward Kamlesh, who glimmered in a sapphire chiffon sprinkled with silver sequins, and the director's nephew surely felt his star dim, for he stepped away to join a small group going down to watch the marriage ceremony. Some people had gathered around the mandap at the bottom of the garden. The groom was seated under the open canopy, leaning toward the fire pot, the pandit sitting on the ground opposite him. The marriage rites would continue for a couple of hours, and most people would take a few minutes out during the party to go and watch.

Having no film to discuss with Vikram Bakshi, Kamlesh stood tongue-tied before him. He had to be in his midtwenties, well spoken, dashing in his dark suit. His questions sustained the conversation: "Oh, you're studying English literature? Which authors do you like?" Had Kamlesh really said "Any of them"? Jaya gave her an annoyed glance. *What about* Jane Eyre? *Isn't that your favorite book?* She could not speak for her twin, nor admonish her as she would have liked, since she felt herself reflected in Kamlesh. *Speak up—as if you have some intelligence.*

"I was studying in Lahore, but I got admission in Sydenham College without too much trouble," Vikram Bakshi replied to Kamlesh's muted inquiry about his studies. He spoke of the change casually, with a lightness about him that made Jaya wonder why he'd chosen to leave Punjab in favor of studying in Bombay. After a minute the year of his arrival sank in—they'd come in '47, he said. He hadn't simply left Lahore; his whole family must have fled. His father must have sought shelter with his brother here—the groom's father, who was performing the marriage rituals along with his wife under the canopy beside their son.

A strong breeze blew off the sea, the girls holding down the long fluttering ends of their saris to the boys' smiles. Heavy-hipped Shuli Auntie trudged toward them. Her thinly plucked eyebrows rose high with her merry voice. "All you girl's people, come and have your food. Our turn now, come on! O! What a nice group you've made, both sides mixing."

Kamlesh's friends giggled, surmising her real meaning—here were the two sexes mixing in a way one rarely saw. Some of the girls, perhaps embarrassed, began moving toward the grand shamiana for dinner. It annoyed Jaya to see Kamlesh slip away from Vikram Bakshi's lingering gaze—didn't she realize he wanted to keep talking to her? Jaya looked hopefully toward his sisters, trying to appear friendly, but they were chatting intently with another girl. She was about to go after Kamlesh when some others came along. Two girls, a chap she recognized from college. Then another fellow from the common room, accompanied by the tall Bengali boy. He was magnificent in a stiff-collared white shirt, his hair trimmed and neatly combed. She couldn't look at him.

Standing in front of a dim arch of the high-roofed veranda, lights shimmering on either side behind her, Jaya wondered how she could escape. It seemed as if Kirti Dasgupta was the only one there, coming straight toward her as her group broke apart like a puzzle. To which fragment did she belong?

He lifted his eyes to hers, cracking a brilliant smile. "You're Miss Malhotra, isn't it? I've seen you around at college."

In one unexpected moment, Kirti Dasgupta had smashed the compact of silence they'd kept for almost six months, sending a jolt through Jaya. He stepped away from his friends and Vikram Bakshi's chattering sisters, toward the veranda steps, as if suggesting they enter the dark corridor together. But it wasn't that. "Do you mind if I smoke?" Mr. Dasgupta fished in his shirt pocket. Not at all—she smiled. "Others might not like it," he explained. "Why cause offense?" A cigarette and a matchbox in his hands. He lit up, waved away the flame, tossed the match on the grass. No one would see her here with him, in the shadows of the veranda, the others forming a screen shielding them.

Which side was she connected to? he asked. She told him and he laughed, confessing, "We hostelites have been feasting this evening. Very delicious food." The groom's brother was a year senior to him, but they'd become good friends at the Old Boys Hostel. His parents stayed in town; they had an army bungalow in Colaba. His father was an officer. Not fair that girls living in town were allowed to enjoy the comforts of home, he teased, while boys were required to slog it out in the hostel. Jaya laughed, admitting she was lucky. Five years in a cell like Hema's, without her family, would have been hard to bear. She kept fingering the tarnished gold cord around her neck from which a round pendant hung, aware of him watching her stroke her throat, and she felt she had some power over him. She told him things about herself. She liked to draw, paint. He'd noticed her sketching in the Boys Common Room, it surprised her to hear. In his first year, as an anatomy student, Kirti said, he'd been impressed by how beautifully Dr. Rekapalli could draw bones, like an artist, her illustrations making you see their shapes better than the bones themselves.

Jaya laughed. "Perhaps she should have been an artist."

Kirti turned his head away from her, as if he found the remark silly, but it was only to blow smoke out of his mouth. The thick strokes of his eyebrows, his strong nose, and his curvaceous lips made her catch her breath.

"That's a lovely sari," he said, as he took in her sand-colored silk. It felt as if he'd touched her when he spoke. She glanced around to see if anyone was watching. The group near them had grown smaller, but it was still noisy with laughter and talk. Some ladies slipped from the veranda, shadows coming down the steps. A defiance took hold and Jaya went on talking to Kirti, despite the worry that someone would notice them. Five minutes must have passed.

He stamped out his cigarette with his shoe and flicked his head to indicate they should move out of their secluded spot. Jaya followed him, deflated by the prospect of separating. He raised his hand to a passing bearer, and the man came around, lowering his tray first to Jaya, who put her hand out to decline. Kirti plucked a samosa from the tray and dunked it in the dregs of a chutney bowl. He broke the pastry shell in two, holding half out to her, as if it were natural for them to share food. A thrill went through her as her fingers brushed his, and she put the piece of cold pastry and spiced potato into her mouth.

6

ARMED WITH LARGE scissors, Jaya ran downstairs to Sea Castle's cement forecourt the next afternoon. The palm trees inside the boundary wall leaned yearningly toward the sea. She clipped stems of bushy pink and orange zinnias from the least conspicuous flower bed along the wall that separated their building from Warwick House. Imaginary flowers could fill in the arrangement—she needed only a spark of something real to set her off. Mhatre Sahib's instruction about drawing from nature could be ignored. Why hadn't she realized that before?

When she turned, Heerabai was watching her from the gatepost. Jaya guiltily wagged the bouquet in her hands. The maidservant and her friend from the fourth floor were on their afternoon break, sitting on their haunches, smoking. Two sinewy Marathi women wearing threadbare saris pulled taut around their slim, girlish bodies. Heerabai's deep-set eyes stared out from a bony face, her hair scraped back in a small gray knot. She drew a bidi out from between her teeth, the burning tip pointing inside her mouth. It always amazed Jaya to see her smoking a cheroot with its lit end turned the wrong way.

Why did you cut the flowers? Jaya understood the question without comprehending Heerabai's Marathi. "Painting," she replied in English. Heerabai nodded, grinned in approval. A word she knew. Geometric patterns were tattooed on every part of her face—rounded forehead, chin, both cheeks. Her arms hung over her haunches, inscribed with a country idiom of crawling snakes, lotuses, squiggles. Jaya used to ask what the tattoos meant, but neither she nor Kamlesh could understand the stories Heerabai told as she touched the marks, her remembrances made of hard, rattling Marathi words like stones.

IN THE SIDE balcony, an amethyst glass vase crowned a tall stool holding five globular zinnias. The flowers had multiplied on the sketchbook propped against the board in her lap, mixed with imaginary stalks of cosmos whose bluish petals hovered above stippled light-green leaves. After talking to Kirti last night, she had felt swollen with excitement, her heart racing with a sense of her own power. Now she felt a familiar, dismal sensation of plummeting, staring at the pretty, gaudy flowers floating in white space, lifeless to her eye. She had been moving backward over the last few months, the size of her pictures diminishing as her doubts grew. She had shrunk away from using medium-sized pieces of wood board to scraps no bigger than books, or sheets of oil paper. Lately she had returned to drawing paper and colored pencils. It shamed her to think she was back to her earliest days as a pupil of Mhatre Sahib.

She turned. The old, unsmiling man in kurta-pajama was watching her from his balcony in the opposite building. He gripped the railing and leaned forward, as if absorbed in some grand theater she was presenting. Jaya ignored him as always, shoving the sketch inside the sideboard that held her jumbled stacks of old drawings. Only the bottom shelf was well ordered, with sections for hog-hair and sable-hair brushes, boxes of oil colors, trays of pencils. Against the side of the cabinet stood a splintered wooden board, about two feet by three feet, salvaged from a packing crate in which machinery had been shipped to the factory. She had primed the board with glue and texture white days ago and had later drawn a thick circle in zinc white on the white ground. She'd drawn a cobalt line placing the sea—and then what? She hadn't known what to do. She'd smashed the brush into more cobalt, making little slash marks all over the board as if it were a paralyzed body she could explore with incisions. The markings had dried into dark crusts.

Abandoning her balcony studio, Jaya carried the twisted-glass vase back to the drawing room and set the flowers on the corner table next to the radiogram. Pulling open the balcony doors, she watched gleaming water heave to shore, the green sea high on the horizon. Inside, the furniture was arranged in a tight rectangle, a gloomy old sofa and deep chairs with great curving wooden armrests, the side tables covered in stained embroidered cloths. Mhatre Sahib would lay a cherished book of black-and-white reproductions on the center table, dwelling for half an hour on a single masterpiece like Botticelli's *Birth of Venus*, pacing around the table as he lectured, imprisoned by the bulky furniture. All their lives they'd had the same furnishings, even the shabby settee with tears in its cane back that was lodged beside her mother's curio cabinet, crowding the room. Only the modern, stiff-backed, upholstered light blue sofa had been purchased new when they moved here. Otherwise their old Colaba flat had been faithfully reproduced inside the sprawl of a grand Marine Drive apartment, Mummy's frugal habits ingrained.

High above the curio cabinet lined with ornaments, her mother had prominently displayed her painting of dahlias and cherries in a silver bowl. That was a nice painting—that and her fat pink mangoes piled in a basket. The only two paintings of hers that she liked.

In the dingy sconce-lit dining room, Jaya surveyed with a cold eye her earliest still lifes, done when she was fifteen or sixteen years old. Over the trolley hung white and purple chrysanthemums in clotted strokes, in the corner was a study of asters outlined in dust. and beside the door, a garland of marigolds curled on a banana leaf inside a white frame. A sickening monotony connected the images—the flowers lit by a dusty beam of light, the background a murky area of shadow. Like an antiquated grammar, the stale techniques once taught to Bombay art students had been passed on to her by Mhatre Sahib, who had promised to train her in the manner of the best British art academies. In the absence of life-size plaster casts like those he'd sketched from at the J. J. School of Art, he'd bought her clay figurines of the local Marathi people's gods for her light and shade studies. She'd started off drawing simple geometric forms emphasizing tonal values, and from there she had progressed to foliage from nature, shading first in monochrome, using a pencil, then twig-like charcoal sticks, then pastel crayons, then watercolors. Finally, two years later, she had dabbed a brush in oil paints and learned how to gesso sailcloth for canvas.

At the back of the bedroom, Bebeji was taking a nap. The fan whirred in her alcove. Jaya partially closed the curtains between the two sections of the room. From the shelf above the writing table, she pulled down two hefty books. On her bed, she thumbed through *The Harper History of Western Art*, then the color plates pasted inside the more interesting volume, *Picasso: Man and Vision*. Her most treasured possessions, brought back from America by her father. She had given him the names of a few artists who intrigued her. Picasso's monstrous women wielded hands like shovels hewn from rock. They thrust themselves out, solid in their stances, each plane of the body a hard shape, a change in color. Three stripes conjured the rigid volume of a breast.

In self-disgust Jaya shut the book, shamed by all she was afraid to do. At the dressing table, she pulled her hair up in a bulging roll, grabbing a fistful of bobby pins from the hairpin dish. "Should I wear it like this in the evening? With Mummy's little silver pins poking in it? So pretty for the reception," she jeered at herself. She drew two lines of coral lipstick over her mouth then smeared it off with the back of her hand. She combed her hair flat against her scalp, plaiting it and pinning it taut behind her ears so not a strand could fall loose, nothing to distract or obstruct her from painting her picture.

"Let me see." Kamlesh lifted her head from the magazine she lay reading on her bed.

"You know those lovely silver hairpins with bells on the ends?" Jaya continued to mock herself, smoothing down even flatter her tightly pulled-back hair.

"What are you doing?" Kamlesh frowned.

"What happened to Meher's friend—that Persis Vakil?"

"What do you mean? You met her—"

"I should have rung her up after the lunch." Meher had arranged a girls' luncheon at her house, introducing Jaya to her father's portrait painter, whom she had raved about—the prize-winning graduate of the J. J. School of Art now married to a businessman.

"You want to talk to Persis again? Why?" Kamlesh, too, wore her hair combed cleanly back from her face in a plait, her eyes prominent, darkly wary.

"She may know of someone through her college." At the lunch Jaya had discovered Persis's studies had intersected hers at one point: anatomy. Persis had learned the Latin names of muscles and bones from a medical college lecturer who taught elementary anatomy to art students. That common learning had bolstered Jaya's hope that she could turn medical college into her own school of art—make herself a student of the human body as an artist was.

A short, gossipy, pushing girl, Persis had talked nonstop about the personalities heading the Bombay Art Society, deliberating over who on the Hanging Committee she might persuade to select her portrait of *A Gujarati Lady in Traditional Costume* for the society's annual exhibition. Persis mentioned winning first- and second-place prizes for a watercolor and an oil painting at J. J. School of Art, and Jaya spoke little, recognizing her distance from the actual study of art and the world of exhibitions and prizes real artists competed in. Finally she dared to open her mouth, telling Persis of a modern art exhibition she'd seen at a gallery at Kala Ghoda. "Some very abstract landscapes and village scenes. One was only blurry shapes in soft, muted colors."

"Which painters?" Persis had said in a challenging tone.

"Zaidi and some others. Dhasal." Jaya couldn't recall the other names, feeling hollow before Persis's dazzling self-assurance.

"Zaidi started out painting nursery furniture," Persis informed her with the knowing air of an insider, "and now he's the cat's whiskers. That entire modern group is made up of J. J. graduates. Zaidi learned everything about Cubism, Surrealism, Expressionism from them. How else could a furniture painter learn to paint like Picasso?"

"I didn't know how he began," Jaya confessed. She wondered if that made Zaidi, India's best-known artist, a fraud. Wasn't she herself a fraud, thinking she was an artist? The question she'd been burning to ask Persis—could she recommend a master—died in her mouth.

Studying her multiple images in the dressing table's triple mirrors, she told her twin, "Ask Meher for her telephone number. Ask Persis if she knows any teacher, someone from J. J. School of Art or the Art Society or anywhere—someone who knows about modern art."

"A drawing master?"

"A new teacher—one of those modern painters she was telling me about." She wanted to hear a different voice, to break away from Mhatre Sahib's withered techniques, from the gloom in which he had taught her to insert objects as if they were stillborn.

"Will you talk to him again if he's there?" Kamlesh asked, feigning great interest in a booklet about Queen Elizabeth's coronation that summer, laid out in a feast of photographs.

"I can't ignore him. If I come across him, I might say hello." They'd had the same conversation last night as soon as they got home, Kamlesh wanting to know who that boy was she'd been talking to. What if he was invited to the reception? No one had heard of receptions given by the boy's side, but Leela's husband's family apparently moved in the most elite circles, where receptions were known. They were throwing a party for the newlyweds at the Willingdon Club.

"No, I mean talk to him all alone like that. Everyone noticed."

"Who's 'everyone'?"

A couple of Kamlesh's friends had seen her chatting with Kirti and reported back to Kamlesh: "That boy looked very interested in Jaya."

"You don't want people to start gossiping, that's the only reason I'm saying this. It would be very embarrassing."

"What about your suitors? People must have noticed that also."

Kamlesh frowned, staring intently into the booklet with the queen's gilded horse carriage on the cover. Though her silence conceded her nervousness about male attention, she persisted. "Mr. Dasgupta—that fellow you said used to look at you in the common room. He's that same fellow you were talking to?"

"Maybe." Jaya moved away, not wanting to think about Kirti Dasgupta in her sister's presence, the desire he provoked. It was a nice name—Kirti. She liked it very much.

She returned to the balcony, hot sunlight glaring on the red stone floor tiles, searching anxiously through sheaves of old drawings in her hobbled sideboard. Everything was there, all the sketches she'd made since childhood. In the farthest corner, beneath blank sheets she'd neglected to use, she discovered her pencil sketches of the family people who'd taken shelter with them. Her first grown-up drawings. A large iron key appeared in a few pictures, the key to the locker full of valuables left in plain sight for Sarojini to find.

It was in those days of Partition, when she had been drawing a lot, making images of the terrible things she overheard, that she and Kamlesh had fought most bitterly. Together they would escape the flat, the ladies' silences worse than their tears, their appeals to God. Home lost, land lost, gold lost. The whereabouts of a daughter or a brother unknown. *What happened to them? Where are they?* The atrocities they had seen—*Everyone went mad!* One morning, she and Kamlesh wandered far from their locality, following a small road straight to the sea. A jetty of black rocks extended enticingly from the land's end far away into the waves at high tide, and Jaya excitedly ordered Kamlesh to walk out there. They were alone, free to do anything. Puffed up with a sense of power, she wanted to make her twin obey her. Kamlesh submitted, despite her fear—persuaded to act bravely, screaming only when she reached the jetty's tip and crashing waves soaked her. Jaya, terrified that Kamlesh might be swept away, ran out on the loose, wobbly rocks to bring her twin back. Later, a fight erupted at home, and Kamlesh flung a shoe at her in a rage, cracking the glass on the print she and Mummy adored of a little English girl looking lovingly upon a kitten playing in a basket of wool. That was when Mummy separated them, placing their two beds against opposite walls and positioning their relatives' cots between them. Kamlesh continued to join Jaya on the balcony, watching her sitting on the dirty floor to sketch. When she told Mummy about the pictures, their mother was horrified to find distortions and fragments of the incidents their relations had endured illustrated by her daughter's hand. She rightly connected Jaya's sketch of a boy striking a weak, bent-backed man with a long stick to the silent boy who'd visited their flat. He'd come with his parents, a college-age boy who didn't speak, who looked like he was blind, his eyes empty and unfocused. The RSS had lured him into their cadre, his mother whispered among the ladies, and she didn't know what terrible things he might have done to Muslims. Maybe beat them, maybe more. He must have done terrible things, she cried, look at him now. Vidya had studied Jaya's drawings closely. "Why do you let these things trouble you?" she scolded Jaya. Jaya looked at the drawings in her mother's hand and couldn't formulate an answer. It lay buried within. How could she keep absorbing people's despair and not respond? "You're safe and sound at home," her mother tried to assure her. Mummy found Mhatre Sahib through an acquaintance, hoping a drawing master could dispel her fears and guide her to things of beauty. At their first lesson, Mhatre Sahib looked over the drawings she was looking at now—of a terrified girl fleeing downstairs, of a girl staring at a key in her hand as big as her palm, of a flaming house that was not quite Bebeji's glimpsed through a train window. Her bespectacled teacher had gazed at her, a thirteen-year-old girl, and said without a smile, "Do you know, you're an artist?"

Jaya returned inside with a sense of trepidation, aware she had an urgent matter to attend to. In her parents' room, a tea tray set with a fruit plate was laid on the rug. Her mother sat on the dhurrie, leaning against the footboard of her bed, her sari spread out loosely around her. Jaya asked if she could wear her meenakari necklace to the reception. She leaned against the glass doors of her father's book cabinet, waiting for him to put aside his reading—he was at his writing table, an ink pot set in front of him. He always made margin notes. Jaya's hands, hidden behind her back, traced a line on the glass she could follow, a line back into her painting with a new teacher. Persis Vakil, with her connections and cunning, was the right person to approach. But she would need her parents' permission; the absence of their permission was probably what stopped her from asking Persis about a teacher when they met.

"Yes," Jaya said to her mother's offer of tea. Vidya shouted out for Heera-bai to bring an extra teacup for "Didi" and got up to unlock her cupboard, murmuring enviously, "They've found such a cultured family for Leela, very fine people—members of the Willingdon Club. Can you imagine?" If her daughters weren't careful, she meant to say, they would be cheated of boys from such fine families, too old by the time they finished their degrees—particularly Jaya in a five-year MBBS course—and overeducated for the liking of some families, their father placing too much importance on their studies. No one wanted a girl better qualified than their son.

Her mother handed her a velvet pouch from which Jaya extracted the collar she would wear in the evening: enameled blue lozenges studded with pinpoints of uncut diamonds and trimmed in seed pearls. Lowering her voice, Mummy said, "That Mrs. Bakshi, the groom's massi, seems quite keen on Kamlesh for her son. How handsome he is, and doing so well in a British company. Five hundred ships they have! She found me again later and was asking, 'For how much longer is Kamlesh in college? What is she studying?' I hated to say two years for her BA, and probably another year for her teacher's training. She didn't mind, she said, 'Let's stay in touch'—it seems Vikram has to complete one full three-year contract with his company before they give him permission to marry."

Jaya was puzzled. "His company will decide when he can marry?"

"Some of these old British companies have funny rules. They want a lot of control over their employee's life, it seems. In any case, three years suits us fine. Shuli was saying the father was managing director of an insurance company in Lahore. Now he's got some small office job. What can he do? The main thing is he educated his son well. Vikram seems to have excellent prospects at this steamship company."

Jaya nodded. Everyone understood the older generation's enormous difficulty in rebuilding their lives after Partition. They had been left penniless, homeless. It was their children who were expected to succeed. She smiled at the idea—a boy for her twin? How striking they had looked together for the few minutes Kamlesh was able to talk to him.

"Later on, you talk to Mr. Bakshi," her mother said to her father. Her tone was deferential. She would relinquish her role, leaving it to the fathers to negotiate their children's marriage.

Harbans took off his glasses, rubbed his eyes, looked at Jaya without a smile. He'd been absorbed in his reading. Jaya waited for her mother to cut a guava then took her father the creamy wedges on a quarter plate. "Are you having breathing trouble again?" His journal was open to an article on asthma, the small print set unevenly on the rough yellowish paper, underscored and annotated with his blue fountain pen.

"No, this just discusses the foods to be avoided by asthma sufferers." Above the desk hung his revered image of Mahatma Gandhi as an ascetic. He was bare-chested and walked with a wooden staff. On either side of it hung smaller prints of Jesus baring his bulging heart and Lakshmi rising from her rosy-pink lotus, the pictures affirming her father's faith in the sanctity of all religions. A follower of the Arya Samaj like Bebeji, he rose at dawn to sing his hymns, followed by a two-mile walk along the sea. His self-discipline was exacting and meant to tame his temper, Jaya had come to believe. Perhaps it lingered from his stalled government career, or went further back to his father's financial problems after he lost his income tax job. He would explode at Mummy over a trifle, then the next day announce a weeklong salt fast, insisting all his meals be prepared bland.

"I was trying to finish a drawing." Jaya paused, burning to ask his permission. Inside his book cabinet two art prizes she'd won as a schoolgirl were displayed—tarnished medals mounted on wooden shields. "I was thinking, Daddy, I'd like to have a painting teacher again."

"Why do you think of a master now? After so long?" His tone was harsh.

"I keep on going over the same things I learned from Mhatre Sahib. I'd like to develop my own style." A new teacher would force her to seize her ambition, force it out, the weight of it trapped inside her.

Her father pushed himself back in his chair, scraping the heavy wooden legs on the polished stone tile. "What is the need? You're in medical college now—you must know your purpose. You're old enough." She and Kamlesh would celebrate their nineteenth birthday in a couple of weeks, on the last day of November.

Jaya nodded, adding expectantly, "I was thinking someone new could teach me a different approach."

"Don't let yourself become confused." Harbans returned his gaze to his journal.

"I won't let my studies slip." Jaya faltered. In her mind lurked a belief that she had cleared a way for her own aims by gaining admission to medical college. She had done as her father dictated—now wouldn't he allow her some liberties?

"What is the harm in letting her have an art master?" Her mother shut the almirah door, rehooking the lock on the latch.

"I was thinking of a lesson just once a week," said Jaya, encouraged. Perhaps it was because of the boy, Kirti, that she could summon the bravado to declare what she wanted—because of the way they'd spoken so freely to each other.

"That way, Daddy always encouraged our interests." Her mother fell into a familiar reminiscence about her own father as she folded the bedsheet that lay rumpled from her afternoon rest. Just as her father had engaged teachers to develop his children's hobbies, Mummy had done for them, although in her eyes whatever their father could provide faded against her own daddy's indulgences. "*One interest?* My word, Daddy had a thousand interests. Piano, badminton, billiards . . ." He was her idol, dying of tuberculosis when she was just sixteen.

"She must still her mind and set it to one purpose," Harbans replied firmly.

"Look at her eyes, see the dark circles," Vidya lamented. "I've always said medical college is the wrong place for a girl. It's ruining her face, making her tired all the time. What is the harm if she wants a diversion?" She paused as Heerabai carried in Jaya's single teacup grandly on a tray set with a tray cloth. The maidservant offered the cup to Mummy, who poured Jaya's tea, adding hot milk and a spoon of sugar. Grinning, Heerabai carried the cup to Jaya beside her father's table.

"Pinting?" Heerabai flicked her head from side to side, meaning: *Is it finished?* No matter what the medium, they tossed the word "pinting" between them, Heerabai curious to see her pictures. Yes, Jaya replied, it was finished.

"Girls need pleasant things in life as well," her mother appealed to her father after Heerabai had slipped barefoot out of the room. It was her mother's elegant personality talking, the side of her that pampered them, disappointed at how few luxuries her children had compared to those of her fabled childhood. She had grown up like a princess in a mansion graced with rose gardens, tennis courts, stables, seven cars in the garages, and that rarity in the 1920s in Kanpur, a swimming pool. A house named Dreamland by her father, a sugar mill owner and distributor for the prestigious Begg, Sutherland and Company, hailed the "Sugar King of U.P." All beauty in Vidya's life had been left behind there, in Dreamland, before her father's world collapsed, his managers swindling him and the banks hanging locks on all the mansion's doors. Both her parents had died within a few years of the bankruptcy. Vidya had fallen ill and missed several years of high school. Then she had rallied, determined to study, and had passed her Matric exams through sheer will and effort, for which Jaya deeply admired her mother. Her uncles scraped together the money for her fees, and she was admitted to the best women's college in Lahore. Still the early shock of so many losses lived inside Mummy as a dread of losing whatever she had.

So, to her daughters' perpetual embarrassment, she locked up the flour and ghee from the servants, argued with shopkeepers, accused merchants of overcharging her.

"His fees should be reasonable. There may be a new graduate of J. J. School of Art giving tuitions. A modern artist."

Brusquely, her father turned to her. "Why were you talking to a boy by yourself last evening?" His eyes were hard and piercing.

"Which boy? I didn't see her with any boy," her mother said.

Jaya's head was warm, her ears burned. Her father continued to stare at her. He'd been taking his sweet dish with some friends, he said, when Mrs. Sagar came by and remarked to him that Jaya seemed to be "engrossed in conversation with some very tall young man."

"There was a group from medical college," Jaya replied hoarsely. "Leela's brother-in-law's friends."

"You must think of how things look in front of others—it's not good for a young girl to be seen speaking to a boy alone. Don't turn into a dreamer, painting and drawing—drifting around. A restless mind spins from one thing to another, accomplishing nothing. You're becoming an escapist."

Her mother did not intervene. Seeing Jaya's humiliated face, she lowered her eyes, indicating Jaya should let the matter rest. Her slight nod meant she would settle it for Jaya later.

Jaya left the room, the necklace and teacup in her hands. At her dressing table, she scorned herself: *dreamer, escapist.* Her father saw straight through her. She had dedicated herself to nothing. She was weak. In the mirror, she saw herself hunching like an animal, her hair pulled back in a sleek cap, her eyebrows pushed together in two deep folds.

Early in the evening, she returned to the balcony, her breath falling heavily as if she were chasing something. The first marks she made on the primed board were two long slashes in cobalt blue and a hard line connecting them: the blunt sides of a face and a chin. She drew a rigid neck and two meager humps of shoulders at the bottom of the board. Then she dipped her brushes in azure, yellow, and burnt sienna to scrawl a mouth drawn back in a grimace, the teeth clenched between parted lips, caught in the act of grinding. Vermilion shaped the high bones beneath the eye sockets and the bloodied, tightly coiled ears. Pulling the planes of his cheeks away from his tensed mouth, thrusting his jaw up defiantly, Jaya recognized the face of the man she dissected every morning, limb by limb, nerve by nerve. Her hand flew in all directions, scribbling paint as she moved around the easel in a feverish rhythm, remembering this man who surrendered mutely to their shiny scalpels. He was a head of two blues, burnt brown, and red: wild-eyed. His royal blue nose flared above his mustache, two black knife incisions slanted above his nostrils.

In the dissection hall, he would be whittled to a torso-stump raised on blocks of wood then flayed to a branch of tarnished ribs. Only here in her painting was he not dead. He was furious, his face a combustion of slashed brush strokes, his eyes a livid yellow. Around his neck she strung a metal amulet on a string like the kind villagers wore. When she peeled back his skin in the mornings, she saw a hard-boned, lean-bodied Marathi man who had moved to the city from an unknown village, to a shanty colony near the railway lines, the kind of man you could see running with a loaded handcart on the roads, shouting at whoever swerved too close to him—a raging man in public.

7

INSIDE THE LUCKY Restaurant, the green malodorous air grieved her as they sipped boiled tea and shared a plate of samosas blistered in oil. Jaya propped an elbow on the table, fanning her fingers against her face to shield herself from the smirking men who openly stared because she was the only woman in the room. Sweating clerks and small businessmen battled their chicken chop masala and veg pattice with a spoon in each fist. A bearer with a curry-stained towel flung over his shoulder was beckoned in all directions: "Rafique!" Rushing from table to table, he dealt out plates like playing cards and carried water glasses in clusters, a finger dipped in each. Kirti Dasgupta called out, "Rafique!" He tapped the marble tabletop to indicate something was missing: "Ashtray."

Eyes narrowing intently at his match, Kirti lit a cigarette, offering Jaya the illicit pleasure of watching tendrils of smoke unfurl toward her. The searing heat of June invaded the café through the open doorway, carrying the din of yelping horns and shouting roadside touts, the street noise nearly drowning the nostalgic lament of Rafi's song on the radio, which so stirred Jaya. Every sense of hers was aroused by Kirti's presence, by the controlled cadence of his voice. He shot her a look, letting his story about his surgical experiment on a dog hang in the air.

"I don't know how you could do it, without any experience treating animals."

He'd taken things into his own hands, cutting a tumor out of a dog belonging to the caretaker of Farrokh Wadia's beach shack. Kirti was twenty-three and fearless. He immersed himself in any subject that interested him—for this operation reading everything he could find on the anatomy of dogs and canine malignancies. Last year he'd been named winner of the Dr. R. Desai Medal for Clinical Medicine. His ambition, after completing his final year of medicine, was to secure a house job in surgery at J. J. Hospital, to become a Master of Surgery, and afterward win a fellowship to the Royal College of Surgeons in London or Edinburgh. Leaning closer to Jaya in his green-checked bush shirt, Kirti came near enough for Jaya to stroke his cheek as he spoke, to feel the deep gray shadow around his mouth, his firm burnt-reddish-brown jaw, so close she had to resist the urge to touch his skin, as dark as earth. Her hands settled heavily in her lap.

Months and months ago, after he'd approached her at Leela's wedding, he'd started inviting her out, the two of them banding together with Hema and Farrokh Wadia and three or four older students, boys and girls, all of them sitting around a table at a tea shop near J. J. Hospital, his knee grazing hers. She'd discovered there were a few couples at college among the older students, romances publicly covered up by going for a group meal. Lately, Kirti had begun asking her out alone to this rundown Irani joint in the red-light district on the fringes of the hospital. If he invited her more than once a week, she declined. Every time she walked into this place, her stomach dropped in fear of being seen by someone she knew. She'd always sit with her back to the doorway, half in dread of a passing student discovering them together.

Kirti glanced at his outstretched fingers, pausing to consider something, then thrust his gaze on her. "Are you disappointed about something?"

Jaya squinted, recoiling from the question. She was reluctant to speak directly of herself.

"You seem tired," he said.

"Do I look so bad?"

"Somehow dejected."

She sometimes woke up feeling a cord of pain embedded in her bone. A yanking ache traveled along her right arm at night, and in the day, her arm felt heavy, as if she'd strained her muscles. For three months she'd been waiting for Meher's friend Persis Vakil to refer her to a painting teacher. She'd rung up Persis several times after Kamlesh spoke to her, politely asking if she'd come across anyone. Each time Persis promised to fix her up with a master in a few weeks, but no teacher appeared. Recently she'd phoned Persis a fourth time, feeling like she was begging. Persis's curt response—"I've been trying to find you someone, okay? Can't you also look for yourself? "—had been mortifying.

Jaya looked at her hands resting daintily on the marble table, her slim fingers tapering above her glass bangles, and asked Kirti, "I don't have a surgeon's hands, do I?"

"No," he agreed and she felt vaguely demeaned. If he'd pointed to some evidence of natural competence in the shape of the digits or the breadth of her palms, it might have encouraged her. All last month she'd been on holiday from college but hadn't dared to attempt a painting.

"I've done some sketches of your hands," she teased Kirti, trying to sound buoyant. Her eye went to the blood-red coral ring on his left hand. His hands, hard and slender, slightly knobby at the knuckles, were a rich mahogany shade even darker than his face.

"My hands?" He appraised them, looking flattered by her interest. "Wouldn't you rather draw other things?"

Invariably Bebeji or Kamlesh was in the room with her when she drew Kirti's hands in small notebooks or on loose pieces of paper, remembering the peculiar way he held a cigarette deep in the "V" of his fingers, or the shape of his hands bridged together in front of him when he was being serious. She would put the drawings away before anyone grew interested in looking. Some of the characters in these cafés also turned up in her sketches: Rafique lunging at a table with plates thrust out, the hefty proprietor guarding the till beneath a portrait of the Shah of Iran, the clerks hunched over their food. Quick jottings, like notes scribbled in a lecture hall.

"I've done a picture of my sister I call my 'self-portrait'"—a laughing glance at him—"it was easier than looking at myself in the mirror and trying to draw at the same time."

"You said there are differences—"

"Minor ones. Though you'd be able to tell who's who."

"Bring your 'self-portrait' next time. Let me see if it's a good likeness of you."

"It's too big to carry around." Despite what Jaya had told him, she had sketched her own face reflected in the dressing table mirror, comparing her features to Kamlesh's to try to discover where the differences lay, the points at which their features and personalities diverged, became discrete. It baffled her that she had continued to meet Kirti behind Kamlesh's back, betraying not a word about it for the last six months. She had never imagined herself capable of living so separately from her twin.

"So?" Kirti stretched out the taut word, an elastic sound pulling her toward him. Jaya shook her head, refusing more tea, knowing she had to disentangle herself from him. Kirti slapped his hands down on the table as if he were asking for hers, picking up the chit Rafique had tossed down. Beneath his outspread fingers was the same yellowing, gray-veined marble the cadavers slept on. A man at the next table spat out fragments of chicken bone onto a pile of scraps garnishing his plate, reminding Jaya further of mortal remains.

In the dissection hall, one of the boys in her group had stuck a toffee in the mouth of a wiry man with sunken cheeks who exposed his abdominal viscera to them—a new body to dismember—turning him into a child sucking on a sweet. Everyone had laughed. Remorsefully, Jaya recalled the prank, asking Kirti why medicine began with the study of dead bodies, as if death was all medical science could deliver. "Why begin at the end?" she asked. "With failure?"

"Not failure," he contended. "With understanding. You have to look inside a person to know anything."

It was impossible to go home straightaway after their meetings, so Jaya often walked half the long distance through the smoky evening city coming alive with lights—exhilarated, flustered, gripped by an excitement blindly sexual. A chaos overcame her, elation mixed with fear that she had dared to meet him alone again. This evening, she waited on the crowded footpath for the Churchgate bus, painting Kirti in her mind, tilting his face to angle his glance suggestively downward, turning his broad shoulders back to the left, exposing his darkly grained chest and arms softened with hair. This time, with the painting of him in mind, she jumped off the bus near the J. J. School of Art. She carried Kirti's image through the gates, past monstrous weeping banyans, into the deserted campus of hulking Gothic buildings, their arched windows shaded by palm-mat awnings, into the greatest art school in India, straight into the Department of Drawing and Painting.

Colossal portraits hung from copper chains in the foyer, each an homage to a vanished professor, Englishmen in armchairs so gravely shadowed against piteous black backgrounds that she could scarcely make out the sitters' faces. A view of two steamships under a violent red sunset was captured in a heavily carved gilt frame. Where were the copies of the Ajanta murals that Mhatre Sahib and his class fellows had painted in the caves? Where were the fruits of that twelve-year-long labor to reproduce the masterpieces of ancient Indian art? To steal them out of the darkness in the form of facsimiles? What had happened to those murals replicating the royal processions of dark princesses and dying princesses and dancing girls and music makers and princes on elephant-back? Jaya climbed the stairs, trembling with a queer nostalgia, half expecting to see her old teacher waiting for her at the top.

A theatrical scene had been set up in the main hall. A swath of yellow satin fell in folds over a three-step pedestal on which a model apparently was to sit. A light mounted on an iron stand spread its glare on the flaming cloth. Both the model and the artists were absent, the students' empty benches with attached easels arranged in a half-circle around the small stage. It was nearly six o'clock; the professors' offices were shut. No real chance, of course, of finding a teacher who might agree to tutor her in painting.

Pushing open a door, Jaya walked into a long gallery lined with classrooms on one side and arched openings looking over the garden on the other. At the far end of the passage, a woman plunged a dipper into an earthen pot set on a stool and filled a tumbler. She turned aside and drank. The missing model, perhaps. She appeared to be young, elegant in her movements, and was wearing a chaste white sari like a sister in the wards. *Are you the model?* Jaya decided she would ask her. *Where is the teacher?* When the woman approached, Jaya glanced away to study the minaret of a date palm in the vacant evening garden.

"Are you looking for someone?" The woman had the dry voice and flat gaze of a college administrator. Yet she was almost beautiful, her complexion a milky coffee color, her crinkled hair a soft, light chestnut brown. On her forehead was a stunning caste mark of solid black and red circles overlapped by a powdery, pear-shaped splotch of saffron, the large circles topped by a crumbly bar of ash, a bold layering of pigments.

"I came to meet the model," said Jaya.

"Are you a new student? We'll be starting our class for casual students at six-thirty."

"I didn't bring anything to draw with." She couldn't think properly, but she didn't rush away, hoping to instigate a conversation about who she might approach as a teacher.

"So you haven't come for sketching?" The woman tilted her head sharply.

"Someone suggested I observe a session to see if I'd be able to draw from a live model." A wooden chest filled a niche between two classrooms opposite where they stood, a squat, splintered box trimmed with iron fittings that gave Jaya the idea the charcoal and ink she needed were buried inside.

The lady administrator or instructor advanced a step as if to appraise her, looking steadily at Jaya. "You came to observe? You're a student? Or are you an artist?"

"I do sketches," Jaya replied, a quiver in her voice. "At some point, I'd like to join the class. I thought I'd come today just to look at the model, see what sort of subjects the students paint." The woman grew impatient with her confusion, her face closing off. Jaya's gaze fell to the decrepit chest that stood under a painting of a dancing goddess who brandished a different weapon in each of her four hands. If she raised the lid, she imagined finding in place of drawing materials an array of sickles and axes, weapons with which she could lay claim to her future, to herself.

Later that week, she sat on her grandmother's bed, pressing Bebeji's legs. Bebeji had drawn up her white sari to her knees and sat propped against a pillow as the setting sun burnished the sky gold outside the wall of windows in her alcove. She couldn't deny she was exhausted; her thick hands lay folded over her stomach like a piece of statuary. Accompanied by Dipi, who helped her climb the hill every month to meet her five-member residents committee, which provided some leadership at the shanty colony, she had spent half the day on the hill. Today they had watched donkeys transport bricks up the rain-washed slopes to the site of the one-room primary school she was building.

Tending to her grandmother, Jaya felt like her old self—the obedient girl who did not deceive her family. Manu sat in a chair at Bebeji's bedside in his school shirt and trousers, a notebook on his knee like a professional journalist. He asked in which order she would implement the various pieces of her welfare scheme—*What will come next after the school is finished?* Since he wrote well, Mummy had suggested an essay contest in the *Indian Express*, "The Living Character I Most Admire." Manu had chosen Bebeji, who waved off his questions and forbade him from writing about the colony. "I don't want to make trouble for your daddy. He wants to keep a distance publicly between the factory and the busti, so let it be. You write about my work with the Congress in Lahore. Those old stories he won't mind my telling. All that can't hurt him now."

Manu, determined to appear mature at fourteen, restrained his gestures, yet still had a habit of talking a lot in his high, young boy's voice, and persisted in questioning her about Ganesh Murti Nagar. Jaya straightened up from massaging her grandmother's soles to admonish him. "Don't push like that, Manu." Yet she, too, wanted Bebeji's work on the hillside to become known. Over the last six or seven months, they had all noticed an abiding change in her. Bebeji had revived herself, drawing strength from the planning and activity. The tiny glass containers of ear drops and eye drops, and the brown bottles of health tonics that she used to depend on, had gone dry from disuse. Jaya had shaken them earlier, a litter of evaporated vials on Bebeji's night table collecting dust. "Ask Daddy if he minds you writing about Bebeji's plans for the colony. You can connect it to Gandhiji rather than anything to do with the factory."

"Listen to me," Bebeji said forcefully, sitting up, addressing both grandchildren. "Your daddy doesn't want any publicity about our work in the colony." By "our work" she meant that Kamlesh would volunteer at the school and Jaya at the clinic, once the buildings were constructed, the factory providing a small amount of funds to run those facilities as a charitable donation.

Manu relented and asked about the first protest march she remembered taking part in. Jaya cupped her hands around Bebeji's shiny, dry shins as her grandmother recalled seven British MPs visiting Lahore as part of a bogus commission on government reforms. Bebeji was among thousands of Congress supporters who greeted them at the railway station with black flags that said "Go Back." In response, the British police beat the demonstrators, including Bebeji and her friend Satya, though they were peaceful. Scott, the superintendent of Lahore police, repeatedly cracked his baton on the chest of the great leader of Punjab, Lala Lajpat Rai, who died of his injuries. Bebeji's work in the shanty colony was the culmination of her role in that struggle, thought Jaya. It was her small piece of the "constructive program" she believed was Gandhiji's true genius, linking the freedom struggle with the mission to uplift the weakest members of society. Liberation had meaning only if the poor were also liberated from misery—that was the message Bebeji conveyed to her grandchildren.

Since no government school was available to the children of laborers in the "Thana Industrial Belt," a fantasy of manufacturing power that might take twenty years to achieve, Bebeji had decided to build a school first. She had insisted on paying for the bricks, and Mummy had been upset with her for spending from her limited savings. A school was the responsibility of the municipality, of the government, she argued, not of private individuals. "Let me make this one donation," Bebeji had insisted. If they waited for the government to take action, they would have to wait for years. What resources did the government have? Everyone was poor. Bebeji deeply regretted Harbans having to ask Khosla Sahib to allow the factory to bear all the other costs of construction. The least she could do, she said, was buy the bricks.

The shanty colony should not be seen as an appendage of their factory, Harbans cautioned, since its residents were employed by various factories in the area. He didn't want to antagonize the other owners by presenting himself as a champion of the labor class. Quietly, though, on the side, he suggested the factory would pay the class teacher's salary. Fortunately the doctor Bebeji had approached about the future clinic was adamant about volunteering his time, refusing to accept payment for attending to the poor.

The entire scheme had sprung from their search for a doctor for the electrician's feverish baby boy that day they visited his hut. They had taken the child, Shankar, to a clinic in Thana township. The doctor advised that he be hospitalized; he was very ill. At the civil hospital in the main bazaar, the doctors who saved Shankar later confided that he had been brought just in time—a day later and he would have died of encephalitis. It caused Bebeji to realize that she still had the power to help people.

After her interview with Manu, Bebeji got up to jot some ideas down in the long, cardboard-backed register that contained her notes on the progress of the colony. Jaya did a quick likeness of her grandmother sitting intently at the table. When Kamlesh came home, she went straight to the writing table and called to Bebeji, "Why is your diary lying open like this? You've written something new?" She slapped the register shut and walked away, behaving as if Jaya, who was now sitting at the table reading a volume titled *Surface Marking*, was an untrustworthy character who ought not be privy to Bebeji's thoughts. In Jaya's portrait of her twin—her "self-portrait," as she had described it to Kirti—Kamlesh sat on her bed, as she did just now, her hair loose, chin lifted up, eyes darkly wide, and mouth closed in a despondent line. As Jaya drew her twin, she'd felt herself becoming what she portrayed, taking on the expression of injury on Kamlesh's face. Many times she'd wanted to tell Kamlesh about Kirti, but the secret had become a habit she clung to. She was afraid to release his name into her twin's ear, out of her control. By some intuition or suspicion, Kamlesh seemed to know about him already—the way she questioned Jaya about where she'd been, or burst into anger if Jaya borrowed a pair of sandals or a kameez without asking. Once Jaya had come close to confessing, speaking about couples at college and wondering what might happen if the parents on one side or the other didn't approve. "Are there many such couples? Do you know them?" Kamlesh had asked. Jaya had hesitated then retreated, saying simply that one got a sense of who was involved with whom. "Are you involved with some boy?" Kamlesh had demanded. Jaya had turned stone cold, feigning offense at her sister's question.

"Where have you been?" Kamlesh lay on her side now, her head propped in her hand, observing Jaya.

"At home," said Jaya.

"I mean earlier, before I left. You must have come back late. I left at a quarter past six."

"I was at the library. I came back by six-thirty—I must have just missed you," Jaya said.

Kamlesh wrinkled her nose as if the answer stank of a lie. "Some fellow rang for you."

"Who?" Jaya withered—had he phoned here?

Kamlesh got up and moved toward Bebeji's alcove, deliberately holding back the information, seeing Jaya was keen for it. "Some Mr. Tule," she finally mumbled. "He'll ring again tomorrow."

"Tule? Who's he?"

"Persis told him you were looking for a teacher. He was quite a loud, irritating fellow. Just banged the phone down in my ear," she said, blaming Jaya for the caller's rough manner.

THE FIRST THING Namdeo Tule announced at their meeting three days later was his political affiliation: "I am a Communist! My paintings are shown at Communist Party headquarters in Parel for ordinary millworkers and sweepers to see! Every picture of mine is true to the lives of the proletariat; it reminds them of the injustices done to them on a daily basis by our own homegrown capitalists!"

"I see." Jaya nodded. They were in the drawing room, Tule's back to the paintings and sketchbooks she had displayed for his examination along the top of her mother's curio cabinet. He started shouting about the need for artists to cultivate a political consciousness, so she got up to half close the doors, afraid her father would hear and throw him out. It wouldn't matter to him that Tule was a leader of an avant-garde painters' group whose name she had read in the papers. The same group Mhatre Sahib had called "madmen," saying they tore apart images rather than put forms together. On the phone, Tule had offered no explanation as to why he was taking on students, and Mummy doubted his ability to earn a living from his paintings.

"Why are you in art? Do you believe in art for the people, or only for the high society capitalist-bourgeois elite?" Tule was a good-looking man, narrow shouldered and short, his hair oiled and combed to the side, his mustache sleek—a man possessed by a ferocity so theatrical it had to be faked. He wore a cloth bag on his shoulder as his artist's badge, but his drab pants and shirt were the cheap garb of an office clerk.

"No, not just the elite. I think art should be for everyone. It is for *everyone*, really. Even villagers paint the walls of their huts."

"Have you read Marx, Engels, Lenin? Why did we found Group 47? Because India needed a revolution in art! That's why Dhasal and I got together with four other rogue students from J. J. School of Art and organized a union of modern artists. We called ourselves Group 47 because that's when we banded together—'47 was the year of our political and artistic liberation. Together we were a rebel force out to annihilate all the third-rate art flourishing in this country. We'd had enough of that dry, bloodless British art they were churning out at J. J. School of Art, and enough also of the sentimental, anemic, folkloric Bengal School, and Jamini Roy, and that entire group of impotent, effeminate Indianized painters. And we've had our revolution! We've created a modern movement in Bombay. We were like a streak of lightning—in two years half the fellows had gotten scholarships to study abroad, chased by the top galleries in London and Paris. Do you know two of my paintings are hanging in the Venice Biennale right now? All six of us who originally organized Group 47 are being shown there."

When he realized she didn't know what the Venice Biennale was, he erupted ferociously. "It's the biggest art fair in the world! This is the first time India's been invited to hold an exhibition. They've given us a space with some other countries still chafing under the colonial yoke. You didn't hear what Nehru said?" Jaya shook her head. "'Modern art is a part of making India modern.' You didn't read in the papers that he said that?"

Jaya had to admit she wasn't aware of that statement by the prime minister; she only knew that he'd called factories and dams the new temples. Privately she felt a thrill that art could have such importance.

Tule demanded, "Have you seen my paintings? Are you familiar with Zaidi's pictures? Do you go to exhibitions? We have our own Picassos in India." He paused fleetingly to consider the bowl of cherries and dahlias in her painting over the cabinet. He glanced at the other flower paintings she'd put out for him. On the phone, he had asked to see her work before he decided whether he would tutor her. "How serious a painter are you? Miss Persis didn't seem to know much about you."

"I want to free up my approach—learn some modern techniques."

A shadow moved in the doorway. Her father must have heard Tule shouting; he would order him to leave the flat. Heerabai entered the room with two glasses of lemonade on a tray, bending to serve them in the thin maroon sari she wore like a second skin, its tail end pulled up between her legs. Jaya feared that Tule would condemn her as one of the capitalist-bourgeois elite crowding his mind, but he merely took his glass and went to appreciate the sea view through the open balcony doors. A minute later, he asked to see any other pictures she had, and in the dining room he viewed her chipped and flaking flower studies done in cheap paint on canvas and board.

"You refer to all the dry, passionless, sterile academic painters who came before Cezanne, before Picasso, before the modern revolution," he said, offering his diagnosis. "Your marigolds are shriveled up with your stilted brushwork. You show a good sense of color, a way of handling line, but where is the desire in your painting? Modern art isn't pretty, it isn't timid and sweet—it's virile, bold, emotional! It's not afraid and it doesn't hide anything. These paintings of yours—they're dainty bedroom pictures!"

They returned to the drawing room in silence. Jaya tried to remain hopeful and retrieved two pictures in cardboard frames that Dipi had propped against the radiogram on the corner table. She took them to the curio cabinet and stood them in front of her other pictures. A pair of watercolors she'd done for Dipi's office at the factory that he'd brought home for her to show Mr. Tule. Looking over the rural market scene of vendors squatting amid baskets of overflowing vegetables, and her portrait of turbaned village musicians holding their long-necked stringed instruments, Tule asked, "Have you seen these people yourself?"

"No." He knew she hadn't. "They're copies of pictures from my father's magazines."

"They're exactly the sort of sentimentalized Indian scenes that have flourished for decades thanks to the insipid, effeminate aesthetics of the Bengal School. Bunk. All bunk. They deserve to be burned."

Jaya couldn't answer him or meet his eye. To end her humiliation, she decided not to show him her sketches of hands and figures, desperate to get rid of him. "You have nothing else, Miss Jaya?" he said with mocking sharpness. His tone enraged her; she was afraid of shouting back that she didn't care what he thought of her. Instead she opened her sketchbooks on the cabinet, furiously displaying herself in her "self-portrait," which was a three-quarter profile of Kamlesh looking over her shoulder, regarding the viewer with quiet resentment. Turning over loose sheets of sketches, she stopped at one of a male hand beckoning her.

Tule held the images of Kirti's hand drawn in hard charcoal lines up to the light like a doctor examining X-rays. He paged through her quick sketches of men in cafés, of her own hands, of her grandmother entranced at the writing table, then shuffled back through sketchbook pages of Kirti's hands, pausing at a drawing of his masculine hand brightened by a square coral ring in deep red pastel. "These are quite good. Realistic, humanistic. Expressive—that's good. This is your strength: human features, the human figure. Have you done any figure paintings besides those storybook villagers?"

Ignoring the sting of the question, Jaya confessed, "One other." She had thought it too raw and unformed to show anyone. From its hiding place on the back balcony, she carried out the fastest painting she had ever produced. She pulled back the old, torn bedsheet that covered it. A wild face of blue and crimson slashes, mounted on hunched shoulders.

"This is a modern painting. It has the power of an outburst," Tule bellowed. "Why didn't you show this one to me first?" He took it from her arms and placed it on the cabinet, covering her village scenes with a portrait of the first cadaver she had stripped apart in the dissection hall.

Tule rummaged distractedly through his shoulder bag, preparing to leave. She felt her stomach tighten, a hollow trembling at her core. "Will you take me on?" she burst out.

He flicked his head as if to say yes. A slight movement, easy to misread in a man given to paroxysms of speech. A twitch of his hand, a gesture at her portrait of the cadaver. It was assumed: *yes.*

Jaya followed him to the door, her heart racing, and nearly stepped out with him, forgetting she wasn't also on her way out to the street.

8

AT THE HEIGHT of the rainy season in July, Jaya entered the hospital wearing dark glasses, hoping to see less. The entrance hall swarmed like a railway station with crowds of the sick and their relations, infants shrieking, skeletal boys trapped in ramshackle wheelchairs or propped on crude homemade crutches. Women in burqas concealed their afflictions beneath their black robes. Old men sought directions from her to guide their old wives urinating blood or leaking stool to a doctor in the outpatient clinic. Kirti would meet her in the interstices of the building in the middle of the day, stealing ten minutes from his duties in the surgical ward. With most of the staff at lunch, the passageways were empty for minutes at a time, and he didn't hesitate to take her hand for a moment. He grew bolder and grazed his fingers across her cheek; then he stunned her with a kiss on the forehead. Once, when the sister-in-charge had been absent from her desk, barricading the entry to Ward 4, he had slipped her inside, though it was a violation of hospital rules for second-year students to enter the wards unsupervised by a staff member. Jaya had felt a bleak nausea seeing the iron beds lined rigidly against the walls, the exhausted bodies at rest, a black foot lashed to a bedpost with bandages to stop the patient from fleeing.

One lunchtime, he took her to look in on a patient awaiting surgery in the isolation room. "He's taken a liking to me. Somehow he's gotten it in his head that I'm his doctor," Kirti said, sounding flattered. Though he had no patients of his own, only attending to them as part of a group headed by an honorary, this particular man had become attached to him. Perhaps it was because he took a few minutes during his morning rounds to talk to him.

"Why has he been isolated?" Jaya was concerned.

Kirti tapped her head with his pen and smiled. "Not to worry. The ward was full, they didn't have a cot for him." They knew they would both be trespassing in the isolation room unsupervised by a doctor. Square-shouldered, his stethoscope stuffed casually in the pocket of his white apron, Kirti made it clear with his firm gaze that he expected her to accompany him. She felt partially grateful for his guidance, her interest stirring when he told her the patients in the wards were his teachers.

In the cinema-hall dark of the isolation room, Jaya could smell Kirti's sweat tinged with the musk of tobacco. Stepping deeper into the large room, she could make out a grainy square of window light showing through a gauzy black curtain. To her right, a single weak bulb hung from the ceiling. A labored sighing filled the air, each breath accompanied by a strained whistling. The silver-haired patient sat on his haunches at the edge of a cot, his knees neatly fitted under his armpits. Coming nearer, Jaya saw that he was hunched over a small table on which she caught the glint of a metal jug and bowl.

"Who brought you the food, Chetty Sahib? The sister?" Kirti asked, announcing their presence.

The old man lifted his head slowly. "My son came," he managed to say, wheezing harshly. They watched him finish his meal. His unshaven face had a bluish cast in the dark, a grizzled stubble covering his lean cheeks and jaw.

"Are you all right in such darkness, Sahib? Should I put on another light?" Jaya said, as she searched the wall for the box of light switches.

"I don't need the light," the man replied in a voice that sounded difficult for him to produce. They heard the whistling exhalations of his breath again.

After a couple of minutes, Kirti shifted the table of dishes away to begin his exam. The old man, still squatting on the edge of the mattress, lifted his kurta and allowed Kirti to press his stethoscope to his chest. Though his limbs were pared down to the brutal outline of his bones, he had the inflated barrel chest of a proud, well-fed man, a mockery of his disease. The moment Kirti shifted the position of his stethoscope, the man was overcome by a coughing spasm. His coughs grew louder, wrenching. A thunder of coughing shook him, made him rock back and forth. Jaya stepped toward him in alarm. Kirti laid a hand on his curved back. There was half a minute's silence, then the renewed fury of his illness. He raised his head for an instant, struggling for breath, and Jaya saw the helplessness—the plea—in his eyes.

"I'll wait outside," she murmured to Kirti in English. Her legs were shaky, and she felt her knees might give way. She clutched the iron bars of the bed. The man dropped his head between his knees, coughing. It was unbearable to witness his agony and be unable to help him. Was it possible, too, she could absorb his illness from the air? Jaya motioned to the doorway. "I'm going," she said to Kirti, but he was concentrating on the patient, and she slipped quietly out of the room.

SHE FELL ILL for four days. Fever kept her in bed and a relentless itching drew blood on her arms and legs. When Kirti had found her outside the isolation room after he examined the old man, he'd dismissed her fears: "You're not risking your life every time you walk into a ward." The patient was sick with emphysema. All his life the poor fellow had worked in a mill, inhaling cotton fibers, Kirti explained. His lungs were covered with blisters that could be removed only with surgery. But she'd caught something. The doctor from the C Road clinic nearby came and applied his cold stethoscope to her chest. Her father prescribed vapor baths to reduce her fever, sitting Jaya in a chair with a heavy woolen blanket wrapped around her body and a tub of scalding water placed under her feet. The heat rising to her head made her moan in pain. For strength, Harbans ordered her to drink whey, almond water, and raisin water, which Kamlesh brought to her in tumblers whenever she was home from college.

"It's these paintings that are making you sick." Kamlesh had discovered the pair of portraits Jaya kept under her bed, covered by the dust-shield of an old towel. A portrait of the cadaver wearing an amulet around his neck, and a newer one, another recollection of a corpse, with an invented mask-like bronze face. The nose and lips jutted to an aggrieved point from which the shriveled planes of the cheeks slanted away, marred by deep umber-red cuts. Tule had recoiled, calling the second picture "morbid" and "grotesque." She'd lost control of her subject, of the form, conveying only a sense of hysteria. Nonetheless, Jaya grabbed her twin's wrist, pleading that both pictures be returned to their hiding place under her bed. They were her foundation, these two views of dying and death: her two modern paintings.

Inside the hospital campus, the dead were her subject and the sick her world. On the roads were starving dogs and crouching bodies eaten by disease, whose suffering she could smell as she walked by. Victims of accidents and illnesses sat without their arms or legs, begging on the footpath. Inside and outside the hospital compound, she lived in the ruins of other people's misery.

When Jaya recovered and began a new portrait in oils, Kamlesh made no secret of her hostility to the picture. "Another sick man," she called it. Jaya had to abandon it on the balcony with the other two portraits Kamlesh objected to. The painting, done on scrap plywood, showed a man's mortally hollow blue face with a head of shining bristles, a thin crop of luminous hair. After studying Rouault's thickly outlined figures in a small book of black-and-white plates that Mr. Tule had pressed on her at her first lesson, hissing that "Rouault and Soutine are the two greatest painters of our time," after painting thoughtfully, incrementally, Jaya had completed her fictitious patient's head, his gaunt face and sunken eyes illuminated by a glistening black line. The image had emerged as a slow summation of her fears, the ravaged face of illness.

Her painting teacher arrived for her third lesson after a delay due to her illness, his weekends reserved for his few students. During the week he painted on his own chaotic timetable, it seemed, staying up the whole night and half the day. Scratching his stubble apprehensively, looking frayed, Tule studied the sketchbooks and loose drawings she had laid out on the center table in the sitting room. He praised her quick new portraits of Kamlesh. Still Jaya was apprehensive about showing him her portrait of the blue patient, remembering his previous attack on her bronze cadaver's head with small wounds. Afraid of further condemnation, she asked a question she'd been contemplating, "What makes art modern?"

Tule laughed. He spewed ideas about demolishing perspective, turning an image into a feeling, an impression into a spectacle. Her excitement grew. "Like this," he said and sketched her face in soft pencil on an empty page in her sketchbook. A fractured Cubist head, her hair plaited in diamond shapes, her chunni lashed across her throat. Her raised eyebrows sharpened to naive points, her mouth misaligned in two pieces. She laughed to see how good and fast he was.

Next he rendered the room for her amusement, made the furniture bulbous, allowed the great, curving armchair to swallow her. The Japanese doll holding a parasol sprang from the top of the curio cabinet to the position of a lamp beside her head. The boat-shaped cut-glass dish expanded into a barrier on the table. *"Bourgeois Trappings Trap the Artist"*—he recited acidly what might have been his title for the picture. Jaya felt the slap. She felt the strike against her father. Was his achievement a trap for them? Would they have been better off in their cramped Colaba flat? She felt the force of Tule's resentment—a spectacularly talented artist staying in a rented room in someone's flat. Who was actually trapped?

"I'll bring something," she said, pushing down her anger. She went to the back balcony, returned with her picture of the blue patient. It was nearly dry and she propped it on her mother's curio cabinet, moving aside the knickknacks.

"It's a bold picture." Tule stepped back to gain the necessary distance from the image. "Shadows are pronounced, there's a lot of drama in the face. See what the black line does!" Then, remembering himself, he cried out, "Every painting I do, I paint in one go. I become obsessed, I don't know how much time passes—three, four, five, ten hours. I'm not conscious of anything except attacking the canvas, but always with two principles in mind: aesthetic order, plastic coordination. In this picture, you've paid a lot of attention to form." He made chewing motions with his mouth, giving her picture a second thought. "But when we look at the face, we feel afraid. Such a boiling expression of illness, such menace in the poor fellow's suffering. We should feel his anguish. We shouldn't feel repulsed by him."

Jaya went to shut the drawing room doors. What could he tell her about how to bring out the pathos in her subjects? How she should look at things? What should she paint? "Are there any lady painters in your Group 47?"

she inquired, wondering if her fears were a consequence of being female, a condition she was destined to live with.

"None. There are none. In any case, we've more or less disbanded now. Everyone has gone off in their own direction."

"You don't know of any lady painters in Bombay?"

"There's Sringara, of course. She's one of our circle—we might have an exhibition together. I don't think of her as a 'lady painter' as such. She's come up very well in the last few years. You've not heard her name?"

"No." Jaya regretted her lack of familiarity with Sringara.

The double doors made an abrupt noise like a bark. Her father pushed them open and walked into the room. "Why do you keep the door closed? I didn't know if there was anyone inside." He had come home after being out somewhere; he swept his handkerchief around his neck. He gave Jaya a withering look, seeing her alone with Tule, whom he barely acknowledged with a nod. She was aware of the impropriety of shutting the doors while alone in the room with a man, but keeping their conversation confidential had felt necessary. Now the anxiety returned that her father was going to dismiss Tule, refuse to pay fifty rupees a month in tuition to a braggard whose booming voice they could hear at the back of the flat.

"Oh, I didn't realize—" Jaya said, as though she hadn't been aware the doors were shut. Her drawings of Kirti's hands were spread all over the center table, mixed up with her charcoal sketches of Kamlesh. The patient's blue face was in full view on top of the cabinet. She took a step in front of it.

Her father approached the picture with a slight grimace, then turned away, satisfied he'd seen what was going on. He threw open the balcony doors. "Let the breeze in. There's such bad air in this room," he said.

OUTSIDE THE PRINCE of Wales restaurant, Kirti flung out an arm to scatter the onlookers watching Jaya hoist herself onto his sputtering motorcycle. The spectators lingered on the road, street boys standing at a slant with their arms folded across their chests, waiting for the action to begin. Motorcycles were a rare sight in Bombay, the vehicle of a movie hero or an army officer. A girl in a sari riding side saddle was a curiosity. Because it was Kirti's only form of transport, borrowed from his father—a lieutenant colonel—Jaya had to risk exposing herself. Someone whistled loudly. She nestled her handbag in her lap and hesitantly circled one arm around Kirti's waist. The thin hood of her sari, drawn around her head, offered faint concealment. The bike leaned sharply left and they pulled into traffic. Only after they'd cleared the congested bazaars, swinging onto Love Grove Road, traveling along darkened blue stretches of the sea, did Jaya relax enough to enjoy their speed. Kirti's bush shirt bloused out in the wind and her hand, pressed beneath his ribs, followed the reassuring rhythm of his stomach swelling and sinking as he breathed.

North of the reeking fishermen's enclave at Mahim, thick green fields with palm trees replaced derelict markets and agglomerations of crumbling tile-roofed houses, the land baring its original wilderness as the city disappeared behind them. Yet even burrowing through this flat green passage as the sky turned to dull tin, Jaya feared she would be seen. She hung her head, pulled her black-and-white print sari to her brow, shielding herself from the eyes of anyone who might report her to her father. Leaving the main road in Juhu, Kirti wove through a network of lanes paved in loose gold sand, turning corners around old bungalows, until they were roaring down a narrow sandy drive toward Farrokh Wadia's beach shack, the immense sea visible ahead.

An old man, short of stature, gripping a bamboo staff, hobbled out of a shed. It stood across the drive from Farrokh's tile-roofed holiday shack. The man was naked except for a light cloth drawn around his hips, his chest slack and withered. The taut convolutions of a white turban gave his head enormous prominence. Kirti rushed forward to greet him as he bashed his swollen turban with his fists. Jaya couldn't understand his lament.

"What is her condition?" Kirti's voice rose in response to the man's distress. He gestured to Jaya for the packet he'd asked her to keep. She opened her purse and handed him the small paper parcel.

The caretaker started shouting in pidgin Hindi about his dog. "I didn't let her go near the water. I followed your orders—"

Kirti rushed toward the black maw of the shed's doorway. "Is she inside?"

"She's gone, that sweet child of mine. She was in too much pain."

Kirti stopped and removed an ampoule of milky penicillin from the package. "This medicine cures everything." He held up the glass like a treasure, as though he hadn't understood what he'd been told.

"Then shoot some in my head. I have the pain of the whole world in here." The man slapped his turban with both hands, his puny jaw jutting out in contempt for Kirti. "That smell came back. She started smelling so badly where you cut her," he shouted at Kirti. "I thought you'd come back in a day or two. I kept waiting." The old fellow's mouth fell open, and Jaya braced herself for a cry. But he only hammered his turban with his fists. "Her misery was too much even for a clever doctor sahib like you."

On the beach, a surging wind carried bitter sweeps of sand and rattled the dark ribs of palm trees. Jaya had suggested a walk and they'd taken off their shoes, although rain clouds pressed low on the sea. The air and water had turned the dark color of smoke. She held her beige purse by the handles, a weight in her left hand. Kirti lit a cigarette, too entangled in the question of what had gone wrong—at which step he'd made a mistake—to drive back into town. The dog had been sick with an ulcerating tumor the size of a mango on one of her teats. He had thought he might be able to save her. It had felt good to give the old fellow some hope, he recalled; the man suffered from terrible migraines. Four or five times in the last month he'd come to check up on her, take out her stitches, change her bandages. She was a gentle dog, gone all white around the face. Every time he came he had to borrow his father's motorcycle, keep aside half the day for the trip. Last time, the wound had shown signs of infection, so he'd bought the syringe and penicillin. Spent twenty-five rupees. He'd intended to come right away, but his hospital duties had gotten in the way. Jaya listened, nodded. *A lot of money, twenty-five rupees.*

Someone was watching them, a man standing on his lawn above the beach as the sky contracted in darkness. The wind raged anew through the gallery of palms below the houses. They turned back toward Farrokh's cottage, Kirti tossing the burning stub of his cigarette into a deep pit in the sand. Something landed between her shoulders. His hand. Jaya laughed uncomfortably and straightened her back. His hand fell away.

It wasn't likely he'd told Farrokh he was bringing her here; he would have been careful about protecting her reputation. Still, he shouldn't have asked her here. She should never have agreed to come. But she wanted to know what it would feel like to be completely alone with him, far from town. What if the old man said something about a girl to Farrokh? Thankfully he hadn't acknowledged her presence, saving her the discomfort. Kirti took another cigarette from his shirt pocket, lit it, tossed the match in the sand, and walked ahead of her.

The prospect of returning to the city under a dimming sky seemed remote to Jaya; Kirti seemed remote. A tall man in white trousers and white shirt who did as he pleased. He continued to move away from her, absorbed in his own thoughts. When she slowed her pace to let him walk ahead of her, up the garden steps onto the lawn, she meant to chart the distance she felt from him. Climbing the cement stairs a minute later, she found him sitting on the top step, putting on his shoes. "We'll have to wait," he told her. She nodded and stepped past him to retrieve her sandals from the grass. Thunder blasted over the sea. Jaya glanced back over the garden's low barbed-wire fence. The water rose in a black gleam. There was an instant's perfect silence before the deluge unleashed. Suddenly they were running against a stinging rain toward Farrokh's cottage, Jaya's arms flung over her head, her purse held up for cover. Kirti shouted many times for the caretaker from the veranda. Finally he ran across to the servant's quarters and reappeared with the old man, who came to unlock the shack, tented in a piece of gunnysack, clutching his bamboo staff.

The plaited-palm wall panels were pulled back. The caretaker extracted two cane chairs from the jumble of furniture strewn around the cavernous room and set them on the threshold of the covered veranda. He searched through drawers and shelves in the back for a spool of wire to mend the fuse with, but there wasn't a scrap to be found. Kirti discovered candles and paper lanterns on a kitchen shelf, leftovers from one of Farrokh's parties. Lighting them, they watched the old man jerkily propel himself back through the flumes of rain on his bamboo crutch. With three lanterns, Jaya composed a bloom of light on a side table set between their facing chairs, trying to dispel Kirti's black mood. She lit a fourth and fifth lantern against his pessimism; it was a quality they intensified in each other.

Nothing could be done about her drenched sari, but she went on blotting her upper body with a sheet Kirti fetched from a bedroom at the back. His shirt clung to the broad planes of his chest. They would have to wait until the rain stopped to drive back to town; no point in trying to read her wristwatch every two minutes. She gazed out at the lawn and vast, eerie sea under shuddering spasms of rain. Kirti disappeared inside the shack again and returned with a bottle of raspberry soda from the kitchen. Another party leftover. She didn't expect him to pour the first warm sip into her mouth.

Their attempts at light conversation couldn't divert Jaya from the worry of how she would explain her absence at home. Making up a missed lung dissection due to illness didn't stretch from afternoon into evening, or however long they would be stranded here. "Farrokh's parties must be good fun," she said self-consciously.

"A boys' get-together. The old fellow makes a lovely fish curry." Without asking, Kirti took a swallow from her bottle. It felt invasive, exciting. "Cards going on the whole night. Only once we had some dancing."

"Dancing? With whom did you dance?" She spoke against mounting blasts of thunder, uncertain if he could hear her a few feet away.

"Some nurses from St. George's Hospital. Narula knows them. We played the radio. It was a long time back." He let it go—uncomfortable, it seemed, to talk to her about other girls.

"My sister met Ashok at that wedding. She's mad about films." He smiled—he'd heard that a few times. "You must meet her some time."

"That would be nice. Why not?" Kirti went along with her pretense, as though they had nothing to hide.

Over the sea's black abyss a blaze of silver light flashed, brightening their universe for a moment. A minute shift of time back toward day. She had something for him, it occurred to her. She opened her purse. "I hope it hasn't gotten wet." Jaya wiped the binding with her hand, offering Kirti a small tablet of her drawings.

He laid the book on the side table and thumbed through the pages in the lantern light. She glanced across at the sketches—then at his face—a hand imprinted on each page: her own, or Kamlesh's hands taking the shapes of dance mudras. It was his first glimpse of her twin. Somewhere in the middle of the sketchbook was a drawing of the top half of Kamlesh's face, her eyes downcast and evasive, the disturbed expression of an argument or a wounding, perhaps of the mournful distance they felt between the two of them. Kirti lingered over a picture Jaya couldn't see—perhaps that one—then continued flicking through the pages. He went quickly; he might have expected more of her drawings. "It was the only pad I had small enough to carry with me—"

"You read a lot into hands." He nodded as he stopped at a page. She smiled—it seemed her drawings didn't make her small in his eyes. He held up a charcoal sketch of a lean forearm supporting fingers unfurling like branches. "Whose hand is this? Yours?"

"Yes," she admitted.

He went on staring at the image as if it were a code he was trying to decipher then put the tablet aside. "May I keep this with me? I'd like to go through it on my own."

"Sure." She gave him a tentative smile, not knowing what to think; perhaps he found it tiresome to go on dutifully studying her sketches in front of her. A formality descended between them as they sat isolated on the verge of the veranda, a dark room behind them.

When she asked for the toilet, wanting to move away from him, Kirti ushered her through the dim main room to the back of a narrow bedroom. She opened the bathroom door into a deeper darkness smelling of the earth. A bowl recessed in the floor, rain spattering the clay roof tiles. She stayed there longer than she needed to, glad to be alone for a long moment, then stepped back out into the galley-like bedroom. He surprised her, standing between the bed and a low mirrored dressing table, toweling his hair. "You haven't dried yourself properly," he said.

Jaya let him touch her for a moment, drying her head with the towel, then stepped away to arrange her hair with her hands. "I'm all right," she said.

The lantern he'd brought into the room painted an arch of light on the brick wall above the bed. His arms made black fronds in the glow. Her face was warm with anger at herself for having come here with him. But when he reached for her from behind, she allowed herself to be held, following the pleasant sensation of his hand moving down her hair to her spine. She tilted her head back, relieved by some constriction coming loose, and Kirti stood stroking her for some time.

On the bed, an unsheeted cot, his mouth over hers tasted warmly of cigarettes. An earthy, ashy odor she first shrank from, then sought out with her tongue, savoring it because it was the scent of him, clinging to every pore of his body. His hands, stirring across her face, moving to her throat, pushed aside the long, loose end of her sari, exposing her brief white blouse. Jaya lay on her back, clutching Kirti's waist, following the trails of his slow caresses in concentrated silence. A haze softened his eyes; his face was somehow transfigured. She pressed her mouth to the wet shoulder of his shirt, running her hand along his neck. He was sighing, rubbing his leg between hers. His hands rounded her hips, moved across the limp pleats of her sari falling between her legs. A fear revived. She watched him shift down her body, smothering his face in folds of soft cotton below her waist. How utterly strange to have a man this close. She had never borne the bulk of a man before—she tried to slip out from under him. "Do you want me to stop?" Kirti's words were hoarse, private.

Jaya glanced down at the wet tips of her blouse where he'd sucked. Yes and no and yes. She couldn't speak, couldn't accept the strangeness of exposing herself so completely to him. She shifted onto her side, facing the lighted wall.

A conversation began, a long aimless murmuring, Jaya keeping her back to him. Eventually Kirti swept an arm over her, turning her around against his chest, wrapping her in his luxurious heat. His shirt was there—flung on the dressing table. She laid her face against his cushioning chest and drew his finger with the coral ring on it into her mouth, tasting metal and biting into flesh. He shifted and she raised herself for a moment, to remind herself where she was. In the mirror, she caught a glimpse of her hair falling in damp hanks over her blouse, her lipstick smeared, her sari strewn around her waist. She had never seen herself in such disarray. "The door," she whispered in alarm.

Kirti got up to bolt it shut. His chest softly rose and fell with his breath. She loved him for the shape of his breath and reached up to his dark, solid chest to feel him breathe when he returned. He sat down cross-legged on the bed and lifted her head into his lap, fanning her long wet hair across his thighs.

PART 2

On the Precipice

9

KAMLESH WAS ATTEMPTING to dash across Victoria Gardens Road when she got caught between intermingling streams of traffic, oncoming drivers swerving around her, taxis blowing smoke from their tailpipes, horse carriages clattering by on enormous wooden wheels. A line of clerks and shop assistants who'd been standing behind her on the footpath darted across the street in the fleeting gaps between vehicles, while she stood immobile, hesitant to run ahead. A tram came to a halt a short distance away, disgorging passengers, and Kamlesh stepped in front of it, waiting for a moment's clearance. The driver's horn forced her to retreat. She caught sight of Kirti Dasgupta for the first time after the tram passed, standing on the other side of the road near the outpatient clinic's entrance. Jaya anxiously gestured for her to stay where she was. She looked small next to him, like a doll in her dark red sari, gripping her bag of books. He held his head very straight, a tall, broad, dark-skinned boy, looking like a naval officer in a white bush shirt and white trousers. Before Kamlesh could make sense of his movements, he'd run across the road in front of a double-decker harshly striking its bell as it neared its stop. "Come quickly," he urged, pressing a hand on her shoulder.

"Now?" She stiffened under his touch. He caught hold of her upper arm, digging his fingers into her flesh as he pulled her past two lanes of motorcars, buses, and lorries and a bullock cart transporting blocks of ice wrapped in jute.

To their dismay Jaya had disappeared in the rush of people in front of the hospital. Standing together at Gate No. 2, waiting for her, felt deeply uncomfortable. Kamlesh was relieved when Kirti asked her to remain by the gate that patients passed through while he went to search for Jaya. Anonymous men passing by sucked the air loudly, making kissing sounds in her direction. Someone rubbed his body against hers as he passed her from behind, and she sprang away, then turned warily to trace a persistent kissing sound and saw a lanky boy in pajamas smirking at her. "Hello, phency lady, hello"—a thin man passing by, showing off his English, mocked her, standing there in her flounced skirt and puff-sleeved blouse among women covered in saris and burqas. As she waited, it felt as though Jaya had deliberately abandoned her to these stares and hisses, to punish her for asking to meet Kirti. It was only some minutes later she learned that Jaya had run up the road to catch an empty taxi, which had gotten blocked in traffic as it turned around at the signal to return to the outpatient gate, where they were all to meet.

Jaya threw open the taxi door, crying out for Kamlesh. Kirti spotted them from the footpath and took the seat beside the driver. The taxi turned right, following the sprawl of the bazaar. They skirted a green mosque that rose in the middle of the road and continued through the evening rush past shops selling burqas, electrical goods, sequined prayer rugs, oil products, books. Kirti glanced back at the twins from the front seat, his elbow pointing sharply at Kamlesh. "Jaya tells me you're at Sophia College."

"I'm doing my BA." Kamlesh heard the tremor in her voice. "In English literature."

"You're passing out next year, is it?"

"Yes . . ." There had to be something she could add. "I'll be doing my teacher's training after that. There's a new institute of education attached to St. Xavier's my father's found out about—it's a one-year course." She crossed her arms, ashamed to have brought up her father in front of him. Her hand unwittingly went to the spot where he'd grabbed her, clenching his fingers so tightly below her sleeve he must have left marks on her skin. She didn't look.

"Kamlesh just started teaching at a hutment colony in Thana," Jaya said to Kirti. She was fidgeting with her beaded earring, nervous to mediate. "She's the singing teacher."

"I've heard you dance, but I didn't know about your singing," Kirti said, glancing back at Kamlesh again in a friendly manner.

"I teach songs and games." Kamlesh smiled, encouraged by the thought. "I have my class on Saturday afternoons—just for an hour, before the school closes. It's a class of laborers' children. I don't know if you've heard about this place." She refrained from speaking about her grandmother, hesitant to make family people known to this outsider. He nodded as if he knew about the hill colony.

The soft, sad blue shadows of dusk descended as the taxi stalled in traffic-crammed lanes, and they pretended not to see the women displaying themselves in doorways. A taut silence fell between them. Kamlesh hadn't expected to be taken through the red-light district, and she stiffened in shame. Yet she couldn't help glancing at the girls in petticoats, wearing very dark, heavy lipstick. She looked at her twin. Jaya felt like a stranger, artificial in her appearance. She had pinned her hair up meticulously, her bun held back neatly in a black net cap, her coral lip color applied too thickly. Her batik sari, a modern design of wavering lines and blocks of paisleys, was one she wore to nice lunches. She probably felt anxious about introducing Kamlesh to him after the uncertainty over the meeting. First Jaya had been eager to arrange the tea, and then she'd tried to cancel, saying it was the wrong time since she and Kirti were both under pressure studying for exams. He was locked away in his hostel room, and she hardly saw him. A distance had grown between them as he devoted himself to his final MBBS papers. Then they'd had a conversation to straighten things out, because Kamlesh couldn't wait—wouldn't wait—until after their exams to meet him. For ten months Jaya had been going around with him without her knowledge, and it felt as if a part of her own life had been lived without her.

"She's actually become very popular with the children," Jaya said about her teaching. Kamlesh grinned, touched by Jaya's effort to build her up in Kirti's eyes.

The taxi ride terminated at a battered Irani café open to the road—not an elegant hotel coffee shop, as Kamlesh had imagined they would meet in.

Abrasive voices inside the Prince of Wales echoed the frenetic tempo of the roads. They sat at a table under a wooden balcony overhanging the back of the long Victorian hall, the air penetrated by the steamy odor of bitter tea and the shrill whistling of trains from Bombay Central Station across the street.

Casting quick glances around the room, Kamlesh heard the boisterous talk with a twinge of discomfort and a budding sense of excitement; she had never been to a restaurant like this—full of loud, talkative men. You could say a lot to a man in a free atmosphere like this. A distracted bearer came around, and Kamlesh modestly ordered a plain tray of tea when Kirti asked what she would like. In his capacity as host, he insisted she have something to eat—a cheese toast, mince samosas? "You must take something," he said. "Their snacks are very tasty."

"I like their pineapple cake," Jaya encouraged her.

Sponge cake was listed on the board, so Kamlesh decided on that. Kirti leaned over to say something privately to her sister that Kamlesh couldn't hear, nor did she catch Jaya's reply against the uproar of feuding voices in the front. What was he saying to her? Kamlesh gave them an open smile.

"We Marathi people will prevail over Bombay! The Marathi language will prevail!" shouted a man at a crowded table to the left of the entrance. Some men at a neighboring table shouted back that the city was theirs, probably Gujaratis. A fight was erupting over how state lines should be redrawn and whom the capital, Bombay, belonged to—the Marathis or Gujaratis. The angry Marathi man shouted the pro-Maharashtra slogan: "Mumbai amchi hai!"

"You swine," cursed a man at the other table. "You're nothing but illiterate fishermen, what else are you? Drinking in your jhopadis and taking your stinking boats out at night."

As if deaf to the shouting, Jaya and Kirti laughed over something that seemed to dispel whatever tension or exam fatigue had been pushing them apart. When the bearer brought their order, Jaya spooned some of Kirti's peas and mince onto her plate, and he went on intently discussing a matter with her that remained unknown to Kamlesh.

If she wanted to, Kamlesh could tell Jaya something quite interesting. But Jaya had kept secrets, so Kamlesh kept her own. No one knew of her encounter with a man. A film director. She'd taken a bus to Bandra a few weeks back, then walked all the way up Hill Road to Tanvir Studio. She'd worn her lovely blue and green bandini sari, changing clothes quickly at the Ritz hotel bathroom so no one at home would know. At the studio gate, the chowkidar with the red paan mouth and khaki uniform wouldn't admit her. *You girls are always coming around, asking to meet a director.* Despite her insistence that she had an appointment, he waved his stick to shoo her away. As she was leaving, a polished white sedan surged out of the drive. A man opened the door. He seemed to know of her wish to speak to someone about going into films—how could it hurt just to talk about it?—and offered to take her to his office. She'd heard his name—Kishore Sehdev. She dropped the bag stuffed with her college clothes on his front seat. He was a small, spare, quick man, smiling keenly at her. She recoiled when he greedily held his hand out to her just as she was about to climb in and she shut the door. Sehdev angrily lurched away. After a moment, she realized he'd driven off with her clothes like a captive figment of herself.

Two scornful lines like scars formed between Kirti's eyebrows; he was listening attentively now to the shrill battle between the tables of Marathis and Gujaratis over who would take possession of Bombay city when the state was divided. "Bloody mad people," he said, frowning. "They should all be thrown out. Where's the bearer?"

Jaya, peering across at the two raucous tables, said she'd thought for an instant that the churlish man standing up at the Marathi table was Tule. Her teacher lived just over the bridge in Tardeo, a paying guest in someone's flat. It did look like him, Kamlesh agreed, concerned it might be the painter, but when the fellow turned to argue with the bearer, who was exhorting him to keep quiet, she could see it wasn't Tule. They both laughed apprehensively, thinking of the mess they'd be in if someone they knew discovered them with Kirti Dasgupta. Tule was having an exhibition at the Jehangir Art Gallery in November, Jaya said, trying to divert Kirti's mounting anger.

"Oh, is it?" Kirti turned his attention back to them.

"With a friend of his, a woman he says is one of the best painters around."

"What about you?" Kirti teased.

"Do you think I'm ready for the top art gallery in town?" Jaya laughed dryly, looking ticked off by his question. Kamlesh would have liked to say something in her defense, but she shied away from speaking to Kirti directly. "Her name's Sringara, she's from Mysore," said Jaya. "Her paintings are inspired by the South, he says, by village people—women working in the fields . . ."

"Which place inspires you?"

"No place." Jaya resisted his probing with a mischievous lift of the eyebrows. "They're just faces. I suppose it's the hospital, if I had to name a place—"

"That was before—" Kamlesh paused, stopping herself from divulging that for the last ten days she had posed for Jaya every evening. Jaya would put aside her medical books and lecture notes, taking off on the wave of an idea, and sketch Kamlesh as well as their mother, Bebeji, and even Heerabai, filling one sketchbook after another, despite their father having suspended her lessons with Tule until after her exams in October. "First professional," the exams were called, as if she were already a qualified doctor.

Jaya picked up on the thought. "I've been drawing a lot of Kamlesh. She's going to be the model for my next painting."

"After her exams, I'm going to be put up for dissection." Kamlesh laughed, feeling a faint titillation in telling Kirti something he didn't know about them. For half an hour at a stretch, Kamlesh held her dance poses for Jaya, demonstrating a catalog of eye movements for Jaya's close studies of emotion. This is *sankita*, uneasiness, Kamlesh would say, lifting her pupils timidly. This is *vismita*—astonishment—her eyes opening wide, pupils staring upward while she held her eyelids absolutely still. Sometimes Jaya would turn Kamlesh's face upon itself in the dressing table mirrors, her eye continually traveling from Kamlesh down to her paper, pausing a moment, then roaming again, taking in some new part of her. Sometimes Kamlesh shifted and Jaya immediately recast her in the mirror panels, her movements circumscribed by the arc of Jaya's gaze. Jaya would pull Kamlesh's elbow back, turn her by the shoulders to angle her face more sharply into the glass, press her back so it arched more deeply. Kamlesh was Jaya's subject: she was subject to Jaya. But she didn't object to doing what she was told, because when she glimpsed the charcoal line Jaya drew, she thought of it as a solid black thread connecting them.

Though it felt as if the line stitched them together, she had sensed her twin's distance from her, sensed Jaya was withholding something, before she found out about Kirti. To punish Jaya, Kamlesh would push her away or question her in a distrustful manner. But the day she received a letter from Leela, after not hearing from her for months, she read out the most worrisome parts to her twin, unsure what to do. *I've never felt so cut off from the world*, Leela wrote. *It's raining all the time now. I feel so sad I don't even bother getting out of bed.* The quarry town in the jungle was a dreadfully lonesome place. Leela and her husband were forced to socialize only with a few middle-aged British couples, her husband's rank too high for him to mix with Indian professionals. They couldn't even take a ferry to the big steel mill club across the river to meet other Indian couples, because the river flooded in the rains. *I feel like sinking to the bottom of the Brahmini River.* When Kamlesh read those words, Jaya frowned and wondered if Leela's mother knew how depressed she was feeling. Something about Leela's isolation or sadness prompted Jaya to confide in Kamlesh the same day. "There's been something I've been wanting to tell you," Jaya said. Despite her suspicions, Kamlesh was surprised to hear about the boy, Kirti Dasgupta; what hurt her most was Jaya's long deceit.

"Are you going to tell them? You should tell them," Kamlesh said. She meant their parents should be informed because if other people found out Jaya was meeting a boy, their name would be ruined.

"No," said Jaya firmly. "Not now. We have exams, he has a big paper to write—something about body temperature in heart surgery."

Kamlesh didn't press her. She knew from Jaya's tone that she wouldn't give in. He was Bengali and dark-complexioned, which their mother wouldn't like. Their parents might not accept him at all—perhaps that worried Jaya. He was outside their community, their Punjabi language, their customs. A Punjabi khatri of a good family, like Vikram Bakshi, was the kind of boy they were both meant to marry.

"I want to meet him," Kamlesh told her twin.

Jaya immediately agreed. "I didn't want to keep it from you," she said, "but I didn't know what to do." Her eyes were moist. The secret seemed to have hurt her, too, or made her feel lonely at home.

At the table, Kirti leaned across to brush something out of Jaya's hair, a fleeting gesture whose intimacy took Kamlesh by surprise. She leaned away in her seat, feeling out of place.

Kirti turned to her, as though there were nothing unusual about his touching her twin. "Jaya's shown me some drawings of your hands. The fingers very intricately bent and twisted. It conveys a strong impression of your dance—just the hands."

Kamlesh's glance fell to her plate of half-eaten cake, as if he'd spoken of an intimate part of her body. A red coral bloomed in the square gold ring he wore on the hand that had caught hold of her on the road. His fingers were restless and dark-skinned under the nails.

"What's happening over there?" Jaya was alarmed. The entire Marathi group, shouting spitefully, stood up, making a move toward the Gujarati table. One of the Gujaratis sprang out of his seat, chest thrust forward and fists cocked. The proprietor stepped out from behind his till and walked swiftly toward them—a rugged man with heavy shoulders and a protruding stomach. Every ethnic group, every language community was clamoring for its own state. Now that the country had been broken in two, Bebeji would say, people's appetite to tear things apart had grown. How many partitions could India bear?

Kirti stood up, pulling rupee notes out of his wallet and laying them on the table. "Let's make a move before they start throwing the bloody chairs around."

The distant tram on Bellasis Road approached through the darkness. Its piercing beam outshone the feeble yellow light of apartment windows that washed dimly over the signboards for dental surgeons and palmists tacked to some balconies. Facing the railway station's blocky modern facade, Kirti seemed to have an insight into a brighter future. "In twenty years' time, people will be flying everywhere, and trains will become obsolete." He was carrying Jaya's bag for her, stuffed with her notebooks and papers, and he settled it between his feet to light a cigarette.

Jaya raised her eyes skeptically. "My, what grand ideas you have. Where shall we fly to?"

"So when does one see you next, Miss Malhotra?" Kirti asked.

Kamlesh didn't reply, not knowing which of them he was talking to. After an instant, it was clear by his gaze resting on her face. "What will happen with him?" she had asked Jaya, and Jaya said he'd brought up the word *marriage*—which had gone unspoken between them for all these months.

In his mind, their relationship had always been about marriage, he'd told her, and he would meet her sister only if she shared that understanding. He wasn't going around with her just to have a good time. The word had startled Jaya—such an important word—but she was happy that they'd spoken openly about their future. After their exams, Kirti wanted her to meet his parents. That seemed to make her uncomfortable; it would mean drawing Mummy and Daddy into the equation too. But she'd "agreed to his demand," as she put it. Kamlesh smiled to think it was the prospect of meeting her that had provoked Kirti to declare his intentions—to give her sister's future a shape they could both begin to imagine.

Her twin glanced at her sharply, wondering at her lack of response to Kirti's question. "Anytime," Jaya spoke up for her, knowing that was an impossibility.

"Anytime," Kamlesh added agreeably.

"We'll go somewhere peaceful after exams." The glowing orange tip of Kirti's cigarette drew a curve in the air. Kamlesh stood between him and Jaya, and he pressed an inch closer, brushing Jaya's arm as he handed her the bag and ushered them toward the approaching tram. For an instant, they came together as a trio, Kamlesh included in their confidence, their romance, as if it were something she belonged to.

10

SUNLIGHT FELL THROUGH two unglazed windows, brightening a picture of Durga riding a tiger that the class teacher had nailed to the wall. Jaya counted thirty-two children sitting cross-legged on the floor inside the small brick primary school, an abacus of dark heads lined up in neat rows, the boys on the left separated from the girls on the right by a crooked aisle down the middle. The class teacher, Prabha, who looked no older than a college girl, and Jaya observed the singing lesson from the back of the room. "*Dravida ukala banga*," the children recited after Kamlesh. Sitting on the floor at the head of the class, beneath a chalkboard mounted in a wooden frame, Kamlesh patted the beat on her thigh. In municipal schools, the national anthem began the day, and she had been teaching them the song, as Bebeji had asked, to help them see that India was both a very old society and a very new country.

"What is the meaning of *Dravida*? Who are they? Show your hands." The electrician's daughter, Lakshmi, vigorously shook her head inside the drape of her green chunni to confirm she didn't know the answer. Her baby brother lay on a mat in front of her. He was small for a one-year-old, Jaya thought, and appeared to stare upward without ever moving. Lakshmi squeezed his feet, tiny silver anklets shimmering around them. "No one?" Kamlesh put on a disappointed look, an actress's puzzled exaggeration in the eyes. "*Dravida* are a community of people from the south of India, from Madras," she said and continued with a simple description.

Jaya smiled at her efforts to follow Bebeji's instruction to single out a few phrases of the anthem for explanation each week, though not so many that the children wouldn't remember. "Bebeji, you would make a much better teacher than me," Kamlesh had gently teased their grandmother.

A chorus of thin, humming voices followed as Kamlesh clapped the beat, picking up the song again. Holding a pause at the end, Kamlesh called out dramatically, "*Ek sath: Jai Hind!*"

"*Jai Hind!*" the children shouted back.

Another baby began to grunt, shaking her arms in distress. The girl cradling her infant sister in her lap cried out in a mother's exasperated tones: "*Arre, Ma, rukhja na zara!*" Oh, Ma, just stop it now! "Ma, Ma!" the older sister wearily implored the groaning baby.

Jaya smiled to herself, turning to catch Prabha's eye, but Prabha got up to sort out a problem between two boys in the back swatting each other's arms.

A surly boy shouted at the girl cradling her sister, "Hey, you with the mustaches, shut up your baby!"

"Don't talk to Wasima like that," Kamlesh softly admonished him.

Prabha returned to her place beside Jaya and said the girl often brought the baby to class; their mother was employed as a sweeperess at the table fan factory. Since the school was brighter and sturdier than their huts, the floor of cement rather than dirt, Jaya imagined, the girls might feel the little ones were better protected here. Lakshmi leaned over to her baby brother, Shankar, and clapped her hands sharply in his ears, trying to provoke a reaction. She brought him to class whenever her mother allowed, and always on Saturdays, Prabha whispered, hoping the singing might get through to him though he appeared to be deaf. Jaya watched the girl try to animate the child by moving his hands and legs around. The baby had given her a broad smile as she held him, Kamlesh reported one afternoon, and she sensed his intelligence hadn't died with his bout of brain fever; it was merely buried, sleeping.

Kamlesh led the children in a game of passing a word around the room. A girl in the row in front of Jaya turned herself in circles on the floor, thick scabs on her arms, some roughly peeled away to show raw pink spots. The face of an older boy, on the other side of the aisle, was spotted with sores as if a small animal had pecked at him. The living conditions on this hill, the lack of clean water and the layers of dirt coating the children's hair and bodies, must be behind their skin diseases and infections. She would ask Kirti if he could propose any simple solutions to help them until the dispensary opened.

"*Pani!*" cried a boy urgently. *Water!*

"Go," said Kamlesh, and he ran outside to urinate.

Immediately other boys started shouting, "*Pani! Pani!*" When Kamlesh told them to stop, they squirmed around the floor in a mime of discomfort.

Prabha stood up beside Jaya, her hands on her thin hips, a vermilion bindi between her pinched eyebrows, and gave the boys a stern glare. "How badly you're all behaving! What will Kamlesh Didi think? She won't come back to teach you anymore!" Some of the girls piped up yearningly that Kamlesh Didi should keep coming to school. All but two giggling boys fell silent. "Quiet! Behave!" the class teacher commanded again. Jaya could see by Kamlesh's glance that she, too, was startled by this slender young girl's imperious air of authority. Perhaps it was necessary for her to take charge in an environment that didn't offer children much security.

Outside, after school concluded, a few boys chased each other giddily, one in pajamas with a split seam that showed his buttocks.

A dozen chattering children lingered around Jaya and Kamlesh, who stood in the shadow of the whitewashed school in the hot red dirt. The harsh sun blazed upon them. The class teacher remained inside, latching the window shutters. Kamlesh allowed some curious children to empty her bag of teaching props and make noise with a small drum, tambourine, and bell, and Jaya found herself laughing at their antics. For weeks Kamlesh had been urging her to visit her classroom—wanting to reveal something of her separate life here to Jaya—and Jaya was glad she'd accompanied Kamlesh to the colony on the first Saturday she was free after exams. She'd loved being among the children inside Bebeji's schoolhouse, with its faintly crooked walls and slanted door. It sat seven or eight hundred feet up the hill, on a level patch of parched ground.

The two girls carrying their siblings on their hips chatted away in the bare yard like impish little women. Jaya and Kamlesh went over to speak to them. Taking Wasima's struggling infant sister in her arms, Jaya gasped as she peered downhill, the lopsided shanties resembling shoddy boxes tumbling down the slope.

"No value for education—these people," Prabha said in her terse school-girl's English, coming over to say goodbye. She was headed back down the hill, while the twins had to climb farther up to fetch Bebeji from the hut where she met with the Ganesh Murti Nagar Residents' Committee. By "these people" Jaya understood Prabha to mean the children's parents. Kamlesh showed sympathy for Prabha, praising her in front of Jaya for going around to every jhopadi for forty minutes before school, calling the children to class. Otherwise many of them wouldn't come.

Prabha shook her head over the parents' ignorance. She complained about a new group of men from Ratnagiri, living just below the path to the summit, who gave her dirty looks whenever she passed by. Jaya commended her for rounding up the children for class every day, and Prabha shrugged matter-of-factly. "I will try to bring them to level of reading newspaper, writing letter." The teacher turned and clapped her hands for the children to return Kamlesh's instruments to her, and Kamlesh accepted them from small, reluctant hands, promising to bring them again next week.

HER FIRST SET of MBBS exams behind her, Jaya was on a two-and-a-half-month holiday from medical college, not due back to the J. J. Hospital campus until January 1955. A couple of weeks after her first visit to the colony's school, Kamlesh pressed Jaya to visit again and take a look at the new construction. Jaya readily agreed, first accompanying Kamlesh to her Saturday dance lesson, trying to capture in a few lines the still, sculptural poses Kamlesh held. "Gesture drawings," Tule called them—pure shape, no detail. After the lesson, Dipi picked them up to drive them to the hill colony, Bebeji riding in the front seat with him. He'd been in the mood to celebrate for days, the factory producing near capacity now—ten tons of glass per day. "We can only go up, up, up," he imagined. "In five years' time, we may decide to open up units in East Africa, the Middle East, anywhere."

Bebeji laughed, his jubilant mood contagious. She kept turning around to look at Jaya, her khadi sari draped chastely over her hair. "It's good you also came today," she said. Or, "I'm so happy you're joining us." Jaya smiled, well aware her grandmother expected her to involve herself in the affairs of the colony.

At the factory, they waited half an hour for the arrival of a local politician. Yashwant Halde strode into the front reception room, a tall, loose-limbed, loud-mouthed member of the legislative assembly from Thana district, and within minutes boasted that he could help Bebeji procure water supply and a power connection for the hutment colony. Bebeji nodded, breaking into a broad smile. Her grandchildren knew he'd given her the same assurances on the telephone when she contacted him at his office, prompting her to invite him to visit the colony. Earlier, Bebeji had been dealt a great blow when the collector of Thana, who headed the District Planning and Development Council, rejected her request for assistance. He'd condemned Ganesh Murti Nagar as "an illegal squatters' colony" the government would not condone. At home, Harbans actively discouraged Bebeji from pursuing what he called "an impossible task": bringing water to a remote hill colony of a thousand people at most when much bigger slums in town, around the Byculla mills, for instance, had neither taps nor electricity.

The politician Halde Sahib wore round wire-rimmed spectacles like Bebeji's—like Gandhiji's—brushed by disheveled locks of faded gray hair. He wore the freedom fighter's white dhoti and kurta though it might have been only a costume for him. The five of them passed through the factory compound and, from the back gate, crossed the open land under a hot sky. Halde Sahib was surprised at the distance they had to walk without the relief of much shade until they entered the dim grove of trees at the base of the hill. Women were gathering flocks of dry sticks from the baked earth for firewood, and they pulled their chunnis over their faces to shield themselves from the gaze of unknown men. Halde ignored their inhibitions, inquiring about the living conditions on the hill. They stared down and mumbled replies. At the first sight of the rough shanties among the burnt rocks, as they climbed, Halde blustered that these slum-dwellers were the ones who came out to vote, not the sahibs in their bungalows.

Later that afternoon, Kamlesh concluded her hour of songs and games, and Prabha padlocked the schoolhouse door and turned downhill. A horse-drawn tonga waited at the factory every afternoon to take her back into town. The glassworks paid her monthly transportation fee. The sisters walked around to the back of the school building, trailed by a gaggle of children whom they kept shooing away from the steep drop at the rear. A few hundred feet down a staggered decline of rock and brush lay a new construction site, where women laborers balanced pans of building materials on their heads. Men were laying the foundation for the dispensary amid cindery red mounds of dug-up earth. In about six months, when the dispensary was complete, Jaya would assist a physician there on Saturday afternoons.

The children looked up at the sisters with wide eyes, unsure what to make of the word *doctor*, when they heard he would give them check-ups to make sure they kept well. They happily abandoned the thought of this probing man as they followed Jaya and Kamlesh around to the front of the school and ascended the dirt track with them, running ahead in zigzagging lines. Shanties and mud huts appeared in clusters, the open doorways letting in fresh air and light. Some mothers called their children home, but the children wouldn't listen. Kamlesh explained to the women that they were only going as far as Kalpana's hut, where the residents' committee met, and the mothers agreed to their children's wishes. The children clamored for Kamlesh's instruments and passed them around, a ragtag entourage in torn and soiled clothing raising a thin musical hullabaloo. Jaya breathed in the nauseatingly sour odor of human feces drying in piles behind the scanty brush along the track. It mixed with the fishy smell of blood soaking the pad between her legs. She smoothed the back of her tunic, hoping it was not stained. A few yards ahead, a little child bunched her skirt around her waist as she squatted to urinate on the path. The earth was all the people had for their needs—a vessel for their waste, a bed for their bodies. Its fine red powder dusted their skin and hair.

As the group approached a shack cobbled together from timber scraps and patches of tin, its thatched roof weighted down with broken objects so it wouldn't fly off, Halde Sahib's booming voice could be heard through the open doorway above the children's thumping and squealing. Kamlesh disappeared inside while Jaya waited with the children. Half an hour ago, the politician had burst into the classroom, startling the children. Bebeji and the other committee members had been touring him around the colony, and he'd stomped around the school, offering hearty praise, then exited as quickly as he'd entered, as if his interest had drained. He liked to rush to the next thing, before he could take in what was in front of him.

Kamlesh returned from the hut and told Jaya the residents' committee had just sat down to talk. Bebeji suggested they wait for her and Dipi at the factory. Kamlesh told her they might do that. Ignoring their grandmother's instruction, Kamlesh turned to the children, hands on her hips, eyes twinkling with a sense of fun. "You all tell us, what should we do now?"

Some begged the twins to visit their huts; one boy offered to show them the spot where he'd seen a snake, and a second boy described a remote area where an enormous tiger had sprung out from the trees, making him run faster than he'd ever run before. His classmates hooted with laughter. Lakshmi half twirled with her baby brother hoisted in her arms, sweeping her tattered chunni over the crumbling stones. "Let's go to the top to see the Ganesha statue," she cried. "It's really beautiful up there."

Neither Jaya nor Kamlesh had seen the summit, deterred by others from undertaking the difficult climb with their grandmother. Now they were intrigued by the prospect of finally viewing the shrine—or perhaps only a stone carving—for which the residents had named the colony. "Come, let's go! You show us the way!" Kamlesh implored her students.

"Leave him at home with your mother," Jaya told Lakshmi about Shankar. "We'll wait here for you." The tiny child with the flattish head and bulging brow wore the few protections his parents could afford him—black kajal smeared around his eyes and a black stain painted between his eyebrows, unsightly marks meant to ward off the covetous evil eye. A metal amulet on a black string hung around his neck. There were days he suffered two or three seizures, Madan had told Bebeji. While hospital doctors had failed to reverse the brain damage caused by encephalitis, the electrician held out hope an herbalist's medicaments could cure his son.

Lakshmi threw her head back and gazed uphill, her small face full of longing. "I want to show him Ganeshji's statue too."

Kamlesh reached out and took the boy, who was dressed only in a grimy chemise in the heat. "I'll carry him. You go with your friends." Lakshmi ran across to Wasima, who was free of her sister today, and grabbed her hand with a great upward swing. The two older girls took pleasure in swooping their arms up and down in great arcs as they moved up the hill.

For at least a quarter of a mile, the children led the sisters on a level path that followed the contours of the winding ridge past clumps of shanties. The hutments sprang up wherever there was a shelf or even a slender strip of somewhat level ground. To the left lay empty land and the ghostly shapes of various factory sheds beyond, while closer by, to the right, behind the shanties, rose the scrub-covered grooves of the taller hill. At a different angle sprawled another hill, blurred in mist, a mile or two away. If they turned around and looked below, they glimpsed the gray-blue flatness of two ponds to the south. Jaya watched in amazement as the children dashed barefoot over the searing dust and stones, accustomed to gripping the earth in a way she was not. She had to keep stopping and shaking the dirt out of her sandals. The boys snaked around a line of veiled women bearing terracotta pots on their heads, their arms encased in bone bangles from their elbows to their shoulders. The sisters hurried past them to keep up with the children, quickly greeting the women. They had probably spent two or three hours walking barefoot across the burning earth to fetch a little drinking water. The last woman, masked by a sheer scarlet veil that drifted over her face, moved behind the others with a stately grace. "How beautiful they look," Jaya said to Kamlesh, because their languid gait, their orange and red veils, made them beautiful, their suffering invisible.

The women squatting outside another collection of huts greeted them bashfully. A couple of mothers held their children back, hearing their group was climbing to the summit. The shanties thinned out. They came to a cluster of thatched huts strewn beneath a jagged rock wall from whose cracks drooped withered vegetation. A group of dark-skinned men in lungis fell silent as they approached. Lakshmi had planted herself between the twins, holding Jaya's hand, her head turned to Shankar. Kamlesh held him low on her hip, growing fatigued. The men with yellow eyes and wide, jutting cheeks glared at them as though they were intruders. Jaya understood now who Prabha was talking about; these must be the Ratnagiri men living near the top who made her so uncomfortable. The twins picked up their pace, forcing Lakshmi to take high, galloping steps to keep up with them. She was a thin, almost weightless child in a tiny blouse and flared skirt, the whole of her slight frame draped in her billowing, hole-pocked, bright green veil.

The gradient steepened, the narrow path cobbled with scorching stones. The children ran ahead. Jaya offered to carry Shankar, but Kamlesh said she was all right. She kept sighing with the effort of the climb, her face glowing with sweat. "You're still meeting him these days?" she said to Jaya, speaking in English.

Jaya smiled quickly at Lakshmi, who looked to her expectantly, amused to hear an alien language. Wasima turned her sharp, tight, womanly face to Jaya too. Jaya looked past her to her sister. "Why do you bring him up now? In front of these children?"

Kamlesh swept an edge of her chunni against her damp neck, looking hurt. "Shouldn't you tell them something now?" She meant that Jaya owed their parents a confession of the truth. "What if someone sees you with him and reports back to them?"

"No one's going to see anything," Jaya declared as if she had the power to decide that.

"If he wants to marry you, why go on hiding him?"

"Do you think no one's going to object to anything?" Jaya snapped. "Neither his parents nor Mummy and Daddy? To a Bengali boy?" The children's eyes jumped from her to Kamlesh, hearing argument in their tones.

At home, they had little privacy to speak about Kirti. Whenever Kamlesh brought him up, Jaya grew nervous they might be overheard and refused to engage in the conversation. She didn't understand Kamlesh's impatience for her to confide in her parents about her relationship. Was she eager to see a big fight erupt at home? A real-life melodrama?

Kamlesh placed a hand on Lakshmi's covered head. "Tell me, does your Ganesha really exist? Where is he? We've been walking so long."

"Our Ganeshji dances," cried Lakshmi, dragging her flared skirt over the stones. She and Wasima—two small, veiled figures—ran ahead to show them the way, the other children already far up the path faintly engraved in the slope.

From the summit's scarred stone bed, a ragged, broken-off terrace, Jaya could see in detail the steep slopes of the neighboring hill, whose rougher terrain was bare of shanties. Its angled tip looked as if a giant had broken off a wafer of rock like a biscuit. Strewn across the parched earth at her feet were blocks of basalt that might have been the fragments of a collapsed shrine. Kamlesh called out to the larger group of children not to go too far, but they were already a hundred yards away. Lakshmi took Shankar from Kamlesh's arms and planted him on her narrow hip. The twins followed her to the statue of Ganesha, the elephant god wearing a dancer's anklets slipped around his stone toes. He was carved deeply into a slab of rock a foot taller than Lakshmi, resting against a mound of stone blocks people must have piled up to support him. The tendril of a vine crawled down Ganesha's earflap.

"I wonder how old this is," Jaya said hesitantly, afraid of provoking Kamlesh. With her right hand, Kamlesh formed a mudra, her palm facing out, mimicking the gesture of Ganesha's only intact hand. A multitude of small figures and creatures were sculpted around him, framing his singular magnificence. Kamlesh taught the name of the mudra to Lakshmi and Wasima, who mimicked her. Wasima amused herself by inventing fanciful gestures, making Lakshmi laugh. "See how happy he is?" Kamlesh said to the girls. "This Ganesha will dance forever."

Lakshmi sang out the god's physical attributes for her brother, as if invoking them in words would help him hear and understand. After cataloging every feature she could think of–"see his fat belly, see his fat, fat legs, see all his broken hands, still he looks sweet"— earning Shankar's toothy smile, she turned to her friend in excitement. "Come on, let's show him everything up here."

"What is such a little child going to understand about a mountain?" Wasima grumbled, though she obligingly marched off with Lakshmi.

Kamlesh warned them not to go too close to the edge, and to tell the others not to either. The boys were shouting and chasing each other, the girls spinning in circles or walking in little groups. Their giddy movements revealed to Jaya the sense of confinement they must feel, clinging to the narrow margins of space along the slopes of the hill. The summit's flat openness was like a park, inviting them to gambol.

Jaya shook off her sandals and squatted at Ganesha's feet. The weathered gray stone was as hot as fire. A string of wilted red marigolds lay upon the rock pedestal on which he stood, a gift from a worshipper. Ganesha stood on two plump but shapely legs, his stomach hanging low, his hips cocked to one side. Jaya pressed her finger into a splotch of vermilion paste someone had dabbed on his toes, telling Kamlesh, "Such a beautiful red—look," and then she smeared the pigment across the stone.

"They'll get angry with me also if they find out," Kamlesh blurted. "They'll say I knew about it and said nothing."

Jaya was silent. It hadn't occurred to her that Kamlesh might feel guilty for being part of the secrecy she kept. "I don't want to bring this up with them just now," she said firmly to end the discussion. She bent closer to the statue. In his multiple smashed arms, Ganesha held chipped objects she couldn't make out except for a circlet of beads hanging from one set of broken fingers. She stood up, admiring him in full in his barren precinct, his round body swaying with a miraculous energy, the beaded sash of his girdle hugging the bulk of his thighs.

Kamlesh dipped her shirt and salwar in the red dust, crouching on the ground to touch her forehead to the god's feet. Jaya smiled to see her easy gesture of devotion. Then a piercing scream rose in the distance. She turned in the children's direction. At the far edge of the summit, she saw Lakshmi's bent body, a swirl of green, appearing to tumble forward. Wasima sprang to her, yanking her away from the edge.

Jaya ran. When she reached the stunned children, she grabbed hold of Lakshmi. The girl was crying, little Shankar making frightened noises in her arms. "What happened?" It looked to her as if Lakshmi had been about to jump while holding onto her baby brother.

"We were showing Shankar how far down it goes," Wasima said. Jaya left Lakshmi in Kamlesh's embrace and walked a few paces ahead to peer into the chasm between the mountains, which went down hundreds and hundreds of feet, a straight drop until the stony land flared out very far below. "We were telling him, 'Look, don't ever come this far, because you could fall down there,' and then Deenanath came," Wasima cried out, pointing to an older boy in dirty pajamas. "He shoved her and ran."

Kamlesh shouted at the boy, "Why did you do that? Tell us." The boy grew rigid, staring at the ground. He had a head of disheveled coppery hair. Kamlesh walked across to him, demanding, "Why did you push her?" The boy stubbornly looked down, his trembling shoulders the only sign he was crying. Kamlesh cupped his chin and thrust his dusty, blemished face up. "Tell us why."

The boy looked at her, terrified. "She went so close to the edge with that little brother of hers, I thought she wanted to fall. I wanted her to have fun, to see what it felt like to fall all the way down. Maybe they would grow wings and fly—" Kamlesh slapped him, and Jaya recognized a streak of her father's anger in her sister. She ushered the children farther away from the summit's ragged edge. The boy sobbed, staring insolently at the ground. "If her stupid brother could fly, she wouldn't have to carry him around. I wanted to see if he can fly, then he doesn't need his feet." Jaya went over to Wasima, who wore her usual pointed expression. None of the terrible fear she must have felt rushing to save her friend showed on her determined face. "Come, Wasima. Such a brave thing you just did. You were so quick to catch Lakshmi," Jaya said, "and Shankar." She laid a hand on the girl's bony shoulder, and the girl seemed to shift a little closer to her. Together they walked toward the thin path going down the hill.

II

JAYA ENTERED THE exhibition hall with a terrible feeling she had come too late. It was a quarter past seven, more than an hour past the time given on the invitation card for Tule's opening at Jehangir. She was afraid the gallery might close soon.

Namdeo Tule wasn't among the people at the front of the great circular hall, where lights shone on a display of paintings across the curving walls. The name *Sringara* was curled at the bottom of a canvas of two brutally thin women thrashing stones to gravel with crude hammers. Smudged heaps of the same crushed white stone encircled them like a jagged wall, an open-roofed jail. *Stone Crushers at Chamundi Hill,* said the handwritten label below the picture. Which one was Sringara, Tule's artist comrade— the only woman painter of repute in Bombay?

Jaya looked around the Jehangir Art Gallery, wondering if Sringara's face would become apparent to her. Except for the absence of the governor of Bombay, it was the same mix of socialites and intellectuals who usually turned up at Bombay Art Society exhibitions: affluent businessmen and their wives in showy brocades, ghostly Parsi ladies greeting each other in supercilious tones, gaunt professors and writers meditating before the pictures, and a handful of stout, self-assured Europeans. A group of good-looking young men gathered around a petite woman. Jaya couldn't see her clearly but could hear her laughing.

Jaya set off in search of her teacher, keen to see his pictures in person. "Is Tule Sahib here?" she asked a bespectacled man in khaki half-pants, a gallery attendant or guard.

"At the back," she was startled to hear. Going around a partition wall that extended halfway across the hall, she wondered what could have made Tule accept the inferior hanging space in the rear. The gallery was bright and modern, Bombay's posh new art venue, opened just last year, and she had imagined she would find Tule's paintings hanging right in the front as she walked in.

Only a trickle of people had wandered to the gallery's far end, as if the crowd in the front wasn't aware the exhibition extended beyond the partition. Standing off to one side, Tule was caught up in conversation with an elderly European, whose elbow he held in confidence or perhaps affection. He'd made a touching effort to look respectable in a gabardine suit and high-collared shirt and tie, his hair neatly trimmed.

"These people don't know what art is, that is the problem," Tule said scornfully in a lowered voice. Jaya approached him with caution, prepared to apologize. "They think it's a calendar painting of a goddess or a Ravi Varma picture of a maiden bearing a waterpot. Bloody repressed buggers! Our upper classes and Communists suffer from the same Victorian mentality, hiding their eyes like memsahibs in front of a nude picture."

"Da, da," the bald foreigner assented gravely. He towered over Tule with an air of martial command. His hefty mustache angled down to the edges of his chin, and the bulky tweed jacket he wore remembered a frozen climate.

"So, you've come?" Tule acknowledged Jaya in a curt tone. Yet a moment later, the grandiose introduction he gave the European made her think he was including her in a sly mockery of the old man. "This is the great Avanesov, Jaya. He has come down from the mountains to see me! This is Avanesov, whom I never imagined I would have the honor to meet one day. The great Russian seer of the Himalayas!"

Jaya smiled deferentially, pretending to know the name. A well-to-do collector probably.

In outrage, Tule directed the old man's attention to a pair of voluptuous blue nudes hanging side by side that had attracted a few viewers. "Those two! They took those two down as soon as I hung them up!" Deploring "the priggish, asexual Communists" for censoring his recent one-man show at the Communist Party headquarters in Parel, Tule denounced the leader who'd removed his best pictures, prompting his immediate resignation from the party.

Tule's pictures of abstract figures and landscapes seemed to stir a delirious noise—pounding ocean blues and gusting monsoon greens slashed with sunset red fields, cadmium yellow bodies, turquoise and chartreuse faces— the figures tamed by Rouault's black contour line. It was Jaya's first view of her teacher's paintings. His bristling images, which hung in unvarnished frames or were painted directly onto wood board, stunned her—roused her even—assaulting her the same way his voice did the moment he stepped into a room.

Ushering the Russian toward a painting against the far wall, Tule held up a finger to indicate to Jaya that he'd be back.

She went over to look at Tule's Communist-rejected blue nudes. One figure reclined in a chair, facing the viewer boldly, showing wide-open black Indian eyes, the bulbous breasts of a stone goddess, and fat indigo fingers unfurled like palm fronds across her thighs. The other nude, her face a stark Cubist mask, wore her hair in a conical bun and a spiked girdle above her naked pubis, the flesh parted by a black palette knife incision. Jaya thought if she could take home a painting like the seated blue nude, she would hang it on her bedroom wall, knowing this was art in all its sensuality—this arrangement of languid curves and protrusions.

Someone sang out her name, crisply, like a command. "Juy-yaaa!" She looked to her side and didn't recognize the face at first. The woman appeared surprised and announced her name. Jaya laughed, apologetic. It had been a year at least. Persis Vakil had friends with her—other well-to-do Parsi girls. She was chic in a lavender-gray organza and a pearl-drop necklace. "How are you?" Spoken as an order.

Jaya resisted, paused for a moment. "Very well, thank you." She had to chit-chat, of course. She had to smile. Despite the flare-up of her own ego, she was grateful to Persis.

Tule's two nudes drew the women's withering glances. "Quite frank in his depictions," Persis declared with a biting laugh. Her friends passed remarks. "He's your teacher now, isn't he?" added Persis. Jaya acknowledged it was thanks to her. Persis shot her friends a scandalized look. It felt as if she was not only accusing Tule of some moral deficit, but Jaya of the same degeneracy.

Shame flushed Jaya's face, but a sense of loyalty arose at the same instant. A desire to defend not so much Tule as any works of beauty. She looked straight at Persis. "What are you doing these days? Still painting?"

The finely modeled face, the formidable mask of confidence, tightened as Persis took further offense, it appeared, at being spoken to like an equal. She smiled dismissively, brushing off the question—*Of course*. Tule came over, leaving the old Russian's side, and Jaya had to make the introductions, because it turned out Persis had never met the artist, only spoken to him about Jaya on the telephone. When Tule told her, "You brought me my best student," Jaya felt a little light-headed. She felt quite stylish herself, draped as she was in her favorite maroon batik sari with its collage of pattern-blocks that was so modern in design. After the women turned away, Tule spoke dismissively of Persis as a "society painter," and Jaya nodded—yes, she painted portraits. A moment later, he recalled that her husband owned racehorses, and he regretted not speaking to her more nicely. Few people could actually afford to buy paintings at an exhibition.

"Tell me, why did you come so late?" he scolded Jaya. "You missed Dr. Herzfeld's remarks. What a tribute he paid." He led her to a long, sooty horizontal picture of hunched workers plodding through the black gates of a cotton mill like a herd to slaughter. *Wage-Earners' Hell*, which appeared to be his most scathing attack against capitalism—among a group of pictures of poor people—was priced the highest at a steep five hundred rupees.

"I didn't know where the car had gone—my sister wasn't at home. I kept waiting." In fact, Jaya had left the flat punctually without asking Kamlesh to join her, determined to meet Tule's artists' circle on her own. Then she'd taken a bus to J. J. Hospital, sabotaging her efforts to be on time. Though she was not due back on campus until January, Kirti, as a final-year student, had to fulfill his usual ward duties. For forty minutes she searched the hospital buildings, finally tracking him down in the library.

"You're not thinking clearly. Why take a risk?" he said when she asked him to accompany her to the exhibition in a state of agitation.

They could come and go separately, Jaya proposed; no one would know they were together. She felt a new claim upon him, knowing they would be married one day. But Kirti resisted her, under tremendous time pressure. An independent paper he was writing, on lowering body temperature during heart surgery, for a respected professor—under whom he hoped to do a four-year house surgeonship starting next year—was due in three days. He had to prove himself, competing with many hundreds of MBBS graduates for one of eight coveted positions. Still, Jaya clung to him, hesitant to meet Tule's clique of painters alone. She needed Kirti's forceful presence, the aura of his confidence, to gather the courage to present herself as an equal. For nearly half an hour Kirti walked her around the congested bazaar outside the hospital, telling her she'd do fine on her own. Finally he pushed her into a cab. It churned up feelings of anger and insult, since no respectable girl traveled alone by cab in the evening. "Go, before the function bloody well finishes." He shut the door on her protests.

Tule shoved his hands into his jacket pockets. "Did you meet Sringara?" he asked roughly, still not having forgiven her late arrival.

"I didn't look at her paintings. I hardly noticed them in the front. I came straight back looking for you," Jaya said to demonstrate her loyalty. An impression of dry, burnt colors like baked earth stuck with her. Even Sringara's dusty white tones had given off a heat.

When Jaya was introduced to her, Sringara exultantly threw her head to one side and laughed, showing all her teeth. It was a gesture she repeated, looking past Jaya, and Jaya realized it was for the benefit of a short business-man in a jacket behind her who'd come to inquire about one of Sringara's paintings.

"I've told you about her," Tule began again a few minutes later, after Sringara had a word with the man. This time Sringara's eyes shifted to one of the German art promoters in the city, and she replied in a distracted way. "Yes, yes, you're Jaya, is it?" She had pale golden-brown skin and crimped chestnut-brown hair like a foreigner. On her forehead she had drawn an ostentatious caste mark, a plush vermilion bindi overlapping a saffron splotch with a jet-black bead of powder at the bottom, concentrating all the color on her face. Her light cotton sari was as blank white as a canvas, bordered with a thin band of violet—a decorative variation, it seemed to Jaya, on Bebeji's homespun khadi.

Guardedly Jaya watched her, this woman who seemed to have ascended a peak and was laughing down from it, unable to contain her delight: a mirthful, light-bearing creature. Effusive with her friends, flirtatious with her prospective clients, Sringara tossed remarks into every conversation, in Hindi and English and what Jaya realized was Kannada, spoken by a particular cluster of boy artists. Jaya began to feel more and more invisible. After standing by for at least ten minutes, waiting for another chance to speak to Sringara, she told Tule, "I'll take a look at her paintings."

The strain of labor showed in the awkward stances of Sringara's women working, their knobby spines tracing backs submissively bent to some arduous task, or limbs contorted with a ferocity of effort—a woman strenuously pounding turmeric roots with a pole, a thin figure turning a massive grindstone. The women's overstretched arms, long and spindly, accentuated their morbid thinness. They were the doubles of the women laborers constructing the clinic on the hill, whose faces were always coated with a film of dry cement like ash. But in place of a stone-pitted hillside in Thana, Sringara's terracotta women, with smears and gashes for eyes and lips, labored on parched umber fields, under glaring ocher skies, amid singed shadows.

How Sringara had ended up at the front of the gallery, and Tule, the better-known artist, at the back, was not clear to Jaya, since he wasn't the chivalrous type to graciously defer to a woman. Yet somehow the more original artist—perhaps even the superior painter, Bombay's only woman artist of merit by Tule's count—had acquired the place she deserved.

As the gallery doors closed to the public at eight, Tule put aside his hard feelings, inviting Jaya to stay on for the reception. A few other women remained, the wives of art patrons and art enthusiasts, as well as two English girls infatuated with a doe-eyed Muslim painter who cloaked himself in an embroidered shawl and was praised for painting landscapes like Cezanne. The Bombay artists, the skinny, good-looking young painters and art students who had earlier surrounded Sringara, were such voracious talkers Tule almost couldn't be heard above them, announcing, "I sold both nudes to Avanesov—six hundred and fifty rupees." He slapped the notes on a table set with a plate of cucumber sandwiches. Jaya looked out the door, wondering, did he have to do that to prove his worth?

Tule gestured to a couple of men in shirts and ties, goading them in a jesting tone: "You big managers should make an investment. One day you'll see the value shoot up and wish you had picked up some nice pictures."

One of them laughed nervously. The other shrugged, grumbling, "What to do, yaar? Where's the money?" To Jaya, Tule had complained that Indians didn't buy art, not even salaried men made enough. And the businessmen who had the money didn't have the taste. The main clientele for art were European company managers in Bombay, only they had both the money and appreciation for modern painting. A short while earlier, he had placed himself in the path of Persis Vakil in her organza and pearls as she headed to the door, saying an elaborate goodbye, the heretic artist turning into a salesman in an expensive shop, hoping to persuade a customer to change her mind.

A boy who'd come over to talk to Jaya shouted out, "Aye, Namdeo, you go on talking like a gramophone, but you don't say a word about your student? What is this?"

Tule waved the fellow off from his place in a circle of senior artists that included the diffident man in khaki half-pants—the acclaimed painter Dhasal, whom Jaya had taken for a gallery attendant. "I should introduce her to you? Why? You are also just a student. Let me introduce her to some proper painters."

The boy, Vir, shrugged Tule off. "What kind of paintings do you do?" he asked Jaya. His features were fine and delicate, his gray-green eyes like translucent stones held to the light. The single flaw in his appearance was a deformed left ear, which lacked a rounding lobe.

"All kinds." Jaya tipped her head, uneasy with a question about herself. "Portraits, I suppose."

"I am doing figures," Vir said, "and landscapes also. Landscape is more difficult. Where is the interest? You have to make it up in the style. I did Western painting at J. J." He'd finished college two years back, he told her. The year he graduated he won a silver medal in pastels from the Bombay Art Society.

"Jaya," Tule called out. "Whatever he is saying, don't listen to him. He's a bachcha." Tule, chuckling, dismissed Vir as a child.

A ripple of laughter from Sringara sounded like a response to Tule's mockery, though she seemed to have taken no notice of the exchange, absorbed in conversation with one of the two German art promoters. A short, proud-chested chemist, Dr. Herzfeld had promoted the Bauhaus artists in Berlin. Tule always spoke mournfully of the nine Kokoschkas that Dr. Herzfeld had to abandon when he fled the Nazis in the '40s.

Another German Jew who'd come to India to escape Hitler, Fritz Wolfensohn—a distinguished man in a black suit—held forth like a lecturer before a group of eager young painters, slicing the air with his large hands. Tule had denounced him to Jaya as "an absolute racialist," aiming every sort of criticism at his inflated ego and his exploitation of poor boys who dreamt of becoming painters. Wolfensohn had built himself up as a messiah of modern art in Bombay, tutoring young men searching for artistic direction in the most grotesque techniques of German Expressionism, Tule scoffed, yet no one could stand up to this man, whose exhibition reviews appeared in the *Times of India* under the lordly byline "Our Art Critic."

The party was going to shift across the road to Samarkand. Jaya eagerly accepted Tule's invitation to join his group at the restaurant, anxious for a place at the artists' table, ignoring her obligation to return home as it was approaching nine o'clock and she was expected back for dinner. Vir told her of the painters he liked as they walked in a small crowd to the restaurant. Derain and Matisse. He liked the flatness of their paintings, the patterning and intensity of the colors. You didn't find color in British painting, only black and brown.

Jaya heard the chatter about painting all around her, the artists immersed in noisy discussions about art as if it was something significant, meaningful to life, and she found herself stating very confidently to Vir, "I don't like cool painting—not that rigid geometric sort of abstract painting. Klee, for example. I don't like Klee very much, do you?"

Samarkand, a bohemian gathering place where painters offered a sketch if they couldn't pay their monthly tab, according to Vir, brought Farrokh Wadia's beach shack to mind—the same plaited-palm wall panels and breeziness and lantern light. A haphazard display of drawings and watercolors was tacked across a long wall. Tule indicated a chair for Jaya at his table, with Sringara and other senior artists and one of their wives. Vir ended up at one of the two tables of younger painters, each headed by a German. At a smaller table to Jaya's right sat two middle-aged men in ties who looked like company managers out with their wives. One of them, a Levers accountant, had strayed into art, Tule leaned across the table to tell Jaya. He kept threatening to chuck up his job to devote himself to painting but hadn't found the courage till now.

Tule turned to Dhasal, looking annoyed. "What happened to Zaidi Sahib? Why didn't he come?" Jaya waited for the answer, astounded the most famous painter in India had been expected at her teacher's exhibition. Soft-spoken Dhasal made a slight joke, saying Zaidi must be off wandering through some villages on his mission "to paint India."

Jaya glanced across the table at Sringara, who was seated next to Tule, wondering if she would notice her now, but Sringara lifted her plate to a bearer doling out vegetable cutlets with two forks. A second bearer came around with drinks—whiskeys for all the men at their table. Who was this from? Tule glanced around. A salute to the artists from the Levers manager, Chadha, who pulled his fragrant pipe out of his mouth to congratulate Sringara and Tule, particularly, on their magnificent pictures.

"Don't encourage him," Sringara called back to Chadha, apparently speaking of Tule. Tule defiantly raised his glass in a cheers. "Boozer," remarked one of the boys at another table, to the snickering of his friends. Tule waved the youngsters off.

"We're all groping in the dark, we have no tradition to draw from, that's the trouble," Chadha was philosophizing in his Englishman's voice to his colleague, who nodded intently. "Or rather, we've too many traditions to choose from, but no roots in modern painting. We can't make the leap to Picasso and Braque without their foundation, and yet we have to."

"I've just found out about an excellent opportunity—I shouldn't be telling you all," Sringara announced brightly to their table. "The Mexican government's offering a two-year scholarship to study mural painting." That became the subject of the conversation: how to go abroad. How to find a way out. Jaya listened to the growing dispute among the men over the fate of some painters they all knew who'd already made their way to

Europe. Tule had always boasted of their successes, so it surprised Jaya to hear one man proclaim that so-and-so was starving in London, and another fellow was "completely obscure" in Paris. The two tables of young painters jumped into the discussion, Mr. Wolfensohn delivering a stern verdict on an esteemed friend of theirs admitted to Fernand Leger's atelier: "Gaffar is a slow, reluctant painter. He doesn't have the ambition to win a European's heart."

As Sringara bent her head toward the flame of the lantern on the table, a few strands of luminous gray were visible in loose waves of brown hair. How old was she? Hard to tell. In her thirties probably, yet half the time she had her mouth open in a laugh like a popular schoolgirl. Hard to know who she was—carelessly waving around her cigarette in an ivory holder like a socialite, wearing an ascetic's white sari, an orthodox Brahmin's tika painted on her forehead. It was a unique insignia; Jaya felt she had seen it before—that she had seen Sringara before. Wasn't she the instructor at the J. J. School of Art who had asked her what she was looking for?

Sringara said something privately to Tule. Jaya waited for the terrible question: *Was that you I saw wandering around J. J. School of Art one evening? Looking for the model?* She had been a different person there, dry in manner. Sringara spoke to Jaya a moment later. "Deo is quite taken with your painting; he's been going on about it." "Deo" was her pet name for Tule. "What is it you do?"

"Pictures of my sister," Jaya replied, the attention taking her by surprise. "Black-and-white portraits, like snaps, really. I'm trying to paint quickly, as Tule Sahib says to."

"Why quickly? Is that some sort of principle, Deo?" Sringara blew a plume of smoke out of her mouth, turning her gaze from Tule to look straight at Jaya. "There was another girl I knew who used to paint. She had her studio next to mine, but she went into costume design. Actually my friend Yasmin had my studio before me. She's in Baroda now, teaching at the university with her husband. She does beautiful work. Somehow she managed to get me into her studio before she left. Everyone wants a room there, not only painters. Even Ravi Shankar has a studio there. Are you familiar with the place? On Warden Road?" Jaya whispered no. Tule had never mentioned these studios. "Drop by sometime. Bring a few pictures along." The invitation came as a jolt. Jaya didn't hear the rest of what Sringara said, the words buzzing past her after she accepted, but in a voice so small she wondered if she'd been heard. A short while later, as their party dispersed outside, a few painters ran across the road to a paanwallah sitting in front of a darkened arcade of shops. Jaya studied the colors of the night, the dark gray figures walking under the drooping tentacles of a banyan tree, the deep gray-blues of an equestrian statue in the street, everything melting to a violet-black beneath the burning orbs of streetlamps. Sringara's face shone olive in the gaslight, her eyes glimmering black. Her lips, a harsh black-red, were drawn back in a painful smile.

12

A BARE-CHESTED OLD man, shaved bald like a priest—a servant of the artists' compound—silently closed the paint-smeared door behind him. Jaya held the hot glass of tea he'd brought up for her, sitting in a rickety armchair with a lime-green velvet seat. The room wore oil color like a hard, cracking skin, every object encrusted with splotches of dried paint—the two cupboards, easels, chairs, a stool, even the glass jars holding brushes and the medicinal brown bottles of turpentine on a worktable. Dozens of Sringara's canvases stood against the walls, some finished, others just begun or possibly abandoned. "So, let's see what you've brought," Sringara said, crossing the studio to lower the window blind against the afternoon glare, the light sparkling off the sea in the distance.

Jaya had unwrapped her paintings from their tablecloth covering, and now she propped them on top of Sringara's worktable against a wall: her study of a wizened blue man with shorn hair and hollow shadows under his eyes, the patient a reminder of the hospital's anguished environment; and the best of her scribbled black-and-white portraits of Kamlesh, with downcast eyes darkly outlined in an actressy gaze of bittersweet sorrow, her mouth rippling as three gray lines.

"Is it a self-portrait?" Sringara rested her hands on the table, closely examining the image.

"No, it's a picture of my twin sister—it looks a little fake, I know, like one of those film star pictures in magazines."

Casually, Sringara tapped her cigarette. She was surprised and amused by the revelation of a twin sister and gave the portrait another look. "It says something about the Indian woman today, that soft, melancholy look we idolize. 'A face as delicate as a flower blossom,' completely vulnerable like our heroines." Sringara wore the pure white sari that seemed to be her uniform, the widow's or celibate's white sari Jaya had seen her in twice before. Yet she was glamorously cosmopolitan in her ascetic's dress—purple and green glass bangles clinking around her wrists, the cigarette in its ivory holder in her mouth. Her loose, flowing brown hair was lightly flecked with paint where it fell around her face. Now that they were alone, it was possible Sringara would remember her as the girl roaming through the J. J. School of Art five, six months ago. Painting Kamlesh had revived Jaya's hand since then, quickened her impulses. Jaya wanted Sringara to regard her as someone other than that confused, wandering girl, someone with abilities, with a grasp of her subject—whether or not that was true.

Sringara offered no sign that she recollected speaking to Jaya at the old art academy. Tule had confirmed she taught there part-time, two evenings a week. "There's something very intriguing about these faces," Sringara mused. "Something from underneath you've brought to the top, even in the film star one."

Sringara's praise for her loose brushwork, the expressionistic qualities of the blue patient, left Jaya unsettled and disbelieving. Four days after meeting Sringara at her exhibition, Jaya had rushed to her studio at the Gokuldas Daftary Memorial Institute, a three-story mansion with verandas facing the Arabian Sea. She'd brought these two paintings as a small offering, an opening to a conversation, and she was burning to ask Sringara the same question she'd been silently putting to Tule all along: *Do you think I can be a painter?*

Tule had found the blue patient lacking in pathos, Jaya confided to Sringara.

"He's probably just jealous," Sringara said, smiling. "Men are like that."

From somewhere in the building, they heard singing—a woman's tremulous voice winding through a classical Hindustani song at a high, nasal pitch.

"Patak's got his studio downstairs opposite that singer," Sringara reported, "but he says he never hears her. He becomes deaf when he paints. I can pound on his door for five minutes before he hears me. We meet for lunch quite often, and it starts with my pounding on his door to bring him back to this world."

It turned out Patak was the boy—Vir Patak—Jaya had met at the exhibition. "He's downstairs with the novices. He took over Ingle's studio two, three months back, when Ingle left for Paris. And India's Picasso is upstairs above everyone else . . ." Sringara pointed to the ceiling, indicating Zaidi Sahib's studio. "It's quite a democratic house of art, with a number of beginners, one genius at the top—another musical genius down the corridor—and all the levels in between."

The lawyer and freedom fighter Gokuldas Daftary had bequeathed his estate to a trust that made rooms available to all types of artists—painters, musicians, dancers. A resident Communist theater company held performances on the roof. Artists paid a token one rupee a month for their studios; the difficulty lay in being admitted. Sringara's friend Yasmin couldn't simply bequeath her studio to Sringara, she could only implore the temperamental manager of the compound to give Sringara's paintings a careful viewing. The manager, Keshav Mane, was an impresario who planned to open the first curated gallery in Bombay on the premises. No matter how well known the artist, he wouldn't be able to rent the space; Mane himself would select the artists he exhibited. "I'm hoping he'll give even a middling artist like me a solo show one day. He seems to like my work." Sringara laughed to temper her words, in case they sounded boastful.

Jaya sipped her too-sugary tea, the glass in her hand still full. It wasn't her place, as a mere student, to praise an accomplished painter, but Sringara genuinely seemed to doubt herself. "Tule Sahib was saying you've already sold half your paintings," she remarked without making any comparison, although Tule had admitted he'd sold nothing more after the initial burst of sales at the opening. At least he'd made up the cost of renting the hall, he'd groused to Jaya during her lesson yesterday.

"In the beginning, I used to take all my pictures to Deo for his approval, never mind that he's younger than me," Sringara said with a regretful laugh. "I found it difficult to adapt to this foreign tradition—this easel, these oil paints, this European abstraction. I learned painting the old way, sitting on the floor with the canvas at my feet. There was a different ethos in Mysore; once I spent an entire year copying six miniatures to learn about proportion and color. That was my teacher's thinking—there must be complete immersion in what the old masters knew. In Bombay, miniature painting was a dead art. I found it had died a hundred years back, so what good was it for me to go on with it?"

"We had easels even in school." She didn't share Sringara's disadvantages, Jaya realized; hers were different. Only European art had been taught to her at St. Anne's. Long before Mhatre Sahib, her first art teacher, the red-haired, blue-eyed Lady Flanagan, had been so enthusiastic about her drawing ability she'd had Jaya copy pictures by everyone from Reynolds to Degas out of books. The roots of Indian art—temple sculptures, terracotta tribal art, Chola bronzes, Pahari painting from Punjab—were less familiar to her than what the British had grafted onto it. She was trying to educate herself through cheap booklets she picked up at a stall near her college.

An unfinished picture on Sringara's easel was a collage of pencil drawings and roughly painted images in reds, yellows, and grays. "It looks very different from your paintings of women working." Jaya leaned toward the picture. "Almost like a dream image." A scarlet bull occupied the middle of the canvas—a statue of the sacred bull Nandi seated on a dark stone block. The idol was caught in the embrace of a roughly sketched bare-breasted woman who curled her boneless arms around its neck, covering its stone ear with her mouth. Behind the statue and the woman, a shadowy tunnel led toward a dab of ocher yellow, an indistinct flame. Jaya had the impression of a temple, an atmosphere turned inward. "It looks like a sanctum. She's a devotee?"

"I saw a woman like that in Madurai once. Every year I make a pilgrimage there with my uncle and aunt. My cousins."

"What was she doing? Talking in Nandi's ear?"

"She was singing. She was a widow in some terrible distress. She went on lifting up her sari and rubbing puja ashes on her legs, and then hugging Nandi's statue and singing. Some of the things I see down there, I can't get out of my mind. When I return to Bombay, I just start painting those impressions. It's like keeping a diary of my visit." Sringara walked to the windowsill for her ashtray. "I suppose for me the thing is to find essential Indian images and put them down in a modern style."

Jaya nodded solemnly, as if she were receiving instruction. In her studio, Sringara seemed to find calm within herself. She was neither the glib, frenzied character she'd appeared to be at the Jehangir Art Gallery, performing for her admirers, nor the stiff, terse instructress petrified inside the old art academy. She kept walking around her studio as if she was carrying out a search in her mind, retrieving images from memory.

In her own search for Indian images, Jaya imagined, she would have to penetrate deeper into the hospital. That was the core of her India. Her last dissection, of the azygos vein, had been demonstrated in front of her examiners last month, before the start of her long holiday. When she returned to college in January, her muses might be the patients in the surgical ward Kirti had taken her through: poor, gray-haired women lying on their backs, bandaged up after their mastectomies, or brandishing puckered red scars in place of their breasts. Or she could turn to the images burned in her mind of the people on the hill—she had sketches and scribbles, dozens of them. She could paint the children balancing on stones, or the old women whose faces were splintered in a hundred lines by worry. Or she could search for Indian images in the sensuality of classical dance—she might find everything she wanted in the statuesque curves of Kamlesh's poses.

Sringara removed her cigarette from the ivory holder and ground the butt out in the ashtray. She dragged a second empty easel to the wall without explanation, preoccupied with her thoughts. Jaya got up to fetch her pictures, embarrassed that she had stayed too long. As she wrapped the paintings in cloth, Sringara's unexpected invitation came as even more of a shock than the first one she'd extended to visit her studio. Jaya murmured her thanks, excited and wary of what more she would be able to show of herself.

From her sketchbooks, Jaya tore out dozens of charcoal and black crayon drawings of Kamlesh, arranging and rearranging them in variations of four. Well before she'd gone to see Sringara, she had dreamt of doing a large oil painting on canvas. Her big painting would be a composite of images—an enormous canvas in which she would show Kamlesh being transformed by her dance. She could see the picture in her mind, while in reality she wasn't sure which quartet of images to use, or how to arrange the discrete poses to create a flow. It was difficult to achieve any distance from Kamlesh—to view her truthfully, as an individual, rather than seeing her as an extension of herself, or masking her with a film star's exaggerated facial expressions.

All the best painters in Bombay would comment on her picture, she'd told her mother, pleading with her for the money to buy a large piece of sailcloth for canvas and have it mounted on a stretcher made by a carpenter. Her mother had been impressed. "My word," she exclaimed. Everyone had heard of A. A. Zaidi, and although Jaya wasn't sure he would attend the artists' gathering Sringara had invited her to, she suggested hopefully to her mother that he would, saying he sometimes came to these monthly meetings and offered his advice to young painters.

On the balcony, Kamlesh gazed at the blank forty-two-inch-tall canvas like an opaque glass that gave back no reflection. "Why don't you paint my picture? You've got the time to do it."

Jaya felt the gaze of the elderly man in the next building. She recognized the gift of whole days free to paint for weeks ahead, since she was only halfway through her two-and-a-half-month break from college. She felt the pressure of having to paint a bigger painting than she'd ever made before in the span of a month. And yet she found herself at an impasse. Kamlesh couldn't understand her trouble in locating an idea—an aesthetic principle—by which to organize the image. Jaya had done dozens of quick sketches of her, she pointed out, wasn't that preparation enough?

Then, on a Sunday, a few days later, she adjusted Kamlesh in a pose of lunging forward, in the bedroom, moving her sister's limbs as naturally as her own, and she realized she didn't want to differentiate herself from Kamlesh. She didn't want to consider her twin as separate from herself by analyzing and questioning who she was in the process of painting her. A part of her wanted to go on seeing Kamlesh as someone to be turned to or away from as she needed, a familiar distortion of herself.

THE FOLLOWING WEEK, while Kamlesh was at college, Bebeji took Jaya a short distance into the hutment colony to introduce her to the doctor she would assist, on Saturday afternoons, once the dispensary was constructed. Bebeji rested a proprietary hand on her back in the doctor's presence, as if

146

to impress upon Jaya her bond to the colony. The three of them met amid mounds of soil and sand on the raised cement foundation on which the clinic would stand. Some of the residents' committee members gathered to one side, waiting to speak to Bebeji and the doctor. A larger group surrounded them, an inquisitive audience of women and men without jobs or those who had just come off their shifts. Lakshmi's father, Madan, who had greeted them earlier, now lingered in the crowd in his familiar dark-blue factory half-pants and bush shirt with the name of the glassworks embroidered in red.

"So, you are Jaya?" Dr. Pendharkar said. "I've been hearing about you." A spare, compactly built man, probably in his forties, the doctor had clear bronze skin and soft, deep brown eyes. His hands moved calmly in the air, blocking out the shape of his thoughts as he told her about how he'd like to organize the clinic. A compounder from town would accompany him to dispense medicines. Bebeji had been full of praise for the doctor, a local physician who lived in a small flat in the Thana bazaar. He would volunteer his services two afternoons a week and take no payment. Both his parents had been freedom fighters, Bebeji had noted proudly; his idealism must have come from them.

They walked around the neat rectangular foundation, looking down upon the thicket of trees that darkened the base of the hill and across the empty landscape to the dark spears of chimneys marking the factory. "What will be my role here, Doctor?" Jaya inquired.

"You'll bring order to this place," he said in his steady, relaxed manner. "You will take down the patient's name, history, and ailments in the front room before I examine them in the back. You will be the recordkeeper, the organizer."

"That'll be very good." The stress on order pleased Jaya, implying mutinous illnesses could be brought under control if one followed the correct protocol. But it was an open question whether a dispensary could serve more than a thousand people just two afternoons a week.

Jaya knew Bebeji was prepared to search for another doctor to share duties with Dr. Pendharkar. She wanted the dispensary to be of the utmost benefit to the colony people, since she was spending her last couple of thousand rupees on its construction., "Giving away all her savings for these people," Jaya's mother often complained. Her father too thought it a folly to deplete her account of the funds Lalaji had managed to withdraw before fleeing Punjab. The bank had allowed him to take only a portion of his account balance, the rest forever lost. Now Bebeji had opened her fist, Vidya lamented, making a gesture of spilling, and thrown it all away.

"I have enough for the little time I have left on Earth," Bebeji would reply bitterly. Beneath their dispute lay Harbans's loyalty to his mother. Construction costs were three or four times Bebeji's contribution, but he could not ask Khosla Sahib to foot the bill after Khosla had grudgingly permitted the factory to pay for the construction of the school. So Harbans sold some of his shares. It infuriated Vidya. Their investments were small; they didn't have money to squander—they had two daughters to marry. When her father said it would mean the world to Bebeji to see people being looked after by a doctor, Jaya sensed her father meant the dispensary was for Bebeji's well-being too.

Patting Jaya's back now, Bebeji turned to the doctor, saying, "Here she'll be doing something useful for people with you." She indicated the group of thirty or forty colony residents gathered around the clinic's foundation. "I've asked her many times," Bebeji told the doctor. "*What good are these pictures you make? Who do they help?* She's constantly drawing and painting." Bebeji rocked her head wistfully and offered Jaya a familiar instruction, "The only good we can do is help the poor who suffer so much. Isn't it, Doctor?"

The doctor nodded mildly, reluctant to disparage Jaya's other vocation.

An elderly woman got up off the ground as they gingerly climbed down temporary steps constructed of loose stacks of bricks, Dr. Pendharkar assisting Bebeji. The old woman approached the doctor bent-backed, her buttocks thrust out like a horizontal extension of her spine, her crabbed hands clutching a throat strangled by a dense vine of tattoos. She had trouble swallowing, she complained hoarsely, and her throat constantly pained her. The doctor, who translated her Marathi into Hindi for them, felt the nodes below her jawbone.

Watching the woman still herself as the doctor examined her, Jaya awakened with a jolt to the idea that she had found a subject. Instead of Kamlesh, she could paint the woman's gnarled body, her withered neck and chest inked with tattoo vines that spread their tentacles into her blouse, entwining her arms and fingers in creeping blue-black filaments. She was a widow whose husband had died many years ago, she kept repeating when Dr. Pendharkar inquired about her symptoms, as if the loss of a husband constituted an infirmity.

At home the next afternoon, Jaya followed the back passageway to the servants' quarters behind the kitchen. It seemed to her now the woman on the hill had been only a shadow of her true subject, whom she was making her way to. She felt a reluctance, too, to paint a portrait of someone she didn't know and couldn't study continuously. Jaya needed to grip her subject very strongly. The uncertainties she felt about herself could be forgotten with a firm grasp of someone else. The maidservant had just finished washing up after lunch; it was the hour of her afternoon rest. Coughing, Heerabai let Jaya into her room, which reeked of the bidis she smoked and the cloying coconut oil in which she soaked her hair. She stood hunched in her cell, her tattered mangalsutra hanging around her neck—seven fraying strands of black marriage beads tacked together with safety pins, the relic of a husband who had deserted her. Sprigs of gray hair poked out of the knob of her bun. The tattooed scribblings on her arms had pulled Jaya here—the dark green semicircles, feathery leaves, and bands of stars and triangles woven into her skin like a pattern into cloth.

Opening her sketchbook, Jaya asked the maid if she could pose for fifteen minutes. Heerabai grumbled, waving her hands in protest, feeling self-conscious. She indicated the chatai, where she'd just lain down for a nap. Though Jaya felt guilty, she knew it would be hard to get Heerabai to sit for her when she was on duty. She was always occupied with housework. Ultimately, Heerabai conceded. She sat under a broad shelf displaying rows of her gods. Her knees were drawn up to her chin, her palms laid flat on the floor, calling attention to her acceptance of all that befell her.

Seeing Heerabai's eyes wander overhead to the shelf, Jaya helped her bring down her kingdom of gods and arrange the clay and metal idols, and their tiny clothes and cushions, on a low stool used as a puja altar. Heerabai swaddled her Krishna in a shred of flowered cloth and pushed him on a toy swing of wood mounted on the altar. Two icons crudely cast in white metal, her Bhairoba and Khandoba, were given places of honor on a doll's divan padded with cotton wool. Sketching Heerabai in the intimacy of worship, a girlish figure tenderly stooping to her gods as if to small children, exposing a tear in the back of her magenta blouse, Jaya forgot herself in the maidservant's daydream, in the fumes of coconut oil saturating her windowless room, until her mother called out sharply for tea, and Heerabai got up to boil water.

On her third day of working on Heerabai's portrait, contemplating ways to elaborate the image in detail, Jaya sensed a growing distance from her subject, as if she were an onlooker stopped outside the servant's world by an invisible line. As forcefully as she tried to project herself into Heerabai's mind, to forget herself by playacting in a mythic universe, she couldn't enter the maidservant's psyche. "What is the meaning of all these marks?" Jaya confronted Heerabai as she lit the kerosene burner in the kitchen. She gently lifted Heerabai's forearm to inspect the tattooed calligraphy on her skin, feeling the patterns of stars as if they were a braille her fingertips could read.

"What can I explain to you?" Heerabai laughed, placing her hand over her teeth, etched brown from betel nut. "Those are all the things in our world." She meant her world, her village in the Ghats, her village religion, her childhood, her Marathi language and culture. Jaya saw the clear shape of a leaf on the inside of Heerabai's wrist but didn't feel comfortable duplicating in paint a symbol she couldn't decipher. The dilemma of knowing your subject was the dilemma of distancing yourself from the person while placing yourself inside them at the same time. It seemed impossible; it seemed painting was a limited way to know any person. What could her picture reveal to anyone about Heerabai? Wasn't a portrait just a fantasy of the artist? Only once she understood the symbols of Heerabai's world, once she could define the meaning of each feather, snake, and pattern of rings, she thought, would she truly understand her subject—be inside *her* and not merely inside herself.

"Don't ask me to keep posing for you," Kamlesh had snapped, fiercely hurt to see Heerabai's hunched figure displace her on the canvas. After modeling for dozens of sketches, she had expected to see herself finally acknowledged as a dancer in Jaya's big painting. She might have hoped for the portrait to mark a big birthday, but their twentieth birthday had passed.

Vidya frowned, recognizing the figure in the unfinished painting on the easel standing in the balcony. Why had Jaya given such importance to a servant? All that money spent on a canvas and a carpenter to make the stretcher for a painting she could never hang in the house. It only made Vidya angrier when Jaya informed her Tule Sahib and his friends painted villagers and poor people. Anyone could be the subject of a modern painting.

"You mustn't trespass across boundaries," her mother scolded her. "Everyone has their proper place, and you should respect those lines. Even Heerabai will feel embarrassed that you've made such a big picture of her." Her mother turned out to be right. Heerabai shook her head in shame, in deep remorse, at seeing the shape of herself on canvas. She didn't joke with Jaya, she didn't giggle; she knew she wasn't meant to be given this kind of attention.

Tule studied the painting in progress and called it a unique view of the plague of the country: religion as the opiate of the masses. He liked the way Jaya had spread the magenta pigment of Heerabai's sari thinly enough for her limbs to show through, and the way the black line accentuated the servant's bony hands clutching her idols. Yet he was fed up with what he called Jaya's "brooding tendency," shouting at her for wasting his time discussing a picture stuck in the same state of incompletion for two weeks. It worried Jaya how sharply he seemed to resent Sringara for inviting her to the group discussion at Chadha's flat. "If she wants to take you under her wing, that's your affair! Don't involve me in your picture any longer." Once he had saved the fare for a passage by sea, he was going to England, he announced abruptly, threatening her with his disappearance, she felt, to punish her for seeking out Sringara.

13

IN CHADHA'S SPRAWLING drawing–cum–dining room, Jaya squeezed herself onto a settee between Tule and Sringara like their offspring, keeping an eye on her ghostly painting draped in white. It stood a head taller than the other five canvases propped against a long wall, flanked, on one side, by a portrait of a fleshy pink woman reclining in a patterned interior and, on the other, by a hilly landscape in indigo and mustard done in tortured, writhing brush marks.

"Every painter has his hero," Sringara remarked.

Jaya nodded vaguely, detached from the chatter around her, thinking alternately that her picture was spectacular and a grotesque failure beneath its shroud. She was the only one who'd arrived at Chadha's flat with her painting wrapped in two sheets like a bandaged patient. It unnerved her to think the attention of the entire room would soon be directed on her picture, every available seat occupied by a painter, the latecomers sitting on the carpet. Tule debated the relevance of the Mexican muralists' politics to the poverty of the masses in India with an artist to his right. Others discussed whether Zaidi would show up.

Sringara nudged Jaya. "There she is, that Humpty Dumpty." Chadha's plump wife, a heavy-bosomed woman in a peach cotton sari, who Jaya remembered sitting silently at Samarkand, slipped into the room with mincing steps, smiling wanly as she went around to the dining table. Chadha was adjusting a display easel in front of the table, and she moved past him without a word and bent to fetch something from the sideboard. Chadha pulled his pipe out of his mouth to speak to her, and she banged a biscuit tin down smartly on the table, looking harassed. She carried the tin out of the room like a salvaged valuable, bulky-hipped and tottering on heels, an older boy somewhere in the flat calling out "Mummy! Mummy!"

"She's terrified of us," Sringara observed. "She thinks we're after her husband to chuck up his job and take up painting full-time. Her biggest fear in life is losing her lovely company flat and all the perks. You should have seen her when she found out Dhasal stays in a servants' quarter, kicking open his bedroll at night."

"In a servants' quarter?" Jaya was dismayed.

Dhasal painted in the house during the day and slept there at night, Sringara said; the businessman was a patron of his. Jaya glanced at the artist who sat cross-legged on Chadha's carpet in a peon's khaki shorts and felt a deeper sympathy for the inward-looking man in large spectacles. He appeared to be the only senior artist in the group who'd brought along a painting for discussion. It was the loveliest picture in the room, to Jaya's eye—a subdued bluish-green abstraction with dark umber shapes suggesting hazy islands floating above depths of water.

The lush seascapes and thick palm groves and still lifes in the room were done by Chadha, Sringara pointed out to Jaya, who glanced around, admiring the cosmopolitan collection of artwork on the walls—lithographs of English villages and spired English towns, folk paintings on cloth, and intricately carved old wooden corbels mounted beneath the ceiling to evoke a rural landowner's home. Chadha's flat was one of those high-ceilinged, sun-filled old Colaba apartments done up with an ensemble of heavy modern furniture. The air of bohemian luxury was marred by a foul odor of sea muck and rot wafting into the room. It was the stink of fishing boats hauling in their catch at Sassoon Dock nearby, Sringara said. The fish market stood right there on the docks.

"Beautiful, Patak," Sringara called out when Vir entered the room. She swung a ginger-brown foot in a webbed sandal as if to lure him. Vir Patak flashed a grin, setting down a full-length portrait of a turquoise-haired woman wearing a bindi and missing an eyeball.

No one recognized the hand behind the first painting Bal Chadha mounted on his easel: a flat figure assembled from abstract shapes like a collage. The figure pushed a plow in a field of dun-gray soil, his mouth twisted in a ragged black grimace stylizing the agony of the labor class. The animal had plodded off-canvas, the man the beast of burden. Chadha walked around the picture, holding out his pipe contemplatively. "Pardon me for putting myself first—it's quite immodest of me, I realize." A note of discomfort rattled his fluent Englishman's voice. "I find I'm going in a completely different direction . . . I wanted to see what the reaction was." The picture was a startling departure from his lush and innocent tropical scenery hanging on the walls.

"Here you have borrowed from both Matisse and Diego Rivera," Vir said.

The shine dimmed a little in Chadha's eyes at the suggestion that a painting he regarded as a breakthrough could be called derivative of foreign masters. His hand went around his throat, which he'd adorned with a blue ascot. Perhaps he thought himself a fraud, Sringara murmured, compared to men who'd sacrificed everything for their art. On the other hand, she acknowledged, no one else had a flat like his, an income like his. Brilliant artists the others may be, but they lived like beggars.

"At this point, it's permissible to borrow from anywhere, isn't it?" Dhasal shyly pushed back his spectacles on his nose.

"Why do you all talk as if modern art is owned by the bloody Europeans? It's an *international* art," Tule asserted. He was looking straight at Vir, the teacher dressing down a pupil. "We can borrow from Picasso, we can take from Matisse, we can take from Tantric art. Does any European have so much at his disposal?"

Sringara boldly drew a packet of cigarettes and her ivory holder out of her purse, apparently free of any inhibitions about smoking in a room full of men. She called out to Vir for a matchbox. The shortage of chairs had forced him to sit some distance away, on a settee crowded with painters. The matchbox was tossed between a few hands until it reached a smiling Sringara.

Tule shot up off the seat beside Jaya. "Zaidi Sahib has come," he announced to the room. Jaya looked through the doorway and down the passage. Chadha's wife was speaking to a man in white and a black cap near the entry door. Some artists rushed out of the room, an impromptu reception committee to greet India's greatest modern painter, who beguiled everyone with his magical images, his staggering output. A melee of voices erupted in the corridor. After some minutes, Chadha ushered Akhlaq Asim Zaidi into the room—a thin, long-legged, long-armed figure with a cleric's flowing black beard. The master wore a white kurta falling below his knees, a black woolen vest over the shirt, white pajamas. No shoes. It was part of his legend that he went barefoot like the simple country people who were the subject of his paintings. In his hand he carried a small sketchbook.

"My student, a very talented young girl." Tule gestured to Jaya as Zaidi crossed the room to an armchair vacated for him.

"Good to have young people coming by," said Zaidi, looking straight at her.

Jaya's hello came out low and hoarse. She could hardly speak in her confusion. The creases around Zaidi's mouth aged him in a way his newspaper photographs missed, while his eyes had the mischievous, mirthful look of a boyish man in middle age. She felt his quick glance slip away—an unimportant young girl.

The ink drawings in Zaidi's sketchbook took precedence over everyone else's paintings, the artists passing the book around the room. It contained Zaidi's impressions from a recent sketching trip to the Ajanta caves. When the pad reached them on the sofa, Jaya looked on in fascination as Tule went through the line drawings depicting enigmatic confrontations between men and animals, the human faces soft, innocent masks, the animals' bodies chiseled and sharp. In a sketch that made her smile, a group of women, shown in fine black outline, gathered around a well into which a monkey had climbed. It was peeping up from the rim, animal and humans confronting each other in mutual bafflement.

"Your mythology keeps growing, Zaidi Sahib," Sringara said with a flirty scarlet smile.

"The mythology is inside the caves, too esoteric for a bumpkin like me." Zaidi laughed as if to dispel any notion that he'd actually felt humbled. "I had to go to the villages around the caves and eat in someone's hut, or sit under a tree and watch people passing by, to find something to draw." He laughed again. Nothing intimidated him, they knew.

If he climbed up to the shanty colony in Thana, Jaya imagined he would weave it into his myth of village India, find his charming vignettes and fantastical folk figures among the slum-dwellers, turning snakes and stones into quirky elements of his human comedy. She gave him a sidelong look, envying his vision, the certainty of his imagery. He knew what his art should be—a profusion of paintings, drawings, and sculptures sprang from his fingertips as effortlessly, it seemed, as the children's toys, furniture, and film posters he'd once painted for a living as a young man.

"Whose painting is that inside a bedsheet? What are you hiding?" Zaidi jovially addressed the group, tucking one unshod foot under his hip.

In the room's buzzing silence, the tops of Jaya's ears burned. It took her a moment to gain her voice. "It's mine. I should have taken the sheets away," she apologized, standing up as if she'd been reprimanded.

Chadha, nervously stroking the ascot tucked inside his collar, told her to keep sitting; he would remove the sheets.

"Why do you cover it up? Is it something so shocking?" Zaidi teased, turning his head to look at Jaya.

"Just as a protection while transporting it on the carrier." The new driver had tied the painting to the roof of her father's Vauxhall. She had worried it might get damaged if he tried to wrestle it into the back seat.

"Art needs no protection, my dear girl. I've carried oil paintings in the rain. Nothing happens."

She could think of no reply to his rebuke. She looked steadily away from Zaidi at the crockery cupboard that rose behind the dining table. Chadha tilted the painting forward and peeled away the folds of the white sheets. The first sight of Heerabai's figure turned on her side was a shock; the painting's green and magenta forms, Heerabai's legs showing through her transparent old sari. Chadha righted the painting and placed it upon the easel at Zaidi's suggestion that they look at the newcomer's picture. Heerabai's eyes half closed in a stupor, her blue-green vine-covered arms could be seen. Jaya felt fully undressed, like a body stretched out on a table under everyone's gaze.

Sringara inhaled the cigarette burning in her ivory holder and released her breath slowly and deliberately. "Fabulous," she whispered.

Frail and kinky-haired, Heerabai crouched on canvas, pouring streaky yellow milk over the stub of an anonymous idol she was bathing. On a dais constructed of crude brushstrokes—a lopsided altar—sat three lumpy clay gods with spotty offerings of food before them. A blotchy Ganesha no bigger than a thumb, its trunk coiled, stood at Heerabai's knee.

"See the distortion of the arms and hands, how they're covered with vegetation like a forest. The whole expression of the painting lies in them," said Zaidi, stroking his long, kinky beard. "Motion is the energy of life; without motion there is no spirit," he added philosophically. "In this picture, the greenery on the arms seems to flicker with light, the whole figure seems to tremble. It's quite enchanting."

Jaya grew breathless, light-headed with Zaidi's praise.

Vir said in a student's rote monotone, "You have been studying the Surrealists?"

"It seems to be about the world of our villages," Chadha proposed. He held his pipe thoughtfully in his hand. "At first glance, I thought she was an old crone playing with dolls . . . but it's our village religion we see, with its innumerable gods. What are these hieroglyphics on her arms? The asps, triangles, quarter-moons?"

"It's obvious the woman belongs to the urban proletariat," Tule said belligerently, his chest puffed up, appearing to take satisfaction in cutting an executive down to a clerk's rank. "There's an electric bulb over her head, a calendar picture on the wall. She lives among us, not in some remote village. She's like any worker or menial—what is religion for them but an anesthetic? You can see it in the lost look in her eyes."

"At least you paint with a social conscience," shouted a hefty betel-nut-chewing man sitting on the floor beside Dhasal. "In India we should use the bloody dust as our pigment."

"It's a fantastic picture," Sringara burst out and Jaya glanced at her, her head throbbing with too much praise. "They're tattoos on the arms, no? But they seem to grow like leaves. And inside the mouth—look!—there's a small fire burning. See how the mouth is glowing inside."

Jaya had taken away Heerabai's cheroot, which she had first attempted to render literally by enclosing the bidi between her lips and turning its burning tip inside her mouth.

"We become mesmerized by the painter's hallucination of fire in the cave of the mouth, the tattoos flowing like plants from her arms," Sringara went on. Jaya felt embarrassed by the attention, and yet she was hungry for more. "You can see the old lady as Mother Earth playing with the gods she's given birth to. For me it's a painting about the power of illusion—all the illusions that make up our existence."

Sringara's interpretation astonished her; she could never have put it in those words herself. Perhaps it was true that she'd seen Heerabai as a figment of the earth, uncomplaining, worn down, lost in her dreams of other worlds.

Later, Chadha insisted on carrying her wrapped painting to the lift, refusing the help of his servant. Jaya stepped into the wooden cabin ahead of him. His wife was visible through the folding metal gate, standing watchfully outside their door. Her eyes flashed with hatred, or envy, of Jaya's painting, or the attention her husband was paying to another painter. Jaya was grateful when the lift slipped down, out of sight.

Chadha carried her painting down the entrance steps into the afternoon glare. He was thinking of organizing a group of novice painters to meet fortnightly with a senior artist or two for guidance. Jaya smiled, unsure if he was asking her to join this salon. Heerabai's portrait had been a fluke. She'd followed her instincts painting it, sometimes wondering if she was creating a portrait of a madwoman. The more she'd ruminated on the meaning of the tattoos, the less real they'd become, her fancy turning them into vines dripping from Heerabai's arms, an overgrowth sprouting from her secret life among her gods. Next month, Chadha said. Come next month. The novices' group was just an idea, he'd have to talk to his wife about it. Come next month to this same gathering. In the new year!

Jaya beamed. Chadha raised her picture in his arms like an effigy in a procession, and the new driver hurriedly brought the Vauxhall down the drive.

JAYA WAS SURE she would have no painting ready to show at the next meeting at Chadha's place. It existed only in her mind as an image of a dancer sitting deeply on bent knees, poised to jump. She had come upon that pose by chance with Kamlesh in the bedroom one evening. Finishing Heerabai's portrait, she'd turned back to her twin, longing for the fluid motion of the dancer, her ideal free woman. She'd been experimenting with a sequence of five stances she wanted to portray in a circular movement on the canvas, rubbishing her original plan to divide the canvas in quarters to arrange four dancing figures. The full complications of the new composition remained unclear to her; she hadn't settled on which poses to depict. It seemed impossible she could finish a painting riddled with so many unknown elements in a month.

Jaya's attention flew outward, to her surroundings, as she resisted the more difficult task of looking within herself, to the source of her painting. Kamlesh agreed it would be nice to have a sitting area in the bedroom, where they could chat with friends or read. The old settee with the fraying cane back that cluttered the drawing room was moved to their bedroom, and Jaya folded an orange and yellow block-print bedcover over the back for color. To make space for the settee, Kamlesh agreed to join their single beds together into one bed on her side of the room.

With their beds pushed together, Jaya decided the curio cabinet that had long stood as a barrier against Kamlesh's bed should be angled across a corner of the room by the writing table. Kamlesh looked relieved to see the obstacle lifted away. Her relief inspired Jaya to take down the print of the blue-eyed English girl and her kitten pawing a ball of wool that Kamlesh had long ago damaged when she hurled a shoe at Jaya. When Kamlesh and Mummy objected to the picture's removal, Jaya pointed to the big crack in the glass, as if the risk of it breaking further were new. Forcing her way, she deposited the picture among the discarded framed maps of Europe and other household junk heaped at the back of the balcony where she painted. Only afterward did she realize she had overlooked the thing she most desperately wanted to be rid of after exams. Late that afternoon she summoned the driver, a thin Marathi man in a uniform supplied by the glassworks. He carried down the two jute bags, and they drove to J. J. Hospital. The driver gripped the sacks of bones by their throats as they walked across the grounds and climbed up the steps of the Court of the Coroner of Bombay. Medical students were responsible for disposing of the bones themselves, the clerk informed her. Jaya said she didn't know where to leave them, she didn't want to put them out with the household rubbish. He flicked his head, conceding. She left the sacks where she had gotten them from. On her way out of the building, where suspicious deaths were autopsied, she came upon three grim-faced men in salwar suits whose beaten expressions told her they had just identified a body. She had seen the look before. All the old dread of the hospital campus returned to her, and it distressed her to think she would have to return here after her long holiday.

The bedroom regained an air of innocence, emptied of human remains. The first week the twins slept in their joint bed, separated only by a thin crack between their foam mattresses, Jaya kept waking and falling back to sleep, sensing Kamlesh's presence, dreaming she was sharing her bed with a stranger. In the mornings, she awoke very early to find Kamlesh looking at her, round-eyed, astonished by her nearness. They reveled in their intimacy, a physical closeness they had not experienced since childhood, facing each other in the dark with their hands tucked under their heads, their knees pulled up, speaking quietly, sometimes with their eyes closed. Their closeness made Jaya want to draw Kamlesh nearer to Kirti. She was meeting him a couple of times a week, since he'd finished writing his independent paper for the professor he hoped to impress.

The three of them went out late one afternoon to the Prince of Wales again, Kirti treating them to tea. "What will happen with him?" Kamlesh asked Jaya afterward. To Jaya's relief Kamlesh had stopped demanding that she tell her parents about Kirti. Kamlesh's fear that she would be implicated in covering up Jaya's romance seemed to abate. She seemed to accept the ambiguity of the situation for now, although Jaya always deployed the word *marriage* to satisfy Kamlesh's concerns. Jaya herself found it reassuring to consider marriage a distant prospect, the present beautifully unshaped and full of possibility, the closed definitions of the future still far away.

She would recite for Kamlesh all the events that had to transpire between now and then: Kirti's house job at the hospital, then his FRCS in England for another four or five years. Another eight or nine years altogether for him to qualify as a surgeon. Another three years for her to earn her MBBS, then another four years if she decided to specialize. Kirti had suggested pediatrics or obstetrics and gynecology for her specialty. What about psychiatry? she had asked. He thought the idea nonsense. There were less than five departments of psychiatry in the country. Did she want to work in an asylum? No, she did not. She just wanted to understand what made people tick.

It was difficult to turn down the party Kirti invited them both to at

Farrokh Wadia's beach shack on New Year's Day. Although a risk always existed that word would travel back to her parents if Jaya were seen in public with him, Kirti said he didn't expect many of his batchmates to show up. Most of them had returned to their hometowns on holiday. It was going to be mainly Farrokh's school friends and old pals—a Parsi crowd, he imagined. People they didn't know. Jaya had gone on no holiday with her family during her long break from college, since her father couldn't take time away until the factory achieved full production again after some mechanical problems with one of the imported lehr ovens. Only Dipi was enjoying a change of scene, visiting his mother and sisters in Delhi. Jaya's mother had suggested she accompany Bebeji on a trip to visit relations in Punjab, but Bebeji had abandoned the idea, occupied with the construction of the dispensary and an effort to bring water to the colony. Kirti's invitation, at least, offered a daylong holiday by the sea.

OVER THE HOT sands, the air was a white haze, and white-frothing waves plunged to shore in staggered curls as they walked barefoot, at Kirti's swift pace, from Farrokh's beach house toward a distant hilly promontory as if it was their unstated destination. After sprinting ahead of them, Kirti turned, paused, and ran a few paces back, lightly kicking sand in their direction, laughing. Kamlesh smiled, watching him turn and sprint ahead again. Jaya shrugged, not bothering to run after him, feeling carefree in a turquoise chunni snaking around her plaits, showing off her gold hoop earrings. When they did eventually run up to him, Kirti opened his arms like wings to the shuddering breeze. He was flying high into the new year, having gotten what he wanted for 1955, a post as house surgeon at J. J. Hospital, and a room in the brand-new boys' hostel. Heart surgery was the future of medicine, he'd declared in the car on the way here, and Farrokh had agreed with him. It might be his specialty one day. "So, Kamleshji, what are your plans for this year?" Kirti teased, husky-voiced, in a brotherly way.

Kamlesh looked blank, as if it hadn't occurred to her to plan anything. "I'll be passing out in April." She spoke of finishing her BA. "Then I'll start my teacher's training course. Another year."

"She's going to become my full-time model," Jaya joked. "I want to paint some pictures of her dancing."

"She always seems to be your model, you're fascinated with your double—what?" The tinge of sarcasm in Kirti's voice was diminished by a playful glance at Kamlesh, a little laugh.

The waves rolled in with a lush slap, the lather of sea foam dispersing in a map of bubbly lines at their feet. Kamlesh rolled the stiff, soaked cuffs of her salwar above her ankles and sank her feet into the silky sand. Pulling out a broken bangle of shell, she clasped it around her wrist, performing an elaborate hand movement for Jaya and Kirti. They laughed. Crossing one leg in front of the other, lifting her elbows up to mime Krishna playing the flute, tilting her head to the side, she asked Kirti, "Is there something wrong with this pose? This is the way she painted me twice before covering it up with blue. Twice she rubbed me out with her oil colors!"

Over two days, in a frenzy of inspiration, Jaya had sketched her composition of the dancer, hoping to complete the picture in time for the gathering at Chadha's place in the middle of January, just before she returned to college. The dancing figures were so abstract and patchy Kamlesh complained that she couldn't see a single feature of hers in them. Still, she would stare at the figures on the canvas as if she were looking at her reflection in a mirror, trying to discern if Jaya had revealed something she didn't know about herself.

"Let's show them to Kirti," Kamlesh had suggested of the numerous sketches Jaya had made of her. She seemed to imagine the three of them cozily huddled around Jaya's sketchbooks like a diary they were all privy to. Jaya refused, putting away all the sketchbooks lying around the bedroom in her broken sideboard. "I'm not going to carry my drawings around town like a hawker carting his wares."

Her paintings didn't really interest Kirti, she told Kamlesh; he preferred to talk about surgical patients. Her resentment surprised her, because she'd actually been touched that Kirti had kept the sketchbook she'd brought to Farrokh's shack, the first time they went there, for many weeks. When he returned it, he pointed out the sketches he'd read his own meanings into.

Later, they returned to Farrokh's cottage, recognizing no one among the gang playing cricket in the sand yard. The crowd was mostly Parsi, as Kirti had expected. Boys and girls chatted freely, a thoroughly Westernized group. All the girls wore flaring cotton frocks to their knees. Farrokh himself appeared lonely, his straw hat tipped over his eyes, sitting back on a cane sofa playing the harmonica. Hema was still at home in Poona for the break.

More people had arrived, everyone cheerily calling out "Happy New Year." Among the group eating around the center table, Jaya spotted a few of Kirti and Farrokh's batchmates. They were all graduating, having finished their third MBBS exams, and none of them had secured a house job like Kirti, so she wasn't going to worry about them spreading gossip back on the campus. Kamlesh and Kirti set about looking for seats. At home, Kamlesh had reluctantly turned the party into a gathering at the home of Meher's aunt in Juhu, telling their mother she and Jaya were both invited. Jaya had felt a knot in her stomach even as Farrokh drove them out here, a terrible mixture of guilt and anxiety. She buried those feelings on the beach, like a scrap of rubbish in the junk heap on the balcony.

People emerged from Farrokh's shack with plates of food, so Jaya stepped into the main room, heading toward the kitchen. What a temptation to turn left, to find the bedroom where she had lain with Kirti in the rain many months back—if only they could be alone there again.

When Jaya returned to the veranda with two teacups of crab soup, for Kirti and herself, she was surprised to find Ashok Narula in the chair next to Kamlesh. A lock of oiled black hair hung down his brow, the rakish look of a film star. Kamlesh was concentrating on a small plate of prawns the servant was passing around, avoiding his glance. Jaya walked toward them. Narula didn't notice her, giving Kamlesh shy, probing looks as he spoke at length.

Lying in bed at night with her twin a few feet away, Jaya would tease Kamlesh about the steamship navigation boy whose name she always forgot because of this label she'd given him—Vikram Bakshi, Kamlesh reminded her. "If you had a choice, would you choose the steamship navigation boy or N. D. Narula's nephew?" she would ask her twin, recalling Kamlesh's two suitors at Leela's wedding. Kamlesh would cry out and swat her arm to make her shut up. Once she started her teacher's training, their parents would seriously start looking for a boy, Jaya warned her twin—they would want to get her married as soon as she finished her course.

Keeping a little distance from the table, Jaya walked past her sister and Ashok Narula and caught him telling her about steamships arriving at

Ballard Pier. Whenever he read in the paper that big stars were coming on a particular ship, he'd go to the docks—he'd seen Stewart Granger and Lana Turner walking down the gangway. Press photographers were taking their snaps. *Lana Turner*, Kamlesh exclaimed, and Jaya smiled over her sister's girlish infatuation with film stars.

She and Kirti sat together eating their lunch. Among this Westernized crowd, all the girls with their hair cut short, their legs bared, she imagined she was in a foreign country, free of the customs of her own. It worried her how little she cared that people could see her with a boy. Later, Kirti led her around the cottage, and she imagined they were going to check on the caretaker, although she knew the old man had abandoned his job shortly after his dog died.

Kirti wandered into an alley of sorts between the back of the cottage and the side of the garage. Somehow they felt protected there, between two walls. Jaya had an inkling he was going to touch her, that he hadn't brought her here just to talk. He stepped back and clutched her from behind, throwing his enormous shadow on the opposite wall, in which the kitchen window was open. She felt the gentle pressure of his hands on her head, his fingers slowly rolling away the sheer blue scarf covering her hair as if he were disrobing her. He stroked her neck with a strong hand, his warm mouth on her ear. She turned her face away, startled for an instant that someone might be watching them. She saw a girl in the window. The girl—was it Kamlesh?—instantly bent her head down, as though she were washing her hands in the basin and hadn't seen anything. For a moment, Jaya let Kirti go on holding her, because nothing else mattered, their bodies glowing in the afternoon light.

AT HOME KAMLESH was cooler with her, turning away from conversation at night. Jaya took her withdrawal as a confirmation that she had seen Kirti touch her. Kamlesh was embarrassed, or she was punishing Jaya. She never had time to pose now, asking Jaya to use the sketches she'd already made for her painting. Jaya had been mulling over the dancer's poses on her canvas and wanted to change two of them, which now struck her as wrong, hoping to find more telling gestures from Kamlesh's repertoire. She began refusing Kirti's invitations in order to make herself available to her sister whenever she was free from college and her dance lessons, and slowly she won Kamlesh over. She'd been taking too many chances with Kirti, she confessed, become too cocksure that they wouldn't be seen. So she wasn't meeting him much these days. "What will we do?" Kamlesh seemed to believe she, too, would suffer from Kirti's absence. They were silent together, as though they were mourning the inevitable loss of Kirti. But by devoting herself to the pursuit of her sister, temporarily excluding Kirti from their lives, Jaya was able to find in Kamlesh's new rounds of poses the dancing figures she needed to paint her picture.

THE ARTISTS' GATHERING at Chadha's place erupted in a volley of insults bouncing across the room between Tule and Vir when Vir's nude was put up for discussion. "How can you paint so crudely? Do you use your hand or your foot?" Tule barked. His face was greased with perspiration. Others turned to admonish him.

Observing her teacher from the other side of the room, Jaya sensed the trembling wave of his contempt, the force of an attack gathering in the chewing motions he made with his mouth. Sringara shot him a warning glance. She and Jaya sat next to each other on the sofa, Sringara smelling richly of perfume. Vir sat on the carpet at Sringara's feet, like her disciple. Was the brown-breasted woman he'd painted, with a face shattered and reassembled in ultramarine, umber, and emerald shards, a rendering of Sringara? He hinted at a resemblance in the crimped waves of her red-brown hair.

The first thing Jaya noticed about her own painting when Chadha raised it on his easel was the rhythmic sweep of her brushstrokes. Thick, wavy dashes of cobalt blue, sea green, and violet shaped the atmosphere around the dancers' burnt-brown silhouettes—five dancing figures joined by a musical beat of arcs across the canvas. The dancers' shifting images drew Jaya into the painting as if she were not their creator and didn't know what they were meant to suggest.

"It's full of a searching after a form, it seems obsessed with the search, you feel it in the twisting, turning brush marks—" Tule shouted across the room, his voice still vibrating with unspent anger. "When I saw it earlier, I didn't know what you had in mind. You've improved your handling of color, the hues are pure and clear. Look at the depth of the violet and the blue, like the colors of the sea."

Others saw in the abstract dancers the embodiment of elements of Hindu philosophy. In Dhasal's interpretation, the dancing figures were an allegory for the artist's life, the stages of her development, and Jaya had been intrigued by his understanding of the final receding figure she had painted, of the dancer squatting with both arms thrust out in front of her, as a symbol of the mature artist giving all she had, her hands themselves her last offering.

Sringara concentrated straight ahead on the picture. "If you think of it, the dancer is an ideal symbol of life. She's in constant movement, the source of rhythm, and all life is movement, change, illusion after illusion that deceive us. There's a book on aesthetics, the *Vishnudharmottaram*, ancient, ancient . . . You know it, Deo?" She addressed Tule by her pet name for him, a gesture of reconciliation perhaps. "It says that since rhythm is the essence of painting, a painter cannot create the right mood in his pictures without knowledge of classical dance." She turned to Jaya as if to inquire about her motive for portraying the dancer.

"I was thinking of a sequence of movements leading to a dancer's freedom, how she frees herself through the pure motion." Jaya spoke quickly, sighing heavily in her self-consciousness before the group.

What she'd tried to expose in the image of the dancer might be *shakti*, it occurred to Jaya when she awoke in the early morning dark the next day. Bebeji had made her aware of the word, as she opened and closed her arthritic hands slowly, lamenting that she had no shakti left. No power or energy or strength. Jaya would cup her grandmother's hand and massage it, promising her that shakti would return.

Chadha had pointed her in the direction of this idea, praising the "tremendous energy" in her picture. As she was leaving his flat, he had mentioned several young artists, including Vir, with whom he was organizing an exhibition. A showing of the new generation, the post–Group 47 batch. The Young Turks, he called them. "Why don't you join us?" he proposed. It would be a group of five or six painters; and the first time he'd be showing his own pictures. "Never mind the gray hair," he said, running his hand over his head with some embarrassment. "I'm a Young Turk at heart."

"I have very few paintings," Jaya apologized. "Not even half a dozen. None of them can be put up in an exhibition." Both the pictures she'd brought to his flat were worthy of display, Chadha said. He, too, would have to create a new body of work, setting aside what he called "the juvenilia of a middle-aged man." All of them would need time to prepare, so he'd booked no venue yet. He was considering the frame shop near Parsi Dairy, or possibly the much grander space at the Jehangir Art Gallery, for next October or November. Ten, eleven months. Nearly a year from now. Renting Jehangir for ten days would be expensive, but affordable if they split the cost by five or six.

Disregarding the matter of cost, as though it didn't matter, Jaya grabbed at the opportunity. "How many paintings should I plan on showing? I mean, roughly?" Overcome by swirling pride, excitement, and fear, she wanted to show him how good she could be, show him everything she was.

"No fixed number," Chadha replied in his airy manner. He mentioned half a dozen, then a minute later went up to ten, fifteen, twenty.

To Jaya it seemed unlikely each artist could display fifteen pictures in the tight confines of the frame shop. But it might be possible at Jehangir. "Fifteen," she agreed. It calmed her to approach the offer like a class assignment with clear parameters. Immediately she changed her mind about the number. "No, sixteen." Sixteen was a better number, the six closed and definite. Sixteen paintings to be made from now until October. It would consume her, which was what she hoped for. An enormous artistic undertaking to counterbalance the resumption of her studies in a few days, marked by rotations in the wards, which would fully immerse her into the agonies of the hospital.

Outside Chadha's building, Tule and Sringara joined her in the drive as she looked around for her missing driver, her picture perched against a column at the top of the entrance steps. The shrill cries of egg and vegetable men rang in the lane. "Chadha tells me he's giving you a place in his exhibition," Tule said in a raw tone that accused her of going behind his back.

Jaya tried to smile and wondered, with a guilty intake of breath, if she should have declined Chadha's invitation and waited for her teacher to decide when she was ready for a show. "You'll be coming for my lesson tomorrow, no?" she asked Tule.

Sringara congratulated her. She looked fetching in a high-necked jade silk blouse and gold paisley earrings worn with her sexless white sari. Her crinkly hair had been pinned up in a bun. Tule was taking her for a Chinese lunch, she'd mentioned. He'd lost a bet.

"You still require me as a master? What for?" Tule joked, despite the tight expression on his face.

"Why does she need you at all?" Sringara needled him under her breath.

"Are you managing all right on that balcony? You'll be able to do your paintings there?" Tule inquired, reminding her of her limitations.

"Oh, yes." Jaya turned away apprehensively. At Chadha's gate, one of Colaba's ancient bow-legged Kolis set down from her head an enormous basket of fly-speckled fish for a servant to inspect.

Sringara waved her cigarette toward Tule, offering him a drag. Through some unexplained turn of events, he had regained his place next to her, and Vir had hung back in Chadha's flat. Sringara's wrists were thin, her knuckles protruding. In the harsh glare of noon, her boniness seemed a sign of fragility, a need for sustenance. Squinting in the light, Sringara asked her, "You paint on your balcony? You've got enough privacy there?"

"What is private about it?" Tule scoffed, telling Sringara about the clutter at the back, the old man in the neighboring building whose pastime was staring at Jaya painting.

"I've always painted there." Jaya smoothed her chunni flat over her shoulders. Sringara might think her at a disadvantage, her circumstances a hindrance to the task before her. She didn't want any doubt cast upon her. She had to believe she could paint her sixteen pictures. "It's quite a large balcony," she asserted. "There's enough space for me."

Sringara looked at her intently. "Why don't you use my flat if you like? I'm in my studio the whole day. Deo can stop by in the evenings sometimes to see your work."

"Oh, that's all right, I wouldn't want to disturb your parents." Jaya's pride rose. She wasn't going to burden outsiders with the practical arrangements for her painting. Not Sringara, not Tule. The idea of her teacher dropping by to see her in the evenings was unseemly—she recoiled from it as her father might.

"There's no one at home. I stay alone."

"Oh. I see." Jaya didn't know what more to say. She knew no woman who lived alone, separate from her family. Sringara wasn't married, so she'd assumed she lived with her parents. Immediately Jaya felt a distrust of this woman who had no one to answer to.

Vir appeared at the top of the entrance steps, waving but apparently deterred from joining them by the presence of Tule, who stood bullishly beside Sringara, his thumbs hooked into his trouser pockets. Sringara's life seemed to wind uneasily between these two men—an unbridled life, neither connected to a family nor curbed by their expectations. Jaya found it disturbing to imagine being such a woman, without any limits upon her, living entirely on her own.

14

KAMLESH STEPPED FORWARD, imploring Krishna with a wide-eyed glance. She took a slight leap—*Why doesn't he let me pass by?* She smiled, opened her arms in a plea. She pictured the dark blue god strutting in front of her as Masterji sang his praises. She jumped, lunged, leaped to the side. Afterward she was surprised to see the strand of white jasmine buds she'd looped around her plait lying on the practice room floor like a wisp of cloth. She hadn't felt it slip off. She bent to retrieve the flowers and tried to pin them back in her hair, remembering how Kirti had rolled away Jaya's chunni from her head and caught it in his fist. She'd felt like she was watching an intimacy between a husband and wife.

Masterji beckoned her from his place on the floor. He sat majestically straight, wrapped from his waist to his ankles in the cottony white sheet of his lungi, his deep brown chest bare and smooth. "I think you enjoy the padams to Krishna more than anything," he said, anticipating her response with a faint smile. Kamlesh was surprised by the interruption in her practice and stopped fidgeting with the flowers she'd failed to pin in place. She sat down cross-legged in front of him in her damp practice sari. He wanted to teach her a new padam to Shiva, *Natanam Aadinar*, the dance of creation, which was his favorite padam and would be the centerpiece of the group of padams he wanted her to present at her debut. But the most difficult dance she would have to work on, her moment of glory, would be the varnam he had selected for her. She would play the role of Sati, who had chosen Shiva for her husband and gotten into a battle with her father for the right to decide things for herself. Kamlesh was smiling, uncertain still if he meant what she thought he did. Masterji said he would arrange the orchestra and the singer, fix up a mridangam player for the rehearsals. She must see to booking a hall and putting the announcements in the papers when the time came.

"Am I ready?" Kamlesh laughed, elated. What a lucky start to the year. She would be ready by September or October, Masterji said. It would give her eight, nine months to prepare. "I'll get my bells." Kamlesh bounced the strand of flowers in her hand. A dancer was permitted to tie bronze bells around her ankles to articulate rhythm for the first time at her stage debut.

Masterji spoke to her in detail about the preparations, the six or seven new pieces he would teach her in addition to *Natanam Aadinar*, for a repertoire of eight dances. Two and a half hours of solo dancing—he had full confidence she was ready. In her excitement, Kamlesh revealed the news that Jaya's exhibition would be held around the same time, picturing their coinciding debuts as a collaboration. Something they could create together. Jaya had thrown herself into sketching Kamlesh, but she couldn't seem to get started on a painting. She was wary of asking for money for another canvas, afraid their parents would stop her from taking part in the exhibition if they found out about it. Kamlesh realized she had to protect her sister's secret. She told Masterji, "My parents haven't yet given their approval for the exhibition, but I think they'll agree."

Jaya was a talented girl, Masterji said, and she was devoted to her art. How intently she'd sat in on Kamlesh's lessons, trying to capture her in motion, her hand moving the entire time without pause. Kamlesh nodded and laid the flowers in the lap of her sari. The thought of Jaya's devotion launched her teacher into a reverie about the purity of a dancer's life in the past. He ran his fingers through the fringe of gray curls at the back of his neck. "In the olden days, the dancer lived in the temple, she danced for the temple god every day. You could say she lived inside the dance." He recalled that Kamlesh was finishing college in April without remembering she would begin her teacher's training course after six weeks of summer holidays. Kamlesh didn't interrupt him to remind him of that, nor was either of them disturbed by the loud clang of utensils falling in the kitchen as her teacher proposed to her the ideal way for a student to immerse herself in the preparations for her arangetram: living in her guru's house. He laid out in elaborate detail his notion of a perfect discipline.

"I can come—I'd like to," Kamlesh said, moved by his vision. She would have a sanctuary in his home, in this room where she felt closest to herself, conscious of her strengths.

In the car, which picked her up on its way home from the factory, Kamlesh sat in the back seat with her father. Dipi was in the front beside the driver, his briefcase propped up like an armrest. It was after six, and the evening air was smoky, a man with a ladder lighting the gas lamps that lined Masterji's quiet street, edging a cricket field. Dipi was discussing some factory business with her father, so Kamlesh waited to give them the news. Her thoughts drifted until she heard the word *vultures*. The Communist trade unionists had set their eyes on Thana, Dipi told her father in English to keep the driver from understanding, seeing a clutch of prosperous factories to get their claws into. It was all politically motivated, her father agreed. These union leaders would make absurd demands, threaten a strike—all a big show to impress the workers—while behind the scenes they would extort a payment from the owners to call off the strike. Rumor had it the Communists were meeting with Madan, the electrician, whose promotion to operator of the annealing ovens had put him in the kind of respectable position they liked their stooge to have.

"Let's wait and see what happens," her father muttered to Dipi. Kamlesh sensed he was reluctant to discuss labor matters in front of the driver even in English. "If Madan starts causing problems, put him on the night shift. Isolate him a little, he'll get the message."

The mood was wrong to bring up the news of her debut, so Kamlesh held her tongue. The question of appearing on stage wasn't the worry, really. It was the question of whether she would be allowed to shift away from home to prepare for her dance recital in Masterji's flat.

When they reached the coast, she could no longer contain herself. "I've got a bit of good news," she told her father.

He relaxed, hearing of her arangetram. His hand went to pat her shoulder in congratulations.

Dipi turned his head around, raised his eyebrows. "Where and when will the show be, Madame?"

"I don't know where," Kamlesh admitted. The other, more difficult, question receded as she pondered where she wanted to present herself in public. "Why not C. J. Hall?" It was a grand venue for concerts and stage shows in the heart of town, right down the road from the Jehangir Art Gallery, where Jaya might have her debut exhibition, showing her paintings of Kamlesh dancing. *The Shakti Cycle*: her paintings about the powers of the dancer. It made Kamlesh smile.

Her father agreed, seeing how happy she was. "Yes, we can hire C. J. Hall for one evening." He smiled, then added, "If the cost is bearable, why not?"

Kamlesh laughed and opened her fist full of flowers. A few jasmine buds shone like pearls among the browning petals.

THE SISTERS WERE careful to talk softly at night. Every evening Jaya drew the curtains between their half of the bedroom and Bebeji's alcove in the enclosed balcony, to keep from disturbing her. These days Bebeji slept very early, an hour after taking a frugal evening meal. The growing conflicts at the shanty colony had discouraged her despite her small success in bringing two handpumps there. The twins were sensitive to their grandmother's need for rest and didn't talk long. But the evening Kamlesh learned about her arangetram, she told Jaya everything she could not tell their parents, and they spoke till late in the night. Masterji had offered to train her like a true dancer, in the way dancers traditionally prepared for their debuts. After her exams in April, she could shift to his home, share his daughters' room. For four to five hours a day she would practice new dance pieces, sit with him and learn his interpretations of the slokas and shastras, the dance theory in its detail. He would teach her singing, and his wife would instruct her on playing the veena. Learning an instrument was important, he said, because dance in its purest form was considered a visual embodiment of music. Jaya kept sighing in awe over such an intricate and elaborate discipline, enchanted by Masterji's ideal. "To become a true dancer," Kamlesh recalled her guru telling her, "a girl's surrender to dance has to be complete."

"I wish you could live like that for a few months," Jaya said. "It would be out of this world. I can talk to them for you."

Kamlesh was hopeful but remained silent. She doubted Jaya would succeed in persuading their parents to let her take residence in Masterji's flat, yet she'd already started fantasizing about shifting there. She could take her books along to study for her exams, dipping into Hazlitt's *Of Persons One Would Wish to Have Seen* and De Quincey's *Levana and Our Ladies of Sorrow* and Dickens's *Bleak House* while she learned the new padam to Shiva.

Jaya asked again if Kamlesh wanted her to speak to their parents about Masterji's proposition. They always felt more courageous to speak up for each other than for themselves. Jaya had not said a word to their parents about her exhibition. As long as Daddy didn't forbid her from participating, it seemed to Kamlesh, she could go on imagining she would create her *Shakti Cycle* of paintings and hang them in the Jehangir Art Gallery.

"Why don't you ask about your own exhibition first," Kamlesh said as gently as she could.

"I'll have to tell them soon," Jaya conceded. "I suppose I should tell them the whole thing."

When Kamlesh asked what she meant, Jaya murmured that Sringara had offered her the use of her flat to paint her exhibition pictures. She would have more privacy and space than on the balcony; she could spend an hour or two there every afternoon after college. "And Sringara could look at my paintings and give me her advice," said Jaya.

"You'll do all right at home. You've always painted here." Instinctively Kamlesh opposed the idea of Jaya leaving the flat with her paints and canvases. She wouldn't like to pose in someone else's flat with strange people around. She was accustomed to collaborating with Jaya on her pictures at home, holding long poses in the middle of their locked bedroom.

The next morning Kamlesh went to join her parents for tea in their room, keen to carry on the previous evening's conversation. Her mother was sitting up in bed with a cup and saucer. She set it down on her bedside table before telling Kamlesh they had been thinking over the venue. "It's such a big hall in the middle of town—foreign orchestras perform there. It doesn't seem the proper place for a student to give her recital."

"What?" Kamlesh was baffled. "Why? Arangetrams are also held there. I've seen announcements in the papers."

Her father, who sat on the edge of the bed with one leg folded up, lowered his newspaper. "Your reputation will be spoiled. It's better you don't go on the stage."

"Your daddy is correct." Her mother looked at her seriously. "There's no need to give a performance. It can hurt you very badly."

"Yesterday—I thought," Kamlesh stammered, "you were happy about this."

"Since last evening we've been thinking over what to do," her mother explained, keeping her tone neutral. "This year the most important thing is we find a good boy for you. By next April you will have finished your teacher's training, and within a few months of that you should get married. The time to look for boys will be this year. We're hoping things go well with Vikram Bakshi, but I haven't spoken to his mother in a long time. We don't know the details of his situation now. If any difficulty arises, we'll have to look for someone else. We'll need to take the help of our friends to find well-placed boys."

"Anyway, I'll have my show in September, October," Kamlesh cut in. "After that I'll have all the time to meet whoever you'd like me to."

"You're not understanding," Harbans admonished her, his voice rising. He threw his newspaper aside on the sheet. "If you go on the stage, then we'll have a very difficult time finding anyone to meet you. A few families may accept a girl who dances in public, but most will not. You'll spoil your name."

"Your daddy is correct." Her mother could see her distress, could see she felt betrayed, and beckoned Kamlesh to sit by her on the bed. "We don't want you to be hurt by what other people say."

Kamlesh remained standing where she was, hesitant to approach her mother. "So, what are you saying I should do?"

She would have to cancel her arangetram. People in the Punjabi community were not familiar with Bharata Natyam, they didn't regard a girl dancing on stage as an artist. No respectable girl displayed herself like that in public. Even the few families who let their daughters learn Bharata Natyam only allowed it as a hobby. Kamlesh would become the subject of gossip, people would question her character.

"All these years I've been learning," Kamlesh said. "You knew about the arangetram." She spoke only to her mother, trying to avoid her father's tense presence on the bed. She would never dare complain to him in this way. Somehow Vidya had imagined her arangetram would be a group dance program with Masterji's other students: a small show for families. Her father eased a little, his shoulders dropped, he leaned back. He'd been preoccupied with factory matters yesterday, he explained, when he agreed to renting a hall. He hadn't been thinking properly. Kamlesh asked if he would speak to Masterji.

"What good will a discussion with your Masterji do?" He raised his voice, as if her question offended him. "He doesn't know the thinking in the Punjabi community. You don't have any shame?"

"You'll ruin your future." Her mother pressed her lips together to say the matter was closed.

The tears slid soundlessly from Kamlesh's eyes. She hadn't expected to start crying in front of her parents. The sorrow simply befell her, beyond her powers to suppress. They were taking away from her the very thing she had dreamed of for years. Now, suddenly, it was not going to happen, though yesterday Daddy had patted her on the shoulder and agreed to hire C. J. Hall for her show. She had pictured herself standing on the stage in that magnificent theater with its stone columns and galleries, the lights shining on her, her hands tucked in at her waist. Everyone would know, then, who she was.

15

THE PHOTOGRAPHER PROWLED around a new cement washstand in the shanty colony, capturing a woman in a sopping-wet sari squatting beneath a stream of cold water that poured from a handpump. Jaya glanced at Kamlesh, smiling over the woman's young son vigorously working the pump's iron handle, licking his lips with the effort. Behind him frustrated women queued up for water shouted at the bather to fill her pot and go away. A line of clay pots balanced on the heads of forty or fifty women snaked crookedly up the hill. Sarvi Singh, the son of Nihal Devi's old friend Satya, had come to write a story on the hill colony for the *National Standard*. Bringing water to the colony was both an accomplishment and a further problem—Bebeji told him she hoped the article would raise the issue of the lack of clean water for factory workers in Thana. The sight of flowing groundwater on the arid hill amazed Jaya, but her attention kept slipping to her sister. Kamlesh had been ill for more than a month, and this was her first time back at the colony since she'd recovered.

Every small affirmation of her recovery brought Jaya relief. She felt lifted by Kamlesh's laughter, her animated tone in speaking to the children. At home Kamlesh was more subdued, so Jaya was especially curious to see how she responded to the children in the colony. Here, she was reassured to see, Kamlesh seemed almost back to her usual self. When some of the children asked her why she had missed her songs lesson again, although she was here on the hill, Kamlesh smiled. "Today, we've brought a sahib who works for the newspaper. He's going to write a story about all of you."

The children looked around in puzzlement—*Who's going to write a story about us?* It was the photographer who'd caught their eye with his big, boxy camera, and they had to repeatedly be told not to follow too closely behind him.

"Get up! Fill your bucket and go bathe at your jhopadi," a woman in line for water yelled at the obstinate bather, who dropped her head between her knees and scrubbed her hair. Another woman swatted her little boy on the head to make him stop pumping.

Dipi stepped forward in his white office dress, flapping his hands for calm, the young manager trying to restore order. He chastised the woman who had hit the child, ordered the unrepentant bather to allow others their turn at the handpump. Jaya and Kamlesh walked over to their grandmother's little group. Fights were constantly breaking out at the pump, Bebeji was saying. The district representative, Yashwant Halde, called out to Sarvi's photographer to take all the pictures he liked—soon the lack of water would be only a memory for the people. The pictures would remind them of what their lives used to be like.

"Halde Sahib, you're a very hopeful man," Bebeji said lightly, not wanting to alienate the person whose help she needed most in negotiating with the local government. Jaya caught her sister's eye, both aware what Bebeji really thought of the blustering Halde. In his pious garb of a dhoti and white Gandhi cap, he probably expected to be photographed as a dedicated Congress politician serving the poor. When he boasted to Sarvi that the district planning council had sanctioned a power line and pump house for Ganesh Murti Nagar, Bebeji offered a correction—Halde Sahib had been assured those things would be sanctioned, but so far Ganesh Murti Nagar had not been officially recognized on the development plan. An article about the colony's hardships in a prominent newspaper was Bebeji's attempt to shame bureaucrats into paying attention to the settlement.

As they began climbing the track up to the dispensary, a troop of children followed. Sarvi stopped to speak to a couple of women in the queue who complained about the long lines for water. As Sarvi jotted notes in his pad, Manu stood by his side, an aspiring journalist still, though their father had chosen commerce as his future course of study. So Manu had decided he would write on the side.

The stone-pocked path of dry orange soil gave Bebeji particular trouble today. The sisters each took their grandmother by an arm, guiding her, though Bebeji protested that she was used to the terrain now. Over the last eighteen months, she had found her place here, Jaya realized, despite the strain of making the climb, the frequent flare-ups of intense knee pain. Rheumatoid arthritis was a chronic condition made worse by walking up and down these uneven slopes, which added to the wear and tear on the knee joints, Dr. Pendharkar had told Bebeji plainly. Jaya had brought up her grandmother's condition the one time she met him. Bebeji had not liked her speaking to the doctor about her infirmity. She liked to present herself as a person who could bear anything, indomitable.

Further up the track, a group of veiled women bearing waterpots approached them, walking downhill. The last woman, masked by a sheer scarlet veil that drifted over her face, moved with a soft and fluid poise that so beguiled Jaya she had to force herself not to stare. Bebeji warned the women of the long line at the handpump. One woman, balancing two earthen pots stacked on her head, replied that they still fetched water from the pond off the Agra Road. They preferred to walk a few miles than fight with people in the queue. "You see?" Bebeji said to Sarvi after the women passed. "One handpump is no solution for a thousand, two thousand people. Most of them are still going to the ponds."

The bearded photographer discovered the second handpump off to the side, in front of a stand of thorny brush. Bebeji asked him to take a picture of it—it had run dry from overuse in less than a month. Beneath lay brackish water. The photographer posed some children around the pump, stripped of its iron handle. An engineer who'd tested various locations on the hill for Nihal Devi's private water supply scheme had discovered only two spots where the subsoil water level was high enough for handpumps, and he had warned her the pumps could dry up within two or three months if use was heavy. "Bebeji spent her own money on these pumps," Kamlesh rued, "and the one below might also run dry soon."

Their grandmother had surprised them with this last bit of money squirreled away in her savings account. The four or five thousand rupees Lalaji had salvaged before leaving Lahore, she had spent on her schemes in the colony, so it was troubling to hear her admit now that her efforts on the hill were temporary and provisional. "Unfortunately, there's a lot of politics involved in obtaining water," she told Sarvi in a scratchy voice, some irritant in her throat. "The bureaucrats of the old guard like the collector, Mr. Kundla, aren't interested in bringing water to what they call an 'illegal settlement.' These men were trained by the British to ignore poor people, they've spent their entire lives turning a blind eye to the villages and wadis around here, so it's difficult to persuade them to reform themselves and pay attention. If the newspaper tells how these laborers are being neglected, how desperate they are for power and water, then these bureaucrats might feel shamed into doing something."

Sarvi nodded, while quietly noting the logistical difficulty of drawing a power line to such a remote hill. He turned his ash-colored eyes on the twins and inquired, "You two always come here with Massiji? The next generation of social workers?"

"How can we compare, Uncle?" Jaya said. "They did so much." She meant Bebeji and Satya, and all those of their generation who had devoted themselves to organizing people, fighting for independence. It was a kind of miraculous selflessness. She couldn't imagine devoting her entire self to a cause in that way, and giving up the freedom to pursue her own dreams.

"I enjoy teaching the children songs," Kamlesh said, gesturing to the ten or fifteen children gathered around them.

Approaching the dispensary they were surprised to find a small crowd outside—young women listlessly straddling infants on their hips, elderly people hunched under a parched tree. Others stood stoically with their arms folded across their chests. The crowd parted for their group, and the roofless clinic became visible. A shell of four outer walls, dried mortar oozing between the bricks. Through the open doorway, Dr. Pendharkar, draped in a stethoscope, was attending to a woman patient seated in a chair.

Dipi led them up the cement steps, ordering the entourage of noisy children to remain outside. Their group waited to one side of what would be a two-room clinic while the doctor finished up with his patient, an adolescent girl sitting wearily with a naked baby in her lap. A few minutes later, the doctor stepped across to speak to them, and Bebeji made the introductions. Jaya remembered Dr. Pendharkar's calm method of speaking but had forgotten his modest appearance—a trim man in a faded half-sleeve shirt, cheap trousers, and scuffed leather sandals. Since the clinic's construction proceeded in fits and starts, she had not started working as his assistant, and the doctor kept no regular timings. He showed up whenever he had free time, and his assistant went around the colony beating a drum, letting the people know he was in attendance. The room he worked in was empty except for two armless chairs and a table holding his black bag, some bottles of medicine, and his assistant's odd little drum. For now the few pieces of furniture were stored in people's huts and brought out whenever the doctor appeared.

"There's been a big rush of people today," Dr. Pendharkar acknowledged in a troubled tone, "almost everyone suffering from acute gastrointestinal infection." All of them were collecting water from the same pond off the Agra Road, and some bug must have tainted the water. Fortunately he had a sugar-salt mixture with him to help with dehydration, but not enough, so he'd sent his assistant down to the market on Agra Road. Sarvi arranged a time to speak to the doctor later, after he was finished with his patients and Sarvi had taken a full round of the colony.

As they were about to leave, the doctor turned to Bebeji. "There was a disturbing incident earlier," he said. They all waited, listening. He seemed reluctant to speak, then proceeded. Two hooligans had appeared at the clinic, both drunk. One had gashes on his arm, a crude knife or homemade weapon appeared to have been used on him. Apparently a fight had broken out last night between this man and one of his relatives. Bebeji scowled. When Dr. Pendharkar inquired how he'd gotten the cuts, the man became belligerent. The doctor's assistant tried to intervene, and the injured man struck him in the face. His companion shoved the boy onto the table. The doctor ordered both the men to leave. Now he shook his head and seemed to feel guilty about sending away a patient. Bebeji let out a fearful sigh. "What is happening in this place?"

Jaya was alarmed. She hadn't heard of violent incidents on the hill. Kamlesh said the women sometimes fought. She'd seen a couple of vicious arguments, but never anyone in a physical fight. They all remained quiet, climbing to the school. The sight of the small, self-important building with its rippling tile roof pulled them out of the grim mood. Prabha met them outside. The photographer continued his ballet, capturing the schoolhouse with the teacher at the doorway from many vantage points. When Bebeji mentioned her plans for a women's literacy program to be offered in the building, after the children's school hours, Yashwant Halde took over the discussion. "We will include vocational training like embroidery lessons or making incense sticks," he announced. "There has to be a money-making angle to entice them, these women won't come just to learn alphabets."

They continued onward, introducing Sarvi to the residents' committee at Kalpana's hut. Dipi decided the men would continue up to the summit, so Sarvi could see the statue of Ganesha for which the colony was named, while Bebeji and the girls should return downhill and meet them at the factory. Jaya held her tongue. A thought flashed about the nasty Ratnagiri men who lived near the top. How they'd glowered at her and Kamlesh when they climbed up with the children that one time. Could the troublemakers at the clinic have come from that group? She didn't want to bring it up and add to everyone's unease. Only the men were going up, in any case. When the little boys tagged after them, Dipi turned them away—the hilltop was not a safe place for children to play! Bebeji heaved a long breath and said it was her fate never to see that beautiful carving everyone talked about.

Jaya and Kamlesh gripped Bebeji's arms tightly, the path downhill slippery along stretches of loose, sandy dirt with few stones. The children kept up a chatter with Kamlesh, and listening to the flittering conversation, Jaya felt a deep, whole-hearted relief. Kamlesh had fallen ill the day after their parents denied her her stage debut. Something inside her had fractured. She couldn't get out of bed, couldn't speak. Their father scolded her, thinking she was putting on an act in order to get what she wanted. He ordered her out of bed every morning, and for a few days she was able to comply, attending college as usual. As soon as she returned home, she would lie down. She had to be dragged to the table for meals. Her dance lessons were canceled. No amount of coaxing by Jaya or Bebeji succeeded in getting her up for a walk along the seafront or a drive to Chowpatty for kulfi, which she loved. Whatever had overcome Kamlesh, she was powerless to resist it.

She stopped attending college. She couldn't even sit straight in a chair, spending the day withdrawn, silent, often with a sheet pulled over her head in bed. Their parents were bewildered; they didn't know how to help her. Bebeji would sit at her bedside and take her hand, pleading with her to get up, take a bath. Kirti agreed with Jaya that it sounded like a deep depression.

One night, as she lay awake in bed beside Kamlesh, her motionless body draped in a bedsheet, it became apparent to Jaya what had to be done. The next morning, she spoke to her mother. They had to allow Kamlesh to have her arangetram, otherwise she would continue to deteriorate. Jaya was sure of it. Kamlesh had spent years giving her all to dance—countless hours of practice, lessons three or four times a week all the way out in Matunga. They had to consider all her effort, all her discipline, all her love for dance that went into that. To be denied her stage debut was a big blow. A shock to her system. Vidya was desperately worried. She, too, suspected Kamlesh's breakdown was connected to their decision. She agreed to speak to Harbans about Jaya's proposal. In the evening, her parents called Kamlesh to their room, as Jaya stood by, and told her they had reconsidered. She would be permitted to have her arangetram. They hadn't realized how important this one performance was to her. They hugged her, they held her. They just wanted her to be happy. To be herself.

Slowly, day by day, Kamlesh regained her ability to function. A wan smile returned. It would not be quite the grand stage show she had imagined, but she seemed satisfied. The barrier her parents had imposed between her and the performance she'd longed for had been lifted. That seemed to be enough for now.

A day later, Jaya disclosed to her parents that Bal Chadha had invited her to participate in a group exhibition. She had believed keeping silent about it would shield her from her parents' intrusive questions and admonitions, but silence had only ended up crippling her.

The scare over Kamlesh's health had softened them. She had never expected her parents to ask to meet Chadha. He came over with his wife, impressing them as a successful company man who nurtured younger painters on the side. His respectability, his association with a prestigious commercial firm, made all the difference in the world. Harbans agreed to let Jaya participate in the show as long as painting didn't detract from her studies. Chadha had confirmed that with a cordial smile when he said she must keep up her good marks.

A cluster of shanties, each a sturdy jigsaw of wood and tin with chinks of open space between the scraps, offered them a place to pause. Bebeji lowered herself onto a large stone. Kamlesh waved to some children playing nearby. "Oh, Wasima, I was wondering where you were," she cried out. The girl clutched her baby sister, bangles sparkling on the little one's arms. A flock of boys, aged between about three and twelve, dashed around her in the dust. Kamlesh knew all their names—Ali Mohammed, Yawar, Saeed, Suleiman. Wasima's brothers.

Their mother emerged from the shack, hurriedly draping her chunni around her head. Behind her followed her stooped, blind mother-in-law, turning her face up to greet the visitors. Jaya had not met them in a long time. Wasima's mother was quieter than she remembered and had to be drawn out with questions. Wasima was progressing well in school, her mother noted, nodding her head in small circles of satisfaction. Bebeji said she'd heard Prabha praise her. The mother smiled shyly. "She tries to teach her brothers to read, but they have no interest. No patience to sit down and learn." She cried out to the boys not to run too far, and an older child paused and turned back, acknowledging her tone of alarm.

In her thick, grainy voice, Bebeji, standing again, urged Wasima to take charge. "Make sure your brothers follow your example. Make them sit with you. Do sums with them, count up to one hundred."

"Suleiman is the only one who listens to me," Wasima replied, coming toward them. She swiftly wiped a streak of grime from the baby's cheek to make her more presentable. "The others have straw in their heads."

"Where's your friend?" Kamlesh said. "I haven't seen her today."

"Lakshmi's sick."

Her mother's expression grew solemn. "Yes, she's fallen ill." Immediately Jaya wondered if Ram Shree had been fetching water from the pond off the Agra Road. "I don't know of what," the mother muttered defiantly, as if she couldn't name the illness and shouldn't be asked to speak of it.

The arid ledge where Madan's shanty stood was nearly deserted, backed by a jagged wall of basalt on one side and overlooking the open fields on the other. A couple of anxious men hung about some yards away, near the dirt track. The doctor was inside, they said. Each of them was waiting to take him to a family member too sick to come to the dispensary. The door to the shanty was shut, a plank of weathered gray wood slanted at the bottom. Bebeji knocked. No one replied. "Doctor Sahib? Ram Shree?" A moment later, the doctor called out that he would be out soon.

They waited under the burning sun. Kamlesh passed around the water bottle she'd tucked into one of Heerabai's scruffy shopping bags. The door still didn't open. In a kind of despair, Kamlesh sat down in the hot dust half in the shade of a thatched shelter. The curved mud stove behind her was bedded with ash. Jaya remained standing though her feet ached. Finally the doctor stepped out and shut the door behind him. He squinted against the light, his shoulders slightly slumped. His face seemed thinner, the cheeks and mouth sunk in hollows. He looked different from the man they'd met an hour earlier.

He ushered them around to the side of the shanty, a short distance beyond which the land dropped away. Below lay a vast expanse of green and on the horizon rose the serrated black roofline of the furnace shed at the glassworks. Here they were out of the hearing range of the other two men, Dr. Pendharkar explained. He wanted to take Lakshmi to his clinic in town to do a thorough exam. "They lit two lamps for me, so I could see her inside the room," he said, "but it was like working blind. I couldn't see the full extent of her injuries. I don't think there's any internal damage, but I haven't been able to examine her properly. They don't want me to remove her from the hut."

"What happened, doctor?" said Jaya.

"May I go inside?" Kamlesh asked, as if she couldn't bear to hear an objective description of Lakshmi's injuries. "I'd like to see her."

"Go. It may lift her spirits. But beware. She's in a state of shock."

Kamlesh took her bag and went around to the door. Jaya considered following her, but she wanted first to know what had happened to Lakshmi. In truth she felt pure fear at the thought of confronting a child in great pain. So she remained in the blazing light, protecting herself.

Dr. Pendharkar's hands moved in waves across the air, drawing a connection between Lakshmi's injuries and the belligerent man who'd come to the clinic earlier—that man had fought a brother or cousin of his who had bothered a girl. Jaya was surprised. The doctor had kept this troubling information from them earlier. The doctor now believed that girl was Lakshmi. Not a girl, a mere child.

"The fellow hit her? Assaulted her?" Bebeji asked in the low tone of keeping things secret.

"Everything you can imagine," the doctor said. "He was a terrible man."

A sweat broke above Jaya's lip, and she felt the heat of the sun intensely. There was the woozy sense of plummeting, as she'd experienced in the dissection hall. She stepped back against the splintered outer wall of the shanty, trying to pin herself to something solid. "Does she know who it is?"

"I didn't want to ask too many questions," the doctor said. "She's too hurt. But last night, after she was found, she talked to her parents. It's remarkable how much she could tell them. Perhaps she was in a delirium. She said he had some teeth missing. A small mustache. He's one of those men who lives near the top of the hill, she said."

Madan stepped out of his jhopadi. Perhaps he felt uncomfortable remaining inside with Kamlesh. Bebeji immediately asked him when this had happened. Where had Lakshmi been? Madan began to cough. He turned his head to cough into his hand, and after a moment Jaya realized he was crying. It was a choked, sputtering cry as if he didn't know how to cry, or hadn't cried since he was a child. He wiped his eyes as he replied to Bebeji's question. "Four, five o'clock yesterday."

Jaya turned to go inside the hut, afraid of what she would find. A smell of humid soil engulfed her in the black tightness—a sensation of entering a burrow inside the earth. The boy, Shankar, lay on a pallet of gray cloth, making nonsense sounds. *Tan, tan, han, han.* Kamlesh huddled on the ground beside Lakshmi. She was tangled up in some dirty bedding. "Tell the doctor if it's paining too much," Kamlesh encouraged her. "He'll take you to his clinic. They'll give you a nice comfortable bed to sleep in and your pain will go away."

Two kerosene lanterns illuminated the girl's head. Her hair was combed back in a plait, only slightly disheveled, but there were abrasions all over her face, too many to count, as though someone had held her by the neck and rubbed her face into the stones. The doctor had applied tincture of iodine to the cuts and tears on her lips, so her mouth looked all the more red—a swollen bruise.

"Lakshmi," Jaya said, squatting beside Kamlesh. "You'll get well, Lakshmi. Don't worry. Doctor Sahib will examine you and give you the right medicines. Okay? Will you come out? He can look at you in his clinic down below, in the town."

Lakshmi appeared to be far away. Her eyes were lost in a vacant stare. Jaya wasn't sure if she could hear her. She lifted the girl's wrist to take her pulse and saw her hand was bloodied.

"Let her be, she wants to rest. She wants to sleep." The mother's plea was sudden and vehement. Jaya turned toward the voice and made out Ram Shree, sitting with her head lowered as usual, in the shadows behind the baby.

"I didn't see you," Jaya apologized.

The doctor came in and they shifted away, giving him space. He bent down on his haunches, observing Lakshmi for a long moment. "I'll take you to the clinic. I can carry you, or your father can carry you."

Lakshmi didn't respond, so the doctor repeated himself softly. "No," the child whispered. "I want to stay here."

"Chalo, Madan," Bebeji said, entering the tiny room with the father behind her. The six adults filled up the space. "Help Doctor Sahib with Lakshmi."

Jaya expected Madan to refuse. She thought he would insist on keeping his daughter sheltered inside the room, but Bebeji apparently had persuaded him to let her undergo a proper examination. Over the course of a few minutes, hushing his wife's objections, Madan brought his arms around his daughter. In the periphery of the lamplight, Jaya noticed a shimmery stone, glittering with mica, that someone had probably tried to distract her with. Madan straightened up and lifted the girl from the grimy cloths. One side of her bodice was torn. There was another gash in the cloth at the back. She was wearing her soiled skirt below, loose around the waist so as not to cause her any discomfort. Then they saw it was completely ripped from top to bottom and merely laid around her like a wrap. Madan asked his wife for something more to cover her with. Ram Shree rose, went to a box on the opposite side of the room, and pulled out a crushed yellow veil and draped it around her daughter. Bebeji patted the child's shoulder. "It's all right, Lakshmi."

"You're a brave girl," Jaya told her.

Silently the mother returned to her place in the shadows, watching Shankar. Jaya stepped outside the door. Madan was carrying his daughter toward the dirt track, Kamlesh following him, murmuring words of encouragement to Lakshmi. Dr. Pendharkar lagged a few feet behind. He put his hand out, indicating Jaya should stay back. She was apprehensive about possibly having to assist him with Lakshmi's exam but felt she must ask. "You don't require my help, Doctor?" The doctor instructed her to stay with her grandmother, who remained in the hut with Ram Shree. "It's very disturbing at her age," he said, referring to Bebeji, "to be confronted with a situation like this."

"What exactly happened, Doctor?" Jaya felt compelled to know.

The doctor hesitated, then came closer to speak to her. "She had gone to gather some sticks for her mother to light the chula for the evening meal. There's a patch of trees lower down, where she finds firewood easily. That fellow saw her. He told her that her brother had fallen somewhere and was badly injured. Her mother was calling for her. She followed him around to a track that connects to the next hill. He led her farther and farther away, way down to a ledge covered with boulders. Everywhere she looked were huge stones. Her mother said that's what she was babbling last night. Stones everywhere. She started screaming when he threw her down. There was no one nearby. I don't know everything, Madan doesn't want to tell me. 'He touched her,' he said. He's telling people the fellow tried to push her down from the boulders. He's afraid she'll become a pariah if people find out the truth." The English word *rape* came like a blow. Jaya felt a shot to her stomach, a dull sensation of swaying. She knew of no equivalent word in Hindi, only allusions. *Touched, teased, hit*—she didn't want to believe it could be more than that.

"She hasn't urinated since then, the parents say," the doctor continued in a low voice. "I want to make sure there's no damage to the urethra or any other organ." Jaya's ears burned. The doctor would not have confided this information to her grandmother or to Kamlesh. But she had asked, wanting to know. She was a medical student—it was her duty to understand the clinical details of an injury. As it was the doctor's duty to heal wounds, determine the proper course of treatment. Dr. Pendharkar always appeared tranquil and self-contained, yet even he needed to share the burden of this sorrowful knowledge. "He told her to stay there," the doctor continued. "Never to leave or he would come back and find her. She was so frightened, she obeyed him. She didn't try to climb out of there. But when it began to get dark, she became afraid and started screaming. Two women passing by above, some distance from the ledge, heard her and called back. Somehow she found her way out of that rubble area by following their voices. When they saw her, she was wearing nothing below. Ram Shree went back today and found her ghagra."

Ram Shree was sitting inside the hut with her head uncovered when Jaya returned. Her face was now partially lit by the lamps, which had been moved closer to her and Bebeji. Her fidgeting, babbling boy lay in her lap. "Mataji, she's such a good girl, such a clever girl—why does God make her suffer like this? All the time she was worried about her brother. Any time she was ready to do whatever work I asked. She was my only child for so long, we could have no more children after her. We went to so many devi temples, praying for a son. Then he was born after so many years and his legs are no good. He can't talk. He can't move. He's a son in body only." She rubbed Shankar's bare thighs vigorously. "Now, she is a body only. That man has taken everything out of her. Why did God have to destroy both children?"

"She'll be all right," Bebeji said firmly. "She'll recover. We can take her to a hospital if the doctor says it's necessary."

Jaya sat away from them, beside the closed door, allowing them their conversation.

"No! It won't be all right! Even a hospital can't make her all right." Ram Shree's voice boomed inside the room's black enclosure. It felt as if Jaya were trapped inside the mother's throbbing voice, inside the throat the words sprang from. "Everyone will find out what happened to her. Those women from the other side who brought her will tell people. My husband told them not to say anything, but I'm sure some have already heard what happened. My husband went to kill that fellow, why else would he do that? He tried to burn down all those Ratnagiri people's huts, but that man's relations stopped him. He told everyone the man beat our child, but they'll come to know what really happened. She'll live in shame, we'll all live in shame."

Bebeji leaned toward her. Her words came out in a low rasp, almost inaudible to Jaya just a few feet away. "We can file a police case against him. They'll throw him in jail for what he did."

Ram Shree shook her head vehemently, her hair tumbling out of its loose knot. "What had to happen has happened. He ruined her. Whether he's punished or not, she's been punished forever. So much blood there was. She's torn, all torn inside. I wiped her wounds, I saw it. What more does the doctor need to see? She's completely ruined—isn't that enough?"

16

FOR TWO MONTHS Jaya and Kamlesh stayed away from the shanty colony. Vidya forbade them from returning, terrified they were as vulnerable to assault as a child. Nothing the girls said could shake their mother's tenacious fear that their lives would be in danger if they climbed the hill once more. Their mother's prohibition also happened to align with circumstances: Kamlesh had to study several years' worth of course materials for her BA exams in April. She would have to suspend her songs and games class for at least six weeks. Since the clinic remained unfinished, the doctor saw patients on an improvised schedule, leaving Jaya no predictable role as an assistant. Although the twins hadn't returned to the busti, they had gone with Bebeji to see Lakshmi days after she was admitted to the small hospital in the bazaar in Thana. It was the same hospital to which they'd brought her baby brother the first time Madan took them to the hill a year and a half ago. Ram Shree cooked Lakshmi's meal in the veranda outside her hospital room where patients' families camped. It made them happy to see Lakshmi able to sit up and eat. She looked smaller without her veil, her bruised face plain to see. She ate little but when they heard her say the vegetable was delicious, the simple word *sawad* gave them hope for her. Bebeji pressed some notes into Ram Shree's hand before they left. Kamlesh lifted Lakshmi's scratched fingers and kissed them. Jaya wanted to say, "I'm going to make a beautiful picture of you," but she was afraid that might only demoralize Lakshmi, reminding her of the terrible thing that had been done to her.

The painting of Lakshmi remained an image in Jaya's mind. By making it real she worried she might betray the injured child, remembering the gallant girl she had been. Several other figures from the busti had been abandoned on small canvases on the balcony. Kamlesh stepped out to join her there one muggy late April morning, following her exams, her back obstinately turned to the old man in the next building. He peered at them from his balcony—a bloated, swarthy face with hair as white as cotton wool. Jaya unwound the strings of the bamboo blinds and lowered them halfway to block out his face. Rummaging through shriveled old tubes of Camel paints, she pierced the clotted necks of lamp black and sap green with the tip of a paring knife. Swiftly she wiped the smeared knife with a cloth then thrust the tip into a tube of brilliant blue sealed with a dried callus of pigment. "Hema asked me to share her hostel room with her," she told her sister, "but I can't ask them for that. They wouldn't want to pay for a room when I can stay at home."

It might console Kamlesh to know Jaya was also prevented from leaving home to prepare the paintings for her exhibition. Their father's soft but firm no to Kamlesh's wish to shift to her dance teacher's flat had come as another blow. Jaya felt the full weight of her twin's grief as they lay silently in bed at night, knowing his decision was irrevocable. She worried her sister might fall ill again, but Kamlesh managed to study, though she was noticeably subdued. She was aware she'd lost a great deal of practice time, first because she'd been sick with depression, then due to preparing for exams. When he returned, Masterji would decide whether or not to postpone her performance until the end of November. This month he was away on his annual holiday to replenish himself among the paddy fields in his ancestral village in Madras. On the balcony Kamlesh distracted herself with the paints, lightly squeezing the unclogged tubes for a glimpse of bright pigment. She looked upset, but Jaya was afraid to probe. It had been so reassuring to see her regain her discipline in the absence of her guru. To see her full of purpose, practicing on her own, had soothed Jaya's enormous worry for her sister. Even during her exam study period, Kamlesh had put on an old salwar and sari blouse and closed off the bedroom for an hour every day. They heard the thunderous slapping of her feet, the thuds of her jumps and leaps rattling the furniture. The downstairs neighbors had sent their servant up a couple of times to complain of the noise.

"Share a room with Hema? Why?" Kamlesh glanced up at Jaya, hurt and skeptical. "Is it to see more of him?"

"Not at all. I wouldn't shift to campus for that." Hema wanted to be free of her roommate, Jaya said, a chatterbox who gave her no peace and was always leaving her dirty plates around the room. In May, girls had a chance to change their living situations. Although Jaya was a day scholar, the warden made exceptions for local girls who applied for a room in order to study. Privately Jaya thought Hema just wanted a good friend to lean on in the roommate's place, since Farrokh had dropped out of her life. He'd graduated, started his practice on Pedder Road, and gotten engaged to a Parsi girl to please his parents. Jaya had contemplated asking her father if she could shift to campus, wondering if she might have more privacy to paint in the hostel. But that would be impossible, she quickly realized, with Hema in the room all the time.

"You're still meeting him, aren't you?" Kamlesh sounded concerned that they might lose Kirti. Jaya reassured her. Kamlesh was anxious for Kirti to remain fixed in their lives, yet never occupy the central place in Jaya's affections that belonged to her.

Jaya nodded. Kamlesh already knew they met every morning in the hospital these days, since Jaya had started on a surgical rotation and Kirti assisted a registrar in the ward in presenting patients to her student group and teaching them how to conduct examinations and take down patient histories. He would watch her carefully when the honorary arrived, and she had to answer questions posed by the distinguished, British-educated doctor. In public they maintained the customary formality between an MBBS student and a house surgeon. But Kamlesh didn't know that late in the afternoon, Kirti would take her to the grimy Light of Asia on Girgaum Back Road, its obscure location preferable to the Prince of Wales and also nearer to her home. Every two or three days, he would buy her a full meal for a few rupees—pullao, fried mutton liver, a lemon barley. Talking, joking, touching hands under the table for a moment were the few intimacies permitted them. Desire accumulated in her like an ache and had nowhere to go but into looks and words.

Jaya found their frequent meetings a beautiful escape, since she'd gathered no momentum with her exhibition paintings. A sense of despair bloomed; the possibility of giving up seemed more likely every day. The clear vision she'd had for her paintings earlier in the year had dissolved into confusion. Her paintings of Kamlesh dancing, an emblem of shakti, the raw, golden energy of life, had been disrupted by images of the women on the hill. Some of these she'd rendered as wisps of lines and dabs of color on canvas. But she could discover no principle by which to unite these two sets of images. Her wonder at the notion of shakti had eroded with the shock of seeing sweet Lakshmi lying so terribly wounded on the floor of her hut. A certain faith in life had been stamped out at that moment.

It seemed to be the same for Kamlesh. They'd imagined the worst had happened to Lakshmi when she was nearly pushed off the summit; she and Kamlesh had reveled in her good luck at escaping that catastrophe. Then they'd seen life was more merciless than that. A child could be destroyed for no reason at all.

"He just goes on looking." Kamlesh framed her face in her hands to shut out the old man staring. He had sat down on a chair on his balcony, with a clear view of them.

"Maybe he's the reason." Jaya meant the man's persistent gaze might have inhibited her from painting the pictures she saw in her mind. She squatted in front of the hobbled sideboard and put away the battered tubes of paint. A folded-up newspaper lay beneath some drawings on the top shelf. Taking out the paper, she was surprised by the ink drawing she'd made on the back page weeks—months—ago. A woman, shoulders sagging, sitting down in the dirt with one leg extended. A memory of Kamlesh waiting outside Lakshmi's hut, the leg extended as if she'd taken a dancer's pose. Her body was scarred by dark cross-hatchings that bled into the newsprint. Kamlesh came over to look. Jaya turned the pages of the March 1, 1955, issue of the *National Standard* until she landed on Sarvi's article, "Workers Struggle for Survival in Hillside Slum." Kamlesh tried to smooth flat the large, grainy picture under the headline. A group of women with bulging earthen pots on their heads gathered anxiously around the handpump, their faces contorted in grimaces. A passing goat framed the lower edge of the picture. Straightaway, in the first paragraph, Sarvi accused the Thana government of doing so little for industrial laborers that their safe harbor against eviction from public lands was to occupy a thirteen-hundred-foot-tall mountain. Had the tyranny of British rule been overthrown for a homegrown system of neglect?

"Hai," Kamlesh exclaimed, full of emotion. "Hai, look at them all standing so sweetly."

In a second picture, below the fold, the children stood in front of the school with Prabha, all holding their arms rigid at their sides, proud of their role as students. The signboard emblazoned over the door read, *Ganesh Murti Nagar Primary School.*

Lakshmi had not returned to school. She was too scared to leave her mother's shadow, Prabha had reported to Bebeji. Their grandmother continued to visit the colony once or twice a month, since she was not subject to their mother's orders. The residents' committee members escorted her from the factory up to the hill and back. Early on, Jaya and Kamlesh had asked Bebeji to intervene with their mother, but she had made a rare concession to Mummy's wishes. "If something happens to either one of you, what would we do? As a mother, Vidya has a right to protect you." Jaya had come to understand that any act of molestation could ruin a girl. If others came to know, no boy would want to marry you. A girl's life was a fragile thing; it could very easily be broken.

Still, the day they rediscovered Sarvi's feature on the colony, they took the paper to their mother. Vidya lay on her side in bed during her afternoon rest, reading it once again with absorption. Her fear for her daughters' safety did not mean she lacked sympathy for the poor. Two months back, when Lakshmi had been assaulted, sheer panic had caused her to cry out, "I'm not going to sacrifice my daughters for the sake of those poor people on the hill. Is it our fault they have to live as they do?" After finishing the story, and hearing her daughters out, she agreed to let Jaya and Kamlesh go back to the colony one last time. They would be allowed to accompany Bebeji when she went for her next residents' committee meeting.

To prepare for their visit, the sisters took a bus to Colaba Causeway and bought two dozen tiny colored glass bangles. They bought cotton chunnis in turquoise and orange that a little girl could wear as a veil. A tailor stitched a long skirt and tunic in materials they chose. You couldn't drop out of sight of a child who had suffered so much without seeing if she was better, returning to a semblance of her childish self.

PASSING THROUGH THE belt of trees that circled the base of the hill, Jaya and Kamlesh came upon the familiar sight of women gathering fallen sticks and branches for firewood. One hacked the dry limbs off a tree. They greeted the women, who inquired why the twins hadn't come around lately. "They have to study too much," Bebeji replied. Two of her residents' committee members, who were escorting them, smiled agreeably. On the zigzagging path up the hill, a few goats trekked ahead of them, and women they did not recognize passed by them, carrying large, flat baskets on their heads, as if they were on their way to the bazaar to sell something. Jaya and Kamlesh insisted they would go by themselves to see Lakshmi, so Bebeji and the man and woman on her residents' committee continued onward to their meeting. Ram Shree was sitting in front of her hut with her knees bent up and her head down, as if she were asleep or in a stupor. Hearing the girls, she got up and adjusted her veil around her face, giving them a small smile. She summoned Lakshmi, repeatedly calling her name.

The child emerged from the hut. A faint look of recognition passed over her face when Kamlesh went to her, and then her eyes went blank. They unpacked her presents from their bag, asking how she was. They helped her slip her new glass bangles around her wrists. Her mother asked her to take off her old chunni, and the sisters draped the bright turquoise veil over her uncombed hair. Then they sat down in the dirt with Ram Shree. Kamlesh beckoned Lakshmi to sit next to her, but she preferred to stay at the threshold of the hut, as if to retreat to safety at any moment if she needed to. They had more questions for her—was she going back to school soon? How was Shankar? Was she still playing a lot with Wasima? Lakshmi's eyes were far away. She didn't seem to know them anymore. They wanted her to smile, to talk, to say yes she wanted to go back to school; they wanted her to look excited about the new bangles and new clothes they had bought her, but she wasn't able to do any of that. Kamlesh teased her, went to sit next to her, but Lakshmi didn't speak more than a word or two. They wanted to make her happy, to make her smile, but they couldn't take away what had happened to her.

"Shankar's crying," she said quietly. At first Jaya didn't hear her. Kamlesh repeated her words. Then they all heard the faint cries from the hut. He was almost two years old now, and he couldn't move.

"Go!" said her mother. "Go and see what he wants." Lakshmi remained sitting, staring at the ground. Her mother commanded her again. Kamlesh put her hand on her back, and she finally stood and went inside. Jaya could see Ram Shree wanted her daughter to do everyday things, to move, to be part of life.

"For that," Ram Shree cried, pointing to the chula that stood on the ground under the thatch-roofed shelter Madan had built near the rock wall. The low horseshoe-shaped clay burner she cooked food on. Sticks and ash were piled in the center space. "She used to worry about snakes when she went to collect firewood. How could we ever imagine a grown man would come for her?"

The man had run away, the sisters knew. Jaya had spoken to Dr. Pendharkar the night they admitted Lakshmi to the civil hospital after he examined her in his clinic. She had suffered no serious internal injuries, but he wanted her to be attended by doctors while she healed. She was put on a sulfa drug. Ultimately, neither the doctor nor Bebeji was in favor of filing a police case, although a medical exam at the hospital confirmed she had been raped. Police involvement would bring the incident to the entire colony's attention. People would be questioned. Everyone would talk about it. The stigma would be unbearable for a child. She would be shunned, smeared. The doctor thought Madan clever to portray the assault as a drunken madman's attempt to kill his daughter and said they should all speak of it as that—as a beating—even if a rumor about rape were to circulate. Since the incident Madan had lost his status as a Communist union man on the shop floor. He'd failed to protect his daughter's honor, Dipi explained quietly to Jaya and Kamlesh one afternoon, so his own honor was lost. None of the workers could respect him anymore.

"My husband wants to leave this place. I also want to go." Ram Shree said they had been sending money to their family, in their village, for years to buy bricks to build a house. They still didn't have enough bricks, and if they went back, there would be no work for her husband, but it would be better than this, than living in fear. She didn't know when someone else might try to touch her daughter. They might think her ruined and prey on her. It didn't matter what more was done to her. She was spoiled. Someone had told her there were men talking like that. Jaya felt her throat go tight at the shock of those words.

When they got up to leave, they stood at the threshold and called to Lakshmi. She came outside. She smelled of the earth, of the soil, and when Jaya hugged her she was surprised by the force of the girl's embrace, the way she clenched her arms around Jaya's waist so tightly, full of need and emotion. Jaya held her a long time, feeling the pain of tears in her eyes.

Lakshmi was still a part of life, Jaya thought when she returned home. She had felt it in her hug, the girl she used to be, who had sung to her brother all the qualities of the dancing Ganesha, who had clapped in his ears to make him hear. Wasn't that shakti? She had thought of shakti as physical vigor, the life energy embodied by a dancer leaping through the air, turning, bending, swaying, making her hands flutter, stretching them into bows and arrows. Now it occurred to her the purest energy was emotion. Maybe shakti was all motion fueled by the vitality of emotion.

TOWARD THE END of the first week of her six-week-long half-day holidays, when she attended morning rounds in the hospital but had her afternoons free of lectures in pathology, pharmacology, and forensic medicine, Jaya took a bus down to the sea at Warden Road. She watched the sun's glitter on the water from the back veranda of the Gokuldas Daftary Memorial Institute, listened for a few minutes to what sounded like the recitation of dialogue from somewhere inside. Probably the theater group rehearsing. A little later, she found her way to Sringara's studio, and she shyly inquired if Sringara's offer was still good. "Would it be all right if I came to paint in your flat? I can't seem to get anything done on the balcony, and I've got my afternoons free for the next five weeks."

Sringara rested her cigarette on an ashtray. She was sitting in her chair, contemplating a painting, but she seemed excited by Jaya's query. "I've just gotten rid of my paying guests, a very quarrelsome couple. What a headache they gave me. You can paint in the spare room until I find someone reputable to take it. You'll have more privacy than in the drawing room." She returned to examining her picture and asked Jaya what she thought. A woman stood in a dark forest. Jaya went closer, intrigued.

Since her father had consented to her taking part in Chadha's exhibition, she had decided to ask him for permission to spend her free afternoons at Sringara's in support of that project. The biggest obstacle would be to persuade her parents to let her regularly visit the home of a spinster. That's the name anyone would give Sringara, who was somewhere between thirty and forty years of age and unmarried. Her mother sometimes had odd fears; maybe she'd worry that by going to a spinster's house Jaya might end up one herself.

Her father was sitting at his desk in his bedroom, some office files open in front of him on a Saturday afternoon. "Why do you want to squander your time painting?" he asked as if he didn't remember agreeing to the exhibition. "Why not read ahead in your subjects so you're better prepared for lectures when your classes resume?"

She was dependent on her parents for all her privileges connected to painting—the money for her supplies, her lessons with Tule, the small black-and-white art books she occasionally bought. She was dependent on them for every liberty she had, so she knew she had to agree to all of Harbans's conditions. She would spend an hour a day reading ahead; she would bring all her painting materials home when her holidays ended. A fear that she would not make the grade in medical college seemed to plague her father, as though all his efforts to tutor her in science and help secure her admission would go to waste. He had lived under a similar tension working for the colonial government when she was young; she had always sensed a fear in him that he might err in his job and fail in the eyes of his British superiors. Now he was passing on his worries about failure to her like an inheritance she didn't want.

When Vidya heard where Sringara's flat was located, she put down her novel and pulled off her glasses. "My word, is that where you expect to find peace and quiet? In a bazaar area? With crowds all around?" What baffled her more was that Sringara was not a widow, but a woman living alone.

Vidya wanted to see Sringara's flat for herself. Kamlesh was reluctant to be left out, despite her hostility to the idea of Jaya painting her exhibition pictures away from home. Like most people, Sringara had no telephone so Jaya couldn't ring her in advance. The three of them set off late on a Friday afternoon, pretending it was a social visit. Vidya powdered her face light beige and wore a silk sari as if she had been invited to a ladies' tea. Kamlesh put on dangling earrings and her heeled sandals. The driver fought his way through traffic with his horn. Bellasis Road ran above the northern boundary of the red-light district, Kamathipura. The prostitutes' iron-barred rooms, known as their "cages," were between Sringara's flat and J. J. Hospital, just out of sight. After driving past Sringara's building once, the driver discovered a short lane branching off the main road to a middle-class housing complex. They parked in the sunken lane, the steam engines shrieking out of Bombay Central on the opposite side of the road.

Jaya pushed open a rusted iron gate, entering a forecourt where an ema-ciated cat darted away from small children chasing her. Lines of washing hung on the balconies. Three cement buildings wore layers of black damp from years of monsoons. Kamlesh wrinkled her nose at the compound's shabbiness. It took Jaya a couple of minutes to locate Sringara's building among the three, and to find her aunt's name on a massive wooden board in the dingy foyer listing the occupants. A lot of Parsi and Muslim names, but her mother made no remark. She complained of having to climb four stories, *Ramamurthy* located on the topmost floor. The black stairwell reeked of animal fur, and a dog's frightened yelping sounded in the dark-ness. Someone had drawn delicate rice-powder designs of crescent moons and fishes at the edges of the sagging wooden stairs. Jaya took heart in the images soliciting good fortune as they climbed up.

Sringara came to the door with her hair spilling out of an untidy bun and the top hook of her blouse undone. She appeared to have been napping after her return home from the studio. Despite a slightly dazed expression, she immediately invited them inside.

Struck by the great absence in Sringara's drawing room, Vidya asked, "You've just shifted here?" The room was bare of decoration, sparsely fur-nished with two rows of bent-cane chairs facing each other and a couple of small tables at the ends. A powdery membrane of soot from the road blackened the high blue ceiling and the blades of the ceiling fan. The only adornment was a wall shelf lined with books and a broken clock in a humped wooden case traced with a gilt line.

"No, Auntie," Sringara said. "My aunt lived very simply. I'm used to the same. In the South, we don't go in much for ornaments. But I have the parrots." Two tall domed cages stood on either side of the open balcony doors, a bright blue parrot and a green bird shuffling on their perches.

Quickly divining the purpose of their visit—and confirming it with a glance at Jaya—Sringara summoned her plump, smiling servant girl to bring coffee and toured them through the flat. They stepped into a dining room without a stick of furniture, a tidy kitchen, its shelves lined with brass utensils, and a stone counter occupied by a row of shiny idols before which Kamlesh lingered for a moment, bowing her head. Flicking on the bulb in the storeroom, Sringara suggested Jaya could keep her finished pictures here. Sometimes the Germans brought over visitors from abroad who were interested in buying Indian art.

"You don't keep any paintings at home? Jaya was saying they're quite lovely," Kamlesh inquired, She appeared not to notice a canvas stashed beside some metal trunks in a corner. The top of the painting was visible, showing the thatched roof of a hut. It brought to mind the picture Sringara had been working on at her studio last week. Jaya would have liked to see the finished picture but didn't ask. Kamlesh seemed to be seeking some proof from Sringara, an image by which they could know who she was. The wild depiction of a woman in the picture Jaya had seen would only have horrified her.

Sringara's facial muscles tensed, resurrecting the humorless instructor from the J. J. School of Art. "I paint all my pictures at the studio. I only bring them here if I know some foreigners are coming. At the moment, I've sold most of my pictures."

Jaya offered her congratulations. Mummy wore a pinched mouth full of unsaid words. A strand of pearls glowed at her throat. The question at the heart of her concerns erupted: "You've not gotten married, Sringara? Why not?"

Sringara gazed down regretfully, as if she were enacting the look of contrition people expected of an unmarried woman. "No. It wasn't meant to be,

Auntie. Things didn't work out. That's all." To Jaya's surprise there seemed to be real emotion in her expression—a genuine sense of disappointment.

On their way out of the compound, traffic bleating loudly on the road, Kamlesh made eyes at Jaya. Mummy shook her head in disapproval. The two of them looked as if they felt they had been somehow tricked. "What kind of artist is she?" Kamlesh said. "No decorations on the walls, not even a photograph. Not a single painting?"

Despite her mother's misgivings, she permitted Jaya, who clamored for a painting space, to use the apartment as her temporary studio. The only room Sringara had not shown them on their tour of the flat was the spare bedroom where Jaya was to paint. She was in the midst of putting the room in order, she'd said, after her paying guests shifted out. Her servant girl, Amvi, a friendly young woman, unlocked it for Jaya two days later when she brought Kamlesh to the flat with her again. Sringara was at her studio. The door, which the girl had to push hard to unstick, gave way to musty air smelling of damp and mold. Amvi drew back the thick curtains. In the natural light, they saw the crumbling walls, the green pigment cracked off in huge patches, showing chalky plaster underneath. A tall mound of brown coconuts occupied a dim corner like a strange sculpture. When Jaya asked Amvi about them, she said the coconuts were drying. It took months for the meat inside to shrink to a sweet, oily ball, which was chopped up and eaten like candy in the South. An easel stood nearby, against the wall.

Kamlesh hesitated at the threshold, as though she were entering the room against her will. Jaya wanted the first painting she created at Sringara's to be of her twin, so she might win Kamlesh's approval to continue painting here. If she painted other women first, Kamlesh might become jealous, and unintentionally or even deliberately sabotage her efforts. Kamlesh's dance costume was folded in a valise that she was reluctant to put down anywhere. Finally she placed it on the floor beneath the window and ventured into the murky corner where the coconuts were piled. "Hard as a stone," she said, picking one up and rattling it. "There must be a hundred coconuts here. How many can she eat? There may be rats running around."

A bare bed—narrow for a couple—a tall bedside table, and a plain mahogany chest of drawers were positioned against the walls. The room appeared to be waiting for a new occupant. Jaya carried the easel to a spot where light through a window fell on it from behind. It worried her that such a spacious, private room might not be available to her for very long. Sringara's aunt, widowed young, had always rented out the room for additional income.

Kamlesh complained of the floor being unswept, as she changed into her silky dance sari, a rich violet-and-gold costume her mother allowed her to purchase for inspiration many months ahead of her stage debut. Kamlesh hooked on her jewelry. Without apology, Jaya carried the end table across to her easel and unpacked her cloth bag, setting out paint tubes, brushes, bottles of pungent turpentine and linseed oil, and two palette knives, like a surgeon's ensemble of tools.

When she finished preparing her worktable, she took a long moment to study her twin. Thrusting Kamlesh's hips sharply to the right, pushing her chest out in the opposite direction, bending her body in two lush concatenated curves—an S—Jaya improvised a pose from the spirit of her model. Kamlesh added her own flourish, flinging her arms overhead in joy, the heels of her hands joined together in alapadma, her palms blooming open like lotuses. Her jewelry, Vidya's pearl choker and gold-garland wedding necklace hanging to her breastbone, bell-shaped earrings, and a wide false gold belt pinching her waist, brought glittering lines of definition to her figure. In the painting, her hair came down in long dark strokes with sienna lights, loose and unjeweled. Jaya left off her elaborate costume on canvas, wrapping Kamlesh in thin scarlet cloth trimmed in a deep blue border. Her foot, drawn in henna-red paint, was raised to fall in a loud slap, dispelling the night. She was the dark dancer of morning, Usha, goddess of dawn, her arms thrown up giddily to the skies, her gleaming foot poised to stamp the day into motion.

17

SIX THIRD-YEAR STUDENTS sat in a small classroom opposite the surgical ward, Jaya and Hema paired at one end of the row, near a dust-encrusted pedestal fan. The patient lay flat on his back on a cot, his hands folded under his head, his pajamas pulled down around his ankles. Sir had spread a sheet over his bony legs, leaving his enormous, swollen scrotum and the tiny black hook of his penis exposed. They watched Sir lean over the patient and expertly press his fingers across the boy's stomach, locating a second swelling extending to the right and left of the umbilicus. The quick-moving, sharp-minded Gujarati surgeon straightened up, leaving chalky fingerprints on the boy's taut brown abdomen. The patient, Behram, was a nineteen-year-old village boy suffering from a scrotal mass.

On the blackboard Sir had drawn a diagram of the nine zones of the abdomen in the shape of a shield. Sir rinsed his hands in a basin of milky disinfectant and toweled them dry, recapitulating Behram's case for them. "He was operated on for a swelling in the right testicle one year ago in his village. Three months ago he started feeling pain in the lower abdomen and noticed a swelling there. He began losing weight. Twenty days ago, he started vomiting his food, which means some part of the GI tract is getting obstructed, probably duodenal." He gazed directly at the students for emphasis. "This is a good, rare case of testicular malignancy with metastasis to the abdomen. Knowing his history, we can correlate the two swellings, but this is not always the case. Be open-minded."

Jaya wrote in her copybook, *History of Patient's Anguish* and underlined the heading. She was back to a rotation in surgery after one in medicine, where this title came to her as she took down patient histories in the wards and heard bits about their lives in the narrations of their illness. *This happened to my son. That happened to my husband. We lost our house because*—At the start of class today, when Sir had turned the grimacing boy on his side, enumerating the different types of abdominal pain, Jaya had sketched his whittled body, stressing the curved protrusions of his hipbones and shoulders. She had drawn the black hollows of his narrow back, shading in darkly the skin tarnished by the tobacco-leaf paste his people had applied as a counterirritant to the pain of the tumor in his abdomen. One pain to take away from the agony of another.

An hour later, Jaya had stopped sketching the boy. He had shed his power to affect her, coming to exist as a mere specimen, diseased and weak, subordinate to their need to study him. This was the approach of medical science: it separated you from your subject, inserted a cold space for observation and analysis, bringing you closer to the illness, not the person.

In painting you took a step back from your work only so you could find your way more deeply into your subject. Sringara had been sitting in the lime-green velvet armchair in her studio last month when Jaya went to ask about painting in her flat, her studio in complete disorder, with tables, easels, and canvases strewn everywhere, which Jaya hadn't noticed at first, in her nervousness to request the favor. Sringara had been "sitting and staring," as she called it, at an unfinished picture on an easel. A black figure crouched in a heavily shadowed grove of palm trees into which light sifted like rain, the woman a piece of the surrounding forest, her bare breasts half-visible through her sari. Often an image came together when she stopped painting and let her mind roam, Sringara said. In clear flashes she saw what she must do with it, how to form it, where to lay shadow and where to lay color. Jaya had listened attentively, remembering that sense of revelation that she, too, had experienced.

Sringara had remained in her chair, looking over her painting. "She needs her knife," she'd said all of a sudden. The woman who worked on her uncle's lands in their ancestral village moved through the trees hunching like that, she recalled, with a cutlass in her hand to split open coconuts, maybe to protect herself. Jaya had moved close to the picture, painted in deep tones of green, brown, and black, imagining the curve of a large blade in the woman's hands, like Kali raising her weapons.

At the conclusion of class, Sir invited the students to palpate the patient's double swellings. The boy stared fiercely at the ceiling, refusing to acknowledge them. Jaya held him in her gaze. She was the last in the queue, hesitating to approach him, to subject him to her fondling hands and remarks in alien English. As a kind of blessing, his people had tied thick strands of red thread around his neck and circled his pubic area with a black string. Never before had she handled a living man's organ, never touched Kirti there, had only once nauseously dissected the bulbs and stem of a cadaver's genitalia. She watched Hema palpate the boy's scrotum deeply. "It's hard," Hema confirmed about the swelling in a hoarse, unemotional voice. "Harder to the right, softer to the left. Not pulsating." After two others took their turns, Jaya reluctantly brought her fingers down to the boy's groin, checking his lymph nodes for swelling, brushing over his cowering black penis. Shifting her fingertips to the warm balloon of his huge scrotum, she tried to gain his confidence. The boy shut his eyes. Her fingers moved slowly to his inflated right testis, feeling the softly wrinkled flesh around the tumor, then pushed into the leaden ball of tissue, the malignant hardness whose size she needed to assess. When she was finished, she could breathe again.

As they walked out of the hospital to have lunch, Hema announced that Farrokh was getting married on the eighth of August. He had invited her to tea yesterday to tell her the date, which she didn't need to know. He seemed to be asking for her forgiveness for obeying his parents' wishes, feeling as helpless as she was in the situation. His fiancée was not only a Parsi, she was the daughter of family friends. Again, Hema sounded unemotional, matter-of-fact. Maybe it was just her practical nature to accept what couldn't be changed. Jaya tried to console her, and Hema again inquired about the possibility of the two of them sharing a room in the hostel. Jaya said no, it would cost a good bit of money, so she didn't want to ask her father. They came upon a motorbike parked in the drive near the Pathology School, its forlorn lamp nodding between the handlebars. Jaya recognized it with a start, checked the mark. A Royal Enfield. Kirti must have borrowed it from his father—perhaps he was being sent on some work for the esteemed surgery professor who'd taken a shine to him.

The other day he had found his way to Sringara's flat just from her casual mention of the location. When the servant girl announced a visitor had come for her, she was putting away her paints. She rushed out to the drawing room, puzzled. Who had found her here? Seeing Kirti was always a thrill. An excitement shot through her, diluting her anger. Still, after a few minutes of sitting beside him in Sringara's drawing room, the bedlam of train whistles and traffic surging from the road into the flat, she told him he shouldn't come to see her here. It was only a place for her to paint. She hadn't gotten Sringara's permission to have visitors. He suggested she ask Sringara about him stopping by, and she refused. Kirti was offended. He stood up and pushed his hands into his trouser pockets. "Do you want to stop meeting me altogether?"

The question frightened her. She kept saying sorry, she didn't mean to be rude, she only wanted him to understand that her use of Sringara's apartment in the afternoons was strictly for her painting. His expression softened; he let his arrogance deflate a bit. "We'll find some other place to be alone," he promised.

The painting of Kamlesh had taken more than an afternoon's sketching in oils. Jaya worked new colors into her scarlet garment and jewels and hair, to pull her out of the somber blue-grays and ivory black of the ground. Altering her original intentions, Jaya turned parts of her sister's physiognomy into sculpture, curving thick stone lips in a contented smile, dangling stiff pendants from her long ears, though the figure as a whole was fractured in sharp, angular planes of color, a modern-ancient woman.

Now that Jaya spent hours a day inside Sringara's apartment, it dawned on her what she had feared most when she heard Sringara lived alone was her solitude. She had equated a solitary life with devastation. Painting alone in the spare room gave her a different understanding of solitude, as a condition in which the mind could create. After two or three hours, the street noise that so annoyed her when she arrived at the flat around twelve-thirty every day was absorbed by an inner silence, a fluidity of thought as she moved around her canvas. The true luxury of being alone, she thought, was this escape into an internal landscape.

Sometimes the tempo of her hand quickened of its own accord—the force of suppressed images pushing themselves out. On another canvas, the scarlet-veiled woman took form over a couple of afternoons, wearing the awakened expression of a woman who had been hidden from herself. One hand reached up to steady the swollen clay pot on her head. The other reached inward, beneath her sheer veil, to feel her round belly, the locus of her power. Huge, angular stones, a Cubist collage, thrust up from the ground, a forest of boulders that contained her.

When she needed to pause, Jaya left the room and took down an art book from the shelf in Sringara's drawing room. Over and over again, she read a slim monograph on the half-Punjabi, half-Hungarian painter Amrita Sher-Gil, whom she had never before heard of—a daring girl who abandoned Paris as a twenty-year-old to return to India, traveling into the villages and into the caves, like Zaidi, to find her subjects, her essential Indian images. Her portraits made Jaya gasp, the exquisitely tender, weary, inward-looking young women and men whose humanity you saw in an instant. Their sorrow was so transparent, so true. They were of a piece with the women on the hill, and it was tempting for Jaya, after looking at Amrita Sher-Gil's pictures, to paint the women's sorrow, their burden, because that was true about them too. Yet she had been touched by something different in them—their courage, their energy, their way of walking tall, with a sway, even though they had to walk miles to fill their pots with water. They came back to sleep on the hard ground, and to scrounge among snakes for firewood, or hack at dry branches, and still they had the will to climb and walk and chatter, to laugh and put on their bangles, to embrace all the things in their lives. *Who are you?* she asked the red-veiled woman. *Who are you?* I am alive, the woman told her, and I love many things in my world, starting with my children.

The ring-necked parrots in their tall cages would chat to each other. They would watch the bustling street through the open balcony doors. Sitting in a cane chair, listening to them, Jaya was also fascinated by a study of the Surrealists published in London: a thick, costly book with rich color plates stuck to the pages. She read of the Surrealists' belief that the perception of art was akin to sexual excitement, a convulsive sensation that she thought pervaded the making of art too. The canvas became a second body, painting a sensual act, with oils smearing the hands and clothes and hair, a kind of ecstatic touching. The painter painted in a state of craving—at least she did.

BEBEJI'S TREMBLING HANDS, into which Jaya placed a gift bought to mark the unexpected sale of a painting at the end of May, were withered and dry. Bebeji set the package on her bedside table to remove the string and wrapping. She lifted the round silver box to her eyes, removing the lid, engraved with scrolling flowers and leaves. "What shall I put in this?" Her implacable eyes, embedded in swollen puffs of skin, fixed on Jaya.

"It's meant for supari but you can put anything in it—your tablets?" Jaya suggested. Numerous containers of pills, drops, and tonics were gathered on her grandmother's bedside table. A host of minor ailments had cropped up: an ache in one ear, sudden headaches, an itchiness along her sides. The pain in her knee and finger joints was worse than ever.

"Why did you spend on me for no reason?" Bebeji got up from the edge of her bed, put on her slippers.

"It's from my first pay. I wanted to give a little something to everyone, just like Dipi did." Her grandmother was headed out of the room, apparently to show off her gift. It was Jaya's most extravagant purchase, costing more than the thirty rupees she had budgeted. From a shelf in her cupboard, she gathered up all the small packages she'd been accumulating over the past few days.

"Do you compare selling a painting to a salary?" Bebeji turned to look at her from the threshold of the bedroom, amused. "You should have put your money aside."

The whole family was gathered in her parents' room, as occasionally happened, talking and reading the evening papers, a depleted tea tray not yet cleared away. Her mother was mending the hook on a sari blouse, sitting up in bed, the lampshade tilted up to allow her more light. Jaya went around the room like Father Christmas. "What's this?" Daddy, at his writing table, was delighted to find a fountain pen in a slim box.

"It's from my first pay," Jaya told everyone. "Sringara sold one of my paintings."

One's first salary marked one's passage to a continuing vocation and, for this reason, Jaya insisted on calling the earnings from her first painting her "first pay." For her mother there was a carved Kashmiri picture frame of walnut wood from an art shop in Colaba. Mummy had been generous in providing her the extra money for a new box of oil paints, three large brushes, and five canvas boards of good size as a start, despite her habitual grumbling about the expense of art materials.

Kamlesh was surprised by an oval papier-mâché box painted with glossy orange and gold flowers. "I can keep my trinkets in it," she said. Manu, wearing new spectacles, turned to the first page of a biography of the revolutionary Subhash Chandra Bose. Jaya thought it might provide a model for the pamphlet he planned to write on Bebeji's life as a freedom fighter. Their father was going to have it published on the occasion of Bebeji's seventieth birthday next January.

"All this from the sale of one painting?" Dipi grinned slyly, examining his pen. He sat at the foot of her parents' bed in his office shirt and tie. Gifts embarrassed him; perhaps he felt he didn't deserve them. He was used to pleasing others, doing the work they wanted to avoid. The task of blocking a pugilistic Communist union movement at the works had fallen to him as well as her father, and they would discuss various names as potential stooges for the union leaders, now that Madan had fallen out of the running. Dipi held the pen out, chagrined. "I can't take anything from you, Choti. You're my little sister."

"Oh, come on, Dipi," she said. "It's a small thing."

Everyone was astonished by the price her picture had fetched. Sringara had set it for her on the spot—one hundred and seventy rupees. More than the monthly salary many earned. "Beginner's luck," said Jaya, secretly thrilled.

"No matter the amount." Bebeji was dismissive. "Why should you take that girl's help?" She was convinced a woman living alone could only be a corrupting influence.

Her old pictures were stored at Sringara's place, Jaya explained, without mentioning these were paintings her mother refused to hang in the house. Her portrait of Heerabai and men her mother believed to be sick patients in the hospital. A German art critic in town, a Mr. Wolfensohn, Jaya said, who wrote for the *Times of India*—mention of the country's most prominent newspaper caught everyone's attention—sometimes brought over foreign buyers to see Sringara's paintings. She served them a typical South Indian lunch on leaf-plates and rolled paan for them at the end. "Mr. Wolfensohn says Europeans find it very exotic to come to the artist's house, be given a meal sitting on the floor, then look at some paintings."

"What is the purpose of making paintings for foreigners?" Bebeji demanded.

"It was very good of Sringara to show them my pictures." Jaya said. "They're the ones with the money to buy art."

"Which painting was it?" Kamlesh asked. She hadn't been told about the sale, since Jaya had wanted to collect everyone's presents first.

"The painting of Heerabai." Just today she had found a shop near Sringara's flat that sold the nine-yard sari that Heerabai wore pulled between her legs in the practical way of Marathi working women. A gift for her model.

Vidya looked up from her mending. "Some foreigners wanted a picture of a servant?"

"I didn't paint her working as a servant."

The Austrian couple had asked Sringara who the woman in the painting was, and Sringara had said she was a maidservant in the painter's household. When Jaya had taken her few finished paintings over to Sringara's, she'd confessed that it wasn't until she began painting Heerabai that she realized how little she knew of her—though she had worked for the family for years. What she meant was she had never really considered Heerabai as an individual, with her own past and her own inclinations, only felt great affection for her as their maidservant of many years. Someone who had a role in their lives. So she had made a fantasy person because she didn't know the real person; they didn't even share a language, so how could she say she understood Heerabai?

Sringara had put the notes in her hand and asked how she felt. "I feel freed," Jaya had blurted, exhilarated. The painting had felt more real to her now that someone else owned it, disentangling her from the image. She had felt more substantial, holding the money she had earned in her hand.

Her brother, who lay sprawled across their parents' bed, put down his book and threw off his glasses. He rubbed his eyes, pained by his new spectacles, by this new way of seeing. "You should do some huge big painting of Bombay with the ships in the harbor, the Gateway of India and people milling about, something grand."

"I do want to do some huge, big paintings." Jaya smiled.

KIRTI'S PRESENT WAS not one she could risk keeping at home. She had left it at Sringara's overnight, and when she told him she had something to give him, he looked amused. He suggested going to an out-of-the-way spot with a view of the lighthouse in Colaba. They rode in a rumbling double-decker as far south toward the tip of Bombay as they could, and then they walked. In his chivalrous way, Kirti slipped her book bag into his hand, and somehow she felt like his possession, empty-handed, as they entered the cantonment area where his parents lived. Tentacled banyans grew in the middle of the road, spreading their canopies at the land's end. It all felt serene and provincial, but she shouldn't have agreed to come. Every few minutes a soldier in uniform or a navy man in a white cap passed them on the road. Three jeeps shot by in quick succession. Someone might recognize Kirti, and then her presence would have to be explained. Was that what he wanted? He'd begun pressing her to meet his parents, or to bring both sets of parents together. "Let me finish my paintings at Sringara's first," she had said to put him off. He didn't understand what her paintings had to do with confessing their intention to marry to their parents. But in her mind, the two were intricately connected. If she asked her father to accept Kirti, she was afraid he would deny her her paintings. The freedom to make her life exactly as she chose did not seem a possibility. Her father would have his say over one thing or another.

Kirti pointed to a low building in the greenery with a great signboard in the front—his father swam at the Western Military Command Swimming Pool every day. They continued walking away from officers' bungalows and white military buildings and came to a deserted stretch of sea pines. She followed Kirti, taking off her shoes and clambering after him to the top of a rim of black rock. The surf broke below in soft, frothy showers, and out in the bay a lighthouse rose on its own rocky island. They fitted themselves side by side on a damp slab of stone, crabs barely bigger than ants scampering at their feet. Jaya raised the cuffs of her salwar to keep them dry. Kirti's dark hand, with its coral ring, red as a drop of his lifeblood, was hers. His arm grazing her knee was hers. A moment later, he shifted himself, and his heavy foot stroking her foot made her forget the brown-paper parcel in her bag containing raw silk shirting material for him. She basked in the slow rubbing of his sole over her ankle, her calf, setting off sparks of heat like the pricks of light that marked a ship in the heaving green water at dusk. He had some story about going to see a ship land at Ballard Pier with Ashok Narula. An American director making a travelogue on Bombay for MGM was supposed to be on the steamer, and the two of them spent an hour searching the crowd for him. Ashok was ready to shut his clinic for a week if he could join in the filming; at the very least, he was keen to show the man around town and point out all the sights he should include in his picture. It had all been for nothing, Kirti said, they never found the director.

He himself had only been interested in boarding the *Carthage* to see the kind of vessel in which he'd be sailing to England one day. He'd heard these great steamships had ballrooms and libraries. "I suppose I'll have to wait to see all that until I leave India," he said. He spoke of his ambition to go abroad as if it might be a permanent move, not a few years of study as a fellow at the Royal College of Surgeons.

"Kirti, Kirti, don't say such things," Jaya cried, nudging him with her elbow. "I wouldn't like to leave Bombay for good, would you?"

"Why not?" he asked. "What's keeping me here?" A smile, half teasing.

Jaya made a face, then lifted her eyes questioningly—*What about me?* His hand was in her hair, on her face. And she was laughing, thinking this narrow island a few miles wide suited her, but the magnitude of ocean crossings, a crossing into another life, held little attraction. Behind the sea walls of her city, she had the world she wanted.

18

THE ANGLE OF the line kept changing. It defined the edge of the hilltop above the colony. She had made numerous pencil sketches on paper and thought she had arrived at a definitive image, but on canvas the sketch looked wrong, small. She drew the line from left to right, from right to left, higher and lower on the canvas. She had scraped money together for sailcloth and a stretcher, she'd had a carpenter assemble the canvas, and she had only six days left before her half-day holidays concluded and she would have to stop painting at Sringara's flat. In four weeks here she had painted four pictures, as many as she had painted at home in a year. She had been contemplating this painting since she and Kamlesh went to see Lakshmi but was overwhelmed by the task. How could she portray Lakshmi in a way that would be true to her without betraying her tragedy? She thought she could see the image in her mind, but it started to shift. Until she worked up the courage to paint it, she wouldn't know what it was. The problem was, from which angle should Lakshmi be seen standing on the precipice?

Jaya kept drawing and rubbing out the pencil line across the canvas, retreating to the drawing room and pulling down the volume on Amrita Sher-Gil. That afternoon, standing at the easel in Sringara's moldy spare room, she finally made a decisive diagonal, rising from the left to the right across the primed surface, with the idea that the foreground would be the deep ravine that fell away from the edge. A man's voice bellowed frightfully in her ear. "Are you blind as well as deaf as well as blind?" His black curls were bushier than the last time she'd seen him, his forearms thickly matted with hair. Jaya had the odd sense of looking at someone she knew but couldn't immediately place.

Sringara had brought Tule home. Jaya walked out to the drawing room with him, satisfied the line anchored her picture. She could return to it later, after the interruption. She could hear Sringara and Amvi talking in the kitchen. This was the first time Jaya had seen her teacher in weeks, her lessons temporarily halted while she painted at Sringara's. Once before, Tule had stopped by to see her and made a few critical but astute remarks about her red-veiled woman. But when he barked, "Have you forgotten Rouault already? One should be able to understand a painting form by form!" she became fed up with his dogma about the delineating black line and replied evenly, "I returned your book to you." In that moment she realized she hadn't missed him—his tics, his doctrines. She didn't require his bullying voice to spur her on.

Sringara walked in carrying a plate loaded with wet, freshly washed fruit and a knife. She set it on a small table as Tule wandered to the balcony looking down on the road, the cries of vendors swarming into the room. Jaya went to fetch quarter-plates from the kitchen. When she returned to the room, she was glad to see Sringara cracking open a pomegranate. She rarely saw Sringara before she left the flat in the evenings, since Sringara either stayed late at her studio or taught her casual students' class at the J. J. School of Art. Even so, Jaya had the sense Sringara was watching everything she did. Her lessons were not explicit; they were only in the watching. In this flat, she was Sringara's pupil, though Sringara was not her instructor as such. She was a silent teacher, watching Jaya teach herself.

Sringara drew a tired hand across her forehead, accidentally rubbing off a portion of the gleaming circles of black, crimson, and ocher powders that brought a dazzle to her small face. She laughed, smearing the colors from her hand onto Tule's arm. She pulled her chestnut hair out of a carelessly coiled bun. Should she leave now, Jaya wondered, allow them their privacy? Passing around small plates of cut fruit, Sringara blithely informed them of her plan to apply for an Italian government scholarship to study advanced painting in Rome. She'd written to the embassy in Delhi for the forms.

"Rome?" Tule scoffed. "When was the last time that city was a center for art? How many centuries back?"

The discussion, or rather the inevitable dispute, that followed between Tule and Sringara over which were the best European art institutes seemed to disprove the possibility they were lovers; they spoke so easily of separation. "My first choice, hands down, is the Royal College of Art," Tule declared. "Second choice, École des Beaux-Arts."

"To study? What about your poor students?" Jaya felt possessive out of habit. Sringara's wish for Rome, she put out of her mind. Sringara had to remain here, with her.

She sketched Lakshmi's painting in blue the next afternoon and began to fill it in. A moon would hang in the evening sky over the murky depths of the ravine. She fixed the image in her mind as a talisman she could return to if she lost her way.

JAYA'S HALF-DAY HOLIDAYS finished and two weeks went by; then suddenly, it was already July and she was coming straight home after college, no longer permitted to paint at Sringara's flat, to dedicate herself to her studies. Yet she had deliberately left her supplies and canvases there. Her unfinished painting of Lakshmi had been left on Bellasis Road, too, where it was safe. She remembered the dappled moon in the sky, which would pull Lakshmi's gaze from the terrifying abyss.

One rainless evening she kept her eye on the full moon shimmering gold over the bay, reminded of the moon's importance in her picture, as Dipi drove her down the length of Marine Drive to Chowpatty Beach. Out of the blue, he'd invited her for kulfi, and she was flattered to think he regarded her as more of an equal now that she'd earned a good sum of money from the painting she'd sold. Yet Dipi kept an unsettling silence in the car. Jaya was used to listening to him reel off whatever came to mind, whether it was gossip about his friends, his opinion on a political matter, or a bit of startling international news—inevitably something for them to laugh about or debate. This stern silence, she felt, might have to do with the burden of negotiating with Communist union organizers at the glassworks.

Dipi finally spoke in a grim voice. "I had some work in town about a week back. I didn't go to Thana that day." It was an announcement more than a bid for conversation. His face was greased with sweat, and he wore his crushed office clothes, his tie missing. He gave Jaya a rare scowl when he turned to look at her. Between his meetings that day, he'd gone down to buy a cold drink on Girgaum Back Road. "I saw you coming out of a restaurant with a boy. A darkish fellow, quite tall. I was hoping it wasn't you."

"Of course not. Why do you think it was *me*?"

"Because I know the difference between you two."

"I never said it was her," Jaya replied, taken aback that Dipi thought she was implicating her twin.

A crowd jostled around the famous kulfi stall on the damp sands of the beach, a Petromax lantern casting a glow on the activity. Everyone was shouting their orders at the same time, the harried vendor plucking kulfis from his ice chest without stopping. His assistant chopped the frozen custard on tin plates that he thrust out roughly to customers. "Who was that boy?" Dipi demanded. His arms hung straight at his sides, and he stared at Jaya like an interrogator determined to extract an answer.

"I may have been out with some friends." She grew nervous. "We sometimes go for tea after lectures."

"There were only the two of you. You came out of the restaurant and started walking down the road. You seemed quite familiar with him, I could see from the way you both were talking."

Jaya turned away from the kulfi seller and the anxious customers to gaze at a few cars parked along the road with theirs. How foolish she had been to take so many chances going out in public with Kirti, imagining she wouldn't be seen, or that people couldn't deduce the relationship between the two of them if they never touched each other. You were in love with someone, and you thought it belonged to the two of you alone—that no one else could detect the intimacy you shared behind a facade of propriety.

"Is it serious?" Dipi asked. Jaya didn't reply, remaining sullen with him. "I don't want to interfere in your affairs, but I can't stand by quietly if your parents are going to be hurt by this. If it gets back to them from someone else, somebody outside the family, they'll be shocked. They won't know which way to look. You should tell them yourself if it's serious. They're your parents, after all. They'll look after you."

All Jaya could think of, angrily, as they ate their chopped malai kulfi on tin plates in a hostile silence, was why Dipi hadn't gone to the office that day instead of sneakily watching her come out of the Light of Asia with Kirti. She wasn't going to confess anything to her parents unless he brought it up first and forced a confrontation. How ashamed she would be to tell them about Kirti and how furiously they would react. They might put an end to all her freedoms.

The next day, after classes, Jaya rushed to the new men's hostel on campus, a risk she'd never taken before. She bore her head down against a heavy shower, sandals clogged with mud. Rain washed down the steps of the multistory R. M. Bhatt Hostel in a reddish flow to the drain. A couple of boys ran in past her, and she hoped they hadn't caught sight of her face either. She announced herself as an urgent visitor to the desk clerk, and a peon was dispatched to summon Kirti Dasgupta. She hadn't found him in his usual haunts, the Outpatient Department or the library. They no longer met in the hospital in the mornings now that Jaya's rotation had changed to ob-gyn, her notebook pierced with sketches of the swollen abdomens of pregnant women in distress, suffering complications.

Five minutes later, Kirti came quickly down the steps in a creased bush shirt, his dark arms bare, his feet looking large in chappals. Two loose cigarettes stuck out of his shirt pocket. Something had happened, she told him, breathing nervously, could they go somewhere this afternoon or tomorrow? He wanted to know what but she wouldn't say. They stood behind a column in a gloomy nook in the lobby. Jaya hoped the boys walking past were too bothered about being soaked to notice her. She had to believe she wasn't seen. Kirti said he was working on another paper. It was raining badly, he pointed out. He suggested the Light of Asia tomorrow, but Jaya tensed at the mention of the name. He proposed a few other places. The movie hall sounded suitably out of the way; they couldn't possibly be seen there by anyone they knew.

On the main road past Chinchpokli Station, they found the ramshackle cinema compound pressed between millworkers' tenements and surrounded by the tin roofs of textile mills. The theater, a jerry-built structure set in a dirt yard, had the aura of a village cinema. For a moment, Jaya set aside her worries, enchanted by an ancient pipal tree in the middle of the courtyard that moviegoers seemed to worship like a shrine, its trunk tied with innumerable red threads, each representing a wish. A stream of Marathi-speaking men, thin laborers in undershirts and lungis, cotton millworkers from the area, rushed up the stairs, eager to find seats minutes before the picture started. The valances of marigolds and mango leaves strung over every doorway Jaya took for a good omen. In a sliver of balcony four rows deep and more than half-empty, Jaya sat beside Kirti on a wooden bench, lifted high enough to touch the slanted tin ceiling. The atmosphere softened and grew close in the movie's black-and-white glow. Kirti's neck, where his shirt was unbuttoned, was lightly silvered above the squared white expanse of his chest. It returned like a shock, a shivering sensation, the tangible solidity of his presence. Jaya fought an urge to stroke the angle of his jaw caught in shadow, to tilt her head into his shoulder. He looked at her—a warm glance—and she wished she could pretend Dipi had never seen her with him.

On-screen an innocent village girl, her eyes glistening with unshed tears, was being married to a much older man with a paunch and a long mustache, the Marathi dialogue keeping the story from them. Kirti shifted closer to her and tried to draw her hand down into the space between them, away from the gaze of other men, but Jaya pulled away and settled her hands in her lap. She would take no more chances. They sat silently, his hurt palpable to her, and she wondered why she had imagined they could talk things out in a cinema hall.

At the interval, they went down for tea in the open-air compound, subject to many passing looks. Snickering workers turned around to stare at her—the only woman in their midst, grand in her starched peacock-blue sari. To escape the crowd, they climbed back up the staircase to a roofed gallery outside the balcony. Gripped by a need to speak, but not knowing how to begin, Jaya blurted out, "My cousin saw us coming out of Light of Asia last week sometime. I don't even know how, when were we there? I can't remember any date. He saw us walking down the road. I had to tell him it wasn't me. What could I say?"

Kirti sipped his glass of tea. "Did he believe you?"

"I don't think so."

"You think he'll tell your parents?"

"So far I don't think he's said anything. Things are quite normal. But if my father finds out, he'll stop everything. He'll stop us meeting. He'll stop me from doing my paintings. Everything will just come to a crashing halt."

Kirti drew a cigarette and matchbox from his shirt pocket, let the cigarette dangle from his lips, and lit it. "This may not be a bad thing at all," he said, waving his cigarette away and exhaling. Now was the time to put it all out in the open. Half the college knew about them in any case. It was only a matter of time until a rumor made it back to her parents. She was shocked to hear he'd told his parents a short while back about a girl in college he was interested in. A Punjabi girl. "Let's both put it out in the open," he suggested.

"No." Her tone was definitive, heavy with anger. He had no right to expose her. "Why did you say something to them without telling me first?"

Kirti's gaze grew slightly distant, slightly skewed, as if she'd injured a tender spot and he wouldn't allow himself to show it. "What are you afraid of?" he asked in a cool, unemotional voice. "Is it because we're from different communities?"

A temptation to meet his mother, the sweets-maker he spoke of affectionately, and his father, the lieutenant colonel who liked to potter in the garden, took hold of her. It might be nice to be introduced to his two sisters, to come to know the whole of him. "This just isn't the proper time." The right moment would come after her exhibition, when her father couldn't stop her from painting.

"Is it because I'm a Bengali?"

"No." Her mind was occupied with the thought of protecting her paintings. His being a Bengali was a barrier, of course. Her mother would resent it: he was not a Punjabi. He was dark-skinned. His family would speak a different language, follow different traditions. But the more potent fear was of her parents punishing her for carrying on with him behind their backs, a betrayal they would have never expected. For that she might be denied the thing she most wanted for herself.

"The reason I told my parents is that my father's being transferred to Mau, probably in three, four months. I wanted them to meet you."

"You never said anything about a transfer." She was caught off guard, wondering if he might be fibbing just to persuade her to do as he wished. Men came shuffling up the staircase. The picture was about to resume. Kirti carried on, convinced now was the right time for them to speak to their parents. He wanted everything to be decided before his parents left town. It would be difficult for their families to meet afterward. He came a step closer, cutting an overly large figure, throwing too strong a shadow on her.

She wouldn't meet them, no. Nothing would persuade her to change the equation now, when her exhibition was just five months away, when she might have to ask her father's permission for something else he would hate to permit her. This couldn't be explained to Kirti with the full complexities of her feelings; she herself didn't understand why her paintings meant more to her than anything else. She said bluntly, with great insensitivity, "I've got to prepare for my exhibition. I have about five months left and very few pictures. Mr. Chadha's fixed the date for twenty-eighth November. I told you."

"Am I in competition with your paintings?" He was insulted, his brows knitting together tightly. His cigarette was suspended midair between his fingers.

"You still have three and a half years left for your house surgeonship. Then you want to go to England for your fellowship, no?" She tried to shift the conversation to the neutral matter of a timetable. "There's no rush. I'll meet your parents in good time."

"I'll marry you in three years, four years, whatever your parents say. We don't have to wait until I return from England. I may not even go, it all depends on whether I get a scholarship." It was the first time he'd admitted any doubt about his ambition.

"Not yet, Kirti." She wasn't prepared for this declaration about marriage as a prospect in the near future.

"Why not?" He set his tea glass on the ground by a pillar, making a move to go inside.

"Don't force me like this—"

"Who's forcing you? Who can bloody well dare?" He raised his voice in English, drawing looks from young men in ankle-length lungis climbing up the steps. "You're a selfish creature, that much I can say. You'll never do anything unless it's exactly what you want."

"That's right. I'll do exactly what I feel like." Relieved to be free of the word *marry*, she flung words back at him in equal fury, the two of them staring at each other like adversaries. Kirti dropped his gaze and walked through the parted black curtains back to the lopsided balcony. Worse than walking out alone into the dilapidated mills area would be sitting next to him on the bench in a raging silence, feeling the bitterness accrue between them. Jaya turned down the staircase, not seeing where she was going, pushing into a boy climbing up, and she hurried down the walkway out of the compound, breathing heavily, trembling with anger and sorrow. Out on the road, she came up against the charred smokestacks of the Hindoostan Textile Mill, two filthy black bars thrusting into the sky, bringing her to a halt. She walked for twenty minutes without seeing properly, without knowing in which direction to go, her thoughts at a boil. Then she stopped to ask someone where she was, and he directed her to a bus stand across the smoky, congested road.

TWO DAYS LATER, at home, still shaken from the fight with Kirti, she painted sprays of yellow and apricot roses on cotton luncheon mats that Kamlesh had asked her to design as a wedding present for Meher. The marriage would take place the week after next, in the middle of the monsoons, and Kamlesh was thrilled that Leela would be there, too, coming home for the first time with her baby boy. Jaya sat at the writing table, carefully tracing a stem with a fine brush, as Kamlesh chattered about her friends. Then Kamlesh abruptly stopped to ask, "How will you get them done?" She meant the paintings for Jaya's exhibition.

"I'll find a way out," Jaya said.

"How? I can't be in this alone." Kamlesh dropped her gaze and went to the cupboard. She plucked her sari pleats out of her tightly knotted petticoat. To her teacher's training institute, she had started wearing saris like a grown-up girl, drawing a slash of pink lipstick on her forehead for a bindi. At the end of a long day of college, she would hurry home for a quick change of clothes, into a schoolgirlish skirt and blouse, before rushing off to Masterji's flat for a two-hour rehearsal with her practice clothes in her bag, shedding costumes like an actress.

"But you are in it alone," Jaya said as gently as she could. "You'll be the one up on the stage. I won't be there with you. It's yours alone, it's your dance." For a few weeks now Kamlesh had been complaining that Jaya's lack of practice, her stopping the flow of her pictures after she left Sringara's flat, had affected her. Jaya had noticed that Kamlesh's astonishing discipline had started to crack; she'd make excuses not to practice at home in the mornings before college. Then, a few days ago, a mridangamist had come to rehearse with her, and his drumming had thrown her off rather than fixing her to the beat. Stopping now, wavering over how to keep painting more than a month after leaving Sringara's, could put an end to her exhibition. If Kamlesh was so disturbed by her shattered routine, it could put an end to both their debuts. The dates and times had now been fixed—the end of October for Kamlesh, the end of November for her. Three to four months from now, a short amount of time for what they had to accomplish.

Sixteen was greater than the number of paintings she could ever complete at home, inside the family's protective walls. She must have known, when she declared her aim to Chadha, that on the balcony she would never be able to produce sixteen paintings worth showing at an exhibition. Sixteen paintings required her to find a space outside the home, a place big enough for her pictures. Her paintings would be more prominently on display now, too, since Chadha had whittled the group down to four painters—himself, Vir, Jaya, and an abstract artist named Acharya.

The next afternoon she took a bus directly from J. J. Hospital to Sringara's flat. Her old route, from her half-day holidays. It was pouring rain, and she thought of the difficulties of the colony people as currents of water swept down the hill. Bebeji had shut the school until the middle of August. How was Lakshmi? They hadn't had any news about her.

Climbing the stairs to the flat, Jaya was prepared to wait for Sringara as long as she needed to, but Sringara was home early because of the downpour. Amvi brought them tumblers of coffee in the spare room, which Jaya had come to ask about. She had lost her thread since she'd stopped painting here, she told Sringara; she felt she was losing her direction. The images she'd had in her mind while she painted in the flat were already vanishing. She didn't say Lakshmi's painting remained pinned to her imagination by a crescent moon hanging over the abyss. "If I came here,"

Jaya said tentatively, "I could manage much better than at home. Nothing else would interfere, the family things."

Sringara raised her eyebrows, wrinkling the multiple bindis stamped on her brow. "I'm interested in your paintings, that much you know. In any case, all your things are still here." She meant Jaya's paints and canvases in the storeroom. Jaya smiled. Actually, she felt more divided, having taken some of her art materials home, reckoning with the imperative to paint on the balcony yet being unable—or unwilling—to do that. "If you came here, I wouldn't be alone anymore," Sringara said with a playful look. "Yet you would be in a sense, no?"

Jaya blew on her coffee—this was the only place she drank coffee. What would her father make of this room with its soot-grained ceiling and pile of brown coconuts like a mound of dark eggs? It was an artist's ideal world: bare, a hole, a womb for her creations. She would use this room as her studio and her bedroom, but if Sringara found an acceptable paying guest, she would have to share Sringara's bedroom and paint in the drawing room. "Just until the exhibition."

"As long as you need," Sringara replied. She had a finer understanding of Jaya's needs, Jaya thought, than Jaya herself.

HER FATHER STRUCK the dining table when Jaya told him, five weeks after college resumed full-time, that she had left her canvases and paints, along with an unfinished picture, at Sringara's flat. That's why she had stopped pushing ahead with the paintings for her exhibition. Everything had been left there, where she had a place to paint.

"Bring all your things home. Why have you left them there?" It was after the evening meal and everyone else had left the table. He was in an anxious state; she sensed the union movement he and Dipi were constantly talking about lay behind it. The tension had prompted his decision to discipline himself with a month-long salt fast. All meals had to be prepared completely bland, without a grain of salt. A tiny dish of salt lay on the table for the rest of them, clotted with the humidity of July.

"What is the need to keep going to that woman's place?" her mother demanded. She was carrying small dishes of leftover food from the kitchen to the fridge in the dining room, letting out blasts of cool air.

"If you're not able to do the paintings you promised to do, if you can't manage, then drop out of the show," her father ordered. "Finished?" His fierce stare indicated that there was a boundary line behind which a daughter must remain.

"I'm not dropping out, no matter what," Jaya lashed back, not thinking whom she was talking to. She got up to leave the room. "I'll shift to her flat until the exhibition. I'll just go from here." She felt tears and anger burning her face.

Her father stood up, his eyes piercing her as he took a few steps forward. She received, for the first time in years, a stunning slap—a jarring knock of his hard knuckles against her lips. Jaya put her hand to her mouth, touching the injury. "Insolent girl!" He was shouting at her as if she were breaking everything he believed in. Another slap stung her cheek; then there was another that her mother, lurching toward them, caught in her hand.

PART 3

Dancing Girl

19

A DOUBLE-DECKER SHUTTLING up heat-drenched roads took Jaya past bazaars and tenements from Chadha's flat in Colaba toward Sringara's building opposite the railway station. More people climbed aboard at every stop, men suffocating her as they crowded the aisle and clutched her seat back. The smell of bodies, the harsh words flung between men. So much anger brewing over remaking the borders of Bombay state. Jaya blotted the perspiration on her brow with her hankie, reminding herself to ring Kamlesh from the veterinarian's office. Kamlesh complained that she seldom tried to make contact—it was always Kamlesh dropping by Sringara's place. But Kamlesh hadn't come in almost two weeks, and Jaya worried her sister was upset with her. She might have used Chadha's phone to ring home, but she didn't want to ask him for another favor. It had been embarrassing enough to interrupt his Saturday lunch with his family to tell him that she didn't have her share of the deposit to be paid to Jehangir Art Gallery. Their exhibition would run for a week, the four of them dividing the eight-hundred-rupee rental charge. Fifty percent of her portion was required now, but Jaya could offer Chadha only thirty rupees. She hoped to pay the balance from the sale of her paintings. "Pay me the full sum after you sell a picture or two," he told her, ever the gentleman. "I have no doubt they'll be picked up quickly."

"I hope so." Jaya had exhaled deeply. Never before had she counted pennies like this—even the cost of a bus ticket mattered. Every ten days her mother met her and gave her a twenty-rupee note for her pocket money. Jaya would offer a tenner to Sringara toward food. The cost of art materials simply exceeded the scope of her pocket money, so Sringara had taught her how to make cheap oil paint with pigment cake and linseed oil. She found the paint more lush than Camel tubes. She had offered Jimmy Curimbhoy her head studies of the dead and dying to sell on consignment at his frame shop. A couple of weeks later, he'd given her fifty rupees for her portrait of the blue patient.

Bellasis Road smelled of smoke, the burning coal that fired steam engines. Jaya got off the bus near the by-lane and followed it below the main road into the familiar compound, with its dank gutter smell. Up the black stairwell she went without pausing on the second floor, put off by a deep growling behind the veterinarian's door. Not only did she hesitate to ask for the phone for a personal matter, she dreaded phoning home not knowing who would pick up. Heerabai's gruff, broken "Hu-llo?" would come as a relief. They would make a moment's small talk, before Kamlesh was summoned. Once her father had answered, unexpectedly home in the afternoon, and she was speechless for a minute, until she managed to say "hello" in a dry, hollow voice.

When she opened the door with Sringara's spare key, Kirti stood in the entry hall to receive her. He must have heard her at the door. "You're here?" She was confused.

He ushered her inside, his tone hearty and formal, as though Sringara had visitors in the drawing room. "I thought you'd be at home," he told Jaya. "The girl said you must have gone somewhere, usually you come home by two on Saturdays." Amvi had let him in. Though he was familiar with Jaya's routine, he pretended to be ignorant of her timings. He gestured Jaya into the drawing room, looking at her fiercely.

Kamlesh stared at her from one of the bent-cane armchairs. Jaya faced her sister like a stranger in Kirti's presence, detaching herself from the uncomfortable scene. Kamlesh hadn't seen him in a very long time; almost the whole year had passed since Farrokh's party in Juhu. Kirti ran a hand self-consciously through his hair, acknowledging the impropriety of his presence in the flat. Kamlesh's face was flushed pink; she had a glow to her and an air of exhaustion. The tint of her face, the softness of her fatigue, reminded Jaya that Kamlesh was rehearsing every afternoon, her dance recital in about a week. Jaya had lost track of the date, too involved in her own painting. *Too involved*—Mummy would say that. Jaya gave her sister a smile. "How are the rehearsals coming along? All the musicians are there now?"

"No, that's next week. It's still only the mridangam player," Kamlesh said tersely. She was angry—she didn't want to talk in front of him. Last time she came she'd been excited that she'd been given her ankle bells to wear for her practices. Masterji had blessed them at a puja in his home. It was considered such an important ceremony that Mummy and Bebeji had attended.

"Sringara's not at home?" Jaya blurted, wishing she could escape these two who had come to punish her. Till now they had always come separately, each meting out their own form of retribution.

Sringara was here, Kirti said; she had returned home a few minutes before Kamlesh arrived. "You have your dance show coming up, I hear." He turned to Kamlesh, making an effort to be friendly. "It sounds like a very nice function."

"It's just the standard arangetram every Bharata Natyam student gives." Kamlesh made it out to be nothing, this momentous event in her life, fiddling with the bag at her feet and lifting it to her lap. Her nylon sari was arranged sloppily; she must have put it on in a hurry after rehearsing at Masterji's flat. Her practice clothes were probably stuffed in her bag. She looked out of sorts.

"It's like preparing for a marriage, Mummy says—so many gifts for her teacher and all the musicians in the orchestra, a pandit has to set an auspicious time for the program." Jaya was eager to bring a note of levity to the conversation. To make her sister proud and convey the grandeur of the event to Kirti. Her mother had enumerated to her the many purchases she'd made—a silk dhoti-kurta, fine wool shawl, and gold bangle for Masterji, and gifts of silk for all the musicians and the singer. A pujari had consulted the stars and determined the most favorable time for the performance, just as for a wedding ceremony. Her mother had bitterly called it "a wedding without a bridegroom."

Kamlesh's glance skittered from the muttering parrots in their cages to the bookshelf behind her to the cloth bag in her lap. She seemed unsettled by the comparison of her arangetram to a wedding. In her nervousness, Jaya hadn't considered Kamlesh's sensitivity to the subject of marriage, since their parents had nearly canceled her debut for fear she'd be shunned by the families of eligible boys for appearing on stage. "Sringara's gone to get some of your paintings," Kamlesh told Jaya without looking at her.

Sringara had come over to speak to her parents the day before Jaya left home, hoping to alleviate their misgivings. Vidya had treated her like a villain who had lured Jaya away. "*Our* girls never stay on their own," she said peevishly, referring to unmarried daughters in the Punjabi community. "How many years have you been staying alone?"

"It couldn't be helped, Auntie. Some things happened and I had to come here to my aunt. Seventeen, eighteen years back."

When Harbans had realized he couldn't command Jaya to stay at home, or physically restrain her, he'd ordered her not to set foot in his house again unless she was ready to come back for good. For a few days, Jaya went back and forth between Sringara's place and home, during the hours her father was at the factory, trying to mend relations with her mother and grandmother. Her departure stunned Bebeji. "The culture does not allow this," she told Jaya starkly. "No girl behaves in such a manner." Jaya had felt like a criminal then, violating traditions and expectations that were stronger than any law.

A door banged shut somewhere. Sringara entered the room a minute later, carrying a canvas in her arms, its nailed back turned toward them. "Oh, you've just come? Did you meet Bal? What did he say?" The words came out quick and chatty, Sringara's defense against discomfort. "Kirti's never seen your pictures, he told me." She was fibbing now, for Kamlesh's benefit—of course Kirti had seen her paintings. He had stood in the spare room she occupied, looking at her pictures as Sringara offered her commentary.

"I just stopped by to give you some things you left behind," Kamlesh said stonily to Jaya, clutching her bag with both hands.

Kirti took the painting from Sringara and propped it on a small end table he'd carried over to the opposite wall, to catch the light floating in through the balcony doors. Jaya shrank into silence, unable to look at him

or Kamlesh. Kirti had turned Sringara's flat into an intimate hideout, showing up without warning. Jaya almost wished she could go back to meeting
him at the Prince of Wales, which was just a few minutes' walk from the
flat, because at least she could anticipate the meeting then. Sringara had
run into him in the flat a few times but didn't mind his coming around.
She placed no restrictions on Jaya or herself. Occasionally Vir or Tule came
over in the evenings to see Sringara. Jaya brought Kirti into her bedroom
only if no one else was at home, and they might lie together on her bed
for an hour or two. She had asked him not to drop in without warning
her, as Kamlesh stopped by spontaneously also. She used to come about
twice a week, but her visits had grown infrequent in the last month as she
entered a period of intensive practice and rehearsal. On top of that, she'd
begun practice teaching at a school every day, followed by lectures at college
till five-thirty. Lately she had been missing her afternoon classes, because
of her dance rehearsals. Once she came to visit Jaya early in the morning,
before she reported for teaching at Alexandra Girls School.

The possibility of running into Kamlesh didn't seem to concern Kirti.
He reveled in a new freewheeling sense of independence, his father having left him his Royal Enfield, as he'd received a car with his promotion
to colonel in Mau. Jaya could never turn Kirti away when he showed up
at her door, windblown, smiling his huge, hopeful smile, before his criticisms began, his accusations about what she hadn't done and hadn't said.
He hadn't forgiven her for not meeting his parents before they left town.

Sringara walked past Kirti, who appeared to be ruminating on the painting of Kamlesh. She was cooing and chatting to her parrots, guarding the
open balcony doors. She turned back nervously toward Jaya, shaking her
head in dismay. "You're looking dreadful, do you know?" she said to Jaya.
"Your face is getting thinner and thinner. Such dark circles under your eyes.
The more you work, the less you eat. You're going to fall ill one of these
days. What will Kamlesh think? How am I treating you?"

The small table made a scraping noise as Kirti turned it at an angle, only
one side of the canvas resting precariously against the wall. The dancer
threw her arms in the air. A swift red-brown line plunged from her cupped
hands to the swell of her breasts beneath her sari, the line swinging around
her long, curved hip and tapering down to her uplifted foot. The dancer's

skin was as dark as Kirti's, but more burnt red, the cloth wrapped around her body crimson lightened with orange-gold, the beads hanging over her breasts smears of greenish-gold. Sringara slipped out of the room to get some cold drinks. Kirti continued to gaze at the figure with an uninhibited intensity, as if he were dissecting her, or ogling her, his hands stuffed in his trouser pockets. Kamlesh scowled at him, looking embarrassed at the way he kept on staring.

Jaya leaned over to retrieve a scrap of cloth Kamlesh had fished out of her bag and was holding up by her fingertips. A scallop-necked white sari blouse that resembled a fancy brassiere. "Isn't this yours?" Kamlesh asked. "I found it in the cupboard mixed up with my blouses."

Kamlesh inevitably brought something to throw back at Jaya, to say no reminders of her were wanted at home. Jaya's hand brushing against her sister's felt a lushness like satin, some rich material. Kamlesh's touch jolted her. A stimulus like the sound of her voice, her eyes; sometimes she set to work on an unfinished painting of Kamlesh after her twin left the flat, charged with her vitality. A red petticoat, too, was tossed at her. Kamlesh retrieved from her purse a tiny, glossy photograph and presented it to Jaya. A beautiful shot of Kamlesh posed with her hands formally clasped in front of her, wearing her silk sari and V-neck blouse with three-quarter-length sleeves. Gleaming bunches of silvery beads hung from her ears. "It's my graduation photo," Kamlesh said. "There's a different pose of me holding the diploma also."

Jaya smiled. Kamlesh was radiant. "It's come out very well," she said mutedly, not wanting to draw Kirti's attention to the photograph. Kamlesh's lips were parted slightly in the suggestion of a smile. Her eyes were large and magnificent. A dancer's greatest quality, Masterji had told Jaya once, when she'd come to sketch Kamlesh at a lesson, was something inborn that no one could learn—charisma. God had blessed Kamlesh with the charisma to capture an audience's heart. The photograph served a dual purpose, Jaya knew from her mother—a portrait to commemorate Kamlesh's graduation, and a snap to offer the families of prospective bridegrooms. If, for any reason, a match didn't work out with Vikram Bakshi, the steamship company manager, Vidya wanted to be prepared to look elsewhere. Jaya tucked Kamlesh's picture inside her folded petticoat, out of Kirti's sight. "What time should I come to you next Saturday?" she asked her twin.

"I've arranged everything with Masterji's daughter-in-law. She'll do my makeup."

"You'll need another person to help you put on your jewelry—" Jaya tried to appease her—"the pendants in your hair and all that. I can also help you with the costume change after your varnam." The varnam was the highlight of the show, and earlier Kamlesh had doubted she could pull it off. It was a half-hour piece that alternated between fast pure dance and dramatic interludes where she narrated the story of Sati throwing herself on the fire in her rage at her father. Jaya wanted to be backstage with Kamlesh after that grueling climax to support her and take charge of her costume change during the intermission, since it would be hard for Kamlesh to organize herself after an hour and a half of performing.

"You seem quite occupied here," Kamlesh said. She wouldn't give anything away with her eyes, avoiding Jaya with a distant, abstracted gaze toward the balcony. A few weeks back, Kamlesh had asked for her help backstage, and for this reason, if no other, their father had consented to let Jaya attend Kamlesh's arangetram. Jaya had been part of Kamlesh's dance practice; she was a part of her dance. She knew every pose through having drawn it. But now Kamlesh didn't want to accept any favors from her. It must have to do with Kirti being here. Perhaps she felt offended that he'd welcomed her, as if he lived in the flat. "I don't want that to be put up for public display," Kamlesh said abruptly, gesturing to the painting.

"It's not a picture of you as such, not literally. I don't think anyone will recognize it as you," Jaya said. Kirti walked out onto the minuscule iron balcony looking over the road and the railway station, giving them their privacy. "It's just an impression of your face, but very abstract . . ." Jaya stammered. Kamlesh couldn't forbid her now from hanging the pictures of her in the show. Jaya's exhibition was created around the figure of the dancer, and the portraits of women and children from the hill would hang between those of the dancer in motion—the dancer and the people from the shanty colony joined by the same thread of shakti.

Kamlesh got up to look more closely at her portrait, pushing the table so the full canvas rested securely flat against the wall.

"It's a very nice painting," Kirti said. He stepped back inside the room, joining Kamlesh in front of the picture. Pressing his fingertips to the dancer's hands, he seemed to probe the texture of the paint for some contact with the painting's essence.

"Do you find it so interesting?" Kamlesh took a few steps away from him.

Jaya approached, wanting to defuse the tension. The three of them considered the painting silently, and Jaya became acutely aware Kamlesh had the power to expose her. She might tell their parents about Kirti, thinking Jaya had no qualms about exposing her on canvas for everyone to see.

A little while later, after they'd dutifully consumed the soft drinks and puffed rice snack Sringara brought out, it came as a relief that Kamlesh stood up when Kirti did. She also had to get home, she said, and left the flat with him like a friend, apparently no longer mistrustful of his gaze.

That night, alone in her room, Jaya lost heart, as she occasionally did. She arranged her book bag, selected a sari and blouse for the next day at college, laying them out on top of her suitcase, which sat against the wall near her bed. She grew fearful, feeling the smallness and fragility of herself in the dingy, electric-lit room, the merciless dark at her window. The darkness warned her to return home. Her defiance—her crime—had gone on long enough. *The culture does not allow this*, Bebeji had said. It seemed incredible to Jaya that she had left home on a wild impulse, without considering the cost of what she was doing. She'd had no idea she was tearing herself out of the family; she had thought only of nurturing her paintings.

Her mother said people didn't seem to believe she'd left home just to paint pictures for an exhibition. No girl ever shifted out of her parents' home before marriage, but since she had, people suspected it was over a boy, or due to some trouble or illicit behavior. All kinds of rumors might be spreading about her. Everyone in the Punjabi community had come to know. The news could have slipped out through Kamlesh's friend Leela, who was on a long visit home with her baby. Kamlesh had confided everything to Leela, who might have told her mother, who would have told her sister Shuli. However it got out, acquaintances were pointedly questioning Mummy at gatherings. The jealous ones were pleased that one of her beautiful daughters was implicated in a scandal whose details no one understood—*What is Jaya doing these days? Has she dropped out of medical college?* Some of Dipi's friends' mothers, who might have had an eye on Jaya for their sons, were inquiring: *Where has she gone?* Whenever Jaya saw

Vidya, they'd start off having a neutral conversation—What was the family news? What was Jaya's college news? How far along was she with her pictures? Within minutes, her mother's hurt and anger would surface. "Is this how you want to shame your parents?"

Jaya would remain silent, appear contrite. Her mother would shake her head in disbelief. Her voice would rise to a high, disturbing register. "Do you think anyone will want to marry their son to you after this? You want to spoil your entire future for some paintings? Crazy girl!"

Take only as much as you can bear, Sringara had said, but realize if you go home you're unlikely to paint any more pictures. Something there stops you, whether it's the cramped balcony or some psychological factor. Something inhibits you, she said, or you let something inhibit you. Here, there were now twelve pictures. Jaya had propped them all around the room on metal trunks they had removed from the storeroom, and they had locked up the heap of rattling brown coconuts. The trunks gave the room the look of a way station, a temporary home to paint in. Only a few pictures were incomplete, and a couple she had deemed unworthy of showing were tucked in a corner. She would paint new images over those in the impasto of oil paints she'd made herself, mixing plaster of Paris into the pigment for thickness. She might not complete sixteen paintings, she might end up with just eleven or twelve good pictures, but even that would be an accomplishment.

Carefully Jaya pulled the easel that stood in front of the window to the right. Now the painting resting upon it received the light of the wall sconce. Half the canvas showed the depths of a chasm, deep brown earth and black basalt rock, as if the ground had cracked and split apart. In its depths flew the birds she had painted yesterday, dull birds, swooping gray birds of prey—or as Jaya thought of them, night birds, because the earth at that depth was a darkness. Almost halfway up the canvas, you came up the precipice to the earth's surface, where the child stood, holding her baby brother. His small head and her small, sand-brown face were protected by her veil, a veil the bright green of monsoon grass, a wild green above the darkness. The sky up here was gray-blue, like dusk, and the girl and her brother were turned toward a patchy, purplish moon, not quite full, lit by a faint radiance. *Look at the moon, it's made of mud and silver*, Jaya imagined

Lakshmi telling her brother, speaking of its fine qualities, awakening him to the world. She had pointed out the chasm a moment earlier, warned him to keep away from its edge, to never come here alone. But she cared only for the moon and wanted to look there, keeping herself in love with her world.

Sringara pushed open her door, which was half ajar, to wish her good-night. Seeing Jaya at her easel, she stepped inside. She liked the addition of the birds very much, thinking the empty chasm had been a static image. "Now we're in a different world," Sringara said. "The painter's world. An imaginary world." She laughed. "There has to be a point where the painting leaves the world behind for good."

Jaya nodded. All her paintings set in the colony were for her pure evocations of that place, although some might not recognize the real hillside in her images. They were renderings of her feelings and impressions as far as paint could convey what she held inside her.

"You're okay?" Sringara said.

"I hope she doesn't say anything. I don't know what I'll do if she tells them." Over the evening meal, they had spoken about the unlucky coincidence of Kirti and Kamlesh both turning up at the flat this evening. Jaya didn't know if Kamlesh still felt the loyalty toward her that would stop her from betraying Jaya to their parents.

"I don't know why I brought that painting for him to look at," Sringara said. "I didn't mean to bring Kamlesh's picture out. Very clumsy of me. I should have brought out one of your hill paintings."

"It's all right. I was flustered myself."

Sringara turned her attention back to the canvas. "Who is the child in this picture?"

"A little girl from the colony. She used to attend Bebeji's school. Then a terrible thing happened to her—" Jaya had to stop. "I wanted to remember her as she was before she got hurt."

"There's an ominous feeling, for sure," Sringara said. "But, it's also lovely how she's looking at the moon in wonder."

I should name it for the moon, Jaya thought. She had been thinking of calling it *Girl on the Precipice*, but that only put Lakshmi in danger—it didn't speak of her beautiful spirit, her zeal. *A Moon of Mud and Silver* sprang to mind. Mud and silver rolled up in a big ball, the magical sight of it drawing Lakshmi's gaze away from the birds of prey below.

"So, was Bal happy about Rashid coming?" Sringara asked. Jaya said he had been thrilled. Sringara sounded proud to have succeeded in getting Rashid Ahmed, her friend Yasmin's husband—a painter and scholar who taught the art criticism course at the university in Baroda—to accept Chadha's invitation to inaugurate their exhibition. Jaya had spoken to Chadha about it briefly that afternoon. He appeared to be taking care of the Ahmeds' travel to Bombay, keen to have an eminent figure in the art world lend his aura of authority to a show of unknown artists. Rashid Ahmed's writings in art journals on the place of modernism in Indian art—modernism as a way to rebirth the nation after British rule—had profoundly impressed Chadha.

The painting of Lakshmi drew Sringara's interest again. She peered into the depths, in which the predatory birds swam with outspread wings, and traced the girl's gaze up to the stained moon in the evening sky. "I lost a child," she said.

Jaya was stunned. *"Lost?"*

He was alive, Sringara explained, but she had never been a mother to him. She'd had to leave home when she had him, an unmarried girl. He was seventeen years old now—his childhood was gone. She'd had so little part of it. She met him on her annual trips home, in the guise of a cousin. It was why she went home each year despite her relations disapproving of her, some refusing to speak to her. "I know what it's like to have to tear yourself out of your family," she said. "They wanted me to leave, so I went as far away as I could."

"That must have been quite painful," Jaya said, though she knew she was too unformed to understand the depth of Sringara's emotion.

"You get to a point past hurt," Sringara said.

Jaya was silent, trying to fathom what Sringara must have suffered, having a child but not having him. She had always sensed she shouldn't ask Sringara why she left Mysore. Sringara had told her "I know how difficult it is to be away from home," and now the words had a different weight. Sringara had told her, "Keep going, unless you really can't bear it."

Jaya pushed the easel back against the black window when Sringara left the room, recognizing her debt. It was because of Sringara she was painting—not because of this room, or this flat, but because of Sringara herself. If Sringara weren't here to tell her to go on, to do the next picture so she could see it, Jaya might have stopped and returned home.

20

A SMALL FIRE burned onstage inside the darkened, empty hall, where Masterji, tending the iron pot of flames, sang a Sanskrit prayer of initiation. Kamlesh bowed her head, calmed by his words. The musicians, bereft of their instruments, gathered in a circle around the fire with Kamlesh and her family. In an hour, her family members would become part of the audience in the theater's shadow space. Now Jaya was next to Kamlesh, the two of them warmed by the close heat of the flames, their father sitting opposite them with his hands folded together. It was the first time he and Jaya had seen each other in months, and Kamlesh was relieved that the fire seemed to burn away ill feelings and cleanse the air of their sorrow.

She rose as the singing subsided. Wearing a crown of jasmine buds that Jaya had pinned to the back of her head, her hair smeared with their luscious fragrance, she approached her teacher with a blissful lightness, announcing each step with the sixty tiny brass bells tied above each foot. In her hands she carried a tray containing a folded length of silk, an embroidered shawl, a heavy gold bracelet, and auspicious betel leaves. She laid the tray in Masterji's hands, bowing to seek his blessing. The moment he raised his palms to her head, a radiance spread, the dream of her dance opening like a vista in her mind. Tonight she would become his interpreter, his instrument. Kamlesh paused, slowing herself, feeling as though she was on the brink of a long voyage. This would be her crossing, this evening on stage, from a student to a true dancer. Already she felt different, in her costume of violet silk woven with a swan and lotus motif in pure gold thread, anchored by the many large pieces of jewelry Jaya had fastened on her body. Bebeji, Jaya, and her mother waited with the gifts for the musicians. Slowly, Kamlesh presented a length of silk each to the bald vocalist, the flute player, and the mridangamist with long, sinewy fingers that thundered against the drumheads, and a deep-green silk sari to the lady veena player who betrayed no movements of her hands.

Later the lights spread warmly over Kamlesh as she stood in perfect balance on the low stage, surrounded by painted scenery of stone carvings that created the impression of a temple hall. Her audience sat casually in family groups, on dhurries laid on the floor—a hundred and fifty people or more scattered across the small community hall. Her body became a pillar joined at the legs, her arms jutting out like stone braces, her henna-red fingertips pointed up in hasta pataka. The drum roared to life. Kamlesh stamped her heel forward to Masterji's syllable-beat: *"Ta di teiyum. Ta tan tikka takka, ta di teiyum."* Her head slid from side to side on the stem of her neck. She flicked up her cupped right palm, glanced at it, turned it down, then flicked up her left hand. Lowering her hips into a deep sit, her knees turned out and heels touching, she let an apron of silk pleats fan open between her legs. For an instant, her right arm dropped like an unbalanced scale. Then she rose into a column of immaculate stability, framed by the painted stone pillars and arch that dressed the stage in golden hues. A few rows from the stage, her brother and Dipi were seated to one side of her grandmother and parents, Jaya separated from them by a thin margin of space. Kamlesh could not see much beyond Jaya's huge, shining eyes on her. When she held a pose in the next piece, her arms thrown overhead and one foot raised to her thigh, her head tilted down to the right, making a sculpture of her body, she felt herself smiling instinctively at her audience and a photographer lurking by the stage, who set off his silver flashes. She kept returning her gaze to Jaya's black-rimmed eyes, seeking her equilibrium.

Afterward, following eight solo dances presented over three exhilarating hours, when she inhabited a different state of consciousness, Kamlesh was overwhelmed with flowers. Masterji's eldest daughter-in-law walked on stage as the applause continued, a thickset woman with a beaming smile. She laid a heavy garland of pink roses, marigolds and frangipani around Kamlesh's neck. Bowing to the audience, Kamlesh felt transported by the lights, the attention, the enormity of what she had done. Never before had she danced like this, with such a sense of her own power. When she stepped down from the stage, her mother presented her with a bouquet of gladioli. An older student of Masterji, who had debuted last year, offered flowers and embraced her like a friend. "Kamlesh!" she cried. "So beautifully you danced! We were sitting enthralled the whole time." She indicated a few of Masterji's younger students, their faces shining with emotion. Kamlesh hugged the older girl and pressed the hands of the younger ones in thanks for coming. No relations or friends of hers had been invited, no one she knew aside from her family and Masterji's, for fear word about her performance would ignite gossip that could ruin her future.

Kamlesh was perspiring madly, her head-jewels slipping from her hair. Her mother took charge of the embossed gold-garland necklace Kamlesh had removed without thinking, feeling its weight as a burden now that the flight of movement had ceased. Bebeji kept stroking her back, as a kind of balm. Her grandmother's praise swirled in Kamlesh's mind "*Tue te kamaal hee kardita.*" *What you did was unbelievable.* Jaya stood beside her, holding her flowers, bringing her a glass of water from somewhere.

Her father embraced her tightly. He wore his handsome woolen jacket with the Nehru collar. "What a beautiful performance," he told her with a catch in his throat. She could not remember being held so long and closely by him before.

Members of the local Tamil community, familiar with Bharata Natyam and Masterji's reputation as one of the foremost dance teachers in the country, offered their appreciation in a mixture of tongues—English, Hindi, Tamil. "Punjabi girl better in Bharata Natyam than Madrasi girls," one lady quipped. A few others who stepped forward to congratulate her cried, "Vyjayanthimala!" "The next Vyjayanthimala has come!"

The comparison to the actress Vyjayanthimala, a Bharata Natyam virtuoso, was unexpected and flattering. This audience knew the dance intimately, so the extent of their appreciation unnerved Kamlesh. Praise felt strange;

she was used to striving. Masterji stood beside her at one point, handsome in a white silk dhoti and silk stole over his bare shoulder, and just shook his head, looking at her as if she'd done something remarkable. She could tell he hadn't expected it after the mistakes she'd made during rehearsals.

Now she had to acknowledge her performance herself, see herself differently. She had felt herself rising as she danced, growing like a flame, alive. Some spirit had propelled her. Maybe it was shakti, the energy Jaya talked about—a burning desire for life. Perhaps she had drawn that energy from the audience; what a magnificent feeling to have so many people watching her. Or maybe it was her surging joy in seeing Jaya with the family. Afterward, Jaya had whispered to her, "I feel I've just seen the best dance performance of my life today. Every piece you did so beautifully, especially that varnam you were worried about. I wish everyone could have watched you."

At home, over the evening meal, Kamlesh told the family about a man from the British Council who'd spoken to her after the show. Others had noticed this thin, young Englishman hanging about and wondered who'd invited him. He made a point of attending programs in out-of-the-way theaters, he'd told Kamlesh, finding them often more authentic than the shows put on in the big halls, which tended to be Westernized productions. Commonwealth scholarships were available to Indian artists, he'd said, to go over and give performances in England.

"Now you concentrate on your studies," her father said, less harshly than he might have spoken to her earlier, before she got sick. But he understood that she'd brought up the artist's scholarship as a claim to keep up an intensive dance practice. "Next year, after your exams, you should get married. There's no time to go abroad and give dance shows, isn't it? We've let you do everything you wanted." Kamlesh began to protest, and he fixed her with a sharp look. "You must recognize your limits."

No one spoke—not her mother, Bebeji, Dipi, or Manu. They ate quietly, embarrassed to hear her scolded hours after winning great praise for her performance. Finally, Vidya said to console her, "Everyone appreciated your dance very much. You should feel happy it went off so well. Now you attend to your teaching." Kamlesh wasn't meant to object, so she nodded and continued eating.

That week, while teaching a class of ten-year-old girls, and at other times, observing her classmates teaching, Kamlesh's anger magnified. Her professors at St. Xavier's had warned that this would be the most hectic year of her life, with practice teaching going on till early afternoon and college classes afterward, and now her parents expected her to devote herself fully to her teacher's training. Her dance lessons were to be cut back to once a week on Saturdays, like a beginner.

She knew it was only because she had fallen ill that she had been allowed to ascend to the stage. After saying no to her arangetram, her parents had allowed her to hold her recital, but on a diminished scale they could hide from everyone they knew. Her mother had asked Masterji to choose a venue in Matunga, suggesting that a knowledgeable audience would most appreciate the show—never confessing to him that her own community would regard Kamlesh's dance, the art he'd devoted his life to, as a degrading exhibition of herself.

The Tamil audience in Matunga had been very welcoming, and their warmth had touched Kamlesh, yet she couldn't forget her disenchantment with the small hall, the audience seated on the ground. She was too accustomed to grand Western-style theaters not to think that community hall inferior. Yet it intrigued her to hear from Masterji that the hall was modeled on the performance space in a temple, where people sat on the ground. It had been designed that way partly because the community was used to such temples in the South, but mainly because they could not afford to build a Western-style auditorium. So she had danced in a space that came close to what a temple dancer experienced. She might not have felt disappointed at all if her mother hadn't also limited her audience. Her friends, classmates, relations, the entire community she'd grown up in—everyone she'd imagined watching her onstage—were banned from attending. All the years she'd put into Bharata Natyam, all of herself that she'd poured into this dance she loved, all that she'd wanted to show people, was concealed like a shameful secret.

By a rare stroke of luck, Leela had still been in town, but Kamlesh had also been forbidden from inviting her closest friend. Leela had extended a three-month-long holiday from that godforsaken place in the jungle where her only society was a few English middle-aged people. She had confided the depths of her misery to Kamlesh, regretting that she was hurting her husband, who was a good man, by staying in Bombay an additional month before and after his annual leave. How lonely he was in Birmitrapur by himself. Kamlesh embraced her friend and wanted to confide in her, too, but she dared not. Mummy was afraid that word would slip out once Leela spoke to her mother about the arangetram, as she suspected had happened with the news about Jaya leaving home. Her mother had also stopped her from inviting Sarojini, who had stayed with them during Partition and for whom Kamlesh had a special fondness. Sarojini and her husband now lived in government quarters, separately from his family—who'd always berated her for their losses. Though Sarojini had no connection to the well-to-do Punjabi circle in town, Mummy had considered inviting anyone they knew a risk.

In the days following her recital, Kamlesh checked the papers. Her mother had printed two hundred invitation cards for Masterji to distribute to his Tamil community, of which Kamlesh had kept four aside. Before posting them to the critics, she had added a two-page handwritten biography of her illustrious guru, Tiruvalaputtur Muthulakshmi Pillai, a direct descendant of one of the four brothers who'd created the choreography of Bharata Natyam as it was known today. She had included a black-and-white graduation photograph of herself, the one meant for boys' families. On the back, she'd simply written *Kamlesh Malhotra, October 1955*. She knew the power of her looks. Someone would surely pay attention.

The following weekend Manu got to the Sunday morning papers first. He was in the drawing room when he shouted, "Didi! Look at this! Oh my God." By the time Kamlesh pushed herself out of bed and went to the drawing room, her mother was sitting on the blue sofa, reading a single sheet pulled out of the *Times of India*. Kamlesh stood behind the sofa and leaned over her mother's shoulder to stare at the culture and arts page. "Young Artiste's Masterful Performance." The photograph stunned her—her body on full display in a sculptural pose. Her head warmed. This wasn't the kind of picture she had expected . . . Usually a dancer was photographed in active movement, telling a story. But the photographer had fled after taking a few shots, before she got to her narrative pieces. This was a still moment. Her body a sinuous curve. Both her arms thrown up in pleasure, her head tilted in profile, her eyes enormous with dark makeup drawn in tails. Her full torso was revealed in a long, tight blouse layered with a silk drape and gold necklaces. One hip thrust out.

Her mother flung her hand up furiously. "How did they know about the show?"

"Someone must have told them," Manu replied.

"Who is the writer?" Kamlesh asked in an affronted tone, as if she were too upset to read the name.

Her mother said she would ask her father to ring up the *Times* and ask why this man had been sent to write about her performance. Who had allowed the photographer to take such a photo? After a long pause, her mother inquired reluctantly, "You didn't contact him, did you?"

Vidya turned her head to look at Kamlesh, her face ashen, her hair coming out of her nighttime plait. Kamlesh denied playing any role in soliciting the review. "Can I see it?" She took the single sheet of newsprint from her mother's hands. Still standing behind the sofa, she held it wide open, the offended party assessing the damage. *Kamlesh Malhotra, a young exponent of Bharata Natyam, mesmerized the audience at Madurai Hall last Saturday with a full programme from alarippu to tillana that radiated an innocent beauty and energetic grace, instilling a feeling in the viewer that there could be no more exhilarating day than this one.*

"I was wondering who that photographer was," Manu said. "I thought he must have come from a newspaper, he went so close to the stage. Such a big camera with a flashbulb."

"These newspaper people can slip in and out like thieves? They don't need to take your permission before writing about you?" Her mother was indignant. She had noticed a flashbulb going off early in the show, she recalled, but she'd been watching Kamlesh intently, and then the photographer disappeared. Kamlesh heard the panic in her mother's voice. Manu searched the other papers twice but didn't find any write-ups about her recital. But everyone read the *Times of India*; now the word would get out. No one would miss the picture—she'd never seen herself look so beautiful. She was mesmerized by what she held within her and could express through her body. She remembered the moment the photographer first caught her eye. While she'd waited onstage for the musicians to tune their instruments, he had flicked his head, pointing a finger between himself and the stage to ask if it would be all right to take pictures. She'd replied yes with a flick of her head.

That week, her friends' excited phone calls left her beaming, their words holding up a glass to her in which she saw a new side of herself reflected. No longer a novice, but a flamboyant dancer. A personality. Some of her fellow teacher trainees gathered around her at college the day after the article appeared. One girl asked why she was going in for teaching if she was such a good dancer. A man from an advertising agency rang up to propose a role to her in a tea advert, an elegant scenario depicting ladies at a garden party, but her mother refused. The Handlooms Board phoned to invite her to model in a fashion show at the French consulate, exhibiting the latest French fashions made of traditional Indian fabrics. She was forbidden that too. It was a prestigious occasion any of her mother's friends would have loved to be invited to, but Mummy snapped, "I don't want any more attention brought to you. We've had enough trouble with one photograph in the paper."

Her father failed to reach the dance critic at the *Times of India*. He was an occasional writer who dropped off his articles after performances. He had no phone at home, so someone in the newsroom promised to leave a message for him to contact Mr. Malhotra. Harbans was livid but avoided any mention of the sensuous nature of the photograph. He regretted not getting up during the performance and throwing the photographer out. He'd noticed him but didn't want to disrupt her show. He thought he might be a man from the local community, taking pictures for the hall. Right under their noses, the fellow had undermined them. Now it was clear to Kamlesh her family had seen the photographer, he hadn't escaped their notice, but no one had said anything, as if they wanted to pretend he didn't exist. She had pretended the same, both terrified and thrilled at the prospect of finding a picture of herself in the newspaper. Her grandmother ordered Kamlesh to put the paper away—to be exposed like that, showing her whole body, for everyone to see!

Her mother's friends rang up, awed and mystified and hungry for information. Some ladies had had no idea Kamlesh danced, though others remembered watching the brief demonstrations her mother had pressed her to put on in the drawing room when she was younger. Would this be her profession? Was she going to be a girl on the stage? Giving public performances? The questions appalled her mother. But Kamlesh also detected a streak of pride in her mother when she reported her friends' remarks back to Kamlesh: "Such a beautiful picture." "Like an actress she looks." "Very daring girl." It was Mrs. Khosla, the wife of her father's boss, who invoked her mother's greatest fear, snidely asking if such great publicity about Kamlesh's stage show wouldn't discourage the families of eligible boys from asking about her. Vidya was mortified to hear the words from someone else. Now it was all out in the open. What damage Kamlesh's glorious photograph would do to her reputation, her chance for a good marriage, was beyond their control.

In a state of mourning, Kamlesh understood she would never persuade her parents to allow her onstage again. Gestures that came more naturally to her than words, verses and rhythms she recited in her head, her new dancer's bells on velvet cuffs—all of that had to be piled like logs on a pyre and set ablaze. The whole of her dream burned in front of her, and the hot ashes would fill her lap. Bebeji came to Kamlesh in the bedroom and put an arm around her, sensing her low mood—perhaps they were worried she would slip into a hopeless state again. Anything could be endured, Bebeji said, but not shame.

Only Jaya didn't ring her. Kamlesh waited. The week after the review appeared, she gave up on hearing from her twin and went to Bellasis Road. It was early on a Saturday morning, well before her lesson with Masterji, since Jaya left for the hospital by a quarter past eight. Sringara's mutely smiling servant girl, Amvi, led her to the dining room, which was empty of furniture. It was strange to see Jaya sitting cross-legged in her sari, leaning over her breakfast thali littered with the remnants of hot food. The air stank of fried mustard seeds and burnt chilies. Jaya immediately got up, a wary look on her face. "Did something happen?"

Kamlesh would have liked to retreat to Jaya's bedroom, where they could have privacy, but Jaya led her down the passage to the drawing room. They sat under the black, soot-stained ceiling on hard cane chairs deprived of cushions. She produced the newspaper from her bag, trying not to smile. Jaya let out a little scream, holding up the *Times*, folded to the culture and arts page. "What a fabulous picture," she cried. Then, after a pause, she wondered, "Are they angry with you?"

"You didn't see it when it came out on Sunday?"

"No." Jaya squinted, looking like she was thinking back to something she ought to have known about but couldn't recall. "I haven't been reading any papers." She was spending every minute she wasn't at college on her paintings, she said. She still didn't know if she'd be able to complete sixteen pictures for the show.

They sat in silence. Jaya read the article, staring at the page as if she didn't remember seeing the performance herself. As if she had to be introduced to all the things of the world again, because she'd been lost in the fantasy of her paintings for too long. "Oh—listen to what he says," she exclaimed, and began reading from the review. "'Kamlesh's karanas were brilliantly electrified by the passionate nature of her youth. With the revival of traditional dance forms like Bharata Natyam, which fell into disgrace under the prevailing Victorian morality of British rule, one looks to dynamic newcomers like Kamlesh to popularize this ancient temple dance on the modern stage.'"

Jaya looked up, smiling. Kamlesh's regret that she had no future as a dancer struck her all the more sharply. Masterji had looked at her with his soft, glowing eyes during her rehearsals, telling her Bharata Natyam had almost died when the British outlawed temple dancing. It had survived on the artistry of a few exceptional young dancers who shifted the dance to the stage. If she devoted herself completely to her practice, he believed she had the talent to rise to their ranks. Kamlesh had felt an enormous desire flare at his suggestion, but she'd only laughed. Now she understood better why she had posted invitations to the dance critics. It wasn't only for the sheer attention. She was curious to see herself reflected in the words of people who didn't know her, hear what they made of her abilities, and gain an understanding of where she stood in this world of dance that she wanted to be a part of. She couldn't bring herself to confess to Masterji that her parents would never allow her to appear onstage again. She couldn't accept their decision herself.

"What did Daddy say when he saw this?" Jaya wanted to know.

"I think he thinks that I told the journalist about the show." She didn't mention that the depression she had fallen into months back might have protected her from his wrath. He was a little more careful around her now.

"Did you invite someone from the paper?" Jaya asked in disbelief. "They wanted to keep the whole thing hidden."

"And you haven't done things you don't tell them about?" Kamlesh snapped. She sat clutching her cotton college bag in her lap, tense with resentment that Jaya had made her way out of the house, leaving her behind. She couldn't force Jaya to call her, couldn't make her shift back home; she couldn't ask for anything from her. Jaya had withdrawn into her own life.

What most stunned Kamlesh when Kirti walked into the room with a polite hello was the absence of any noise alerting them of his arrival. The bell hadn't rung; the front door hadn't opened and shut. Jaya mumbled a greeting. Kamlesh wondered where he'd appeared from, his trousers and shirt looking a bit battered—had he come out of Jaya's room? "I wanted to see if Parasmal gave you that parcel for me." He spoke to Jaya casually, as if he were another occupant of the flat.

Jaya got up. "Oh, yes." She went off to her bedroom, presumably to fetch the parcel. Or to invent one, thought Kamlesh. Did Kirti come by every day now, whether or not Sringara was at home? It seemed he was used to being here at all hours. With a withering sense of bravado, Kamlesh retrieved the *Times of India* from the side table where Jaya had left it and presented it to Kirti. "I had my arangetram last week," she said.

"Yes—I heard it went off very well. Excellent. Very nice photo, my goodness—" He stared at the picture, in the same way Jaya had, his eyes narrowed as if he were trying to penetrate the facade of her pose.

She loved being onstage, Kamlesh confessed, remembering how frightening and thrilling it had been to look out at the crowd and try to keep their interest. "I can make a second debut in London!" She mentioned the British Council officer who had suggested she apply for a visiting artist's grant. She laughed lightly at her feeble joke.

"That would be fantastic." A pat on the arm from Kirti. "Well done."

When Jaya returned with a brown-paper parcel, Kirti took it and immediately stood up to go. He had to rush back to the hospital to do his rounds. Kamlesh was surprised to receive from her twin an ink drawing on thick white paper. "What's this?" A figure in a sari she recognized as Bebeji stood at the head of a snaking procession of men and women, a large black flag raised in her hand. On the left side, a policeman reared up on horseback, flailing his baton in the air. The title made a wide arch over the scene—*A Lady Freedom Fighter*—and in the center Jaya had scrolled Bebeji's name, *Nihal Devi Malhotra*. Kamlesh wondered if Jaya was trying to divert her attention with this cover illustration for Manu's booklet. Why was Jaya bringing their family story out in front of Kirti? Jaya asked her to deliver the picture to Manu. Kamlesh declined to take the picture, saying she was going to be out the whole day. She didn't want to spoil it.

When Kirti turned to go, Kamlesh impulsively rose with him. "I have to look for the correct bus going to Matunga," she said. Jaya knew her dance lesson wasn't for another two hours, but it didn't matter to her if Jaya realized she was making an excuse to leave.

On the threshold of the rusting compound gates, Kamlesh paused, hesitating to walk all the way down the by-lane with Kirti. He indicated his motorbike parked along the boundary wall. She resented him for feeling so familiar with Sringara's compound that he parked inside, among the residents. "I'll look out for your picture in the papers," he teased.

The last time she'd run into him at Sringara's, as they'd walked down the dark staircase together, he'd brazenly told her she should consider acting in films. A few days earlier, he'd met Ashok's uncle N. D. Narula, who'd remarked that the best heroines had an innocent girl's charm and a dancer's grace. Now Kamlesh tried to hold his glance, of two minds whether to ask him or not, the temptation to seize the opportunity created by her public exposure hard to resist. After all, a number of girls from respectable families were going into films these days. Acting wasn't only for courtesans and poor girls anymore.

Before she asked Kirti if he would inquire with Ashok Narula's uncle on her behalf, she paused for just an instant, thinking she ought not take him into her confidence.

"I was just teasing you about making pictures." He sounded abashed, reluctant.

A car exiting the compound honked. They were startled to be caught standing together in its path and moved to the side, near Kirti's black motorbike. Children in school uniforms were coming out of the buildings, wearing their satchels. The little ones held their ayahs' hands. Kamlesh tried to compose herself. "It's something I've thought about for a long time," she confessed. "I'd like to give it a try." Kirti was the wrong person to ask, too close to Jaya, but he was the only person she knew with a link to a film-maker. Just now, she had seen him in a bad situation upstairs, caught him out with Jaya again. He might worry she'd tell her parents, jeopardizing his ability to meet Jaya so freely here. Despite the trouble she could cause, she was giving him some power over her, putting herself in his hands. She offered him her carefully folded copy of the *Times of India*. "Please show my photo to anyone who might be interested. I'm quite keen on this."

For a long moment Kirti looked at her, weighing his options or perhaps reflecting on her intentions. Then he nodded soberly, agreeing to ask Ashok Narula if his uncle might be interested in an unknown for an upcoming film. A trained dancer. "I hope it won't lead you into trouble at home," Kirti warned her. In the same breath, he fixed a time to meet her at a particular back gate of the hospital on Thursday evening, by which time he believed he would have procured N. D. Narula's response.

"Will you do it on your own? Don't mention anything to anyone." She was trusting him not to disclose any of this to Jaya. The "unknown" need not even be identified to Ashok Narula by name.

"If you're sure about it." Kirti folded the paper in half again, creasing her image straight down the middle, as if he were splitting her in two.

21

THE SEA WAS a vacuous gray at Versova at two o'clock on a Sunday afternoon, the sand burning their feet like the ashes of a smoldering fire. They
plodded up a slope to a grove of coconut trees above the beach. His body
shifted in and out of bars of sunlight falling between the spindled palms.
Kirti spread a sheet stripped from his hostel bed on the ground and laid
out packets of parathas and idlis and oily red mango pickle bought from
a roadside restaurant on their way out of the city. "A feast," he called the
mixed-up foods. Jaya laughed, wrinkling her nose at the hodgepodge. She
sat at the edge of the sheet, one foot toying with stringy fallen coconut
husks. He reached for her, which was what she'd been waiting for, pulling
her down beside him. His hands pressed on her shoulders so that he loomed
over her. One hand slipped to her breasts, swelling against her kameez. It
moved down her tensed abdomen, smoothed a track over the bunched
cloth from the inner to the outer edge of her thigh.

She couldn't help thinking of the people they'd passed by on the beach—
what if someone came around here? She balanced precariously on the
line between pleasure and unease. The desire to touch; the fear of being
seen. She jerked her head away, made a noise of protest. It was madness
to come to the beach today, when she was so anxious about completing
the paintings for her exhibition. The journey had cost them two hours by

train, bus, and then foot for the last half mile to the beach. She would no longer expose herself on the roads on his motorbike.

Yesterday he had found her on campus and told her very earnestly, as if he were a young boy making an entreaty, "I want you to come." You couldn't refuse Kirti when he pressed you; he wanted what he asked too much. He was full of feeling. Yet he well knew Jaya was under pressure to finish the last two paintings for her exhibition. It would be opening in ten days. And she'd just had a batch exam in medicine, misdiagnosing the male patient she was made to present to the honorary, despite mugging up on the symptoms of diseases. Her marks had fallen—she had to devote more time to her studies. But her mind was always on her paintings. In lectures, she would sketch a composition, rub it out, revise. Sometimes a professor's words worked their way into a picture—this kind of swelling, that kind of nerve malfunction pushing a limb into an unnatural position. But she wasn't portraying the sick; she was painting people who burned with life despite everything they were made to bear.

Kirti sat up and tore into the paratha, wrapping each piece around a bit of oil-drenched pickle. Jaya declined his offer of food, and he raised his eyebrow, looking offended. She drew lines in the sand with the stem of a dried frond. He kept pushing his way into Sringara's flat, and Kamlesh had caught him there last Saturday. He had deliberately shown his face, rather than remain in the bedroom. Jaya had been furious with him. What if Kamlesh thought he'd been there all night and decided to tell their parents? Sometimes he came by in the darkness of daybreak, as he had that day, and lay with her for an hour or two before reporting to the hospital. He would guide her hand to unbutton his trousers, and she would feel him with both hands, his soft wilted rose head, velvety dark and fleshy, a drooping flower growing straight up and firm. She would smell of him the whole day afterward, as his tobacco musk had seeped into her skin.

Later, after he had finished eating, Kirti caught her by the neck in the crook of one strong arm, securing her in his custody. Jaya laughed nervously. He reached for both her hands, roughly inspecting them, kissing the tops of her fingers, which smelled of turpentine, and clutched them forcefully in his.

"What are you doing?" She twisted her hands out of his painful grasp.

"Why is it you never tell me anything?"

"Kirti." She'd hurt him somehow. His face showed it.

She asked what she should tell him, and he said, "Anything that actually matters to you." He was full of resentments these days. "You're completely preoccupied with this exhibition. I don't think you realize your obsession with it has become an obstacle." He brought up a woman they'd seen walking along the sea and questioned why Jaya had said she'd like to paint her. Apparently, she was attracted to oddity. Jaya ignored the slight. The woman had been exceptionally tall and slender, her entire body concealed in the windings of a red sari, no part of her visible except her feet. An enigma, a double of the scarlet-veiled woman on the hill. She appeared to be freed by her concealment, seeing everything but remaining unseen.

Kirti reached into his shirt pocket and extracted a packet of Wills, lit a cigarette. "You're too involved in your art, your own thoughts."

Hiding herself from him hadn't been her intention, though it might have happened by instinct. She asked, "Why should I tell you everything I'm thinking?"

"I don't see you." He turned away to watch the sea through the palm trees. If he hadn't sullenly remarked "Maybe there's nothing there to see," she might have mentioned a thought she'd had, likening painting to taking a patient's present history. In the hospital, you began with this inquiry: *Do you have any pain? How many days have you had the pain? What were you doing at the time you first felt the pain?* Sometimes it felt as if painting a portrait were a way of taking down your subject's history, the picture becoming the diagnosis you didn't know you were going to arrive at.

Kirti continued to sit with his back to her, but he turned his head back to snap, "Make a painting of yourself, then I'll know who you are."

Jaya got up and stepped around the greasy food wrappings, refusing his insinuation that she was nothing underneath. She was something; she could be known. And Kirti would not be the one to judge her. He called after her a few times but she ignored him, walking out of the palm grove, down the slope of sand into the light. The sea had risen in the sky. It seemed to have gained altitude. She wandered into the surf's spreading glaze. The chill of seawater dousing her feet reminded her of the last time on the beach, when Kamlesh had been with them, bending into unraveling lines of froth. Jaya had dreamed of doing a series of dance paintings then, and she had done them, following the dancer as she grew into her dance. Into these she would weave the poor women and girls from the colony, moving from canvas to canvas in their own swerves and arcs across the dusty, stony earth. Kirti didn't understand her—art was no obstacle. She was *there* in her images. There was nothing more to know.

BEBEJI TURNED UP at Sringara's flat for the first time four days later. She had climbed to the top story of the building alone and stood sighing at the front door, out of breath. Her sudden appearance, her face tight with anger, worried Jaya. Bebeji would not step inside or even accept a glass of water. She wanted to make absolutely clear her disapproval of Jaya's life here. She had come to take Jaya home; the driver was waiting downstairs. The family wanted to speak to her.

Jaya ran to close her pots of home-ground paint, to clean her fingers off with a turpentine-soaked rag. In the car, Bebeji's face remained firm with disapproval. She didn't talk to Jaya except to say, "This cannot go on."

A desolate afternoon silence hung over the flat. A new servant answered the door in his undershirt and pajamas, his hair tousled. He must have been taking his afternoon rest. Her father and Dipi hadn't returned home yet from their meetings, the boy reported to Bebeji; Memsahib was taking a nap. "Go and meet your sister," Bebeji told Jaya. She disappeared into the kitchen with the boy to fetch cold drinks. Her gait was more labored, as if she were dragging around a heavier burden.

Jaya walked reluctantly down the passageway, a stranger in her own home four months after she'd left. She was wary. She didn't know what they wanted to speak to her about. In the bedroom, Kamlesh was pulling off her sari. Books and clothes were strewn haphazardly across the settee. The writing table was in disarray, Kamlesh's papers and film magazines scattered everywhere. A new, disorderly side of her twin was being revealed. All the curtains were open, a blinding light slanting in through the back windows and open balcony doors. Kamlesh didn't speak but her eyes grew wide, as if she were waiting to hear the bad news that explained Jaya's appearance.

Jaya went to latch the bedroom door. Kamlesh stood there in her bodice and petticoat. "Why are you locking it?"

"Did you tell them something?" Jaya asked coldly. Latching the door was an old habit, an instinctive desire for privacy. "You had no business going to them. You're just worried about yourself, that they might find out you wrote to the newspapers." Jaya listened to the angry words rushing out of her own mouth, surprised. She had been submerged in her painting, remote from everyone, separate even from this other side of herself, who fought her for remaining apart.

"What have I said?" Kamlesh looked bewildered. She went to the cupboard for fresh clothes. "Stop giving me such horrible looks. I didn't say anything about you."

"What was the reason? Tell me." Jaya stood triply reflected in the dressing table mirrors, her face burning, flushed with heat. She could get nothing out of Kamlesh. The way the afternoon light fell, painting the room in patches of glare and strokes of shadow, she couldn't clearly make out her twin's face. Jaya took a few steps toward her, their bodies breaking into collages, strips of light and shadow. Kamlesh drew away, stumbling backward against the cupboard. Her sun-browned face was turned up, pale lipstick glistening, her reflection openly fearing her. Jaya's hand went out to her sister's shoulder; she moved forward as if to embrace her, smelling her powdered skin and pulling at the thick vine of her plait. This shadow, her twin, threatened the very existence of her paintings, the ones she kept safe at Sringara's. She pulled Kamlesh's plait again, wanting to be free of this reflection, this stifling double, to live on her own, unhindered.

"Are you mad?" A shout escaped Kamlesh's mouth. Jaya released her twin, realizing what she was doing. Kamlesh was in tears, her face sheltered in her hands. "Why do you hit me?" or "Why do you hate me?" Jaya couldn't make out exactly what Kamlesh was saying.

In her parents' room, Jaya stood accused. Kamlesh sat next to Bebeji with a swollen expression, a fingernail scratch on the side of her face shaming Jaya. The room was dim, the curtains drawn against the afternoon sun. "What happened?" her mother asked, disconcerted, pressing her hairpins back into her bun. She had been asleep. She appeared to have had no idea that Bebeji had gone to fetch Jaya, but she supported Bebeji for doing so. "It's good you brought her home. She's caused us so much trouble." In a dry whisper of a voice, Jaya said she thought Kamlesh had been making up stories about her because she never wanted her to move out of the house.

"I haven't said anything." Kamlesh was defiant. "I could have told them a lot of things but I didn't. I don't have anything to say about you."

"She was not the one." Bebeji shielded Kamlesh, stroking her head as they sat together on the foot of the bed. She had hurried to see what was happening when she heard Kamlesh scream. "Why do you pounce on her? What does she know?"

Their mother combed her fingers through her hair, trying to bring herself into form, Jaya could see, to confront her with strong authority. "I always thought you told us the truth, despite your behavior in the last few months. But now I wonder, will you tell us the truth at all? What have you been doing behind our backs?"

WHEN HER FATHER returned home, Jaya was brought from Bebeji's alcove, where she'd been resting, back to her parents' room. Her father was dressed in a khaki jacket and tie; he'd had some meetings in town. "Who is the boy? Tell us," her father demanded. She had not seen her father in almost a month, since Kamlesh's arangetram. There was still a coldness between them, an absence of affection. It was a terrible feeling, odd and unsettling. Yet estrangement made it easier for her to speak.

They were gathered around her, a tribunal of elders—her father, mother, and Bebeji. Jaya faced them from the corner chair with a certain resolve, but her mouth quivered. She had slept briefly after spending much time frantically anticipating what her father might demand of her. In her restless, twisting sleep, a decision had come to her like a revelation: a clear idea of what she must do.

"He's a Bengali boy," she began in a low voice as her mother made a face. "An older boy. I've gone out with him here and there—it's not serious. I don't know who's been saying things about me, but we're just in the same group of friends. That's all."

"You were seen alone with him last evening," her father said. His lean mouth was drawn back in sinewy creases. "How can you say it's nothing? What is the meaning of your going around with a boy at night?"

"I've only met him in the evenings with my friends," Jaya replied, avoiding their glances with an unfocused gaze across the room. It was the gross suggestiveness of nighttime that incensed her father: that she had been out in the dark with Kirti. Who had seen them? Was it Dipi again? Had he decided to say something this time? Her father waited for her to continue. She could confess the seriousness of the relationship, throw off the mask of modesty. Yet if she admitted her feelings for Kirti—which was an intimate matter she didn't want to bring up before them—and even if they accepted him, what would she have to give up? She would do nothing to endanger her paintings.

Dipi was called into the room. He walked in without the usual hint of humor in his eyes. Formal in a jacket and tie. In a quiet voice, he told her he had seen her walking out of a Chinese restaurant on Colaba Causeway with a boy, the same tall, broad-built, dark-complexioned fellow he'd seen her with once before. She'd been on the footpath; he and his friends had been walking on the road to their car. "Satish Bhatia saw you first. He asked me, 'Hey, isn't that one of your cousins?' I said, 'No, no, I don't think so.' You were quite dressed up. The chap stopped to buy a paan from a paanwalla on the corner." She remembered that Kirti had held out the paan and she had taken a dripping bite of it from his hand. He'd stopped by the flat, insisting on taking her out for a good Chinese meal.

Dipi stood in front of her father's glass-fronted bookcases, a reluctant prosecutor, saying he had told her parents this morning and they had decided Bebeji should also be told, since she was close to both granddaughters and this was a matter of the entire family's reputation. He wanted to protect everyone from gossip. "Satish saw you last night, Ravi saw you. What will outsiders say if they see you roaming about with a boy and you're not even living in your parents' home? The things people might make up could be much worse than the truth, and we'd have no control over the rumors."

"Her exhibition will be the end of this experiment," her mother said to defuse the tension, to suggest a resolution was at hand.

"I don't believe it's not serious," Dipi declared with blunt conviction. "That's why I decided to say something."

"I won't see him again." Jaya's voice fell, her throat dry with the fear of what she would have to do. "There's no need to worry that I'll ruin my name."

Her father removed his glasses and rubbed his eyes. He looked at her with disappointment, his gray-brown eyes clouded as though tears were not possible for him—nor words.

"I'll have to talk to Kamlesh," she mumbled, thinking of how brutally she'd behaved. Her terrible mistake in suspecting her.

"A girl in her own house, among her own people, is always in the strongest position," Bebeji said firmly. "Your daddy was going to confront you at Sringara's place, but I decided, no, you should come home and be with all of us. You've always been a good girl. You wanted to do good work in the colony. This painting of yours has swept you away. Don't get lost in the hollowness of yourself—in your fantasies and obsessions."

"This kind of behavior," her father said, collecting himself, "casts a stain on the entire family. People are wondering, what is happening here that has made you go off to stay with a strange woman? In everyone's minds, something has destroyed this family—that's why you've left. It looks like we're shattering. We will lose everyone's respect."

At Sringara's that night, alone in her room, Jaya settled into her armchair. A painting was propped against the wall on top of a scarred steel trunk, of a blind woman in her hut. Looking at her pictures calmed her. The blind woman's body was a hatching of bones inside the shell of her hut, its doorway barred by a grille of gray sticks. The whites of her eyes were shaped like eggs; her head was angled up to the light like Wasima's sightless grandmother. Her hands were coated in bright pigment, and on the dun-brown walls of her hut were her memories—smudged drawings of fields, skies, and people, of patterns erupting from her mind. Though she couldn't see, the blind woman had painted her life, remembering what she had loved.

Jaya got up and removed the painting from the trunk—this one she would show. She placed another canvas on the makeshift easel and sat down to assess the smaller picture. In the bent-cane chair, she felt she was sitting in a cage, deserving punishment. She had finished her last paintings, so she was meant to be leaving this flat. Chadha had said something to her about "salvaging our identity" through art after the end of foreign rule, and Jaya wondered if the same idea could be applied on a personal level—was she salvaging her identity in this flat? Was painting a way of salvaging herself?

It was harrowing to see how her absence had caused her father to suffer. She had injured him, injured the whole family. A part of her hated being here and craved returning home, wanting to be loved by her family again.

Yet she had become accustomed to her solitude. This space to paint and think was the purest freedom she'd ever had.

Before she slept, she went to find Sringara—who was in the kitchen squatting on the floor, cleaning a sickle-shaped knife mounted on a wooden block that she held between her feet, a weapon to split jackfruit. Jaya poured milk into a pan and lit the burner. The room stank of gas and spent matches. Sringara rinsed the cloth she'd cleaned the knife with in the basin. She spooned oil from a metal canister into her hands and rubbed them till they glistened. The jackfruit halves lay on the counter, and Sringara reached an oiled hand into one half to yank out a lump of silken orange pods spun around a seed. Jaya stirred a spoon of sugar crystals into a cup of hot milk. "You're sure fifty will be enough?" she asked.

It made them uncomfortable to discuss money as friends, as mentor and pupil, but Jaya wanted to be clear that if she continued to live here, she would pay Sringara at least fifty rupees a month and not be a complete burden on her. As a matter of courtesy, Sringara had insisted she didn't want to charge Jaya rent, but since she was accustomed to earning an income from paying guests, she'd agreed to accept fifty rupees a month for bed and board. Her rent remained the same low rate her aunt had paid in the 1930s, because of the laws favoring tenants, she told Jaya, so she could afford the flat on her part-time teacher's salary and occasional sale of her paintings. It was a delight for her to have Jaya's companionship in place of the couple who were constantly fighting. Sringara pulled her hand out of the soft womb of the fruit and looked at Jaya. "You're prepared to do this?" she asked in response to Jaya's question.

Jaya nodded. Of course, her plan depended on her selling her paintings at the exhibition. She tried to be optimistic and suggested the possibility of the two of them showing their pictures next year at a joint exhibition. "We could call it Two Women," Sringara proposed. Jaya laughed a small laugh. Could she really do this? The question of money had always stopped her before, a surrogate for other, larger obstacles. She wanted something to stop her now—she was afraid to take her life into her own hands, and yet she was taking it into her hands.

"I like that title," she told Sringara. "Two Women."

22

INSIDE THE DANK fortress of the Pathology School, Jaya searched for Kirti. His colleague on the surgical ward, Parasmal, had directed her there, though he was not sure on which floor the lecturer Kirti had gone to meet had his office. Wandering through a dingy labyrinth of corridors to the back of the building, past the professors' offices, Jaya listened for his voice. It was lunchtime; the massive doors to all the rooms were shut. She went up a couple of flights of stairs, walked down one passageway, then another, went up the stairs to the second floor, followed the fragments of male voices till they dissipated, and found no one in the corridor. She climbed back down to the first floor. He was coming out of someone's office, closing a door, looking down with a smile, his white coat buttoned over a checked shirt and formal tie.

"What happened? How are you here?" He gave a doubtful laugh. He looked different—very neat and trim. He'd had his hair cut, she realized.

They walked without aim as she told him about what her parents had found out. They rambled down one dim passageway, then up another in a building she had never become oriented to. They were circling around rooms they'd passed before, she realized, as they retraced their steps in confusion, searching for the staircase going down.

"Let me speak to them," Kirti said. They found the stairs and he glanced down—no one there. He went ahead of her. "If it's out in the open now, let me make my intentions clear."

"No" was all she was capable of saying.

Kirti gave her another doubtful look, a reprimand: "Why not?" She was now leading him down an empty, shadowy corridor as if she knew exactly where they should go, turning left through the Pathology Museum, past shelves displaying diseased body parts in jars of jaundiced amber formaldehyde—lengths of leukemia bones, leathery scraps of leprosy skin, a cyst like a fuzzy piece of cotton wool cocooned inside a cut section of brain. He followed her past two workers sorting through specimens of diseased organs soaking in buckets, splashing the floor with chemicals. They exited out the back, taking a walkway connecting the Pathology School to the Court of the Coroner of Bombay. Brown betel-nut juice spat out on a shred of paper on the ground looked like splattered blood to Jaya's eye. No one around in the silence of noontime except an amputee practicing walking, leaning on a single crutch.

"I'll stop coming there," Kirti proposed—meaning Sringara's flat. From the walkway they could see that the office of the doctor on postmortem duty was deserted behind its barred window. "We can see each other less often. We'll talk to them once you finish your studies."

His hand brushing Jaya's arm, nervously fingering the bones of her wrist and clasping it tightly, caused a thread of sorrow to pierce her. She had been speaking with little emotion, in a remote state of disbelief, but now her throat tightened.

"You never wanted your parents to accept this, did you?" he accused her.

Jaya let her hand fall into the cradle of his and left it there as they moved blindly down the covered passage. Then Kirti drew away, perhaps fearing that someone coming out of the coroner's building would see them holding hands.

He pulled open the door and they walked in as if they had an appointment on the premises. Inside the white-tiled passageway, standing by a door marked Coroner's Surgeon & Police Surgeon Bombay, he came as close as he could to pleading. "Someone has to look after you—you're always fighting yourself."

Jaya shook her head. Something was extinguished inside her, a breath that was attached to his. "We shouldn't meet each other," she said in a tired voice. Her fantasies had crumbled; she couldn't by a sheer force of will remain unseen with him. People saw, they talked. The rumors swirling around her threatened her family more than her. Without their place in their society, her parents would have nothing. "I can't keep telling lies."

"What is it really? What are you angry about? Tell me—" Some other reason lay at the root of it, he seemed to imagine, sounding remorseful he'd done something to offend her. An attendant flung open the door to the mortuary: a burly man was laid out on a high metal table, blood streaked across his bare stomach and heavy thighs. Another nude man lay with his dark, mustached face gazing straight up to the ceiling. Kirti pulled her away from the sight of the corpses, down the corridor toward the dirty stairs leading up to the pathology lecture hall. Jaya let him keep his grip around her arm.

"I didn't want it to be like this," she said.

"I don't know who you care for." He raised his voice, but it came out sounding choked. "I think only for yourself." Jaya didn't know what to say to this. She was just starting to come to grips with her painting, with herself. She didn't have a grasp on herself yet, on what she could do; she felt in no position to claim him. "You were never serious about this—"

"I was serious," she insisted. They were moving back up the corridor when she was given another view of the bodies as the peon pushed the mortuary door open, wheeling out a crate on a gurney. She found herself taking Kirti's hand, trying to hold on to him, but she felt nothing back, no pressure from him, so she let his limp hand fall.

23

IN THE GLARE of a November afternoon, just two days after her confrontation with Jaya, Kamlesh met Kirti at a horseshoe-shaped complex of filmmakers' offices on the seafront in Tardeo. From his dull, sullen expression, she sensed Jaya had broken things off with him. If that was true, she was surprised he'd turned up to introduce her to Mr. Narula, as they had arranged the previous week.

The absence of an electric bulb in the stairwell of N. D. Narula's building satisfied her desire to become a shadow, a silhouette no one could identify. Waiting for the producer-director in a cramped antechamber reeking of mold and cigarettes, Kirti returned Kamlesh's newspaper to her, saying he hadn't shown it to anyone. She hated to see how he'd creased and folded the paper over several times into a kind of baton, and she smoothed it out on her lap.

To Kamlesh's dismay, N. D. Narula was not the handsome, imposing Punjabi man of tall stature she'd imagined to be behind the powerful name Narula Productions, but an aging figure of a crude, fleshy heaviness, disabled by an injury that required him to walk with a cane. He came around his desk to squeeze Kirti's hand. As a producer-director he was seen as second only to Mehboob, so it was a shock to hear him sighing with effort when he returned to his chair, his lower lip hanging open as if he had forgotten what he was about to say.

"How have you been keeping, Uncle?" Kirti addressed him warmly as a family friend, his nephew's former class fellow.

Narula dropped his head with a kind of shrug, putting his hands out in question. "Since my fall, it's difficult for me to move about. I'm bringing in someone else to direct my next picture." Slowly he turned and gestured to the movie poster hanging behind his desk, appearing to recover his thoughts. He asked if they'd ever seen the film, *Samarpan*, and told them it was his favorite among all his films. They had not seen it—he'd made it back in 1942. On the poster a walled city was shown in flames, frantic people running out of its gates. A warrior on horseback galloped toward the calamity, an army trailing behind him. "Trying to save a noble past from destruction," Narula mused. "It's the story of my father's family, at the time when the British seized Multan, told with a few embellishments. The British I turned into invaders from the Northwest, the city I gave a different name, otherwise their censorship board would have banned it. It would have spoiled my career." He continued to gaze at the image, shaking his head. "The tragedy of history has been my obsession for the whole of my life."

Kamlesh glanced around at the panorama of film posters. They covered the room's green walls, blistered and flaking with sea damp. Beneath each rousing image of lovers or battle appeared the slogan "Narula Productions Presents," or "Premiere Of . . . ," or "In Two Reels." Kamlesh imagined herself as the heroine in *Toofani Raat*, throwing her head back in anguish, her pained face imposed above a horde of men on horses stirring up clouds of dust, swords lifted over their heads—marauders who would capture her.

"That was a beautiful movie," Kamlesh recalled, indicating the poster.

"So, Miss Malhotra . . ." Narula was abruptly forthright. "I understand you are a medical student who would like to go into acting. Are you planning on giving up your studies?"

"I'm afraid I may not have been clear, Uncle. She's not the one doing medicine." Kirti smiled over the misunderstanding. He had cut his hair, trimmed it short above the ears, showing an endearingly boyish face, a naivete Kamlesh had not been aware of.

"That's my sister," Kamlesh said faintly, as if the volume of her voice could regulate how much she gave away of herself. "I've trained as a Bharata Natyam dancer."

Narula's eyes opened wide, appearing to pop out of his face. He put his hands on his desk and leaned forward, assessing them both as though to verify he was being told a straight story. He wanted to know Kamlesh's age, who her father was, what business he was in, where in Punjab he hailed from. *Who was she?* That was the gist of his questioning. Kamlesh grew frightened, improvising answers to distance Narula from her father, making her fictional father the owner of a chemicals business in Chembur. He now hailed from—Sargodha.

"Sometimes in educated families there are objections to girls going into films," Narula explained.

"They have a liberal outlook," Kirti replied, to Kamlesh's relief.

"She's finished her studies?" Narula turned to him.

"I've done my BA in literature at Sophia College." Kamlesh neglected to mention she was in the midst of a one-year teachers' training course, her days not ending till six in the evening. Thankfully she had no practice teaching on Saturdays, although she had to cancel a lesson with Masterji today to meet Mr. Narula. It had come almost too easily to her, ringing Masterji's neighbor to pass on the message; she could feel herself cutting the ties to a dance her parents would never let her possess. To her mother she explained the reason for getting dressed up was a lunch given by one of her trainee teacher friends. "I'll be twenty-one at the end of this month," she told N. D. Narula. In eyeliner and a starched cotton sari printed with wavy black lines and huge, bursting flowers along the hem, she felt fashionable and adult.

"I've not seen many graduates taking up acting, though things are changing nowadays," Narula conceded with a nod. "Personally, I've always found the upper-class attitude toward actresses hypocritical—everyone enjoys watching them in films, idolizes their beauty, then calls them whores."

The word stunned Kamlesh. The heat rose to her face as she stammered, "My parents have no objections. I used to act in all the school plays—they're quite broad-minded in that respect."

Smoothing out the deep creases in the newspaper, she laid the review of her recital on Mr. Narula's table. The photograph of her with her arms thrown up, her face in profile, her sleek waistline, loomed large. "I don't know, Uncle, if you've seen this article—I gave a Bharata Natyam performance last month. It was my arangetram."

Narula drew the paper closer and took a long moment to examine her photo—to her embarrassment—then skimmed the article. He looked straight at her. She hoped Mummy's face powder had made Jaya's fingernail mark near her jaw invisible. "You're quite photogenic."

She couldn't help a smile and dared to inquire, "Is it for your next film you require a dancer, Uncle?" Kirti had said as much when she'd met him at the hospital last week.

Folding his hands upon his great stomach, Narula turned his head to the right to glance out a small, dirty window with a partial view of the sea. For his next film, he was indeed looking for a top-notch classical dancer, not just a chorus girl, and that's why Kirti's phone call had interested him. The dancer's role was central to his story, although very little acting was required. She would have to convey all the pain of her young life through her dance for the temple god. Narula grew reticent about the details when Kamlesh inquired further, saying every filmmaker protected his story—it was his gold.

"Oh, I'm sorry." Kamlesh was unused to thinking of stories as assets anyone might steal. In mythology, in dance, stories proliferated like petals on flowers.

Narula reported that he'd sold his story to distributors in seven territories, had recorded four songs, and would begin shooting in January. He was looking to cast his temple dancer, he said, turning to Kamlesh with open hands. She laughed a slight laugh, incredulous that a few words could change her fate.

Outside, on the road facing the sunstruck sea, Kirti shaded his eyes. He advised her to tell her parents before she signed the contract Narula had spoken about.

"I'll see if I can." Kamlesh hesitated. If she mentioned the contract to her parents, Kirti's name might come out; they would ask how she had met Narula. "Don't say anything to her just now," she implored—meaning Jaya. She couldn't be sure he and Jaya weren't together anymore.

"Don't worry about that," Kirti said in a hard tone. He gave her an odd salute like a soldier following orders and then walked away. He had to get back to the hospital.

"Madhavi." Kamlesh stood on the main road and turned around to gaze in the distance at Haji Ali's tomb rising from its mooring in the sea, a shimmering white dome and minaret. "I am Madhavi." She rolled the name out slowly, delighting in its cadence. Madhavi—the legendary dancer of the *Epic of the Anklet*, whom Masterji had described as "the queen of emotional expression." Kamlesh decided to rename herself Madhavi for films, after realizing the impossibility of becoming a true dancer herself. If you were a girl onstage, in public, if you gave others a view of your body—your being—you were dishonorable. Shameless. That's how others saw you. A whore.

24

JAYA'S FOURTEEN PAINTINGS hung on the curving gallery walls, unframed, each portraying aspects of figures as brown as earth, solid and abstract, dancers in a mythic space, and women and girls in dim hovels or a rough, stone hill, two separate subjects joined under the heading "The Shakti Cycle," displayed on a board. The mythological dancers made up a sequence of paintings to the left, the seven portraits of people navigating life on the hill—on its precipices—on the right, the connections between them left to the viewer to ponder. Jaya was the youngest of the four painters in the show, the one completely unknown, her pictures spanning the back end of the hall, where most visitors finished their round of the gallery. It was a comfort to have hovering around her Sringara and her friend Yasmin Ahmed, the painter from Baroda whose husband Chadha had invited to inaugurate the exhibition. The two of them would return to her corner even after someone pulled them away. Yesterday, as Jaya had been arranging her paintings, Yasmin had called them intriguing and also visually bold and had urged her to increase her prices. Few people could afford art, she said, but those who had the money would not hesitate to pay a hundred rupees more for a picture. She was a pragmatic and astute woman, with a heart-shaped face and long black hair she wore loose around her shoulders. You could recognize her coming from afar because of her straight posture and sweep of black hair. Jaya had heeded her advice, laughing as she wrote up a new list of prices for Sringara, who was managing her sales.

Chadha's pictures opened the exhibition: new paintings of emaciated handcart drivers, disfigured bazaar touts, office workers choked by their ties, encumbered by their briefcases, their undulating forms compressed between other figures or vehicles. "What happened to the mystic touch of Gauguin?" the *Times of India* critic Fritz Wolfensohn muttered as he jotted notes in his pad. In the middle of the room were Acharya's geometric mandalas in clayey impastos, and Vir's still lifes and voluptuous female figures segmented, reassembled, and sometimes stitched together with vines. "An offshoot of Cubism," Vir said of his style to a curious foreigner.

For Jaya, the excitement of the evening came in talking to strangers interested in her art—a thin parade of Parsi collectors, businessmen, company executives, writers, editors, film producers, students from the J. J. School of Art; people whose names flew past her the moment they were spoken. What riveted her were conversations revealing other people's thoughts and ideas about her pictures. A strapping German executive brought around by Dr. Herzfeld compared her work to an Italian Surrealist whose name she wasn't familiar with. Jaya smiled her slow, full smile, feeling older than she was—at least twenty-five. The fear she had lived under these past four months, the unhappiness of leaving her family, had lifted this evening. She felt a benevolence shining upon her.

Despite Kamlesh's earlier objections to publicly showing her portrait as Usha, the goddess of dawn—before which Kirti had stood mesmerized that day at Sringara's flat—she now appeared keen to make the link between herself and the painting. Several times Jaya had noticed her standing near the picture, unconsciously taking the dancer's pose, her waist twisting slightly, her left knee bending in a reflection of the figure, the contours of her body in a flowing skirt to her ankles matching the dancer's pillar-long legs and streaming hair. Mummy would pull Kamlesh away to another spot, seeing the connection, but Kamlesh would inevitably return with one of her friends. Jaya tried to talk to Kamlesh, but she kept her distance. She cast resentful glances at Sringara and Yasmin Ahmed, who sometimes hung about Jaya like guardians. Kamlesh clearly hadn't forgiven her for attacking her the day Bebeji brought her home. They all thought she'd gone mad living on her own, Kamlesh had told her that day, and Jaya was too ashamed of her behavior to begin to apologize to her sister.

"You've given her a darker face, but everyone can recognize it's her. Everyone knows she's the dancer in the painting," Vidya hissed to Jaya during a moment when they were alone. Mummy was elegant in thick silk and pearls and lipstick. "Why display your own sister like that? It's bad enough there was that photograph of her in the paper." Her mother's apprehension was rooted in deep disappointment. Shuli Auntie had run into Vikram Bakshi's mother at a gathering, and Mrs. Bakshi had told her they had been shocked to see Kamlesh's picture in the *Times of India*. The way she'd displayed herself, her whole body showing! Vikram had been taken with her a couple of years back at Leela's wedding. "It's too bad for Vikram," Mrs. Bakshi had said. "He works for an elite firm. We can't have a girl who likes to dance in public." Mummy looked tormented. They hadn't told Kamlesh about the rejection, afraid it might make her despondent. "Such a handsome, well-qualified boy—earning so well—gone! And now you're putting her on full display. Have some shame."

Jaya felt shaken, as if she were to blame for the Bakshis refusing Kamlesh. She was already shaken by the events of the last few days—the whole city in turmoil, a sudden combustion of the tensions the Communists had been periodically stirring up. Though the violence had subsided, some people were still wary of venturing out in the evening. Her mother had sent out over a hundred invitations to her exhibition, eager to restore Jaya's reputation—the whole family's reputation—by proving to her friends that Jaya's absence from home only had to do with her paintings, which were now on display at Jehangir, the most prestigious art gallery in town. Vidya had been hoping for more people to show up. Not satisfied that so-and-so had come, she looked around for all the friends who hadn't. People were still arriving, Jaya said, and Rashid Ahmed hadn't yet given his remarks.

Two days back no one could leave their homes, and cars had been banned from the roads. Twenty-one people had been killed in the rioting. Casualties had overwhelmed J. J. Hospital on the first afternoon, and several hundred medical students had been recruited to assist the doctors. Jaya had helped dress the wounds of boys in bloodied shirts, their chests lacerated by flying stones, pieces of their scalps missing. Half a million workers, incited by the Communists to demand a Maharashtrian homeland, had rampaged through the city—looting shops, torching buses, assaulting police. Now every group demanded its own state, as Bebeji said, calling for partitions all over India. Sringara had phoned Mummy from the veterinarian's flat to tell her that Jaya was all right; she was living on the hospital campus. Her mother had been ringing the veterinarian continuously until Sringara contacted her.

Not long after confiding the Bakshis' verdict on Kamlesh, Vidya returned to Jaya's end of the hall, this time in brighter spirits. Three good friends who'd turned up together accompanied her. "Where's your daddy?" Mrs. Narang pointedly asked Jaya. Tall, dark, athletic, with pencil-thin, arched eyebrows skeptically raised. "Has he come? I haven't seen him."

Vidya pulled out a hankie from her purse and tried to find a purpose for it, dabbing it around her neck. She said she hoped the car hadn't gotten held up by a demonstration on its way back from the factory; those morchas last week had created such havoc on the roads. Jaya said she was waiting to finally show him and Dipi all her pictures, knowing full well that her father refused to set foot in the gallery before she returned home tonight.

"Actually, a lot of people have come, considering all the trouble there's been," Manu remarked. Nearly a head taller than Jaya, he stood in front of her picture of the scarlet-veiled woman unveiled. His wide spectacles enlarged his face. "Where's the veil?" he asked.

"I took it away," said Jaya. Manu gave her a quizzical look.

The missing veil lent the background its hazy cochineal patina and the painting its paradoxical title, *The Veil*. The woman was not literally veiled like her double in another picture; she wore her veil within, protecting the fortress of herself. She crouched on a burning gray boulder, reaching one arm far down over the spiked tips of rock to pull up a small carving of a dancing Ganesha in gaudy colors, its trunk and limbs akimbo. Other small carvings bloomed between the rocks. A rock garden alive with her fantasies.

Later Jaya stood among a different cluster of her mother's friends. Raj Talwar pushed her way into their circle with her loud hellos, asking contentiously, "Did you see that painting everyone's talking about? The woman in the forest? Nothing on top or below. The height of indecency, I tell you." She turned her beakish face to Jaya. "Do you know that artist, beta?"

A term of endearment—*beta*—that gave Jaya the illusion of being embraced. Yet the question put her on edge. *Who did she keep company with?* "No. She's here because Mr. Bal Chadha invited her to be in his show," her mother cut in before she could reply. "He's very high up in Lever's, and a very good artist as well. His pictures are there in the front, as you enter. You must have seen them. This other fellow—who knows who he is? Mr. Chadha may have given a young chap a chance, not knowing what all his paintings are like."

Jaya avoided the troublesome word *nude*. She mentioned the European tradition of painting the human body, as well as temple sculpture showing the female form. Vir's nude couple in the forest had touched her deeply. Mrs. Talwar had avoided mentioning the man. Probably too embarrassed. The woman stood under dark, drooping branches. Her head was turned away from the bare male figure in the shadows, showing a dark backside as indistinct as the bole of a tree. His arm reached out to her, touching her stomach, as men gently touched pregnant women. The woman brought Sringara to mind—the crinkled hair, the vague marking on her brow.

"That picture is nothing like a temple sculpture," Raj Talwar replied acerbically. "No, beta, that kind of vulgar display is called *obscene*."

"Not only that picture is obscene," Mrs. Khosla interjected. "There's another one also. Just of a man. I think the painter himself."

The other women laughed, a collective nerve struck, knowing exactly which picture she meant. Vir's self-portrait had stunned Jaya too—he looked at the viewer, his head slightly turned, eyes watchful and sensual. In his hand he gripped the stems of long paintbrushes, a bouquet claiming his vocation, his easel at his side. Fully exposed, his body and the room flared with color. The checkerboard floor was made of pulsating strokes of red, deep blue, brown, gold, and orange; the same colors had been lavished on his body. In his forthright stance, with his hard, bony chest and prominent, tubular genitalia, he dared people to judge him. It was the first time Jaya had seen in Vir the same hurt and defiance that made Namdeo Tule so volatile.

Zaidi arrived late with friends, close to six o'clock, he and his entourage stirring up a commotion as they moved through the gallery. Everyone recognized the master by his slender physique and prophet's beard. Today, in place of his traditional white kurta-pajama, he wore sleek trousers and a striped shirt, dressed for an evening on the town. When he and a friend came to Jaya's end of the gallery, eyes followed them, and Jaya became aware of the greater attention Zaidi brought her work. "She used to hide herself from us earlier," Zaidi told his friend Mane, his eyes lighting up mischievously. "She would bring us her paintings rolled up in sheets." He turned to Jaya, "Don't take talent for granted, my dear. There is no muse, there is only talent. If you hide it—cover it up with modesty—it'll go." He snapped his fingers and his hand shot into the air like a bird taking flight.

A slender, middle-aged man, bright-eyed like Zaidi, Keshav Mane was an "art promoter" as Zaidi described him, who managed the artists' studios in the compound where Sringara painted. His new gallery would open there next year. Meanwhile, he was making a film about a woman artist's life. Could he borrow some of Jaya's paintings of the dancer? The request startled Jaya, she immediately agreed. "The girl is a woman of the world. She returns to Bombay after studying painting in Paris, and falls in love with a penniless Muslim poet," Mane explained. "She's infatuated with all arts, so the dance pictures would reflect her sensibility well."

"My sister loves films," Jaya said. "She would love to hear about yours." She peered ahead, to the front of the hall, but couldn't spot her twin among the clusters of people.

It was Mane, the impresario who would soon open Bombay's first curated gallery, who stepped up to the microphone in the middle of the hall, summoning everyone to gather. He offered an exuberant introduction to Mr. Rashid Ahmed, the esteemed artist and art historian from the Faculty of Fine Arts at Maharaja Sayajirao University in Baroda. Chadha nodded, arms folded over his chest, looking very pleased the evening was proceeding as he had choreographed.

"All art is history," Mr. Ahmed declared to the crowd of about a hundred and twenty people. He spoke with a gentle authority. An older man with salt-and-pepper hair, probably in his late forties, he looked distinguished in a silk kurta and churidar. Jaya noticed Yasmin Ahmed smiling with affection and pride. "The paintings in this hall are all beautiful and varied contemplations of a single idea: Who are we now? How do we see ourselves now that those who occupied our land and enslaved us are gone?"

The Europeans in the audience, mainly British, stood uncomfortably still. A fair-haired man near Jaya looked off to the side, rejecting Mr. Ahmed's words. "We are rediscovering ourselves, our traditions and emblems," Rashid Ahmed went on, "and making our own modernity. Some people are made uneasy by modernity. Our artists are told to hang a black cloth over their paintings; they're showing too much. We were ruled by a foreign power for so long that we don't dare to look at ourselves and know ourselves and our nation for what we are, what we have been made to endure. Our artists today are looking and showing us who we really are. We mustn't throw black cloths over the truth."

Later, Rashid Ahmed came to Jaya's end of the gallery with a few eminent-looking gentlemen. Jaya wanted to thank him for his talk but felt intimidated in the men's presence. Mr. Ahmed approached her after a few minutes and introduced her to Dr. Sohrabji and his associates. She heard "a great aficionado of modern art" and "father of our atomic energy program." Yasmin Ahmed had told Jaya that her husband had invited prominent collectors—among them a nuclear physicist, one of India's top scientists, who had filled his research institute with contemporary art. It had become a small museum of modern art—the only one in India.

Jaya felt suddenly feeble, her girlish pictures hanging before this rather serious man, Dr. Sohrabji, who wore a double-breasted suit and his hair parted in the middle. He was stocky with thick eyebrows, hooded eyes, and a long nose. His voice was that of an Englishman. He wanted to know what inspired her—where did these images come from? She found herself telling the great scientist about the colony in Thana—these were the wives and children of laborers in the new factories out there. Thankfully Yasmin and Sringara appeared by her side then, offering some reassurance.

Dr. Sohrabji immediately connected the two paintings of Lakshmi that she had placed on opposite ends of her sequence of hill colony pictures. The painting of Lakshmi and Shankar holding their faces up to the smeared, opaque, and shimmery moon, and another picture she called *Little Mothers*. In this one, too, a steep precipice cut the canvas diagonally. Two young girls were running downhill, close to the edge, clutching their infant siblings in their arms as a driving rain thrashed them. Their long skirts flared up, their legs flying along the edge of a drop, trying to get home. Wasima hugged her sister to her chest, a bright blue veil draped over her small head, and Lakshmi held one hand behind her brother's lolling head for protection.

Dr. Sohrabji and his colleague wished to buy the two paintings of Lakshmi for the Indian Institute of Fundamental Research. Jaya couldn't speak for a moment. Something caught in her throat, her lips quivered. Dr. Sohrabji could see she had become emotional. What an honor it would be to have her pictures hanging in his institute, she said, trying to cover up the more tender feeling. She was just a novice. He praised her paintings. She couldn't tell him how much it meant that the pictures of Lakshmi would be seen by others, that she might become known to them for a moment.

The painting of Kamlesh as Usha, which Jaya had titled *Daughter of the Sky*, also caught Dr. Sohrabji's eye. He liked the way Jaya had applied the idioms of Cubism to medieval Hindu sculpture. "My sister's a classical dancer," Jaya explained. He would never know the pain around that painting—the story of its making remained hidden inside the image. He said he looked for only one thing in art: a surge of emotion that transported him somewhere. When he and his associates turned to leave, he said to Jaya in his sober way, "Twenty years from now, when you've made a big name for yourself, I'll look at these pictures and say, 'I got your early works.'"

THE RECEPTION AT Sringara's flat afterward felt like a picnic in the drawing room. A few men sat in the chairs that had been rearranged in a circle, but everyone else sat on sheets spread on the floor. Amvi appeared with cold drinks and fried snacks. Jaya settled into the women's circle, six of them sitting comfortably together—Sringara, Yasmin Ahmed, and mutual acquaintances of theirs working in costume design and set design for films. Jaya had begged her mother to be allowed to attend, and initially her mother had refused. Jaya was supposed to return to Marine Drive with Mummy and Kamlesh. Mummy had agreed only after Chadha assured her he would drop Jaya off at home later. Chadha was the only artist with a car. He'd crammed all the ladies into his back seat for the ride to Bellasis Road, with the three men in the front. His wife had preferred to take a lift home with friends.

At Sringara's, the men talked about fleeing India: looking for money, scholarships, a foothold in Paris or London. Everyone wanted to rush to the source of modern art, to view the paintings of the great masters in life. Here they saw only grainy reproductions in poorly printed books. Everything modern lay over there—they were fed up with being broke, unrecognized. Wolfensohn had written to André Lhote's atelier in Paris, Tule said, recommending him for a position as an assistant. Vir complained of ladies at the exhibition scolding him about his "indecent" self-portrait. A scholarship to the Central School of Arts and Crafts would be his ticket out.

Sringara laughed violently, showing all her teeth. She was worried the longer she had to wait for an answer, the less chance she had of being named an Italian government scholar.

"Why go to Rome when you can go around to the villages in Gujarat?" Zaidi called out with a wry laugh. He'd just made an odyssey around the Kathiawar peninsula, as reported in the papers, piling his paintings in a bullock cart and taking them from village to village. A Muslim artist interpreting the legends of Krishna, bringing modern art to rural India. A genius crossing many boundaries in one stroke. He had power and he protected it.

Jaya gazed at him as he stroked his long black beard, in awe of his self-belief. His friend Mane wandered around the barren room, studying it with his filmmaker's eye, and a triumphant Chadha poured the men whiskeys from a bottle he'd brought to celebrate. Rashid Ahmed, the elder in the room, seemed to observe them all with a bemused detachment.

Yasmin told the women she and Rashid would be making an odyssey too, traveling with two students all over Punjab during the winter holidays, photographing woman artisans. It was part of the Faculty of Fine Arts' project in documenting the living traditions of India. Teachers and students worked together, and eventually they would photograph tribal artists, folk artists, and craftspeople in every state. "Rashid, has the date for the art fair been fixed up?" she called across to her husband. March next year, he replied. Yasmin invited them all to come down for it, and Jaya, who was sitting next to her, was swept up in Yasmin's enthusiasm for the event. Traditional craftspeople who worked in a variety of mediums, like terracotta, hemp, metals, wood, all sorts of raw and natural materials, would demonstrate their arts. "It's the ethos of Baroda," Yasmin said, "we're completely different from the old British art schools like J. J. We want to bring the vernacular arts to our students, so they learn from these living traditions, and we can develop a modern art that is rooted in Indian traditions and not only European. We should have everything available to us."

"And for painters?" Jaya said, lifting her eyes up to Yasmin's face. "What would be the traditional sources?"

Yasmin said there were many. She swung her head and her hair softly lashed Jaya, who felt pleased by the intimacy. Yasmin said she had conducted a small research project in making tempera colors: if you went to Rajasthan they used the gum from a particular tree; if you went to the Himalayan foothills, they used a particular kind of grass. These technologies themselves inspired her painting. "There's no one there to tell us what to do and not to do. There are no European rules hanging over our heads, no restraints. We're a completely self-contained group of artists in Baroda with our hands and eyes all over India. Sometimes it feels like we've set up a big art laboratory there for the purpose of experimentation."

"It sounds fantastic," Jaya said.

"What I've come to realize since going to Baroda is that we're a country of art makers. There's nothing so unusual about what you or I or any of the Group 47 artists are doing—it's in our blood, making art." Jaya was fascinated listening to Yasmin elaborating on her upcoming itinerary across Punjab, the Malhotra family's homeland, to meet a multitude of women artisans there.

Night had fallen by the time the gathering ended at nine. Yasmin and Rashid Ahmed were the last to leave with Chadha, who was slightly drunk and concerned when Jaya refused a lift from him. Yasmin's praise for her paintings meant something—maybe it meant she was truly an artist. Dr. Sohrabji's words had been circling her mind all evening—*Twenty years from now, when you've made a name for yourself, I'll look at your pictures and say, 'I got your early works.'* He saw a future for her in art. She tried to imagine it for herself, a whole long life in art, not just these troublesome days she couldn't see beyond.

White halos of light burned around the gas lamps on Bellasis Road, a foggy radiance that brightened the air between the open balcony doors. Sringara had left off the electric wall sconces, which they'd shunned during the party since everyone preferred the intimacy of darkness. Jaya repeated a question she'd asked Sringara several times already: "You wouldn't mind my staying, then?"

"I'm very happy if you stay." Sringara slipped off her sandals, tucked her feet up in a chair, and sat smoking, dropping ash into her cupped palm. "But sort it out with your parents first. I don't want them thinking I've ruined you, corrupted you, whatnot." Later she left the room and flicked the lights on like a torch in Jaya's eyes.

Jaya turned off the lights again and remained alone in the room. Her own paintings had given her life as she moved among them in the gallery. Hanging her canvases, deciding on the order of their placement, had taken a long time. Every painting was an exposure of herself and her subjects. But she could remain mostly hidden, masking herself behind her subjects' faces. She rose and began to untuck her sari, then paused, studying Sringara's empty walls, considering her refusal to display any pictures inside her house. Was it a form of self-punishment? The paintings Jaya didn't sell, she would hang in her room. She stared at the floor, wondering: Which was her room? In which house?

The doorbell's shriek unloosened the calm. Even before she answered it, hurriedly pleating her sari, switching on the sconces, she knew her charade had come to an end. She would have to collect her purse, her nightclothes, and go home.

"What time did you tell Mummy you'll be back? We've been waiting for you." Her father's lips were drawn in a firm, indignant line. He followed her into the light of the drawing room, and she glanced back, seeing his face tight with anger. He had never come here before; somehow she thought he wouldn't ever find his way to Sringara's flat. Kamlesh followed him in, wearing rumpled house clothes, her hair gathered in an untidy plait as if she had been pulled out of bed. "What time did you give Mummy?"

"By eight-thirty, I thought we'd be finished. But it got later and . . . I wasn't able to do my packing. I couldn't organize my things so quickly after everyone left." She wasn't making much sense. Chadha was meant to take her home tonight, and tomorrow Dipi was supposed to drive her here to pick up her things. She paused, wanting to alter the tone, the mood of the conversation. Dr. Sohrabji's enthusiasm for her pictures had encouraged others to purchase an unknown young artist's work. "Seven of my paintings sold, Daddy. It comes to more than two thousand rupees."

Taking in her words, her father raised his voice. "When did you plan to come back?" Sringara would hear him in her bedroom. A fountain pen was clipped to his shirt pocket, and Jaya looked steadily at the gold clip, neither raising nor lowering her eyes. "Go and get your things," her father ordered. "Bring everything with you. Kamlesh, help her pack up."

Jaya went to the bedroom with Kamlesh—her sullen chaperone, forced to bring her home. The sparkle her twin had radiated in the gallery, striding about in her long, printed skirt, had been snuffed out. Kamlesh spoke her first words. "What do you want me to do?" She looked ill, her nostrils flaring and her mouth curled to the side. Jaya pulled out a limp red leather suitcase from under the bed, unbuckled the outer strap, and propped it open. "Can you put all my clothes from the cupboard into this?" She thought of telling Kamlesh about Keshav Mane's interest in putting the very first painting she'd made of Kamlesh as a dancer in his film, the one which showed Kamlesh in a circle of five dance poses, but she knew even a filmmaker's interest wouldn't please her now. Kamlesh wouldn't raise her narrowed eyes to meet Jaya's, pretending Jaya didn't exist in a room displaying her paintings.

Jaya opened the top drawer in the chest of drawers and studied the contents. Despite a wish to make up with Kamlesh, to be close to her again, to lie down beside her in their joined bed, her urge to remain on her own was fierce. It had nothing to do with a wish to defy her father's authority—it had to do with herself, a respect for her abilities. She walked out of the room, leaving Kamlesh on the floor, vigorously shoving her underclothes into the suitcase.

In the drawing room, Sringara sat with Harbans in her chaste sleeping sari, a light shawl thrown around her shoulders. Her father listened without comment as she chatted about the attention paid to Jaya by Dr. Rustom Sohrabji. His face had still not recovered from his anger. "Finished?" he asked Jaya.

"I can't gather my things so quickly. Everything is spread all over the place. Kamlesh is packing up one suitcase, but I'm tired, I'll do it tomorrow. I'm very tired." She had said what little she was able to say.

Sringara got up. "Let me also say hello to Kamlesh," she murmured. In her ascetic's sari, the white garment of a widow's bereavement, she had the deprived look of a woman who had lost her husband or the chances of one. Her father must have seen Sringara as a pitiable, solitary woman, a fate he might fear for her too. Jaya could postpone the truth until tomorrow, advance in a series of temporary steps. She turned to look at her father. "I don't want to come back as yet."

"You want to stay here? For how long?" he asked in English, incensed.

"A little longer," she said in Punjabi, finding surprising force in the home language. "Some more months." She was dreaming of an exhibition she and Sringara might have next year if Sringara didn't leave Bombay.

Jaya observed a change in her father's eyes as he reconsidered his response, relaxing the fine, shallow creases along his forehead. "Sit for a minute," he said mildly, as if to stop the situation from disintegrating into acrimony. Jaya took the chair opposite him, softening toward him as she felt him soften toward her, but she also felt a certain self-possession.

She had spent four months away from home, her father reminded her. "Your exhibition was inaugurated today, your Mummy told me your paintings were well received. Some important people purchased them. That's very good. Your experiment has succeeded." He paused, began again. "Everyone has an ideal—twenty years ago, I wanted to give up my job, my family life, everything, to live in Gandhiji's ashram. You two were still infants, Mummy was occupied with you the whole day long, but I wanted a pure life, the discipline of a satyagrahi's routine. The idea of nonviolence, of absolute simplicity in living, was very appealing to me. I wanted to spend my days at the spinning wheel, doing those humble tasks Gandhiji had shown us were noble work. I visited the Sabarmati ashram, I talked to Gandhiji's people. I came very close to joining them. But then there was the reality. There was my job, my duties. How could I leave your mother alone? How could I leave you both? Just as you cannot leave your home, alone, unmarried. You're a student as yet. Your aim must be to become a good doctor."

"Couldn't I divide my duties between painting and medicine?" Jaya asked in the same subdued tone.

"No. Don't confuse desires with duties." She must know who she was, he told her: a student of medicine. Still a daughter of the family. "Even two thousand rupees doesn't mean you no longer have need for a home."

"I can't come back just now." The money wasn't the impetus for her wanting to remain on her own, but it was a tremendous boost, and it made it easier for her to state her wishes. She could rely on the money for months. Many people lived on two thousand rupees for a year.

"Is that boy behind this?"

"I'm not asking because of anyone else."

"Who is the boy?" he nearly shouted. "Call him over here. I want to meet him."

"There's no boy involved." Jaya was relieved she could speak truthfully. "I don't have anything to do with him anymore."

In a scornful tone, her father inquired, "Do you intend to leave college as well?"

She shook her head.

"Go and put your things in your suitcase," he commanded her, pulling her hand as if she were a child. But Jaya didn't move, her head burning with the shame and fear of defying him.

"Just let me stay a few more months—till my exams," she proposed. Nothing would induce her to leave medical college, she wanted him to know. To leave would feel like she was breaking away from him completely, betraying all his expectations.

"I won't listen to this!" Her father pulled off his glasses, squinting. "There are some things a father will not accept from a daughter. If you insist on this, be prepared to bear full responsibility for your actions. Think of this place as your home—you will not enter my house again. Is it understood?" He glared at her with such force, his rage gathering, that Jaya tensed, afraid of being struck. "*Eh, tera junoon sanoo sareaa noo lai doobega,*" he shouted.

This obsession of yours will destroy us all.

Kamlesh came into the room dragging the overstuffed suitcase, bent over with the weight. "What's happening?" She glanced angrily at Jaya, waiting for a response. Her father moved to the door, ushering Kamlesh along. "Are you mad?" she shouted when she realized what was happening. "I think you've gone mad. We were ringing that veterinarian's flat, wondering why you hadn't come home, but there was no reply. What do you think you're doing?"

The overloaded suitcase stood beside her, and Kamlesh struggled to lift it with both hands. Her father had to pull the handle out of her grasp and push her down the passage. Kamlesh kept looking back at Jaya, eyes dilated with fear at leaving her behind. "Come on!" she shouted.

The boom of the door shutting echoed in Jaya's ears.

Sringara did not come out to the drawing room until sometime after Harbans and Kamlesh had gone. She sat down beside Jaya, asking her to think over her decision. "Meet your parents tomorrow and speak about it calmly," she suggested. Jaya nodded. She had never before heard of her father's temptation to leave home for Gandhiji's ashram. What would it have been like for him, for all of them, if he had gone to live in the house of the satyagrahis, slipping away from the family? What if he had left them to pursue his ideal of a pure life? And what about her? Was she blinded by her ambitions to the damage she was doing? She had left home without a philosophy or a moral guide—for something no bigger than herself.

25

ABOVE THE RAW wooden edges of the temple walls, lighting boys squatted on catwalks that dangled like rickety swings on ropes. Above them, in
the shed's darkest reaches, Kamlesh's eyes rested on a pitched corrugated-
iron roof like the roof of her father's factory. She gazed into the nighttime
darkness layered above the white glare of the temple lights, feeling hollow,
aware she had created no character for herself.

The cameraman, Abbas, shouted to a technician, "Lights number six,
eight, nine, jalao!" Kamlesh was standing barefoot on Stage No. 1 at the
Living Arts Studio, on the first day of shooting *Akarshan*, awaiting instruc-
tions from the director, O. P. Saigal. A sprightly, slender man who wore his
shirtsleeves rolled up and a jaunty bowtie, he was placing the musicians in
the alcove of a deep, pillared hall. Double rows of sculpted columns plunged
back to a mammoth idol rising from a plinth, a colossus in a skin of gold
paint, bearing weapons and talismans in his eight arms. Icing-pink lotuses
decorated the ceiling. The multicolored plaster of paris pillars were cast
to resemble sculptures of dancing girls and girl musicians holding their
veenas, the temple a showcase of pastel hues since the film was being shot
in Technicolor. Rare, expensive color to celebrate the splendor of Kamlesh's
temple dance numbers. Color to draw in the crowds.

Kamlesh wore a diaphanous orange skirt swirled in gold sequins with a violet-and-gold silk choli, a sheer gold scarf drawn diagonally over her chest. Ornaments pinched every part of her body: double nose rings, forefinger rings, bell-shaped earrings, armlets, stacks of bangles around her wrists. A girdle of brass disks was clamped around her waist, and her brocade bodice was as stiff as a leather shield. The rosy-beige foundation the makeup man had sponged over her face had set like a layer of clay, hardening around the wary, close-lipped smile she had given him in a mirror outlined with electric bulbs.

Clutching his cane, N. D. Narula plodded around the cavernous shed's periphery with a dismal, thumping step, like a watchman making his rounds. She prayed he didn't come across to speak to her, as he had earlier, his lower lip protruding, asking about her sister "the medical student." The door to herself was shut, she wanted to tell him; it was shut even to her. She was Madhavi, the unknown actress. Here, on stage, stood the anonymous Madhavi. A name without a background, a character to play. A ghost wearing a band of false pearls around her hairline, a glittering pendant on her forehead.

When the hero, Prem Kumar, finally swaggered on set, he was in character as a suave lawyer of the twenties, his hair slicked down and parted in the middle, a mustache painted over his lip in two thin lines. He flung his jacket casually over his shoulder. Busy with other shootings, he'd had no time to rehearse with Kamlesh. He was in great demand for the role of the doomed lover, which he played with a tender panache, circulating among many film sets around the city. That was the nature of the film industry— the big stars acting in multiple productions simultaneously. Chaotic, Mr. Narula had said with a resigned laugh. When Kirti had taken Kamlesh to sign the contract at O. P. Saigal's house last month, they had learned shooting would be piecemeal, a week here and there over the course of five or six months, whenever Prem Kumar had some free time in his schedule. The fragmentary production suited her. She could disappear for a week at a time, though her excuses left her with a quivering stomach. To her college she'd sent a note about high fever, in her mother's hand. To her parents, her late return home in the evenings was explained by a group project to construct tabletop models for the classroom.

"Monitor!" Saigal Sahib called. "Fans off! Pin-drop silence!" The unit hands closed around her for the rehearsal. One hung from a catwalk above, angling a klieg light on her.

A melancholy temple bell tolled on the loudspeakers. The tenuous strains of a violin meandered through the air, its solemn high notes rising poignantly as a woman's plaintive voice sang out the first line of praise to God. Kamlesh raised her tiered tray, ringed by flaming clay lamps, to the statue's massive feet. "Stop," she immediately heard. O. P. Saigal sliced the air with his hands.

The dance director patted his lips. She had forgotten to sing out loud. He shook his head disapprovingly, a shaggy-haired boy often scratching inside his ear with a long fingernail. On-screen her lips would be synched to blossom with the great singer's words. Saigal Sahib patted her on the shoulder, told her not to worry. She'd do very well. Kamlesh began again. N. D. Narula, leaning on his ebony cane, looked on with a concerned scowl. The camera, a bulky contraption mounted on wheels with a metal seat for Abbas, followed Prem Kumar as he watched the dancer from a gap between two pillars. On the third line of the song, setting her tray before the deity, Kamlesh stamped her feet in the opening movements of the dance. Prem Kumar dashed behind a nearby pillar so they could be picturized together. Saigal sliced the air again—*Stop*. That was as much as he would want for one take.

Shooting began, the director shouting, "Pin-drop silence!" A boy in pajamas slapped the clapper. The camera rolled forward on its trolley. When Abbas, in his large spectacles, pushed by a grimacing assistant, headed toward her riding his merciless German machine, Kamlesh didn't know what to project into its piercing lens. She felt the stress of lighting, the sizzle of heat on her skin. Men all around her, thin, paunchy technicians scrutinizing her face, her body, stopping her from drawing closer to her character.

No script had been shown to her. She didn't know who she was meant to be. She needed the masquerade of a character, a personality, to save herself from view. Kirti had heard that filmmakers didn't like to discuss a story with newcomers, even after they'd signed a contract, for fear of it leaking out. Saigal sahib had only said she was a humble village girl given to the temple as an offering by her parents. The hero would spy her dancing for the deity and fall in love. Beauty had always been emphasized as the dancer's main quality, but Kamlesh found it an empty clue. How was she to portray beauty?

Over the two days she'd spent rehearsing the dance in a practice room with the dance director, Yoganand, the seedy-looking boy with a profuse body odor, she'd had to break the rigorous form of Bharata Natyam, its strict angulations and triangular movement patterns, to sway her hips, shimmy her shoulders, strut seductively, even bend over backward to bare her stomach, a temple dancer made into a courtesan. The laconic sound man operating the reel-to-reel tape machine grew uncomfortable with the rising disputes between Kamlesh and her dance master until finally the silent man began pleading for calm. Once, when Yoganand had marched across the room and clamped his hands on Kamlesh's shoulders as she knelt in worship of the absent idol, straightening her back to make her chest protrude, she'd thrown off his hands, snapping, "Don't you dare touch me." Not once had Masterji put his hands on her. He either gestured in the air or stamped his hands on the floor to indicate how she should move. The soundman had asked Yoganand to leave the room then, to give her time to regain her composure.

Through many beginnings, over two anxious hours, Kamlesh's panic grew: she had no character. On the twelfth take, she dropped the tiered lamp holder, and an oily flame had to be put out on the floor. She felt on the verge of tears. She wanted to run. There wasn't a single familiar face in the darkness she could turn to. Kirti came only to pick her up. She'd given him the contract for safekeeping, afraid to take it home, but its provisions were inscribed in her mind. *Four dances including two puja pieces and one sad song. The speaking part will consist of one dialogue.* She couldn't execute a fraction of a dance; how would she complete the whole piece in a few days? An astronomical twelve-hundred-rupee fee for a girl who didn't know what to do.

In the shadows away from the set, she spoke to O. P. Saigal. "Who is this dancer?" Kamlesh asked helplessly. Her name was Vijayalakshmi, she learned. Kamlesh smiled at the belated introduction. Vijayalakshmi had lived in the temple since she was a small child, completely devoted to the god and her dance—they were one and the same thing to her.

The character had been left open for Kamlesh to interpret, Mr. Saigal said; he liked to work out at least half the story spontaneously on set. Kamlesh waited to hear more. At first light every morning, the dancer danced to awaken the idol—the director gestured to the monolithic statue—to whom she was ceremonially married. When she set eyes on him, she was setting eyes on her husband. Because the setting was pre-Independence India, when men turned themselves into copies of their British masters, the hero looked a proper Englishman. But when he first saw the dancer in the temple he used to visit as a child, he remembered who he was beneath his mask.

Kamlesh rearranged the twisted necklaces hanging over her breasts, excited by this new knowledge. When she approached the idol the next time, striking her feet loudly on the floor, she felt her legs grow, her step quicken, a person take possession of her. Vijayalakshmi was the dancer who lived to dance, who inhabited her art. Her eyes widened as she addressed her god, her husband, confiding her love of being here in his pillared sanctum, her home.

Every evening that week Kamlesh had to accept a ride home on Kirti's motorbike, clutching his waist, her head wrapped in a scarf to conceal her face. She didn't like being pressed so close to him, her sister's friend, but she had no other way home from the squalid district of spinning and weaving mills where the studio was located. At least it wasn't a studio way out in the suburbs that would have taken twice as long to reach.

Kirti let her off on the quiet, unlit C Road near her building. Six days of shooting had felt as drawn out as a month. She spent half the day idle in her dressing room, waiting to be called on set. In another two days, she would finish picturizing the song. O. P. Saigal had set April as the next month for the shoot. She didn't tell him she would have her BEd exams then.

Walking quickly from C Road to her building, the dismal feeling of home returned. Her mother had been on edge since Jaya had refused to return. She lost her temper easily, banged a spoon down in a dish if you refused more food. Bebeji was disgusted. Two girls living alone in a flat—what was that? She thought of Sringara and Jaya as cellmates, as she and Satya had been in that women's prison in Punjab the British had thrown them in, both of them becoming weak and ill. Jaya's decision to live separately had come as a blow to them all. Her parents avoided social gatherings so they didn't have to answer people's inquisitive questions. Despite their efforts to explain it away, the situation had turned into a scandal. The general suspicion was that Jaya had left home for a boy. The more people envied you, Mummy said, the quicker they were to tear you down. Plenty of people were jealous of her father's position, her mother acknowledged, his travels to America, their Marine Drive flat—and, of course, their beautiful twin daughters. Her parents now even worried about her father's job. Khosla Sahib had directed Harbans to bring his daughter home. People were questioning him about Harbans Malhotra's family— what sort of turmoil were they in? What kind of trouble had Jaya caused? Daddy's family problems were pulling down the image of his business, with everyone speculating about what Jaya was doing. What was the family hiding? Daddy explained that he had tried to force Jaya to return home, but she had her mind set on painting. It was about her painting—only that. Mr. Khosla and he had had this talk several times. Khosla Sahib appeared sympathetic, he believed Daddy. But he was in a bind. He couldn't afford to let the good reputation of the glassworks become tarnished by the scandal around Daddy's family affairs.

Though her father knew Khosla Sahib thoroughly depended on him to run the factory in his efficient manner, and manage the headache of negotiating with two rival union movements now battling for recognition, one Communist and the other independent, he worried that Khosla would lose patience if rumors about the family continued to circulate in the Punjabi community. Stress provoked the return of his asthma, severe bouts of coughing keeping him awake at night. To try to heal himself he'd taken his first holiday from the factory, retreating to a nature cure center for three weeks. Kamlesh and Manu had visited Sringara's flat to try to persuade Jaya to return home before their father did. "You should come back," Manu had said somberly in his mannish voice, his hurt glance falling away from Jaya.

Jaya had been withdrawn. She came to life only for a moment when Manu handed her a published copy of his booklet on Bebeji. Her illustration graced the cover, Bebeji raising a black flag in the moments before the police began clubbing protestors. "I missed Bebeji's seventieth birthday," Jaya realized. Kamlesh couldn't understand her sister's obstinacy. She didn't seem happy at Sringara's, nor could she show them any new paintings she'd done. What was she afraid would happen to her at home?

Standing in front of the apartment door, Kamlesh scraped a fingernail around her nostrils to remove any streaks of Pan-Cake she might have missed scrubbing off at the studio. Despite her anger that Jaya was missing, despite her shakiness in Jaya's absence, she realized Jaya had given her something. She had freed her. Kamlesh had signed on for the picture, because she knew she could dance well and she wanted people to see her dance. She was a Bombay girl, so maybe she could never belong to the world of pure dance, only to something flashy and modern like films.

A few days after she signed the contract at Saigal Sahib's house, Kirti had taken her for an excursion to Ballard Pier to see an ocean liner land, a habit he'd picked up from Ashok Narula. A Port Trust officer he knew allowed them through the gate without paying for passes, and they watched four tugs lure the steamer into port, the captive ship's horn blasting its lament into the sky. In the scattering of cargo ships, dhows, and small craft in the blue harbor, Kamlesh read a message about the magic of distance. Madhavi, her actress-twin, might dare to do anything, even vanish into another world. When she asked Kirti how one could go abroad, he mentioned scholarships in England that physicians applied for. Study, that was the only way. He was now thinking of going to America after he finished his MS, since Philadelphia was said to be the best place to study heart surgery. Under a furious Bombay sun, they watched a foreign city empty onto the pier—fair-haired ladies in frocks and men in straw hats; Indians dressed like Europeans, like actors playing a part; coolies running after them all, crying out to be hired.

Outside the flat, Kamlesh composed herself then struck the bell impatiently, as was her habit. Her mother opened the door, looking anxious. She wore her washed-out mauve sari. "Where have you been? It's nine-thirty. Making the model till so late?" Her mother pierced her with a look. "Have you been going to see Jaya? Is that where you were?"

No, she said, following Vidya into the passage. She'd been at Lucinda Nazareth's place, building the model for the classroom. They'd made clay horses for Shivaji's cavalry, and soon they would be finished with their replica of Raigad Fort. It baffled her that her mother imagined she'd been going over to meet Jaya secretly. Is that where she wished Kamlesh would go? Perhaps everyone saw her as the natural emissary to her twin, the one most capable of mending the family's break with Jaya.

26

JAYA HAD COME to a stop. She had exiled herself to Sringara's flat and sat there day after day, unable to paint, afraid to contemplate painting. Sometimes she would sketch. Sometimes she would force herself to sit down with a year and a half's worth of notes and readings in pathology and pharmacology for her second MBBS exams, two months off, in April. Most of the time, she would come home from college and sit in the room with the door shut and find it difficult to move. She was paralyzed. She sat still on her bed for an hour sometimes, not knowing what to do, full of guilt and shame. In her anguish, she knew she ought to go home. Being at home would put an end to her remorse. But she didn't go. She remained here, her will destroying her.

Yasmin Ahmed had told her, "You can't do two things—make your parents happy and be a painter. You'll have to choose one." She had said that the day after Jaya defied her father by refusing to go home with him. She had chosen to be a painter, she thought, but she had not reckoned with the extent of the damage that would do to her family. Daddy had told her, "Your obsession will destroy us all." Her mother had come over one afternoon to tell Jaya that she was jeopardizing her father's position at the factory. Khosla Sahib had rebuked him for letting Jaya do as she pleased, stirring up a big scandal in the community. She was startled when Vidya said Raj Talwar and Shuli had rung her up to ask, in the course of conversation, if Jaya was involved with a man. Although people had seen her pictures at the exhibition, no one could believe painting would compel a girl to abandon her family. Some friends might even think Jaya was going to have a child, Mummy worried. She shouted at Jaya, "Other men would have physically dragged a girl back home and locked her inside. Later on, you'll realize how tolerant your father has been."

At her worst moments, Jaya tried to remember a critic's remarks about her exhibition paintings. Jaya Malhotra had revealed the "intimate reveries of poor women," the critic wrote. "She has an eye for baring her subjects down to their dreams." The observation had startled her. She had painted reveries she imagined for the women, their true thoughts forever inscrutable to her. Still, it amazed her the critic could identify what she only half understood she was doing.

Kamlesh and Manu had also come to see her, bringing her Manu's booklet on Bebeji's years as a freedom fighter. Kamlesh had kept her eyes down the entire time, and Jaya had looked down too—the lacy cuffs of her twin's blouse, and just the sight of her sister's arms, had made her want to go home. What kind of cold-hearted girl was she? But she stayed. She stayed for absolutely nothing, because she wasn't even painting. And yet it felt as though she were saving her life in Sringara's apartment, as if she would be whittled away at home into a girl who was only conscientious of doing her duties.

She sat cross-legged on the floor and stood an old canvas against the wall, telling herself it was all right to paint. Sringara had learned painting as a practice based on the ground. Sometimes she painted sitting on the floor in her studio. By placing the canvas at floor level, Jaya wanted to see if she felt a deeper connection to her picture that might make a return to painting possible. This was a failed painting of Kamlesh as Shiva, a scribble of one foot sliding over the other, one leg lifted high and her arms spread wide, dancing the world into being within a fiery arch of flames. For a moment she took pleasure in the picture, seeing Kamlesh in it, overcome with a desire to be with her twin. But the painting was stilted; she'd brought nothing new to the dance of creation. She would paint over Kamlesh's image, make her self-portrait over her twin, to see for herself who this hard-hearted girl was who thought she was a great painter—would be a great painter. Present and future in one, trembling with a sense of grandeur.

Selling her pictures to Dr. Sohrabji, the renowned physicist and collector, had crystallized this idea in her heart, though it had always existed, somewhere between a desire and a conviction, a small light burning inside. The Europeans had valorized what she had done. They didn't understand what it meant to live in Indian society. Tule had dropped in some weeks before his departure for Europe, bringing along Fritz. Wolfensohn, who had failed in arranging a paid position for him at André Lhote's studio in Montparnasse but had secured a place for him as a student of the master, like so many talented artists from the colonies. Tule had managed to raise the funds for his passage by selling off at low prices the dozens of his pictures that he, fortunately, had not slashed to ribbons in a drunken rage one night. Most of his work he had shredded. Wolfensohn, the dark-suited German, expansive and rigorous in manner, had praised Jaya for confronting "poverty and sensuality" in his review of her paintings for the *Times*. Now he congratulated her for leaving home. "I thought you were a typical Indian girl, but you are showing a lot of courage. You will be free now to make all the paintings you want. In Europe, the girls are liberated. They leave home and find other artists to live with." Jaya clasped her hands modestly in front of her, trying to look pleased that he had compared her to European girls. She hoped she'd be able to do a lot of painting here, she said to oblige Wolfensohn, still smiling.

He thought all it took was leaving home. He didn't know that inside you were made of your obligations to other people, your allegiances and your debts to them—these were the connective tissues that held a person together. He knew nothing about India. Knew nothing of Indians. He had lived here for years, but he didn't know what it meant to be part of a society where you were threaded together with everyone else. Wolfensohn's naive praise of her angered her. A girl pulling herself out of the web of her family could cause the entire web to tear and collapse.

"Go home," Sringara had told her weeks ago. "You're losing your health, go home."

She would have gone, but a little book encouraged her perversity. Amrita Sher-Gil had painted twelve self-portraits; the book reproduced one of them.

Amrita was stark naked above the waist, her hair tied back to show her full breasts more prominently, her lips swollen and colored deep red. She had called the picture *Self-Portrait as Tahitian*, because she was an admirer of Gauguin who wanted to be liberated from the master's shadow, his influence. Amrita resisted being his captive, painting a transparent shadow beneath her that was assumed to be Gauguin—a large grayish male in a dark jacket. Amrita dominated the canvas, Gaugin loomed beneath. Sometimes Jaya thought she would create an equally startling self-portrait, looking at herself and describing the shadows and hands she could not get out from underneath. Other times, she thought: *Let me just sink into the sea, let me go to that rocky beach where Kirti took me at the tip of the cantonment, and let me climb down those black stones where no one will see me and walk into the water. Let me keep walking and walking till my mouth fills with the tide and I descend.*

If she approached her palette, oil paints, and bottles of linseed oil and turpentine, she felt as guilty as someone about to take a knife and plunge it into a body. She dared not paint. She had destroyed enough. Keshav Mane had invited her to participate in a group show of prominent painters that would launch his new gallery in the Daftary institute. A couple of her unsold paintings of Kamlesh dancing were to appear in his film about a woman artist's life, but it was all raw footage as yet. She hadn't seen her paintings in the movie. Jaya told Mane she wasn't painting these days. Still, he urged her to give him at least three or four pictures to place in his inaugural show. She had no models anymore, so she could only do self-portraits, as Amrita Sher-Gill had done. But she had some sense of decency. She was not so shameless as to keep on painting.

Her paralysis resolved unexpectedly. She was one of six students observing a thoracic surgery in the operation theater one morning, on her third surgical rotation. The air was saturated with the nauseating vapor of spirits. Kirti's eyes shifted with concentration above his green cloth mask, peering into the open red pit in the patient's chest. No one could fathom what was happening at the moment it happened. The head surgeon, Dr. Gadgil, made a cut, suddenly releasing a wild geyser of blood. The doctor dropped a clamp on the floor; he shouted at the nurses. Blood continued gushing from the man's chest. Jaya put her hands up not to see, and the light beamed through her red fingers. Kirti hurriedly changed places with the doctor, taking over from his panicked teacher. "I'm inside the heart," Kirti cried out. Jaya couldn't see his eyes. He was bent over the patient, his cap sprayed in blood. They would later understand Dr. Gadgil had cut straight into the patient's heart, mistaking a thin, protruding cardiac wall for a cyst.

Two days after the forty-three-year-old man's death, Jaya made a rare move to speak to Kirti. He looked like he hadn't slept or washed since the operation when she saw him in a corridor in the surgical ward. They usually acknowledged each other in the wards, but they didn't speak. "It wasn't your fault at all, you tried to stop it," Jaya told him after asking how he was. She meant she'd seen him struggling to stanch the flow of blood. A strong odor emanated from under his arms. He didn't look at her. His colleagues, two postgraduates who had been present at the surgery, were spreading a story that Kirti tried to dominate every situation and had prevented them from applying vascular clamps in time. Jaya had observed those boys in the operating theater. They had let Kirti step forward and take the risk. "They're making you a scapegoat," Jaya said. "But they themselves were too timid to do anything." Kirti nodded. He glanced away at a colleague coming down the corridor. Maybe he didn't like her speaking to him with such familiarity, as if they were still close to each other. He looked at his watch, saying he had to meet someone.

He wasn't going to let her console him, she understood. Her words stuck with her: *it wasn't your fault*. A while back, Kirti had told her to make a painting of herself so he could understand her. Maybe she should do that, to see what she could understand of herself. It was possible she was not at fault. She could no longer remain mute and immobile, doing nothing. She had made the decision to stay at Sringara's flat; now she should do what she was there to do.

27

BEBEJI LOOKED AT Kamlesh in silence, her face a weighty, sagging mask that appeared to be unloosening from the bone, slipping downward with gravity, deep lines cutting sharply from her nostrils to her lips marking the descent. Jaya's continued absence from home had left her so discouraged they could see her aging before their eyes. And now Kamlesh had demoralized her further by applying to study in England.

Bebeji sat on the edge of Kamlesh's bed, watching her at her study table organizing her notes for a theory paper on the philosophical foundation of education. Kamlesh's mind was in so many places—on the next shoot looming and on the prospect of leaving India on her own—that she worried she'd fail her exams. She half listened as Bebeji mused on the protest she and her residents' committee had organized ten days back. About two hundred colony people had marched down the Agra Road, Kamlesh among them, chanting "Give us water! Give us light! We are living in the dark!" and confronted an aggrieved-looking collector in his office in Thana city. He had earmarked the colony for development, but no work had been done. Not even a hole dug for a transformer. Though the protest had yielded no tangible results, in Bebeji's estimation the best thing to come out of the exercise was that "next time they can organize themselves." She had urged the residents to be peaceful in making their demands. "There is a right way and a wrong way," she'd said when one man argued that violence was the only kind of power poor people possessed.

Kamlesh had marched in a line with Prabha and some mothers from the school. As they moved down the Agra Road, she found herself longingly searching the roadside and the wide expanses of uncultivated fields for Lakshmi, imagining she and her family might appear carrying their bundles on their heads or squatting in a field. They had left their shanty some weeks back. At first people thought Madan had moved to a different slum, closer to town, taken a different job, but he had gone away with his family with what little money he had. Another man on the hill had tried to assault Lakshmi. Kamlesh hoped the family was safely back in their home village in U.P., and that Lakshmi was feeling more herself. That she might be all right after some time. "I don't think the electricity board would have brought a power line up to the colony, even by the time you return from abroad," Bebeji said. She didn't like to say *England*. She said *vilait. Abroad.* A foreign land. If she went, Kamlesh said—because it wasn't certain she would—it would be for a full year, which would be a long time to bring power to the hill. Bebeji hung her head in thought, her hands folded in her lap. Her efforts at improving conditions in the shanty colony had come to a standstill. The single functioning handpump had run dry. Although construction of the clinic had been completed, Dr. Pendharkar's twice weekly visits now seemed inadequate. They'd come to realize that a rugged stone ridge, marked by precipices, caused innumerable injuries. Workers returning home in the dark from their shifts were particularly prone to falls. Paying a part-time doctor's fees wasn't feasible for Bebeji; and she could find no other physician as selfless as Dr. Pendharkar who would volunteer his time in a slum that was exceptionally difficult to reach.

"Not in one year. It won't happen in my time." Bebeji's chin jutted up, the curve of her mouth turned down emphatically. She was booked on the Frontier Mail for April 26, two days before Kamlesh sat for her last paper. They were concerned about her making a thirty-six-hour train journey to Ludhiana, where she would spend the summer with her brother Lekh Raj and his wife. Bebeji insisted she would be all right traveling alone in the ladies' compartment; there was no need for Dipi to chaperone her, as everyone wanted.

"Someone should accompany you." Kamlesh would have liked to take Bebeji to Ludhiana if it wasn't for her exams—and other obligations she wished she could evade. As a small child of three or four, she had lived in Ludhiana. Her strongest memory of their house there was the tall pink rose bushes in the garden from whose petals her mother had made rose jam, spooning it into her mouth.

"Who will accompany *you?*" Bebeji said, smiling with regret. A girl shouldn't travel to a foreign country alone, she'd said, like a gypsy without a home. Vidya, too, was opposed to Kamlesh studying abroad. Only her father thought a year away might do her good, implying her marriage prospects might improve. The gossip about her stage show had died down, but people remembered when it came to making a match for their sons. When her mother told her Vikram Bakshi's parents were no longer interested, she was deeply hurt. She had liked that boy quite a bit even though she felt terribly shy with him—and he was very good-looking. Four other families her parents contacted, after much effort on Daddy's part to search out well-placed boys, all made excuses not to meet her. Subsequently her mother wrote to Dipi's mother in Delhi, asking her to suggest boys, since no one there would have heard of Kamlesh's stage performance. Her aunt Lajwanti, being a widow and a refugee, wasn't well connected in the city, but she did put them in touch with one interested family. Kamlesh didn't like the sound of a Sikh boy working in his father's auto parts business. Not a clean-shaven boy, but an old-fashioned one who tied a turban. She didn't want to live in a joint family. The freedoms of a modern lifestyle in Bombay had spoiled her, Bebeji thought; most girls didn't live like that. Fortunately, her mother sided with her. She, too, had expected a well-qualified professional for Kamlesh. *We're not going to throw away our daughter to just anyone,* she had said defiantly. An MA course in London was a tremendous expense, one her parents would never have considered bearing if they didn't think it was the only way to save her future.

By the time Kamlesh returned to Bombay, in a year and a half, her stage performance would be forgotten, they hoped, and Jaya's leaving home, which also reflected badly on her, would be an error that had corrected itself. No one wanted to consider the alternative—that the damage to Kamlesh's reputation was beyond repair and she was unmarriageable.

When she allowed herself to think how the movie might affect her chances for marriage, she hoped it would be one of those pictures that was never released, or was lost to a film laboratory.

Yet she was preparing herself for the consequences. In January, she had run all over town—collecting her school and college certificates, records of her examination marks, and reference letters—to complete her application for the child development course at the Institute of Education in London. It was the same place she'd overheard two girls chatting about in the ladies' resting room at college, without realizing then it might serve as an escape hatch for her.

"You two don't seem to know what is right," said Bebeji, also addressing Jaya's invisible presence in the room, as she sometimes did. "You want to go one way, she wants to go another. What has happened to you both? You don't seem to know what the basis of life is?"

"What is the basis of life?" Kamlesh looked at her grandmother.

"Home," Bebeji put it solidly in one word. "You can do everything you want after founding a home."

KAMLESH AND HER grandmother lingered in the stationery shop a long time, looking for fountain pens for Bebeji's brother Lekh Raj. Imported pens of high quality like the ones Jaya had bought for Harbans to mark the sale of her first painting. Kamlesh had accompanied Bebeji to buy a few gifts for her relations in Punjab, taking a break from preparing for her exams. As the clerk packed up two pens in a handsome case, she stepped away from the door—which let in the noise of shouting in the road. A table in a corner was piled with publications. Among them was a short stack of Manu's booklet, *A Lady Freedom Fighter*. Kamlesh excitedly called her grandmother over to look. Bebeji came and shook her head in embarrassment at the commemoration of her life story. Daddy and Manu had placed the one-rupee booklet with several bookshops around Fountain, and one had sold all their copies and requested a fresh supply.

Outside in the sweltering April heat, Bebeji seemed dazed by the sun. She dropped her face in her hands, feeling dizzy. Kamlesh guided her by the arm down a by-lane of old office buildings. The outburst of shouting they'd heard while in the shop returned with fresh force, the cries of an invisible horde. A voice amplified by a megaphone crackled in the air, but Kamlesh couldn't see where it was coming from. They turned into a lane leading to the main road as a stream of men came running in their direction, raising black flags and shrieking. Kamlesh wanted to turn back toward the shop, but Bebeji thought they could quickly get to the car, parked at Flora Fountain, once they reached the main road.

"I don't know, I think we should go back. My God, look at those fellows . . ." Kamlesh grabbed Bebeji's hand. Glancing down another side road, she saw a screaming crowd struggling to overturn a parked car. A flame sprang out of a window. In another direction, glass shattered. Kamlesh looked up in time to see bricks putting out the windows of a building across the road. Now she understood the mob's howl: "*Mumbai Amchi Ahai!*" *Bombay is ours!* Maharashtrians demanding Bombay city for their own Maharashtra—a new home state.

Men ran amok on the main road, trampling banners. Gangs of boys hurled stones at a cordon of policemen stationed in front of Flora Fountain. Kamlesh, pulling her grandmother along, dropped the parcel in her hands and bent down to retrieve it among feet charging in all directions. Over a booming loudspeaker, police warned that assemblies of more than five people were banned. A shot went off. Then another one. The mob responded with a carnal roar, "*Mumbai Amchi Ahai!*"

A young fellow stumbled against a shop window as Kamlesh banged on the door, shouting to be let in. She shrieked, seeing his shirt soaked in blood. He touched the spot on his back where he'd been hit and cried, "Hai!"

"Come on, Bebeji," Kamlesh pleaded, turning her grandmother around to take her back to the stationery shop, elbowing the men who taunted her and blocked their path. But Bebeji couldn't be pulled through the mass of bodies. They were shoved and jabbed as they changed direction again, trying to make their way down to the rifle-slinging policemen blockading the bottom of the road. Someone snatched Kamlesh's parcel. Another man pulled at her blouse. "Oh God, they're throwing soda bottles!" she screamed, lowering her head. Bebeji's hand broke away from hers.

"No! Don't!" a man cried to someone in warning.

Men surged like a thundering wave between Kamlesh and Bebeji. Kamlesh looked around, unable to spot her grandmother. Bodies shifted and then she saw one man and another charging across Bebeji's back as she lay on the ground, men screaming slogans, drumming the breath out of Bebeji as if her spine were a bridge to their futures. Sobbing and shouting, Kamlesh struck at the men in her way. Someone cried out authoritatively to clear the area—it sounded like a constable. She turned in time to catch the stinging trajectory of a blunt object against her forehead. Her hand went to her brow and came back red. She pushed her way toward Bebeji, shouting her name, tasting blood on her lips. Bebeji lay face down on the road, her white sari marked with the grime of men's feet. Kamlesh tried to lift her, struggling to pull her up by the arms, tears flowing down her face as she shrieked at the men to move away, clawing at their legs.

MEN HAD RUN across Bebeji's back but miraculously broken no bone, damaged no organ. After an overnight stay in the hospital, she had been confined to bed for three days. Now nine days had passed since the riot, and she reported she was feeling stronger. Sitting at the dressing table, Kamlesh could see in the mirror the dark bruises that still inked Bebeji's arms and chest, the red marks where feet had trampled her back. Bebeji was bare of the windings of her sari, wearing only a blouse and petticoat after her bath, a comb stuck in the back of her wet hair. Sitting down on the edge of Kamlesh's bed, Bebeji coughed her strangled cough and leaned her head to one side to comb her long, thin gray hair.

Kamlesh leaned into the dressing table's triple mirrors, pulling down the skin around her wound to examine it closely, a new habit that had become an obsession. A quarter of an inch below the hairline, a raw sunburst marred her forehead. The bloody tear was the size of a large coin, unstitched and half-healed—an off-center bindi crusting brown. It would shrink, but a slight scar was likely to remain, the C Road clinic doctor had predicted. Someone had thrown a stone, or a chunk of a brick, or a lump of tar. To her eyes the lesion was her most remarkable feature; she could see nothing else when she sat in front of the mirror. When she went out, she was mortified to think others, too, noticed nothing but this crushed mark on her face.

"If I leave," Bebeji said, looking vaguely toward the light, "she might feel free to come home, isn't it?"

Kamlesh told her grandmother not to talk like that. Jaya had promised to return home; she wasn't waiting for Bebeji to leave. She was just completing a few pictures for an important exhibition, somehow managing to paint during her exams time. Jaya had asked Bebeji to remain at home, in fact, to take all the time she needed to recover. Bebeji didn't have the stamina for a thirty-six-hour train journey, and the doctor also had advised her to postpone it for a month or two, but she insisted she would be well enough to travel in a couple of weeks. She was determined to return to Punjab after so many years. Sometimes she sounded in a panic about the need to leave soon, as if she feared the family would stop her.

When Dipi had brought Jaya home to see them two days after the incident, the first thing Jaya did on entering the apartment was touch their parents' feet. Kamlesh was taken aback. She had never seen Jaya show respect with that old-fashioned gesture. It seemed Jaya was asking for their forgiveness, or showing her regard for them so they might realize her absence was no indication of how she felt about them. Though she was in the midst of her second MBBS exams, which she had to pass to progress to the final eighteen months of her course, she came to visit again. Alert and efficient, looking like a lady doctor in her plain cotton sari, she came bearing an ointment to heal Kamlesh's wound and a lotion for Bebeji's muscle pain. Her presence felt like a balm, and just seeing her face and hearing her voice raised Kamlesh's spirits, though she did not allow herself to talk much to her twin. An instinct to punish Jaya for not returning remained strong.

In the days after the riot, Kamlesh had managed to sit for four theory papers for her bachelor of education degree, with one paper still left to take, two days from now. She could recall neither the questions nor the answers she had written, still disoriented after being caught in the violence. Forty-three people had been killed in the bloodiest pro-Maharashtra demonstration to date. The entire city was in mourning. Jaya told them traumatic asphyxia was the cause of death in most cases, the chest compressed and respiratory system crushed as people were trampled. The second time Jaya came to see them, she came during the day, careful to avoid their father, who hadn't spoken to her when he saw her last. Mummy couldn't control herself and demanded, "When are you coming back? Do you realize what you're doing to this family?"

"I'll be coming soon," Kamlesh was startled to hear Jaya say. After her exams, she had to finish a few pictures for an exhibition. A new gallery had invited her to take part in its opening show with a group of well-known artists. She would give them just two or three paintings, and after that she would return home. No one asked if she considered it her last exhibition. The mood at home changed with her promise. Harbans didn't show any outward approval of Jaya's change of heart—her absence was too painful for him to speak about openly. But internally, Kamlesh sensed, they all felt hopeful this terrible phase the family was going through would soon be over.

"Jaya's going to come back soon, I feel that," Bebeji muttered quietly, as though rummaging in her thoughts. "She wants to come back but she feels ashamed to."

"If she's coming back, then how can you go off to Punjab?" Kamlesh got up from the dressing table and went across to her. She sat beside Bebeji at the edge of the bed, and Bebeji dragged her rumpled hand lovingly down Kamlesh's cheek.

ON SATURDAY, AFTER sitting for her last paper, Kamlesh found herself inside a "family room" at the Lord Irwin, a nook hidden behind saloon doors where couples met, away from the prying eyes of other café-goers. Kirti poured her a cup of tea. The hank of hair Kamlesh had swept across her forehead had slipped out of place, and she could feel with her finger that the tear was visible. Kirti leaned over the table to examine her brow like a doctor, stilling her face with both hands. He'd been stunned to learn she and her grandmother had been injured in the riot.

They had devised a phone signal, and he'd used it yesterday to let her know he had news of the next shoot and they were to meet here the following day. She already knew the April shoot had been postponed until May, and now Kirti gave her the new dates—two consecutive weeks, from 25th May to 8th June. After that, three more weeks of shooting over the course of the summer.

"I won't be able to come on those dates." Kamlesh shook her head in regret, watching for his reaction. The lies would be impossible to sustain— the absences from morning till night without the ready alibi of practice teaching and group projects. "I can't keep filming anymore. In any case, they won't want a dancer with such a horrible mark on her face."

"Don't worry, in a week or two it won't be noticeable. Even if a small mark remains, they'll be able to cover it up with their powders and creams." The softness of his gaze made her wonder whether he was spending so much time guiding her through the film because it was a way for him to continue his relationship with Jaya. Sometimes, clutching him in the dark on his motorbike, or going on an outing with him to the docks, she felt an attraction she hated to feel and tried to drum out of her head. *Akarshan—Attraction*—was the film's title. To her surprise O. P. Saigal had said it pointed to her. She was the object of the hero's desire, the dancer in the temple. But the hero's great mistake was to compromise himself to satisfy everyone else's wishes—marry the right society girl, accept a bad marriage for the sake of his children, build up his career—instead of pursuing the source of his attraction. "We all compromise," Saigal had said philosophically, when Kamlesh had met him with Kirti at his bungalow and collected a portion of her fee. "But, in the end, compromise makes no one happy. If we follow our passions and attractions, they lead to problems of a different kind." He shrugged. "That's the nature of life—it's tragic. No matter what we choose."

Kirti got up and pushed open the swing doors to shout to the bearer to fetch him a packet of Wills. She wondered if this was the last time she'd see him. The only other person who knew of her role in the picture was Masterji. She had confided in him before she stopped her weekly lesson due to exams. Her parents must be told, he'd advised her; they would find a resolution for her. He had tried not to show his disappointment in her, though her withdrawal from the dance had hurt him. "What happened? You shot up like a bright star and now you're finished?"

She could never tell him the dance tradition he'd devoted his life to was looked down upon by her community, that her parents had forbidden her from ever appearing onstage again. She felt the weight gathering around her hips, a thick lassitude settling over her. The energy that came from daily practice had fled from her.

Kirti returned to his seat opposite Kamlesh, a dark figure in bright white clothing. "You've signed a contract." His voice shed its gentle tone. "Narula could make it into a court case if you walk off."

"Why did you let me sign that paper? A court case because of *that*? I thought it was just a formality." Kamlesh blurted out a half-truth, thrusting the mistake onto him in her desperation to extricate herself from the situation.

"Don't tell me that," he said harshly. He wasn't going to accept her displays of helplessness as his burden.

Kamlesh looked down at her half-empty cup, humiliated at her predicament. She hadn't told him she might have to leave Bombay even before the picture was finished, if filming continued in this haphazard manner of delays and postponements. They couldn't keep her captive to their unpredictable shoots. Kirti didn't know she had posted her application to London. She hadn't told him she was waiting to hear from the Institute of Education there. She didn't want to discuss her future with him. She wanted only to find a way to slip through the knot she had tied her life into. She had come to see herself differently. Every time she looked at herself in the mirror, her wound reminded her she was not innocent anymore.

28

KESHAV MANE'S NEW gallery was pristine. The two large rooms on the ground floor of the Daftary mansion overlooked the sea. Diaphanous white curtains covered the long windows to keep out the sun's glare, while allowing the rooms to fill with a diffuse natural light. At the vernissage two nights ago, the electric lighting to which Mane had paid much painstaking attention had illuminated the paintings beautifully. That evening Jaya had found herself speaking to a mixed group of art, music, and dance lovers. Mane had exploited the advantages of the Daftary institute, joining forces with the well-known theater director, dancer, and musicians housed there, to invite the cultural elite of Bombay. Jaya had the fewest pictures on show—only four—and the other five artists were well-known names. Right next to Jaya's pictures hung the works of Salman Gaffar, a founding member of Group 47. He had abandoned Leger's atelier, exhibited at a top gallery in Paris, and recently returned home for good.

Gaffar, like Jaya and the other painters, came around to Mane's gallery for the first two days after the show opened, interested in catching people's reactions to their work. Here Mane was proprietor and curator, managing the sales of their paintings and taking a commission. One picture of Jaya's had sold to a theater producer yesterday. *Untitled* she called it, because men sometimes gave their nudes that title. As if a person could be so undefined.

Jaya looked over her picture, an abstract figure with long dark hair like hers, painting a portrait on an easel. They were all experiments, these four pictures: attempts to understand the female nude as painted by men. She was asking herself, would women paint nudes in the same way? Women would not be as interested in a long gaze at their beautiful or withered bodies. They might want to say there was more to being a woman than her body.

Gaffar was a tall, placid, saintly looking man, stick-thin, wearing a crisp imported shirt, smoking a cigarette. He came over to tell Jaya her pictures did something different—they forged ahead. Jaya was surprised by his approach, as he was a reserved man who had answered the exclamations of people celebrating his return at the vernissage with polite nods. Encouraged by the overture, she dared to ask him why he'd decided to leave Paris, thinking of Tule, who had just gone over there. Six years was a long time, Gaffar said, he'd had enough of being in a foreign country. "Without contact with one's environment, a slow disintegration of one's self takes place. I had to come back to India. There would have been nothing left of me if I'd stayed." The paintings he was showing had all been made over there, Jaya assumed, as she could identify nothing Indian in them. A soundless world of cubes and cylinders devoid of human presence. There were dirty gray blocks of windowless houses on deserted gray streets. There were European kitchen utensils displayed on cubed pedestals. Gaffar's only figure painting showed a rigid gray nude with a vacant gaze, as inanimate as the objects in the other pictures. Jaya thought she understood what Gaffar meant now—he was saving himself from dwelling in that grim European silence, painting like a man in isolation who viewed his subjects from a great distance. He himself was gaunt and still, as if Europe had taught him to erase all traces of self-expression.

They were speaking quietly, joined by Dhasal and another painter, when a man who reminded Jaya oddly of Kirti—dark-complexioned, tall, with nice features, though his were fine rather than broad like Kirti's—walked purposefully toward them. He had a full mustache, dark pink lips. A few feet from her, he pointed to her painting *Dancing Girl* and asked who it belonged to. Jaya stepped forward. The man had a brisk air about him; perhaps he was a businessman. Dark trousers and a white shirt. A moment after Jaya said, "Hello, yes, it's mine," everything happened swiftly. The man was an inspector from the Vigilance Branch, CID. The picture had to be removed, he declared. The other artists stirred. "Removed?" "Why?" "For what reason?" Keshav Mane appeared from the other room and asked what was going on.

"The artist will take down this painting or she will be arrested on the charge of obscenity," the inspector stated.

Jaya's heart plummeted. The shock of the word *obscenity* detached her from the turmoil of the moment. The artists were arguing with the plain clothes policeman, who identified himself as Inspector N. V. Khadilkar of the CID. A complaint had been lodged yesterday by a lady visitor to Gallery 56 about an obscene painting called *Dancing Girl* hanging in the show. He had stopped in earlier to make his own determination, and now he was asking the artist to remove the picture to avoid violating the norms of decency. The charge would be corruption of public morals.

The painters urged Jaya to leave her painting up—this was censorship, an outrageous control of speech. They demanded of the inspector: *Who is the lady who lodged the complaint? On what grounds is this an obscene picture? Why not the other three? They also depict nude figures. Why not any other nude in the gallery?* "You don't see the difference?" the inspector said. "Here you have a naked woman with so many hands on her. She is being touched everywhere. You don't find that obscene?"

Gaffar asked the inspector if he realized *Dancing Girl* referred to a historical image. A shadow crossed the inspector's eyes, as if he felt he were being tricked on some academic point. He ignored the query, warning Jaya that she could listen to the artists if she wanted, but in that case she would be arrested. Obscenity was a criminal charge. There would be a trial, and she could spend time in jail. Was she prepared for those consequences? Jaya felt the fear rising inside her like water, filling her chest, rising to her head. "No," she said. "No."

Keshav Mane informed the inspector this was his gallery. The paintings in Gallery 56 were his responsibility while they were in his custody, and no picture would be taken down on the whims of a policeman calling it obscene. You had to understand the context of art, and see the picture in that context.

Inspector Khadilkar looked at Jaya. "Since you are the artist, Miss, you must consider your fate for yourself. The only one who will be charged with a crime is you." He seemed to summon a little sympathy for her, offering her until eleven o'clock the next morning to remove her picture. If she didn't, she would be arrested and served notice for prosecution.

After the inspector left, the painters descended on Jaya, urging her to take a stand and leave her picture hanging. They would support her in fighting the case in court if the fellow actually arrested her. Censorship affected them all. The buffoon didn't even recognize her painting referred to a prehistoric figurine. Did he think her dancing girl was some kotah-walli? Jaya found it hard to speak over their louder, more insistent voices. Even Dhasal, normally mild and reticent, urged her to consider this a baseless violation of free speech that she should not be made to suffer. Jaya wished she could ask Sringara for advice, but Sringara was the only painter in the show absent at that moment, teaching her figure drawing class for casual students.

"I don't know," Jaya kept muttering. Her heart was pounding. Others knew more than she did, and she felt she must listen. Keshav Mane then asserted ownership over her pictures, saying this was his gallery, his show, and he wouldn't allow a picture to be removed on the basis of "a hysterical society lady" complaining to the police about a picture she found offensive. Who was one person to make such a judgment?

"I don't know," Jaya said and left, feeling very cold, shivering, though it was a muggy May night. It was raining faintly when she stepped outside, portending the arrival of the monsoons.

Inside her room at Sringara's flat, she sat, stunned, on her bed. Her door was latched, protecting her from the next intrusion. She was remorseful; she grew angry over her naivete. She painted as if in a dream, she painted without thinking of who would see her picture, and then she put those private dreamings in front of people. She bared herself. In her four pictures for the exhibition, she had bared herself completely, although none of the women in the pictures resembled her. No one would have identified any of them as a portrait of the artist—as a self-portrait of Jaya Malhotra. Rashid Ahmed had told her about the ancient dancing girl when he saw her paintings of Kamlesh dancing at her exhibition last year. He held the past in his heart, and he had mentioned the historical roots of the dancer in Indian art. The oldest known artifact in Indian civilization, going back four thousand years, was a small bronze dancing girl found during the digs at Mohenjo-daro in Sind in the twenties, about a decade before Jaya's birth. The story had provoked her curiosity. Sringara had brought home a book from the art school library with a photograph of the recovered dancing girl. A bronze figurine only a few inches high, nude, one arm stacked with bangles to her shoulder. She wasn't actually dancing but posturing, one hand planted assertively on her hip, her head thrown back in an attitude of defiance. On canvas Jaya had painted a more tender version of the girl, more human though still abstract, posturing, nude, hands pulling on her from every direction—one hand upon her breast. The inspector had noted the offense of that—the hands of men and women, of her society, pulling her apart, one hand pressing down on her head. She ought to do this, she ought to do that. No, she could not do that. She could not throw her head back and do as she pleased.

When Sringara came home, Jaya went to speak to her in her room. Her voice quivered—really, she wanted to be held. "Mane won't let me take the picture down," she said. Now there were tears in her eyes, a fear that her future was ending. She had begun to believe the pictures were Mane's property, that he controlled them, because it was his gallery. "He is adamant that I should not be censored."

Sringara stood, listening to her at the foot of her bed. She looked straight at Jaya and told her calmly, "It's not his painting. He's not the one who'll be put through a criminal trial."

Jaya nodded. She understood the men would bear few consequences, so they could display bravado at her expense. She asked Sringara to come to the gallery with her tomorrow to face them. She would need help in putting off Mane, especially, since he claimed ownership of her paintings inside his rooms. "I'm going to pull the picture down," she decided.

Later in the evening, Jaya and Sringara were eating their dinner, sitting cross-legged on the floor in the dining room, when there was a firm, repeated banging on the door. Amvi ran to answer, and they hurried after her. The male voices speaking Marathi in the entry belonged to the police. The inspector led in a few ordinary constables in khaki uniforms. He asked almost politely, "Where is your studio, Miss Malhotra?" Jaya was puzzled and asked if he was looking for something. He wanted to see her other pictures, it seemed, to determine if there was additional obscene material. But these were her private paintings, Sringara said, these were not on public display. The inspector said, "I will start with this room." He moved into the drawing room. Within an instant, he could see there were no paintings in the room, only chairs, two standing birdcages, a few books on a shelf. Jaya was terrified. Would they arrest her right here in the flat?

She led them to her room. The inspector ransacked the small stack of paintings slotted in a corner, about a dozen. Another policeman went into her bathroom, and another opened the doors of her wardrobe and began hunting through her clothes, throwing them on the bed. "What is this?" the inspector said, holding a picture from her stack face out. It was a self-portrait, one that was recognizably her, realistic. She had painted it while looking at herself in the mirror she had mounted on the wall. Kirti had said, "Make a painting of yourself, so I can understand you." So she had depicted herself as a man might, focusing on the details of her body, her breasts and mouth especially, as Amrita Sher-Gil had painted herself. She wore red lipstick like Amrita. Her sari fell around her hips; she was naked above the waist, her dark brown nipples were large. She had wanted to see what the painting would tell her about herself. Her eyes were wide, slightly fearful and slightly defiant. The inspector told one of his men to seize the picture. It was large, and when its back was turned to her, she saw the title she'd painted on the verso, *Untitled (Nude)*, concealing her identity, an anonymous woman a male artist might have painted. But below the title she had made her confession in block letters: *JAYA MALHOTRA, '56.*

This picture would be further evidence to support an obscenity charge, the inspector declared. She must take down her painting in the gallery tomorrow to avoid arrest. What was obscene about this one? Sringara asked, gesturing to the painting in the constable's arms. The inspector said nothing initially. Then, at the door, he turned around and told them, "It is a woman showing no modesty, looking straight out, stark naked. She is not even made unreal, she is very real—anyone can see it is the artist herself. She looks as if she is taunting a man, letting him know she doesn't have to show any modesty. *What will he do about it?*"

At the gallery the next morning, Jaya told Mane she wanted to take down all her pictures. What if the inspector decided another one was obscene? Keshav Mane counseled her not to do that. It would be a sign of cowardice, giving into censorship. The inspector had objected only to *Dancing Girl*, so she should take that down if she wanted. Mane was now more moderate in his views, more understanding of her. She'd expected opposition, but he seemed to understand that she could not risk the consequences of an arrest. She and Sringara had decided not to tell Mane about the inspector's raid on the flat last night, afraid it would make him more aggressive in his argument against censorship with the inspector, disregarding the cost to Jaya. That might provoke the inspector to inflict further vengeance on her, and she was afraid of what new forms his punishment might take. Others showed up, perhaps anticipating a showdown with the inspector. Even Mr. Wolfensohn in his black jacket and small notebook appeared. Someone must have alerted him to the controversy. He urged Jaya to remain brave, to fight for her right to show a picture that depicted the dilemma of the Indian woman free of any lurid imagery that could be deemed obscene. Jaya was heartened to see Sringara take Mr. Wolfensohn aside, and thought she heard Sringara murmur the word "confidential" to him. She would have liked to beg Mr. Wolfensohn not to write about her predicament, because if her name appeared in the paper about an obscenity charge it would shatter her parents' reputation, but she didn't approach him. She didn't have any authority to tell a man like that what he could and couldn't write.

Mane beckoned a peon to take down *Dancing Girl* as some painters bemoaned the surrender. Jaya looked at her picture again, coming off the wall, a tall canvas echoing the elongated figure of the ancient artifact. She had turned the abstract bronze statue into a softer form, a thin flesh woman with faint curves. The hands seizing her were flesh hands not bronze, the hands belonging to all the faceless people who thought they could tell a girl what to do, who could turn her in any direction they chose, who could stop her from breathing. Sringara took the picture upstairs to her studio, relieving Jaya of the worry of transporting it home. Jaya eyed the remaining pictures on the wall and hoped the inspector would not select another one to prosecute, just because it had been painted by her.

Returning to Sringara's flat, she found it impossible to sit down and try to still her mind so she could prepare for her lab exams. She had offered four nude pictures for display at Mane's grand inaugural exhibition, which now struck her as madness. Painting over the last couple of months, she had gone so deep into herself, she hadn't realized she was crossing a limit. She'd had to study for her exams at the same time, restricted by the great volume of material she had to memorize, so she didn't hold herself back in her paintings. So far she'd seen no reviews in the papers, but write-ups often appeared several days after the opening. She prayed all the critics' attention would be lavished on the big artists and no one would think to remark on her nudes. To her relief, Sringara had told her in her studio that Wolfensohn had agreed not to write about her troubles, though reluctantly, because he went on about free speech being the foundation of democracy— and wasn't India the world's biggest democracy? Jaya sat hunched over on the side of her bed, holding her head in her hands. What had she done? Never before had she painted nudes. Amrita Sher-Gil's nude paintings had infatuated her, the first ones she'd seen done by a woman. Then Sringara started hiring a woman from the Cages as a model, and since the woman happened to bring an infant with her, Jaya had painted a portrait of them as mother and child. For male painters, who created the tradition of nude painting, the nude woman was a source of beauty. But what was a "nude" for a woman? She'd wanted to find out.

Sringara came back to the flat, as darkness fell and a light rain softened the air. She brought a newspaper with her that Vir Patak had given her. Sringara had thought about keeping it to herself, but she had decided it was best if Jaya knew what had been written, so she wouldn't be caught off guard if anyone said anything to her. Jaya opened the slightly damp copy of the *Evening Standard,* sitting on her bed. Sringara told her to keep turning the pages. The story appeared toward the back of the paper—only a short piece, a flash bulletin under the heading STOP PRESS.

ARTIST THREATENED WITH ARREST ON OBSCENITY CHARGE

Miss Jaya Malhotra, a notable young artist and student at Grant Medical College, evaded arrest by Vigilance Branch, CID Bombay by removing a painting deemed obscene at the inaugural exhibition of six artists at

Gallery 56. Keshav Mane, proprietor of Gallery 56, along with other artists present vehemently objected to the police demand to remove the
picture as unwarranted censorship and state control of speech. However,
police referred to complaints from members of the public against Ms.
Malhotra's painting of a nude woman. A raid on her studio yesterday
evening resulted in the seizure of another picture deemed obscene.
The artist's compliance with police orders prompted the return of the
seized obscene artwork.

The writer went unnamed. One of those anonymous little articles that
sizzled across the news pages. It felt as if someone had spied on her for
the last two days and reported everything to the paper. Sringara tried to
console her, suggesting things she might say in her defense. "I won't be able
to explain this to anyone," Jaya said, hanging her head. The most shameful
event of her life had been revealed to the entire city, and her parents' name
would suffer the worst for it. No one would speak to them. No one would
want to meet them anymore.

She couldn't think of what she should do, but her fury grew. The writer
had gotten things wrong; actually, he had made things worse for her. Only
one lady had complained about her picture to the police, whereas the
writer stated that complaints came from "members of the public," making
it sound as if the general public had denounced her painting. Her self-
portrait, seized by the inspector, had not been returned. She didn't know
where the inspector had taken it; he'd never mentioned giving it back to
her. She imagined the picture thrown into a dark, damp cell—punished,
as she was meant to be.

"Who wrote this? Do you think it was Mr. Wolfensohn?" How feebly she
had protected herself, afraid to speak up to the great man, the European,
the professor of enormous art historical knowledge.

It couldn't be Wolfensohn, Sringara said, standing close to her, rubbing
her shoulder. Wolfensohn wrote only for the *Times*, as their "Art Critic." He'd
wanted to interview Jaya and the other artists, but Sringara had humbly
requested that he not write about her, because it would ruin her family's
name. Jaya sighed an instant's relief that a bigger article wouldn't appear
in the *Times of India*. Sringara understood she didn't have the privilege of

raising a political point, as violated as she felt by the inspector, as angry as she was, because this was a matter of her family's survival. "This fellow," Sringara said, shoving her hand out toward the paper, "seems to be writing some story the inspector fed him."

Jaya couldn't hold back her tears. She couldn't speak. She was sobbing. Sringara sat close to her, her hand on Jaya's back. If her parents came to know of this incident, she couldn't face them again—a girl who painted obscene paintings of women. Whose room the police had raided for her nudes. How ashamed she would feel in front of them. No one would want to associate with them because of her. What would Mr. Khosla do when he found out the news? What might happen to her father? Her father had said her obsession would destroy them all. A week back—or when was it? she couldn't remember the days anymore—she had gathered the courage to ring home to wish Bebeji a good journey. Bebeji sounded extremely pleased when Jaya told her she would be back at home by the time Bebeji returned from Ludhiana. Now she could never go home, she would only burden the family with more shame. She let out a little cry. Many different forces were tearing at her. She felt those very hands tugging at her that she had painted upon the *Dancing Girl*, each pulling her in a different direction. This was another form of disintegration, different from Gaffar's isolation: being embedded so tightly among others that everyone in your society passed judgment on you, their judgment becoming your sentence.

Sringara regretted showing her the article. She tried to calm Jaya, diminishing its importance. "It's a small, insignificant piece. How many people even read an evening paper? I would never have seen it if Patak hadn't brought it to me." Jaya nodded, but she couldn't think. She only felt. Eventually she felt an easing because a notion of relief came to mind—there was something she could do about this. She could walk into the water and be soothed.

The day was not yet steaming at eight the next morning. Jaya took a bus from the railway station opposite Sringara's flat going to Colaba. At the quiet end of Colaba Causeway, she alighted at a familiar stop and walked to their old flat. It was the third balcony up, on the right, in a four-story building. Red bougainvillea boughs sprawled over the boundary wall. The chiks in the flat's balcony were rolled up, letting in the light. She didn't know who lived here. The flat didn't hold much meaning for her anymore. She had come here to have a starting point. She didn't know exactly on which lane she and Kamlesh, as children, had discovered the jetty going into the water. She would have to navigate her way there by intuition, since she had never seen the lane after that day she'd forced Kamlesh to walk out into the sea. The roadways were quiet, serene. Crows squawked in the terraces of great, spreading trees. The only people out were servants on their morning tasks. Jaya dragged her slippers in the dust of the roadside; she couldn't find the lane. Nothing looked familiar anymore. She stopped to ask an ayah if she knew of the jetty. The woman shook her head and smiled apologetically. Jaya wondered if the jetty from ten years back had been destroyed, or if it had been part of a land reclamation project that was now filled with earth and planted with new buildings.

After wandering down several wrong streets, attempting to follow a few people's conflicting directions, she glimpsed the black jetty, unchanged, at the end of a short lane lined with bungalows and old blocks of flats patched with black mildew. A long promontory of massive rocks lunged into the thrashing green Arabian Sea. She walked to the end of the lane. She had to sit on a cement ledge to jump down onto the wet rocks. They must have done that as small girls, but she didn't remember. She left her slippers on a stone. The breeze flapped her chunni around, and she threw it off her shoulders onto the stones so she could be free of it. The sloping blocks of rock were turned at sharp angles and slippery under her feet, and she walked slowly from one onto the next. She had a very long way to go. All around her the sea boomed, and the waves crashed deafeningly against the boulders, dousing her in salt water. She continued walking, concentrating on where to place her foot next, on keeping her balance. The hollows in the stones were pooled with seawater and crushed shells. The sea roared at her. This was not the velvety, soft, sandy, watery bed she had imagined sinking into. The waves slammed into one another, and the salt spray pelted her like stones. Her hair was now wet, her kameez soaked. What would her parents think had happened to her? Would anyone find out that she had come here?

Jaya turned her head to look back at the lane and the palm trees growing around the buildings. No choice was left to her. She had not been charged with obscenity, and yet it felt as though she had been shamefully arrested. As though she had been made to stand in a court and answer to a judge, her nude paintings displayed for everyone to see in her humiliation. Every word of what had happened to her was in the newspaper. Other writers might come up with their own stories. Who knew who was behind it? She stopped short of the jetty's rounded end. She had only to sit there, maybe twenty feet farther out, to be swallowed by a wave. She didn't know how to swim, so she could not save herself if she tried. She would go, she would go. It was what she wanted. The wind made her cold; the sea frightened her. It roared like the devil against the charcoal boulders. She pushed herself forward, across the sharp edges of the stones, toward the tip of the jetty, her whole body wet, and then she stopped again. Some instinct stopped her. She looked ahead to the sky; it was swollen with brooding clouds. Many shades of darkness. Green, gray, slate. The sea would churn more wildly with rain soon.

29

WHEN JAYA AWOKE on the night train to Punjab, she imagined she was
on a ship at sea and was devastated by the thought that she had left her
country behind her. A moment later, she remembered the death and felt
a helpless despair. Rocking in her berth as the train pulled into a station
in the countryside far north of Bombay, she heard the shouts of railway
workers, and a deep moan from Kamlesh in the berth below.

She's died, she told herself, and felt anew the terror of the admission:
Bebeji had died.

Hours later, the knock of a bearer bringing tea to their compartment
alerted her to daybreak. Her mother opened the door to the man, and Jaya
climbed down from her berth to rouse Kamlesh from a hard, defiant sleep.
Her sister turned away toward the compartment wall. Jaya sat in the side
chair with her tea, pain clawing at the muscles of her right shoulder. Her
back had contracted in tension during the night, and the soreness felt like
the continuation of a tormented rest. Finally Kamlesh got up and had a
wash. Her face was swollen with grief, her mouth turned down in the battered expression of a much older person. "What time is it?" she asked Jaya
without lifting her gaze. Neither of them was able to look up at the other
or anyone else, their lines of vision angled into themselves.

"Ten past six," said Jaya, glancing at her wristwatch.

"When did the telegram come? It was one o'clock yesterday, I think, a quarter to one—I was in the kitchen," their mother recalled, attempting to reconstruct the previous day's sequence of events, as though that might resolve the question of how Bebeji had died eight days after her arrival in Punjab. "I heard the bell and thought, who is this coming at lunchtime? I was surprised when Heerabai said it was very important. I rushed to the door and it was the boy with the urgent telegram."

"It was the will of God," murmured a middle-aged Punjabi schoolteacher in the berth above Vidya's. The teacher was trying to absolve them of their guilt with the notion of inevitability, suggesting none of them had played any part in Bebeji's death. "The moment of each person's death is fixed at birth, it cannot be altered even by a minute."

"She survived that horrible riot last month. Kamlesh managed to pull her out of the road in time," Jaya mused. The telegram from Bebeji's brother did not state the cause of death. Now she would never be able to make things right with her grandmother; the chance was gone. For ten months she had neglected Bebeji, obstinately staying at Sringara's for the sake of her paintings. Last night, at the station, her father had reminded her of her wrongdoing. "She wanted you to come home, that's all. It would have given her peace."

Vidya opened her purse and took out her goggles to shield her eyes from the stinging dust flying in through the barred windows. "She insisted on going back. I was telling her it'll be too hot in May. She hadn't fully healed from her injuries. I don't know why she was in such a rush to go to Punjab." She shook her head in regret. "Those people killed her." She meant the rioters.

"I think she went home to die," Kamlesh said quietly. Jaya reluctantly nodded in agreement. Home for Bebeji was not Ludhiana, the small town, but the region, the land she was born in—the Punjab.

The whole hot day they threaded their way north, passing hills softly wrapped in a blue haze, thick stands of trees, and mud villages in the dark soil of the plains. Then came the parched sand landscape of Rajasthan. Jaya and Kamlesh sitting side by side, collecting the soot of burnt coal in their laps. Imprinted under the sorrow of Bebeji's death was the ill feeling of the past months, a shadow that crawled between Jaya and her twin, preventing them from truly comforting each other.

Their father came to their compartment. He stood in the doorway, his face shrunk to a bony shell overnight. "They won't be able to keep her at home for two days in the heat," Harbans told them. A body was normally cremated before sundown on the day of the death, so he expected Lekh Raj would not be able to postpone the funeral until they arrived. Jaya felt her father regarded her as a stranger, keeping her distant because he held it against her that Bebeji had died disappointed, the family torn apart by her refusal to come home. It was Kamlesh he consoled, gently stroking her head when she went to him.

Bebeji's brother received them at Ludhiana station early the next morning, among the coolies in red shirts carrying people's luggage on their heads, a day and a half after they began their journey from Bombay. Manu accompanied him. Manu had insisted on escorting Bebeji on the train to Punjab, proud to be old enough to do so. "Didi? You've also come?" Manu said, as if he had not expected Jaya to be with the family. He wore white clothes of mourning and an austere expression on his face. Thin creases of grief lined Lekh Raj's face. His thatch of silver hair appeared brighter with age, yet he was essentially unchanged from the last time Jaya had seen him, years back, at Lalaji's death in Bombay. Though he was ten or twelve years older than Bebeji, he was remarkably vigorous still, a quick-moving, sure-footed man in an immaculate white kurta-pajama and black lace-up shoes. "She looked just as if she was sleeping," he recalled about the moment he found Bebeji in her room.

He directed the twins, their parents, and Dipi into two tongas and piled a third horse carriage with their luggage. They jostled through the awakening bazaar at the steady pace of the horse's stride, the vendors' shouts in Punjabi, the lines of turbaned Sikh men starting the day's work in their shops, a past life Jaya was moving through. Muffling layers of dust bordered the sides of the road, and there was a noticeable absence of cars. The sight of the brick clock tower with the tall window above the clock evoked a sharp return to childhood. Where was the house with the big rose garden in which her mother had cut blossoms every day? Silent roads lined with houses and tall neem trees beyond the bazaar led them to a small dark-yellow bungalow in Civil Lines. It was only nine in the morning but already the day burned, and Jaya wiped the sweat from her face with her chunni.

Shrieks of bereavement broke out as they entered the crowded front room, a theater of women's grief. Vidya uttered a piercing wail, embracing Lekh Raj's wife, Bhirawan Devi. Bebeji's three elder sisters, arthritic like her but slighter, more frail, came forward to embrace them, crying in anguish. Jaya stepped aside, bewildered by the sudden, ritualistic purging of sorrow.

Lekh Raj apologized to their father. The son was meant to light the funeral pyre; it was one of the most important duties of Harbans's life. But they couldn't wait two days in the heat, so they had burned her yesterday. Though Daddy had warned them this was likely, Jaya still had expected to see Bebeji in the house, to touch her, and was unprepared for her irrevocable absence. It didn't seem possible she was fully gone from the earth. Later, Jaya would look through an open doorway and anticipate Bebeji's appearance, her stout figure, powerful and heavy, dragging her feet along and adjusting her sari palla decorously over her head in the presence of so many people.

The family was given the bedroom Bebeji had used. Bhirawan Devi, a nimble woman, industrious like her husband, assured them everything had been washed—the floor on which Bebeji's body had lain, the bed linens, the towels. The scent of purifying sandalwood incense lingered in the air. Jaya realized the small khaki-covered case pushed into a corner was Bebeji's. Her face crumpled, tears coming to her eyes. The case's small size inflicted a cutting pain, suggesting her grandmother's presence in the world had been negligible.

Pots of water were boiled for their baths. Jaya squatted on the bathroom floor, scrubbing her hair of sand and soot. Washing relieved her, cooled her skin, and made her believe for a moment that she was free of the burden she'd brought with her from Bombay.

Family members were put up in every room. At night, many slept on charpais on the rooftop since it was cooler outside than in the house. The twins slept on the floor near their father and Dipi, who occupied the same corner of the bedroom where Bebeji's body had lain. Their mother had discouraged them from spreading their bedding on the floor; it was a penance only sons and close male relations were meant to endure, not young women, not granddaughters. But dwelling in her grief seemed necessary to Jaya, and the discomfort of the red cement floor suited her. Jaya felt for her sister's arm, as they listened in their separate silences to the howling of jungli dogs living on the roadside. By a purely physical instinct they stayed close to each other, ate together, slept side by side. A childhood habit of joining drew them to one another; yet beneath the surface they had come apart, each enclosed in her separate husk of sorrow.

Jaya would wake up in an exhausted, sleepless state, having remained awake much of the night on the cement floor, aware she had entered a different life—her recent life, the artist's life during which she had been separated from her family, harassed by the police, and degraded in the papers, withering away. She was back in the circle of her family where she belonged, no matter how strained her connections to the others. Here in Punjab, she was safe among her relations. She was the girl everyone thought they knew. Dipi's mother had embraced her warmly, pressing two hard, bony arms tightly around her. Surely Dipi would not have told her that Jaya had left home, or that she'd nearly been arrested for painting pictures people deemed obscene, immoral—a degenerate's work. Dipi had never wanted to undermine her, she knew that. No one here had heard her bad news. She could breathe without shame.

More than a week of mourning lay ahead. On the thirteenth day after Bebeji's death, they would hold the final puja to mark her soul's migration to its last home.

At night, lying in the dark, Jaya thought she heard Bebeji's last cry. She must have known what was happening at that moment, Jaya thought— that her life was finished. The swiftness of her end baffled Lekh Raj and Bhirawan Devi. Since her arrival, Bebeji had surprised them with her energy, making it hard for them to believe she had been badly injured a few weeks earlier. They'd taken her around town to meet her old acquaintances from Lahore who had settled in Ludhiana after Partition. On the morning of her death, Bebeji had awoken early, taken her bath, done her puja, and sat down in the courtyard to read the paper. She had complained of feeling dizzy in the sun and gone inside to lie down. Twenty minutes later they had heard a small cry and gone running to her room. "Just one short cry," Lekh Raj told them. The doctor called it heart failure.

During the day, the twins attached themselves to Satya, the friend Bebeji used to call her younger sister, nine or ten years her junior. The one with whom she had organized groups of women freedom fighters in Lahore, and with whom she had been jailed in the forties. Satya had come from Amritsar for the full thirteen days of mourning, as only the closest relations did. Her round and luminous face and her soft eyes were as comforting as they had been to Jaya as a child, though she now had many fine lines pinched around her mouth. Her hair, rolled back in a twist, was brushed with strands of gray in the front. Satya recalled her son Sarvi had sent her a cutting of an article he'd written on the remote hillside slum where Nihal Devi had opened a school. "You know, your Bebeji was a younger woman than me at heart—she kept on fighting for something. What have I done since Partition? All these years have gone by just trying to secure a house for ourselves."

With Satya the twins wanted to look inside Bebeji's small suitcase. They lifted the khaki-covered box out of the corner and set it on the floor in front of them. Satya clicked open the rusted latches, the little finger of her right hand a stub, her fourth finger cut off at the top joint. As children her damaged hand had held their frightened gazes; only later did they learn a policeman had clubbed her. Bebeji had been struck across the back. Lala Lajpat Rai, the beloved "Lion of Punjab," who led the demonstrators had been clubbed to death by the British superintendent of police. It was this protest against the Simon Commission that marked the start of Bebeji's activism in Congress, which Jaya had illustrated for Manu's booklet, showing Bebeji in a moment of rebellion before she fell.

The contents of her suitcase were meager. Four khadi saris, rough to the touch. Her night garments, two cotton petticoats. Nihal Devi hadn't always dressed so plainly, Satya told them. Before she dedicated herself to the spartan white of the freedom fighter, she'd worn colorful saris with beaded blouses and brocade vests. There was one silk vest of violet and blue flowers with mother-of-pearl buttons that Satya admired so much, Bebeji had gifted it to her. The twins softly laughed to think of Bebeji as a young woman in pretty saris. Behind the suitcase, in the corner where it stood, the girls discovered a short piece of a bamboo pole, which puzzled them. Bhirawan Devi was surprised it had been overlooked, not yet discarded. A bamboo pole had been brought from the market and cut down exactly to Bebeji's height. By custom, it had been laid beside her body before she was carried to the cremation grounds, a surrogate companion for her in death. The pole had been burned with her, Bhirawan said, to accompany her on her journey. Jaya placed the section of golden cut-off bamboo in her suitcase, cherishing it as a last token of her grandmother.

As the days passed, she recognized her isolation within the family. Her mother's anger had resurfaced; she was short with Jaya and Kamlesh. When their father entered a room, it took Jaya a moment to recognize him. He'd shaved his head, according to custom, his razored scalp exposing his gaunt physique, giving him the look of a sick man. He had come to Sringara's flat the day after the article appeared in the *Evening Standard*, indicting her paintings as obscene. Just an hour or two after she had returned home from her walk on the jetty, wet and trembling. She had packed up her things, as he ordered, and followed him out of the flat without protest. All her paintings were left behind at Sringara's flat, as he instructed, implying he didn't want them to pollute the house.

On the day she returned, after Mummy had tired of fighting with her, she told Jaya of the calamity of Kamlesh's movie role. They could not pull her out of a picture in which she played a temple dancer, because she had signed a contract. The producer would not accept Daddy's offer of a ten-thousand-rupee settlement. Mr. Narula threatened to make it a court case, confident he'd win a swift judgment since production was underway. Kamlesh had come to their room very early one morning and told them everything, panicking about the next shoot coming up. "What did we do to deserve daughters like you two?" Mummy had hissed. The next afternoon she had screamed in the passageway, holding the telegram announcing Bebeji's death. The day after Jaya tried to die, Bebeji had died.

No one in Ludhiana could see that the family was shattered within. They were mourning the loss of Bebeji, and mourning what had broken between them. Outwardly they behaved as normal—only they felt the emotional distance they kept from each other. On the ninth day after Bebeji's death, the men went to the cremation grounds in the morning to collect her remains for the kirya ceremony they would travel to Haridwar to perform the next day. Vidya forced the girls out of the house for some fresh air, sending them to post announcements to a couple of distant relatives in Bombay she had neglected to write to earlier. An edge of each postcard was torn to forewarn the recipient of a death. At times, the intensity of Jaya's desire to see Bebeji overwhelmed her. Walking down a quiet road, she peered into the distance, past the stray dogs lying in soft, sandy blankets of dust on the roadside, and conjured Bebeji shuffling toward her with her peculiar side-to-side rocking gait, raising her head in surprise to see Jaya there.

The sisters walked to the Civil Lines post office in their salwar kameezes, their heads covered in long chunnis. Jaya felt she'd slipped into an old life here, a life before the break of Partition, stretching back to their childhood. Where was their old house? She felt an urge to look for it, to find her way back to the life they'd had here as if it could be hers again. She turned over a postcard to check the date. "I've missed my practicals," she told Kamlesh, remembering her lab exams. "They were yesterday and today." Before they left Bombay, six hours after receiving the telegram—her father rushing home from the factory, rushing to the station to book their seats on the Frontier Mail—he had dispatched the driver with a note for Dr. Rao, the dean of Grant Medical College, requesting a postponement of Jaya's lab exams due to her grandmother's death.

They passed a short row of open-fronted shops selling foodstuffs and stationery, and Kamlesh turned to her, saying, "I don't think I'll have to leave." She meant for England. Jaya didn't understand why Kamlesh's eyes brightened with hope at the thought of staying home when she had been eager for admission to a teacher's college in London. "Bebeji didn't want me to go," Kamlesh said, leaning against the letterbox. She shook the fine dust and pebbles out of her sandals, scraping her heels clean with a finger. She, too, seemed to be seeking shelter in these slow, still days, in this past, leaning back as if to anchor herself to the red cylinder of the letterbox. She might have felt, like Jaya, that it was the beginning of a new life for her.

On their return home, they found two tongas standing outside Lekh Raj's bungalow. The men had come back from the cremation grounds, and the group was dividing: Bebeji's elderly brothers-in-law were getting off at home before Harbans, Dipi, and Lekh Raj continued to the railway station. Their father spoke seriously to an intent-looking Manu in the drive, probably explaining to him again that he was too young to travel to Haridwar for the death rituals. Nearer the entry to the house, Dipi's younger sister closed her eyes inside the circle of his arms, resting her head on his shoulder. The commotion of arranging luggage in a tonga ensued, Bhirawan Devi running outside with a handbasket of packed food and a flask of water for the journey. Jaya and Kamlesh stood on the roadside, the smell of dry dust filling their nostrils. In one covered tonga, Jaya glimpsed on the seat beside her great-uncle Lekh Raj a gunny sack that she realized, with a start, must contain Bebeji's remains.

She and Kamlesh walked over to the tonga. The thin white horse showing his ribs stood patiently at the head of the scarred old carriage. They spoke to Lekh Raj. He untied the gunny sack to show them the round clay pot holding Bebeji's ashes. The mouth of the pot was covered with a white cloth, tied up tightly with windings of a soft, thick red rope. Jaya climbed onto the footboard of the carriage to lay her hands on the pot but felt nothing radiating from the clay shell. No energy remained in ashes. There was a white cotton sack, too, much smaller than the gunny bag, in which the fragments of Bebeji's bones were collected. *Phool*, they were called. *Flowers.* Kamlesh wanted to hold the bag, so Lekh Raj passed it to her. She clutched it against her chest for a long moment as if she were clutching Bebeji herself. Jaya took the sack from her and cupped its weight in her palms. Nothing of Bebeji's spirit vibrated against her skin; there was no chance for communion anymore. Reluctantly she returned the bag to Lekh Raj, who placed it on the seat beside him. At the end, there was no meaning. There were only these rituals left for them to show their respect.

Jaya and Kamlesh stepped away from the carriage. The men would transport Bebeji's ashes and bones to Haridwar, where they would immerse them in the river Ganga, all traces of Bebeji eventually dissolving in the sacred water flowing down from the mountains.

30

FOR OVER TWO hours, Kamlesh had been emptying her side of the wardrobe, folding clothes into a black metal trunk, sorting through papers on the writing table. From Bebeji's narrow cupboard in the alcove, she pulled out a dark red shawl Bebeji had worn before she was widowed, a shawl Kamlesh now claimed as hers. She draped the soft bolt of embroidered wool around her shoulders. At the dressing table, she drew a comb through her hair, astonished by how quickly the movement ended with a scratch at her nape, the body of her hair missing. She repeated the gesture to convince herself of its absence. Her face was a revelation to her in the triple-paneled mirrors, her pageboy giving her a sauciness, a swank glamour she hadn't adjusted to. A fringe hid the crushed mark the stone had imprinted on her brow. Pulling her shoulders back and clasping her hands below her breasts, like a model in front of a camera, she studied herself in the center mirror panel to consider how English people might view her when she arrived. In three days, she would set sail on the *Himalaya*, making the six-week voyage to England alone, a student of child development and early childhood education at the Institute of Education. "They say it gets cold there by September. I hope a shawl will be adequate," she said, reducing her great uncertainty about going to an unknown place to a question about the weather.

Her twin passed behind her in the mirror without responding. Jaya's hair was combed back from her forehead, and her thick plait hung down her back, giving Kamlesh the startling impression she was looking at two photographs of herself: one of her old self before she cut her hair, the other of a foreign self she didn't yet know. At unexpected moments like this, she felt a jolt of excitement at the prospect of discovering who she would become over there.

Later, her mother walked into the room, trailed by the servant bearing a hefty bundle tied in white sheets. He set it on Kamlesh's bed, as her mother instructed. Vidya bent to the task of untying the twisted ends of a bedsheet pulled into tight knots. The cotton flaps fell away, showing a stack of brocades, transparent silk tissues, satins, and rich Kanjivaram silk weaves, which she had been collecting over the years for her daughters' dowries. "Take two with you," her mother said. Kamlesh complied, afraid of questioning her mother's command. She chose from the lower half of the stack that was her portion of the collection—a turquoise Benaresi silk and a dark-yellow satin to which a broad black-and-gold-thread border had been applied. "Find yourself an Indian boy there," her mother said harshly.

Kamlesh went very still, feeling as if she were being discarded. *Make your marriage on your own*, her mother seemed to say. Her mother had chaperoned her to the studio every day for three weeks during her last shoot, forced to stand by and watch the filming. "Now you'll have these kinds of uneducated men to choose from—some actor or director," she had shouted at Kamlesh in her dressing room. "Is this what you wanted for yourself?"

Vidya approved the two saris Kamlesh had chosen and said they would go to their tailor in Colaba to get the blouses stitched in a hurry. It had occurred to her there were Indian boys living in London, too, and they might be more liberal in outlook. "Find a boy from a family who doesn't mind a natchnai walli," her mother snapped. Kamlesh's mouth quivered. To be taunted like this just as she was about to leave—she wanted to go and never return. *Natchnai walli. A dancing girl.* Available to men. "Find a family who doesn't mind a girl that plays prostitutes in films."

Kamlesh felt as if she herself were being mocked as a prostitute. She looked at her mother, wounded, trying to hold back tears—Mummy had become someone else, bitter, capable of cruelty. "They never narrated the full story to me, I told you." Kamlesh struggled to defend herself. "They tricked me in a way. I was told the character was a temple dancer, she danced for the god every day." Her mother ignored her and busied herself with wrapping up the sari bundle securely in tight knots. Kamlesh stood quietly; she was meant to accept her chastisement.

O. P. Saigal had sprung the surprise of the dancer's fate on her as he coached her for her one dialogue scene—her few minutes of actual acting in the film. The lawyer played by Prem Kumar, grown into an old man in the final scene, would come across a destitute old woman begging in the street. He'd stop, drop a coin in her cup, and some gesture of hers would remind him of the dancer who enchanted him as a young man. Kamlesh, the old beggar—in a white wig matching Prem Kumar's—would admit she was the temple dancer and ask him why he hadn't saved her. Englishmen had installed her in a brothel they ran for their soldiers after they outlawed temple dancing as an immoral practice, accusing the priests of being corrupt. She'd been held captive in their brothel for years until Independence arrived.

To her mother's distress over this last-minute revelation, N. D. Narula replied it was only a confession—Kamlesh never appeared in the role of a prostitute on-screen, not even as a back thought. The film centered on the hero's unhappy marriage to a society girl and his reveries about the dancer he'd been in love with from afar in his youth. When he thought of her, the camera looked down the pillared hall of the temple as if through the tunnels of memory, to create that nostalgic sensation of looking at something very beautiful very far away in time. He encouraged Vidya to feel proud that Kamlesh had a personality for film, a talent for dance.

In the studio, N. D. Narula glorified Kamlesh to her mother, but a couple of months earlier he'd shown a vicious side. When Kamlesh had accompanied her father to the studio to plead with him to release her from the contract, Narula had threatened to spread bad publicity about her. "I'll make Kamlesh Malhotra infamous not famous!" He'd degraded her in front of her father, insinuating she was romantically involved with Kirti. "That Bengali doctor or surgeon, or whatever he is, was coming morning and night to the studio for her. Why did he make all the promises on her behalf?" As her father stormed out of the room, Kamlesh turned around to apologize. N. D. Narula glared at her from the divan where he was convalescing in a dressing room. "I'll ruin your face if you don't report to the set!" he hissed. "I'll have one of my boys throw acid in your eyes." Kamlesh didn't move. It felt like the words themselves had seared a new mark on her face, and she cried out.

"Let's hope that picture never comes out," her mother said, holding the two saris she'd chosen. "Let's hope Narula runs out of money shooting his expensive color film."

Kamlesh nodded. Maybe there would be no film, just as there would be no reel-to-reel tape of Masterji's songs. The sound man could make her a tape in Masterji's practice room, it had occurred to her, so she could keep practicing her dance in England. Then she had asked herself, where would she play that tape over there? On whose machine? In whose house? When she went to take leave of her guru last week, bringing him flowers, he opened his palms to say everything was up to her now. "You may find what you want over there," he suggested. Kamlesh quickly replied that no, she was going only for a year. She told everyone she was going only for a year, perhaps because she was afraid of the alternative—of not returning.

FOLLOWING A RUSHED visit to the tailor the next day, Kamlesh stood in front of the wardrobe she shared with Jaya, cramming into one deep shelf all the clothes she was leaving behind. She called Jaya to take a look at the extra space she was leaving her for her clothes. Jaya got up from Bebeji's bed—she slept in the alcove, letting Kamlesh use their double beds. In her fastidious way, Jaya searched through the empty shelves and found a hankie, an old chunni squeezed in a corner, some stray letters from Kamlesh's friends married in other cities. "Why did you give your contract to Kirti to keep?" she asked, taking Kamlesh by surprise.

"I didn't want it here with Mummy-Daddy not knowing anything about the film," she stammered. Jaya had learned from their parents that "that Bengali doctor," as N. D. Narula called Kirti, had introduced Kamlesh to Ashok Narula's uncle and transported Kamlesh to and from the studio, assisting her in betraying them. Kamlesh couldn't show them her contract, as her father demanded after she confessed her role, until she went to the hospital to retrieve it from Kirti. Jaya knew all this from their parents, and though she was usually pointed in her questions, to Kamlesh's relief, she hadn't asked her about him, in her quiet, subdued state, as if she didn't realize his importance to her acting in the film.

"What happened with Kirti?" Jaya threw the question out as she yanked away the old, yellowing sheets of newspaper that lined Kamlesh's shelves. Jaya used to wonder if Kirti was attracted to her twin, and since they had spent so much time alone going to the studio, meeting film people, she wanted to know if they had been involved. Till now she had been too overwhelmed by her own situation to confront her doubts about Kamlesh; it was too much to think about. The hardest questions were those no one wanted to consider—she could consider them in a painting, maybe, but not in life. Still, she wanted some certainty before Kamlesh left, so she wouldn't be left wondering, hating Kamlesh.

Jaya listened to Kamlesh ramble, mentioning places Kirti had taken her—an outing once to Ballard Pier to see a liner come into port. Then she stopped. She seemed to know what Jaya was asking. "Nothing happened with him," she said.

Jaya glanced at her twin, who stood before her, wide-eyed, still girl-like in her ankle-long skirt and blouse, and considered the possibility she was lying. She had lied about so much. Kamlesh seemed to shrink a little in fear, but she didn't budge. She wasn't lying. She gazed back at Jaya and asked in a soft tone, "What will you do by yourself when I'm gone?"

"Nothing. I'll do nothing with myself," Jaya breathed out fearfully. She had existed for the last couple of months, since they returned from Punjab, without doing much of anything. She had given her paints and canvases to Sringara to dispose of, and Sringara had rolled up *Dancing Girl* and taken it with her to Rome to try to sell it there and relieve Jaya of the impulse to destroy it. Jaya was deeply happy to see her painting survive. That picture, with all the hands seizing her, was her true self-portrait. More true than the realistic, semi-nude self-portrait the inspector had seized.

The three paintings that had remained hanging in the exhibition had all sold, so Mane had paid her a substantial sum when she saw him. She saw a few hundred from the frame shop for old, not very good pictures. There was a little money still left from the sale of paintings at her first exhibition in November. She had almost two thousand rupees to her name, an incredible sum, but she had no drawings or canvases left. She had no vocation anymore. Despite the money, her confidence was gone. Both in herself and in the purpose of painting. What was the benefit of looking at who you were? Of who someone else was? What good did it do to expose any truth you discovered about yourself or someone else?

"You'll find something to do," Kamlesh said to encourage her. "You won't sit idle."

Jaya crumpled up the pages of newspaper into balls. She would line the shelves with new paper. She had stayed at Sringara's flat for almost a year, and she had both created and destroyed her life there. The *Evening Standard* wasn't the only paper to publish an article about her obscene paintings. When she returned from Ludhiana, Keshav Mane showed her cuttings from three other papers. The debate that the threat of her arrest had stirred up excited him, shining a bright beam on his new gallery. She told him the incident made her never want to paint again—she was stopping. Mane was taken aback. He apologized if he'd played any role in what had transpired. Sringara's studio would be reserved for her, he promised, once Sringara left for Rome. Though Jaya told him not to keep it for her, he said he would let it out on a month-by-month basis until she was ready to take it. She wasn't going to give up for good, he told her; she was just in shock over what had taken place and had become afraid.

But Mane had no idea what was happening at home, and she didn't tell him. She read the cuttings he gave her. In these articles, the writers considered the question of censorship as an intellectual issue, interviewing prominent artists about constraints on their expression in a conservative society. Zaidi was quoted defending Jaya in one story. Some artists attacked the upper classes for adopting a "Victorian mentality," while others pointed to the erotic sculptures of Hindu temples as an indicator of the permissive Indian temperament before the country was colonized. An artist's right to free expression and speech—that was the topic of discussion. None of them had any inkling of the consequences when the word *obscenity* was attached to one's name. They spoke of lofty ideals, and she hated any of them who invoked her as a martyr for free expression, because each time they did, she paid a price.

Her father had been put on a sort of probation after they returned from Punjab. Mr. Khosla at first had accepted Harbans's clarification that nothing actually had happened—Jaya had not been charged with any offense. He needed her father to manage the two rival union groups, neither of whom had a clear majority, and whose underhanded tactics kept the factory in a continuous state of low-level unrest—labor leaders manipulating management and management manipulating union activists, neither daring to show weakness. Khosla Sahib relied on her father to maintain control. But the articles kept appearing, as if the topics of obscenity and an artist's right to free speech, once raised, should not be dropped, and Jaya's name, accompanied by an account of her near-arrest, would appear in these stories. In one article a picture was even published of her other nude paintings in Keshav Mane's exhibition. So Mr. Khosla decided to give Harbans three months to see if the "bad publicity" around Jaya's paintings subsided. There was too much chatter in the Punjabi community about Jaya. Since her parents avoided gatherings, isolating themselves at home, Mummy saying she was too embarrassed even to raise her head among her friends, Khosla Sahib was being made to answer for Harbans, for his daughter. *What is happening with that family? Has Jaya gone mad? Painting obscene pictures?* The image of his glassworks, a factory operating on the latest American tank furnaces and producing top-quality sheet glass, was being corrupted by irrelevant talk about his manager's daughter and her indecent paintings. He couldn't bear the taint. "Why is your daughter painting obscene pictures now?" he had asked Daddy to shame him. "She used to paint portraits of Gandhiji, I thought."

He should stop his daughter from painting, her father was told—stop her from taking part in exhibitions, from speaking to journalists. Of course Jaya was doing none of those things; she didn't need to be told by anyone to stop. She had stopped herself. But no one could stop journalists from writing about a topic. Just when she thought interest in the controversy had waned, having seen nothing on the topic in the papers for a month, an article appeared in the *Illustrated Weekly of India*: "The Woman Artist? Modernism's Darker Side." It featured two women painters in Delhi as well as a couple of paragraphs about her, considering whether women artists better presented the hurts of a woman's existence beneath the passive surfaces of femininity. Something like that. Jaya had hated to see her name mentioned—she was afraid of the consequences for her father's job.

She gathered the crumpled-up balls of newspaper and filled the straw wastebasket beside the writing table. The dean of Grant Medical College, Dr. Rao, had sent her father a letter demanding a meeting. It awaited them when they returned from Punjab. Jaya went to Dr. Rao's office with her father, and there she was expelled. The college had its own disciplinary standards, Dr. Rao stated, so it was inconsequential whether or not she had been arrested. She had brought dishonor to the college. Written complaints had been received from faculty members and parents. Nothing her father said could sway Dr. Rao, a man with a long face and heavy cheeks, normally smiling, who showed them his stern, inflexible side. His subsequent letter to her father, dated 26 June 1956, had been official notification of her expulsion.

Her mother came into the bedroom, her hair disheveled, the pins falling out of her bun. These days she always looked like she'd just gotten up from a deep sleep in the heat of the afternoon. She'd brought Kamlesh a blue cardigan that was tight on her. Kamlesh tried it on and accepted it, tucking it into her steel trunk, which yawned open against the wall next to the dressing table. When the bell rang and the door slammed, they knew Daddy had come back. He'd been called for an afternoon meeting at Khosla Sahib's office in town—at Ballard Estate, close to the docks. Her parents had speculated it would be a talk about his position at the factory. Drawing in a breath, Vidya said, "Let's hope it went well."

Heerabai looked into the room, saying sahib had returned, should she make tea? Yes, Mummy said. Heerabai went away, unsmiling, absorbing the uncertainty and tension of the household. "At the age of forty-seven your father might have to start looking for a job like a new graduate," Mummy had shouted at Jaya when Khosla had called him for a meeting after stories first appeared in the papers concerning the obscenity scandal. "Who will hire a man eight years from retirement?" Fifty-five was the mandatory age. If he was dismissed, not only would he lose his income but they would lose this home, a company flat provided by Khosla Sahib. "Where will we go?" her mother had cried.

Vidya ordered Jaya to ask her father what snack he wanted with his tea. Jaya was reluctant. Normally she avoided contact with her father. They never made special snacks at teatime, but Mummy said they could fry onion pakoras quickly, or send the servant out to buy samosas. "Let him have something nice after his meeting," her mother said. Jaya combed back her hair, brushed her hand over her plait. In the mirror, she took a hanky and wiped the oily sheen from her face. She had broken the whole family. With one painting. Whatever had happened to the confiscated painting—the nude painting of herself—she didn't know. She'd asked Sringara to retrieve it for her before she left, but Sringara had not been able to trace it at the police station. No one there knew the whereabouts of that picture. Jaya hoped the inspector had burned it.

Jaya knocked on her parents' bedroom door and glanced in when her father said, "Yes, come." He was unloosening his tie.

"Hello, Daddy," she said formally. He looked at her as if they were strangers to each other. He didn't want either of the snacks she suggested. "Or some sandwiches, I could make," Jaya said. "Cucumber sandwiches?"

"Nothing. Just tea."

"Something, Daddy?" She couldn't discern from his expression if his discussion with Khosla Sahib had gone well or not. He was a man passing her in the railway station, with no regard for her. Her mother would find out the result of the meeting. He walked away, taking his tie to hang up in his wardrobe. He returned for his jacket on the bed.

"You spoke to Mr. Khosla?" she dared to ask. Now that they were almost face-to-face, she wanted him to know she was sorry for what she was putting him through.

Her father came away from his cupboard and looked at her. "Yes. What do you want to know?" He spoke in an unfriendly tone, as if he suspected her motives.

"Nothing, I was just wondering how it was."

He flung his arm out forcefully, as people dismissed beggars who pestered them. Jaya walked away, her stomach twisting. She sometimes imagined herself in a courtroom, being tried for obscenity. Her pictures would hang before the judge, and she would be made to answer for the crime she had committed. On the basis of one lady's objections, she would say, in her defense, the inspector had come to the gallery and decided her picture must be removed. Then there was the picture in her apartment he also had found objectionable. It was his opinion. The opinion of Dr. Sohrabji, who was building the greatest archive of modern painting in India at his institute, was that her pictures belonged in his collection.

In front of the dean of Grant Medical College, she had quietly answered questions. His pronouncements were severe, he was very sure of himself, and she was too humiliated to try to defend herself. Only her father spoke up to Dr. Rao. In her innermost heart, Sringara pointed out, perhaps Jaya was glad to have been expelled. Jaya at first took offense at Sringara saying that, until she realized it was true. Medical college had been her father's chosen path for her, not hers—though she had been moved by the patients, by the piteous struggle of the poor who were cared for at the hospital. She may have remained passive in front of the dean because a part of her was waiting to be set free. Expulsion had freed her.

"It's what you wanted to happen, isn't it?" Sringara had made her aware of that truth before she left for Europe. Sringara had forced herself to go, though she was tearful over leaving her son for two years, or maybe longer if she found a way to stay on there. She feared she would lose touch with him completely. Jaya went to see her off at Alexandra Docks with a small group of artists. It felt strange to be among them after months. The great white ship bore its name, *Victoria*, on the funnel, and its dressing of colorful flags fluttered happily in the sea breeze. Sringara mounted the long gangway with her back to them, moving toward her future in her radiant white sari, as Jaya hung back with the Bombay crowd, watching her disappear.

Baroda

JAYA KEPT A clay pot inside the room for drinking water, and a window open to a view of jackfruit trees in the garden and the bright blue gleam of the sea beyond. When she was finished in the evenings, she opened the door to let a breeze blow through her studio. The painting against the wall stood six feet tall, raised on a makeshift brick plinth, and as she climbed a footstool to reach its heights, throwing her body into the picture to stroke on color, she felt she was working on the scale of a movie screen. The patchy, layered ocher-gold sky spread over a breadth of indigo and pale blue sea. She stepped down from the stool and moved back toward the closed door, seeking distance from her canvas to assess what she had done.

A couple was caught embracing under the spiked roof of a palm tree, the inky green-black fronds flying in air currents. Shadows and leaves were scattered at their feet. Another figure walked out of the sea, draped in a thin scarlet cloth, thigh-deep in water that brightened to turquoise where she stood. Her hands were sketched in mudras, her right palm cupped beneath her squarish umber breasts. Her left arm extended to the side in a curve, palm down in a gesture encompassing the ocean. Between the dancer in the water and the lovers on the beach, a round pot dappled in clay colors tilted in the sand.

The man, the lover, reached into the shadowy tree like a monarch to pluck a golden-red coconut hanging high above. His other arm, streaked deep blue, was curled around his lover's waist. The woman's back arched out of his one-armed grasp, her head turned longingly to the woman emerging from the sea. The two women's terracotta faces were smooth, oval, and identical, their white almond-shaped eyes defined by a sooty black outline, their gazes joined over the hollow earthen pot, their bodies curving to the same linear rhythm. The sisters had been born together and could not be parted by any man or body of water. They loved each other's reflections down to the way their greenish-umber beads coiled over their angular breasts—their flat, modern-ancient bodies.

In an alert gaze of contemplation, Jaya saw the man's thigh was too smoothly massive, like a length of driftwood. She went to the canvas with a palette knife from her worktable and scraped it along the inside of the leg where it curved into shadow, revealing a crack of bone-white canvas. Putting down her knife, she flicked moist oil color off the canvas with a fingernail. Pigment was scratched off the bodies in various spots to create the impression of chipped figures in a cave. In two or three places, the blue outlines of the bodies, the picture's morphology, were exposed beneath the weathered skin of paint.

It was the first time she had pitted a man and woman against each other on a canvas, seeking the natural tension between them. But the dancer in the sea was the pillar of the picture. She was a woman coming to life, and the woman planted on the beach looked to her, to the sea, as if to her dreams.

At her worktable, Jaya wiped off smeared tubes of paint, swirled one brush after another in a dirty glass of turpentine. Her eyes shifted again to her painting. The figures constructed no tangible narrative, but a mood was invoked, a myth of longing unfolded. Sensuality was its own kind of beauty, perhaps the purest type. She gathered her brushes to clean them off in the washroom downstairs. Rushing past the other studios—past the tentative, rising notes of a bamboo flute, and the thumping of a dancer's feet—she ran into Keshav Mane. "Tomorrow, eleven o' clock?" he wanted to know.

"Anytime," Jaya said. "I'll be here at nine." She smiled and continued moving. Mane would bring around a man who would be curating the Indian pavilion at an international art fair in Paris. A few artists, chosen by Mane, would present their work to the curator, and Mane, who was enthusiastic about her big painting, felt confident it would be selected.

Jaya was almost finished with the canvas, and she was excited to show it to a man who had the power to bring her some recognition.

In the washroom, she scrubbed her brushes with soap and water, and she returned upstairs holding them like a handful of stiff flowers. Her painting startled her—swaths of bright pigment laid against each other. Color in all its luminosity. It felt like a change, an advance.

An urge to go out, take a walk, watch the sun slide into the sea struck her. All day she had painted barefoot in her studio, her feet gliding over the freckled terrazzo floor glazed with light. Now she bent down to slip on her sandals. Deep violet-blue pigment was caked around her fingernails. She liked to see her hands soiled at the end of the day, clotted with dry paint. In the mornings she would enter her studio, the paint still embedded under her nails, and latch the door behind her, settling into her freedom—a space to think, sketch, pace, and paint. About six months back, she had returned to this mansion, where she'd been disgraced, to ask Mane for a studio. He had reserved Sringara's studio for her, just as he'd promised, letting it out to various artists on a monthly basis. He opened the door to the studio one morning and she stepped in, releasing herself from the jail of her own making at home.

She told her parents about the studio only after she took it. They were not pleased, yet they didn't want to see her dwelling inside a sort of void in the flat every day. Don't hold any exhibitions, they told her, still afraid. Her father had not lost his position, but the fear had shaken them all thoroughly; it had numbed them. She had been punished for a long time, and she had punished herself. She had remained at home, avoiding the Punjabi community she once fit into so naturally and easily. People considered her a pariah, a curiosity, a stranger. A girl who painted obscene pictures. No one could forget that. She had dwelled in her own death for ten months, a year—she'd lost track of time. She'd fallen into a state of despondency as Kamlesh had once, a despondency that dragged her down and buried her in its silky sands. She couldn't move. She stayed still; time remained still. One day blurred into the next.

Her mother saw it, and she eventually pushed Jaya out of the flat. There was a clinic in a slum at the edge of Cuffe Parade, and Mummy took her there to volunteer her services. Jaya did what she was meant to do for Dr. Pendharkar—take down the patients' information, their present and past history. It began with those poor patients. In the margins of her register, she found herself sketching a hollow-eyed woman or a small, frightened boy staring straight ahead. When she realized what she'd done, she would take a rubber to the drawing.

Drawing brought her up from the depths, up through layer upon layer of silt and water, into the air. She drew faces, she drew bodies. She came alive, noticing people—noticing the things around her—again. Week by week, sketching, the desire to live grew. She had no friend close by. She could not turn to Sringara for advice, though they wrote to each other occasionally. Then the Baroda Circle came to hold their first exhibition at Jehangir Art Gallery. It was a new group formed by members of the Faculty of Fine Arts at Baroda and their friends. She met Yasmin Ahmed again. She saw Yasmin's surprising and spectacular paintings—they were made on paper, like scrolls, and included lines of text in Hindi and English written above and below the figures, houses, statues, and mythological animals, a variation on a Gujarati folk tradition. "What do you mean you're not painting?" Yasmin chastised her.

Jaya went out and bought canvas and colors and pastels and other materials with the money she'd saved from selling her pictures last year and the year before. Her brushes and knives she'd kept in a bag in her cupboard, never giving away her precious implements because she must have sensed there would be a time when she would come back to life.

Outside, she walked down Warden Road to a small public beach. There was a stream of cars, people returning home from the office. Roasted peanuts scented the air; a hawker squatted behind his smoking tray of plain and spiced nuts on the footpath. A sand fort built by two boys stood on the rim of a slope leading down to a vast ruin of sea rock. Jaya removed her sandals and walked on the hot, rough sand, past candy-flower sellers, ayahs carrying children, and a distraught woman muttering to herself on a bench. "What is art? Is art a *life?*" her mother had shouted at her after Kamlesh left for England. She meant that Jaya should open her eyes and see that art was not a life. It was a pastime for vagabonds like Tule or a spinster like Sringara. A family was a full life. A family was the law. Everyone must have a family. It was how their society was built—upon families. Without a family, you were no one. You didn't matter. But Jaya had never said she didn't want a family. She would have a family one day—it was not impossible. But art was a life too. It was a life made of impressions and dreams and color. It was a life made of feeling.

The humped islands of stone protruded far into the sea's blue galaxy under a bitter orange sun. Lifting her sari above her ankles, Jaya crossed from one pitted crest of stone to the next, keeping above the gullies cracked between them. The jumble of squared rocks went on and on, the sea still far away and almost silent. Wind brought the odor of salt water, the brine from which her painted woman had arisen. In her last letter Kamlesh said she had made an Indian meal with some Indian friends in the flat where she let a room in Maida Vale. After graduating from the Institute of Education, she had decided to stay on in London, finding work as a supply teacher in the schools, earning three pounds a day. She wanted to gain some classroom experience before she returned to India. "It's remarkable how quickly one adjusts," she wrote, without saying she was happy.

Jaya climbed to a high, flat expanse of stone, a rough little island. She imagined that when she saw Kamlesh again there would be a natural distance between them, the distance of two people growing into themselves. She was waiting to see Kamlesh on-screen, to watch her move, hear her speak. After a delay, *Akarshan* would be released in three or four months. March or April 1958. The editing was nearly complete. Kamlesh would be billed as "Madhavi," Mr. Narula had assured her father—her good name would not be attached to the role of the dancer. It would be as if she had never made the film.

In his film about a woman artist's life, Mane had let the camera roam again and again over Jaya's picture of the multiple views of the dancer, because it related so well to his heroine's psychological uncertainties. Jaya had viewed the short film at a special screening at Eros, among many artists in the audience, and written a letter to Kamlesh about the thrill of seeing a moving image of her painting, and watching Kamlesh's image appear to come to life through the sweeping movements of the camera. And, though Jaya did not want to upset Kamlesh by mentioning her movie, she longed for the picture to come out so she could set eyes on her twin again.

A trembling road of light laid over the sea fell apart in narrow bands of reflection as Jaya neared the water. The sun was warm on her face like the pressure of human hands. Jaya sniffed the residue of turpentine on her hands, the skin rubbed coarse as homespun cloth from cleaning off oil color. She was tired, she realized; she had been painting for seven or eight hours. Some mornings she didn't paint but came out to these rocks, painting in her mind as she walked, her mind the canvas, and the image would emerge in sections that day and the days that followed. A bridge of angled, sharp-edged stones spaced widely apart led her to the water, past a beached fishing boat. In a long stride, Jaya leaped onto a flat stone edging the sea. She was leaving the city too, going elsewhere. She had written to Yasmin Ahmed a few days ago, once she was sure of herself: *I would like to come to Baroda to meet you.* Maybe she could study in the painting department; maybe she could serve as a paid assistant. When she met Yasmin in Bombay, Yasmin had invited her to come down for a visit. Jaya wanted to be more than a visitor. She wanted to be part of that society of artists, part of their great experiment of art-making. *What do you mean, you're not painting?* Yasmin had said. She had worn her black hair straight down her back at her exhibition and a bright-red sari like a bride. In her letter, Jaya had replied to that question with her deepest wish: *I would like to come to Baroda to meet you. I'd like to see what I might be able to do there.* The words kept running through her mind. It was unsettling and also exciting to acknowledge she wanted to make a new life for herself. She would go and see if she could belong in Baroda, paint her paintings there, unearth the unknown images inside her.

The wind flapped noisily around her, pulling her seaward. The sea was coated in light, water flowing with light, the warm light she would put in her paintings. All the things she loved would have a presence in her paintings, all those who were gone. None of them were lost. In life she wanted the future, but in art, time was preserved.

Jaya stood on the scored black stone, holding up her fluttering sari in her hands, dipping one foot, then the other, into a sea intensely blue under a sky that held the falling circle of the sun in its span. Squatting down on the rock lapped by the surf, she plunged both hands into the rushing cool waters of evening, splashing droplets high up in the air.

Acknowledgments

THIS BOOK IS my phoenix. It was written over many years, was rewritten, lay buried in rejection and disappointment, then unexpectedly soared to life one summer day.

My deepest gratitude to Brandon Hobson, who chose the manuscript for the 2022 AWP Prize for the Novel. Without Brandon's regard for the story, it would remain unseen. I owe enormous thanks also to Eric Neuenfeldt, the first reader for the prize. Thank you to the Association of Writers & Writing Programs for the honor.

I am profoundly grateful to Marcia Butler for her guidance, advice, and love as I brought the story to its final form during a tumultuous time. My two sets of writer comrades, Geeta Kothari and Sangu Iyer, and Heather Bell Adams and Pam Reitman, have offered much warmth, light, and comfort over the years, making a solitary occupation shine with moments of happiness and companionship.

I feel extraordinarily lucky to have had filmmaker Deepa Mehta among my few early readers. Deepa's thoughtful critique, informed by her astute sense of narrative, became my map for revision. My heartfelt thanks to Deepa for her insightful letter.

Thank you to my agent, Julie Stevenson, for her guidance and enthusiasm for this story. I am grateful to Courtney Ochsner, my editor at the

University of Nebraska Press, for her careful attention to the manuscript. Many thanks to editor in chief Bridget Barry and to Rosemary Sekora, Tayler Lord, Kayla Moslander, Stephanie Marshall Ward, and the entire team at Nebraska for helping launch my book into the world.

My thanks also to Leslie Wells for her editorial guidance.

During the course of my research, many people in India and America generously shared their expertise and recollections of an earlier era. The wayward process of making art intrigues me, and I feel lucky to have spoken to some of India's great modern painters. The late Mohan Samant invited me to his apartment in New York City and spent a day unearthing memories of his youthful association with the Progressive Artists' Group, India's rebel band of modernists. My thanks to Nalini Malani and Gieve Patel for reminiscing about their artistic beginnings in the old, leisurely midcentury Bombay, long before it became Mumbai. Anjolie Ela Menon enlightened me on the ways in which domestic life can work its way into an artist's imagery.

The trailblazing F. N. Souza gifted me Geeta Kapur's *Contemporary Indian Artists*, the only significant book on modern Indian painting that existed in the 1980s, which became a prized resource of mine while I was writing the story in the States, and then in Europe. Fortunately, the situation has changed today, with long overdue recognition accorded the first generation of Indian modernists at auctions, art fairs, and galleries and in the scholarship of art historians. I found intriguing new information about Amrita Sher-Gil and Akbar Padamsee, particularly in *20th Century Indian Art* by Partha Mitter, Parul Dave Mukherji, and Rakhee Balaram. *The Progressive Revolution*, an impressive catalog accompanying a 2018 Asia Society exhibition on the Progressive Artists' Group, by curators Zehra Jumabhoy and the late Boon Hui Tan, offers a revealing investigation into the early years of Indian modernism.

The gallerist Kekoo Gandhy changed my life with a single anecdote. I was a young reporter for the city magazine *Bombay* in the mideighties when we met by chance at the Jehangir Art Gallery. He recalled in rich detail the turbulent birth of India's modern art movement, which he'd witnessed forty years earlier as a confidant of the fierce personalities at its center. No woman painter appeared in Kekoo's remembrance, so I couldn't help but imagine, *What if there had been at least one determined girl?*

Kay Poursine, a disciple of the legendary Bharata Natyam dancer Balasaraswati, introduced me to this stunning dance with ancient roots in an introductory dance class at Wesleyan University. I am indebted to Nalini Aiyagari, a pioneering Bharata Natyam teacher in America, who spoke to me about the traditional method of training with her guru, Pandanallur Swaminatha Pillai, a descendant of the illustrious clan of dance teachers whose forefathers taught the temple dancers at Thanjavur for centuries.

As vital as art is to self-expression in India, so too is politics. I had the honor of interviewing the eminent freedom fighter Aruna Asaf Ali at her office in New Delhi and learning of her activism as a leader of the Indian National Congress during the oppressive years of British rule. I have the greatest admiration for that now-vanished generation of selfless elders who sacrificed their personal dreams and ambitions to the collective struggle for independence.

My great thanks to Dr. Padma Patel for her recollections of life as a medical student in midcentury Bombay and to the staff at Grant Medical College in the 1980s for allowing me to observe dissections and lectures. I am deeply grateful, as well, for the many wonderful conversations I had with my aunt, Dr. Manju Patney, about medical college and more in 1950s India.

My thanks to Payal for her guidance on the intricacies of Punjabi culture.

Within the impressive memory of my grandmother, Shakuntala Dewan, lived the complex history, stories, and lineage of her vast extended family despite the fact she had been orphaned in her teens. At my request, she began to write everything down, producing a vivid though incomplete memoir that is one of my treasured possessions. What my grandmother remembered informs the history of the fictional Malhotras, who are named after her natal family.

I owe my greatest debt of gratitude to my father, Jatinder Nath Kapur, whose kindness and generosity in answering my endless questions and recalling at length, over years of conversations, India of a bygone era gave me a surer footing in my fictional landscape. Without my father's enormous love, nothing would have been possible.

AWP Prize for the Novel

9 781496 236784